ABOUT THE AUTHOR

Jeff Dowson began his career working in the theatre as an actor and a director.

From there he moved into television, and after early Channel 4 commissions he became an independent writer/producer/director. Screen credits include arts series, entertainment features, drama documentaries, drama series and TV films.

Turning crime novelist in 2014, he introduced Bristol private eye Jack Shepherd in *Closing the Distance*. The series developed with *Changing the Odds*, *Cloning the Hate* and *Bending the Rules*.

The Ed Grover series, set in Bristol in the years following World War 2, opened in 2018 with *One Fight At A Time*. The second book *New Friends Old Enemies* was published in 2021.

Born in northeast England Jeff now lives in Bristol. He is a member of BAFTA and the Crime Writers Association.

www.jeffdowson.co.uk

CLOSING THE DISTANCE

"Fast paced with an explosive ending, this is compelling reading."

Mystery People Magazine

"A clever modern thriller where nothing is as it first seems"

Cathi Unsworth

"Brilliant, tough, private eye thriller with a great sense of humour, and a tension which grows and doesn't let go until the devastating ending"

Marian Jones

"A masterly thriller. Hard to put down."

David Kitson

"A cracking good read. Laced with just the right amount of toughness. An assured style that has echoes of Chandler."

Andrew Hickling

CHANGING THE ODDS

"A pacey and absorbing thriller. Jack Shepherd is an excellent addition to the ranks of fictional private eyes

Crime Review

"Another fast-paced Jack Shepherd novel by Jeff Dowson.

John Archer

"Another great book from Mr Dowson. Excellent story, full of twists and turns."

Steve Timmins

"Great stuff. This is an engrossing thriller featuring private eye Jack Shepherd."

Peter Nash

Closing the Distance and *Changing the Odds*
previously published by Williams & Whiting

This edition published in Great Britain in 2022

by Diamond Crime

ISBN 978-1-7397448-5-4

Copyright © 2022 Jeff Dowson

The right of Jeff Dowson to be identified as the author of this work has been asserted in accordance with the Copyright, Designs and Patents Act 1998.

All rights reserved.

No part of this publication may be reproduced, stored in a retrieval system, or transmitted in any form or by any means without the prior permission in writing of the publisher, nor be circulated in any form of binding or cover other than that in which it is published.

All characters appearing in this work are fictitious. Any resemblance to real persons, living or dead, is purely coincidental.

Diamond Crime is an imprint of Diamond Books Ltd.

Thanks to…

Caroline Montgomery, Fen Oswin, Mike Linane, Bob Price, Alan Brown, John Bone, Peter Nash, Andy Hicking,

Steve Timmins, Phil Rowlands and the team at Diamond Crime.

Mariette and Andy at JacksonBone.

Inspectors and Staff at the RSPCA in Bristol.

The Staff and Volunteers in Bristol Night Shelters and Drop In centres.

All the places in the West Country whose names and locations the stories have plundered.

Book design: jacksonbone.co.uk
Cover photograph: Matt Boyle/Unsplash

Also by Jeff Dowson

The Bristol Thrillers Series
Cloning The Hate
Bending The Rules

The Ed Grover Series
One Fight At A Time
New Friends Old Enemies

For information about Diamond Crime authors
and their books, visit:
www.diamondbooks.co.uk

To Mary… Always

Closing the Distance

The Jack Shepherd Collection
Volume One

JEFF DOWSON

PROLOGUE

The Balkans 2000

Kosovo is an impoverished, desperate place. The haves have it all. The peasants, mostly ethnic Albanians who make up ninety percent of the population, have what they stand up in.

It had been this way since the days of the Ottoman Empire. The years of Serb control between World Wars 1 and 2, did nothing to relieve the tension between the ethnic groups. Absorbed into the Federal Republic of Yugoslavia in 1945, the country existed in a Balkan limbo. Tito's police cracked down hard on nationalists throughout all Yugoslavia's provinces. Slobodan Milosevic's vision of a 'Greater Serbia' plunged the Balkans into civil war, brutal ethnic cleansing and NATO bombing raids.

In the summer of 1999, the United Nations took control. A mass exodus of Serbs followed, in the wake of revenge attacks by what was left of the Kosovan Liberation Army. Serbian police and Albanian militants kept up the regimen of reaction and reprisal, despite the UN peace keeping forces insisting there was a cease fire in place.

* * *

The white Mercedes truck had a red cross painted on each side of the body and a plastic strip across the top of the windscreen which read *Médecins Sans Frontières*. It had travelled 140 kilometres northwest from the Macedonia border. As it crested the hill, the left front wheel dropped into a hole and bounced out again. The truck swerved to the left, as the driver attempted to keep the rear wheel from doing the same, fishtailed sideways and slid to a halt.

Inside the cab, the driver looked across to his passenger. The young man had been thrown sideways. His head had thumped into the right-hand side window. Dazed, he sat upright, leaned back against the seat headrest, raised his right hand and gently prodded at his temple.

"Are you alright?" the driver asked, in heavily accented English.

He was Albanian. In his mid-50s and a little overweight, with heavily tanned skin, close cropped hair and dark eyes. The passenger was English. Early-20s, white faced by comparison, with a mass of thick brown hair which dropped over his forehead. He closed his eyes, massaged them with his thumb and forefinger, opened them again and squinted ahead of him.

"I'm seeing stars," he said.

"We will go slowly down the hill," the driver said.

He found first gear, changed up into second and let the engine revs act as a brake. The truck trundled down the hill, into the village of Donjica.

Or rather, what was left of it.

The road into the square was lined with stone skeletons which had once been houses. Jagged holes blown out of the walls by mortars, splintered sections of roof timbers, blackened by fire. What must have been some kind of memorial in the centre of the square, was now a pile of rubble. The driver navigated his way around it and stopped the truck. He climbed down from the cab, knelt by the front wheel, dropped his head to the ground and looked under the engine.

He rolled over, lay on the ground and shuffled backwards. The passenger walked around the front of the truck and looked down at the driver's legs. There was a muffled curse and the driver shuffled forwards again. He re-appeared, with oil smeared across his forehead.

"There is a leak," he said. "Somewhere along the road, we hit the sump." He wiped his forehead with the back of his right hand and got to his feet. "We need to find a garage."

The two men looked round the square. Donjica was a tiny place, only a dot on the largest scale map. The heart of the village was blasted to pieces. The small mosque was the only recognisable building left. Arranged in front of it was a line of bodies, each one covered by a blanket, bed sheet, piece of tarpaulin – whatever had been to hand. Two old men, well into their seventies, were doing the best they could to give this row of shapes in the road as much dignity as possible.

Moving towards the truck, from the opposite side of the square, was another man. Late forties, tall and slim. Dressed in a dark suit, the left sleeve torn at the elbow and the rest of it coated with dust. The driver took a couple of steps forward. The man spoke to him in Albanian. The driver translated for the benefit of his passenger.

"I'm a doctor," the man said. "Have you got medicines in the truck?"

The driver shook his head.

"It's empty. Everything in it was delivered to Brazda refugee camp, over the border in Macedonia. We're on our way back to Pec."

"That's a pity," the doctor said. Then he lifted his arms and spread them wide. "At least, you can be witness to this. And the rest. Let me show you."

He led the driver and the passenger to the line of bodies. He knelt down by one of them, pulled back a bed sheet crusted with dirt and revealed the head and shoulders of a middle-aged man. The top of the man's head had been blown off.

Further along the line, the old men were going on with their work as if the driver and passenger were not there. The doctor pointed to one of them.

"He says, that this man, Adem Mehmeti, was dragged out of his house by three Serb policemen, pushed to his knees in the street and shot."

Gently, the doctor drew the sheet back over the man's head. He pulled a blanket off the next person in the line. The driver looked at the body and instantly turned away. The passenger, steadfastly, stuck to the purpose.

The doctor looked at him and switched to remarkably fluent English.

"This is Sadik Hajirizi," he said. "Those wounds were made by an assault rifle. I know this, because the bullet I took out of the back of his neck is a 7.62mm calibre. Probably from an AK-47. The Serbs are supplied with old Soviet army guns."

The passenger looked at the doctor. Stunned into silence.

"You must write this down. Be a witness. To all, to all of this. I will take you round the village. There is more, much more."

The passenger remained rooted to the spot. The doctor went on.

"You work for *MSF*, yes?"

The passenger nodded.

"Then you are in a position to talk with people. Please help."

The passenger finally found his voice. He pointed across the square.

"That's just a truck. I just help out. I'm not important."

"But you can tell what you see."

The passenger nodded again.

"Yes. I can do that."

He turned away from the row of bodies. Walked swiftly back to the truck. Opened the passenger door. Dragged a battered holdall out from behind his seat. Found a ring-bound notebook in a side pocket. Dug deeper and found a pencil. Pushed the holdall back into place, straightened up and shut the truck door.

The doctor moved to his shoulder.

"Are you ready?" he asked.

"Yes."

CHAPTER ONE

Bristol 2016

Marvin Starratt was a despicable human being.

An assessment Judge Chambers heartily agreed with and sent him down for eleven years. Apologising to the court, the public gallery and the journalists on the press bench for not being able to incarcerate him longer.

"Unhappily, this is the maximum sentence I can impose," he said. "I can only recommend that you are made to serve the full term."

I watched from the public gallery. Starratt had beaten up and raped a client of mine. And four other women, over a period of seven months. I helped find him and get him arrested. A small victory, and you have to hang on to those, but Starratt had brutally invaded the lives of five women and changed them forever.

My client and I met downstairs in the lobby. We shook hands.

"Thank you," she said.

"My pleasure," I said.

She turned, negotiated the big glass swing door and stepped out into the street.

The chances are, Louise and I will never meet again. She came to me in distress, frustrated and angry that the police were making no progress in finding the man they considered their prime suspect. Upright coppers have to work by the book. I'm liberated from that kind of consideration. Admittedly, I don't have their resources, but I can go places they can't. I found Starratt in a flat in Stokes Croft. He swung at me with a cricket bat. I took it from him, hit him with it and delivered him to the police. Louise gave me a cheque, the Inspector heading up the investigation team gave me his thanks and Starratt got his day in court. It was a job satisfactorily done. But I couldn't help to manage the fall-out. This is always the bit that bothers me. And the bit that never lets go entirely. My client cases get filed away in my office filing cabinet, and each time, I hope there has been something about the case that has added to my learning experience. Something that will short cut the route to a successful conclusion of the next job I take on.

There was an angry bellow from behind me. I looked back across the lobby. A man in a brown tweed suit was squaring up to a barrister who was taking off his wig. He ripped the wig out of the barrister's hand it and threw it across the lobby.

"Call that a fucking defence?" he yelled.

Lloyd Starratt was laying in to his brother's brief.

None of the Starratts can be described as nature's noblemen. The family has lived in the Forest of Dean since Noah was a lad. Earning a living down the years, as woodsmen, charcoal burners, farmers, miners, landowners, petty criminals and local terrorists. The whole tribe of head bangers and hard cases operates, without much correction, like the bad guys in a Kentucky backwoods movie.

This one, Marvin's older brother Lloyd, was the head of the clan. In his mid-50s, at the moment in his default setting and making his presence felt. As hard as nails and a seasoned scrapper, he had a lot of clout in his neck of the woods. A member of the Rotary Club, a big noise in the

Severn Valley Hunt and briefly, the local Tory party agent – for a particularly barmy right-wing MP who got in at a by election, but was ousted at the following general election, when the good people of the constituency returned to their senses. Perhaps more damaging, for a while he contrived to get himself on to the JP's bench. An alarming west country re-creation of Elmore Leonard's Maximum Bob.

The barrister took a couple of paces backwards. Lloyd squared up to him again. A couple of security men sped across the lobby and intervened before he could do any damage. He elbowed one of them in the chest and attempted to kick the other in the crutch, before they pinned his arms to his sides and hauled him across the lobby to the swing door. As Lloyd passed me, I was given the benefit of his opinion too.

"As for you, you fucker... Just you fucking wait."

The security men heaved him into the revolving door and swung him out into the street. He completed a full 360 on the pavement before he regained his balance. Then he focused on me through the glass and malevolently gave me the finger. I gave him a cheery wave.

The barrister had retrieved his wig. He stepped towards me.

"Mr Shepherd," he said. "I'm sorry about that."

I told him he had no need to apologise.

"If people like Lloyd start inviting me to dinner," I said, "it will be time to take a serious look at what I do."

We shook hands.

"I'm truly glad you lost."

"In truth, so am I," he said.

I stepped out into the street and walked the three hundred yards to Charlotte Street Car Park.

I had left the Healey on the top floor. My mobile rang from inside the glove compartment as I slid behind the steering wheel. It was one of those 'movie moments'. Like when a character switches on the car radio, immediately to have the music interrupted and a news announcer tell him something the plot badly needs to know.

The call was from Trinity Road CID. Detective Sergeant George Hood. I had known him a couple of years. He was the first-choice hound dog of an old friend of mine, still on the force – Superintendent Harvey Butler.

"How are you today Jack?"

"I'm alright."

"That's good," he said.

What he meant was, 'at least that bit is; the next bit is likely to be less jolly'.

"We want to talk with you about Philip Soames," Hood said.

Philip Soames... A psychiatrist with a private practise in Clifton. Recently a client of mine. Filed under S in the middle drawer of my office filing cabinet.

"Talk away." I said.

"No, not right now," Hood said. "Are you busy later?"

"I hope to be."

I pictured him grinning down the phone line

"Well… It's not our policy to keep the private sector away from paid work. But we would be obliged if you could get round here tomorrow. At noon."

The request was certain to prove a lot less routine than he was making it sound.

"Okay," I said.

He thanked me and rang off. Distracted for a moment or two, I listened to the buzz on the line. Then I closed the call and dropped the mobile onto the passenger seat.

As Scarlett said - tomorrow is another day.

The Healey's engine fired up as soon as I turned the ignition key. It settled into a rhythm and began to rumble softly. I listened to it for a while, then reached up and unclipped the front of the soft top, raised it and pushed it back.

A 1967, classic 3 litre, is an indulgence I know. Expensive to run. I can sit in traffic and watch the fuel gauge needle go down. No breeze to service either, but for that, there is Mr Earl – twenty-five percent Jamaican and seventy-five percent south Bristol. A man of few words, laid back and totally unfazed by the complexities of the world around him, he lives above his workshop in a cul-de-sac in Southville. His son Hamilton works for him, his wife Alesha runs the local soul food café. A more well-adjusted bunch you could never hope to meet. Each time he presents me a bill, Mr Earl shakes his head sadly. But I've had the car fifteen years. Yes, the Healey pumps out more CO_2 than my neighbour's wife's Nissan. But he flies to Toulouse twice a month. My personal carbon footprint is miniscule by comparison.

I drove out of the car park.

* * *

Saint Edward's Church is a tiny place, in a quiet part of Redland. Where Emily and I were married and where her memorial stone is placed. Chrissie and I stood side by side, in the corner of the churchyard and looked down at the stone.

In memory of Emily 1969 to 2015.

Chrissie reached out with her right hand, brushed my hip, found the fingers of my left hand and squeezed gently.

"I can't believe twelve months can go by so quickly," she said.

It was a serene, mid-September day, with a soft breeze

barely stirring the branches of the old yew tree behind us. Summer was stretching on, refusing to let go. So were the memories. Emily had loved, cared for and looked after all of us; mending and healing and resolutely not regretting.

Chrissie let go of my hand and reached into the inside pocket of her jacket. She produced a small photograph, set in a silver frame.

"This is the picture of Mum you always liked."

Emily smiled at us from inside the frame. A photograph taken eighteen months ago in the Cotswolds, before the cancer took its final unbeatable grip. No sign of pain on her face. A little gaunt perhaps, but still beautiful, and at 42, far too young to die. Twelve months on, the grieving had distilled into remembrance. And Emily's legacy was substantial. Her continued presence in most things I did most days, was positive and welcome. Chrissie and I were closer than we had been in a long time. Adam and I were good friends. A relationship which had evolved and matured, in spite of my best efforts to strangle it at birth.

Adam is a senior reporter on the *Bristol Evening Post*. Eleven years older than Chrissie. When she met him two years ago, I decided it was a relationship to be discouraged. She said Adam was the best thing that had happened to her. Emily tried to keep the peace between us and we should have taken note. What began with an argument, was followed by a series of rows, ending in a big fight. Furious with me, Chrissie left home and moved in with Adam. I raged nonsensically in return. And in all of this, Emily was the loser. Neither Chrissie nor I recognised that. Emily watched over us, counselled us, but couldn't knock any sense into us. Driven by our own concerns, we failed to see who was really hurting the most. Chrissie leaving home was a simple disagreement. Emily's cancer which came swiftly afterwards, was a matter of life and death. It took something so deadly to bring us back together. We had time to prepare, eight months to be a family again. At the eleventh hour we did the best we could, but time ran out. Through all the nonsense and eventually the grief, Adam was at Chrissie's side. He kept her grounded and together.

In silence, we looked at the photograph for some time, then Chrissie put it back into her pocket and we stepped away from the stone.

"I think Adam means to propose," she said, as we were about to leave the churchyard.

I pulled open one of the big, cast-iron gates and stared at her.

"Does he?"

"He's working up to it."

"And do you feel disposed to accept?"

"Somewhere down the line, yes, of course. But I've one more year at uni. Then debts to settle and a job to sort out. Or maybe a post grad year. In which case we're looking at a hell of a long engagement."

"You'll still only be 23."

"You married Mum when you were 23"

"And Auntie Joyce said I was far too young."

"Was she right?"

Auntie Joyce is right about almost everything. But back then, she took to Emily instantly, loved her to pieces and put aside her misgivings. That was no surprise. Generous, big hearted and open to everyone with a problem to share, she and Uncle Sid had gathered up a distraught child and given him all the love in the world.

Suddenly, other memories were crowding in...

The day before I started primary school, my father came

home with a new family car. A 1972 Ford Zodiac. I stood at his side, my point of view level with his waist. He, my mother and I, surveyed the gorgeous, chrome trimmed machine. The image was burned on to the back of my retina and has never been dislodged. Not even, when three days later, my father hit a patch of ice on the top of Mendip and the Zodiac side-slipped through a fence and down 100 feet onto the floor of a stone quarry. It burst into flames on impact. That day, I walked the few hundred yards from school to Auntie Joyce's for tea. I was still there the next morning. Whereupon she said I wasn't going to school that day and she had something to tell me.

I closed the church gate behind us.

"She called me yesterday," I said. "Auntie Joyce."

"Of course she did," Chrissie said. "She wouldn't forget."

We walked to her car, a ten- year-old Honda Civic. She pointed the key fob at the front wing, waited for it to bleep, then spoke again.

"How long have they been in Suffolk? Three years?"

"Four... Uncle Sid is making things in his shed."

"What things?"

"Metal things. He says he wants to move house. Needs more space he maintains."

"Why?"

"To make bigger things I guess."

Chrissie opened the driver's door.

"Why doesn't he just get a bigger shed?"

She got into the Civic. Closed the door, pressed a button to her right and the driver's window slid down.

"What are you doing now?"

"Taking the rest of the day off. Come and have some tea."

"I haven't got time," Chrissie said. "I have to pick up Sam. Call me."

She started the engine, let in the clutch, found first gear and the Honda pulled away.

* * *

I live in a brick and stone Edwardian semi, with a curved bay window facing the street and three bedrooms upstairs. The only house Emily and I ever bought. Just before Chrissie was born. There is a small garden at the front. A more substantial garden at the back, leads to a gate into a lane which runs parallel to the street at the front. The garage sits at the end of the garden and opens directly into the lane.

I stowed the car away, walked across the lawn and let myself into the house through the back door. I made some tea and sat down on the living room sofa to drink it.

Out of work again.

Or to be more accurate, currently not being paid by anyone. The self-employed person always has work to do. The question is, whose money is he spending? Right now, indeed for the foreseeable future, I was spending my own.

The sun was shining and the lawn needed cutting. Seize the day.

I got to my feet, went up to the bedroom and changed into an old pair of jeans and my gardening shirt. I fished my gardening shoes out of the cupboard by the back door. My mobile rang from the hall.

"Where are you?" Adam asked.

"At home. Just about to cut the lawn."

"Got anything on this evening?"

"Nothing more exciting than cutting the lawn."

"I think I can help there," he said. "Come for supper."

"Going to be that good is it?"

"There's something I want to talk to you about. Or rather,

someone. You remember Philip Soames?"

I took a moment. Sat down on the chair by the phone table and stretched out my legs. Adam asked if I was still there.

"Yes," I said. "What about him?"

"Tell you when you get here. Soon as you like."

He disconnected. I stared across the hall. Pressed the call cancel button.

Philip Soames... Again...

Saved from cranking up the lawn mower, I de-dressed and re-dressed. Decided on a change of shirt and trousers, collected my jacket and car keys and left the house the way I had come in.

I managed to avoid the city centre, crossed the suspension bridge in light traffic, then turned west up the hill through Leigh Woods and on to the Clevedon road. A few minutes before 6 o'clock I pulled up outside Adam and Chrissie's house on Dial Hill. As I reached for the doorbell, there was an explosion of barking from inside the hall. That could only be the force of nature that is Sam the Bearded Collie.

Indeed so. Chrissie opened the front door and in a whirlwind of noise, swirling hair and thrashing tail, Sam launched himself over the threshold. He reared upright, planted his front paws on my chest and we danced backwards – him Fred Astaire, me Ginger Rogers. I managed to get my hands either side of his neck and slow down the mad fox trot. Sam dropped on to all fours. I bellowed "Sit!" And he did, staring up at me, tongue hanging out, panting like an idling steam engine.

Chrissie was hanging on to the door jam, convulsed with laughter. Adam appeared at her side.

"I did tell you I was picking him up," she said.

"Is he on holiday again?" I asked.

Chrissie pulled herself together and stepped on to the drive.

"Likely to become a permanent fixture," she said. "Our friends with the Australian connection may be emigrating. They're out there now, looking for a house. In which case, he'll stay here, with us."

She addressed the beast directly. "Isn't that right Sam?"

Sam spun around, looked at Chrissie, threw back his head and barked in agreement.

"Come on," she said.

Sam dipped his head. Looked back over his shoulder towards me, considering his options. I stood up as straight as I could and gave him my best severely disinterested look. He took that on board, reversed his point of view, then loped past Chrissie and back into the house.

"On the button," she said.

"Sort of," I said.

I followed Adam into the hall.

* * *

Chrissie had cooked linguini carbonara – bacon, peas, red peppers and basil in some kind of cream sauce. We paid serious attention to the meal and conversation was minimal. At one point, Sam padded into the dining room. He looked around, decided there was no mileage in his 'Hey, here I am' routine, lay down in the doorway and dozed off. Adam made the coffee. Chrissie poured a cup for herself and took it into the living room. As she stepped over Sam, he woke up, got to his feet and followed her. Adam passed a cup across the table to me and turned to the subject of Philip Soames. He had a minor bombshell to drop.

"Your ex-client, Philip Soames, is dead."

I stared at him. He went on.

"Dragged out of the mud in the Severn Estuary yesterday morning. He was discovered by the man who checks the speed camera on the approach to the second crossing. You remember, it's up on the gantry above the toll barriers."

"He saw the body from there?"

"Mr Conway is a bird watcher. Takes his binoculars with him every time he goes up to the camera. Apparently, he's the Westcountry's foremost expert on migratory wading birds."

Adam stood up, moved to the sideboard and picked up an envelope folder. He opened it, took out a page of A4 and passed it to me.

"My copy for tomorrow. Best I could do. The police press statement was a little thin."

I read it... Mr Conway had climbed the gantry to collect the camera data at 8 am. Low tide. His binoculars had revealed a man's body, mid channel, partly submerged in the mud. He had been weighted down. The police statement posited that the deceased had been transported out into the channel at high tide, around 2 am, and dropped into the water... I looked back at Adam.

"The wrong thing to do," I said.

He nodded. "You noticed."

Presumably those who had accomplished this, never intended that Philip Soames should re-appear. Not with weights strapped to his chest and his pockets full of gravel. That being the case, the enterprise was a huge mistake. The perpetrators had reckoned without the second highest tidal range in the world; something around fourteen and a half metres. Even though there are two miles between the English and the Welsh at that point in the channel, at low tide you could walk across – presuming you had mega waders and didn't get sucked into the mud.

Out in the hall, Sam sloped past the dining room door on his way to the kitchen. Adam looked at me, raised his arms and turned his palms outward.

"So our rationalisation of the situation would be?..."

"Those who did this deed were extremely foolish."

"Or extremely ill informed."

"Which leads to the most obvious assumption. They weren't local. Any west country person in the removals business would know about the estuary tides. No one would dump a body any closer than five miles out at sea."

"That was my conclusion too."

"You can't let this theory loose on your readers," I said.

"Not without getting into trouble. But in the meantime, the piece needs some colour. I was hoping you could provide a little of that."

I looked at the A4 page again.

"There are no details of how the police managed to identify him."

"Not released."

A further couple of seconds consideration was gate-crashed by the rattle of a choke chain, followed by extreme barking from the hall.

Chrissie yelled out, "We're going for our evening stroll."

There was a lot more barking and panting and squeaking, followed by the sound of the front door opening and closing, and then silence.

Adam linked his fingers, put his hands behind his head

and leaned back in his chair.

"So why would Philip Soames, eminent Bristol psychiatrist, incur the wrath of a bunch of out-of-town enforcers?" Then he grinned. "Surely not because he was once a client of yours."

"Is there any burgundy left?"

* * *

It was half an hour before Chrissie and Sam returned. By which time, we had finished the rest of the burgundy and Adam had the bones of a page one story.

"Was Soames married?" he asked.

"No. He was gay."

"In a relationship?"

"Not when I worked for him."

"And that was when... nine months ago?"

"About that."

"Can you talk about what you did for him? Or is that confidential?"

"I traced his aunt."

Adam looked at me in amusement. Obviously not the sort of high-end criminal activity he was expecting to hear about. I explained.

"Philip's mother died early summer last year. The only surviving relative, apart from him, was her sister, his aunt. Neither he nor his mother knew where she was. There had been a big family bust up years earlier. Philip was his mother's sole beneficiary, but he wanted his aunt to know she had died. He did some digging himself and got nowhere. So in the end, he hired me to find her."

"And being the super-sleuth you are..."

"She lives in Ambleside, in the Lake District. I went up to see her."

"How did she take the news?"

"She said 'Thank you for telling me', and made me some tea. I reported back to Philip. He smiled, said 'So be it' and asked me to send him my invoice. In return, he sent me a cheque. Since then, I've passed him in the street, met him in the foyer of the Colston Hall and had a drink with him on a couple of occasions. The last time, erm… three weeks ago. We were not close by any definition."

The front door opened and Sam's choke chain rattled again. Seconds later, he was in the dining room, looking for trouble. Chrissie called him into the kitchen. He gave us a resolute 'I'll be back' stare and reversed out into the hall. In the kitchen, he downed his supper biscuits and slurped away in his drinking bowl. Then he re-appeared in the dining room doorway, his soaking wet beard dripping water steadily onto the carpet. Chrissie materialised behind him with a towel.

"Sam," she said.

The beast turned to face her and she wrapped the towel around his muzzle. This was clearly part of the late-night routine. Sam waited calmly until Chrissie had finished drying his face, then he stepped back, barked once, shook his head fiercely, circled round three times and sat down in the hall. He dropped his head onto his paws, his ears stretched out flat on the carpet. He let out a contented sigh and lay still.

"Is that it?" I asked.

"Usually," Chrissie said.

I got up from the table.

"Are you going to stay over?" she asked.

"I'd love to," I said. "But not tonight."

I turned to Adam.

"I'll look into this Philip Soames business. If I find out anything I can tell you, I will."

He nodded in acknowledgement. "Thanks."

I moved to the dining room door.

"Good night," I said. I looked down at the dog. "And you Sam."

He offered a soft rumbled response, a kind of grace note to the evening, and lay quiet as I stepped over him. Chrissie escorted me to the front door.

CHAPTER TWO

Scarlett was absolutely right of course. Tuesday was another day. In all respects. To begin with, summer seemed to be over. I woke to the sound of rain. Stair rods battering down on the roof. I opened the front door into the onslaught of the prevailing wind and got comprehensively soaked collecting the milk. While I dried out, I made coffee, toast and scrambled eggs.

I took my mobile off charge and switched it on. It rewarded me with a message saying I had missed three calls. I finished the eggs and poured my third cup of coffee. The mobile rang.

A woman's voice, low register, asked if I was free to talk. I replied that I would be in my office within the hour and we could talk there. There was a pause. I waited. A car drove past the front window. The voice came back to me and said that would be fine. I asked who I was talking too. The voice said that was the issue at the heart of this. There was another pause. So I made a suggestion.

"How about nine o'clock?"

"Yes. Nine o'clock," the voice said.

"Do you need directions?" I asked.

"I know where it is," the voice said and the line was disconnected.

I put the mobile into my jacket pocket and finished my coffee. I hadn't much to consider, other than the mystery woman I was about to meet, so I got on with the day.

At ten minutes to eight, I sprinted across the back garden lawn to the garage, getting marginally less soaked than I had done half an hour earlier. I drove to the office, the ancient demister on full and wipers at maximum speed and still not managing to shovel the water away.

Bristol's traffic problems border on the irredeemable. And in the rain, the snarl-ups spread like runny tapioca.

The city was built on a swamp by the Avon and across the hillsides surrounding it. John Cabot sailed to the New World and ushered in Bristol's 'golden age'. Slavery. Fortunes were made by merchants who built more churches per square mile than anyone before or since, to salve their collective conscience. The slave masters identified the docks as both the hub of commerce and the centre of town. They drove from their enormous mansions on the Downs to their places of evil employ in gilded carriages; before which the traffic made way and members of the underclass stooped and tugged their forelocks. The rest of the populace struggled to get on and get by. The motor car arrived and jammed up the city centre completely. The Luftwaffe did its best to sort out the problem; but the town planners of the 50s and 60s reversed the process, filled the holes with concrete and built one of the most user-unfriendly city centres in Europe. And now, barely half a mile east, is a new retail complex the size of a small airport. Cabot Circus. A monument to the enterprise culture, appropriately named after the man who started it all. So we've come full circle. And commerce is, as always, top of the agenda.

It took so long to get to my office the clouds had rolled away and the rain had stopped by the time I arrived. A bright morning sun was out and the day was warming up.

The office is located in a converted, multi-storey, red brick tobacco warehouse on the north bank of the Avon, west of the city centre. An optimistic pre-millennium development, now rented out at £15 per square foot because times are hard. It looks out across the river; towards Coronation Road and the Victorian built terraces which crowd the hinterland between Asda's hypermarket in Bedminster and Bristol City's ground at Ashton Gate.

The urban renewers were making another assault on the banks of the river. Tearing brambles and nettles out of the ground and hacking away optimistically at wild hedging clogged with plastic bags, empty food cartons, battered drinks cans and materials much more insanitary. A bunch of men with a generator and heavy-duty sand blasters, were bombarding the graffiti on the ancient iron footbridge which links this side of the river with the old badlands of South Bristol.

"They've promised to do our car park before they leave."

I turned back into the room. Linda was standing in the office doorway. 42 years old, smart and funny and by some miracle, my friend as well as my accountant. And in spite of numerous threats to move, still occupying the office next to mine. She is five feet six, has dark hair and dark blue eyes, a composure and an instinctive body language that gives her all the confidence in the world. She and Emily had been close. Her mother died of cancer when she was fifteen and her empathy with Emily's condition was instinctive. She supported us, day after day, right down to the wire.

She was dressed for business, in a charcoal grey suit which wasn't remotely off the peg. It would have looked like just another expensive statement on anybody else. But it fitted Linda like Versace had sculpted it on her. She spread her arms wide and stuck out a hip.

"Sexy, yet purposeful is the intention. What do you think?"

"I think you look terrific. Knock 'em dead."

"That's the mission. I'll be back before lunch."

She swayed back into the corridor and slipped out of view.

I got to my feet, returned to the window and looked down three floors to the tarmac that did duty as an access road to the building, before it fetched up in the 'car park' – in reality fifty square yards of pounded down hardcore enclosed by corrugated iron sheeting, proudly displaying the efforts of local graffiti artists. I didn't mind the work, I thought it cheered up the place. But Banksy it wasn't. So it was next in line for an assault by the men with the sand blasters.

The wet tarmac was steaming and the warm day had encouraged tenants to throw open their windows. I could hear Patsy Cline's *I've Got Your Picture* drifting up from the office below, underscored by the distant throb of engineering. Patrick, the web designer, had a library of torch song CDs, which he played to help him through his labours at the pc keyboard. We didn't socialise exactly. We met in corridors, in the lift and in the lobby. I didn't know much about him. But he didn't seem gloomy per se...

A blue Mondeo with a taxi light on the roof, swung round the side of the building, out of my line of sight, presumably to park. I looked at my watch. If this was my 9 o'clock appointment, she was dead on time.

I left the window open, stepped to the office door, swung it round until it was almost closed and looked into the dress mirror hanging on the back of it. It seemed only courtesy to check I was presentable enough. I stared at the face in the glass, nine years older than the face that first moved in here. I was 37 then, still young. 46 is middle aged. I decided my hair was tidy enough. I turned through ninety degrees and looked at the body profile. That was okay. I wasn't carrying any extra weight. Still comfortably straight backed and half an inch short of six feet tall.

I swung the door open again, moved back across the office, sat down in the chair behind my desk and waited. I don't make any attempt to appear busy at moments like these. Doesn't fool anybody.

The phone rang. I picked up the receiver. It was Jason, on the security desk.

"Mr Shepherd..."

Jason's politeness is resolute. No one in the building has managed to persuade him to call them by their given names. He is young and the smartest member of the day shift, by a mile. A real bonus at the front desk, for tenants and guests alike. He has a sports management degree from Bath university. An accomplished kayaker, he missed 2014 World Cup qualification by a whisker. So while he figures out what to do next, the building can rest secure.

"There is a Ms Thorne here to see you," he said.

"Thank you Jason. Send her straight up."

I put the receiver back in its base and waited.

Two minutes later, I heard the rumble of the lift, followed by a couple of judders and a thump as it came to rest. The door slid open, then slid closed again. A determined visitor takes twelve seconds to stride purposefully to my office door. A worried guest takes longer. I couldn't hear the sound of footsteps, and it was some twenty-five seconds before my putative client appeared.

The lady made something of an entrance nonetheless. She glided into the office like a ballroom dance champion, stopped, and waited for a moment or two. She was wearing a linen jacket over a white tee shirt and washed-out blue Wranglers. She had a pink silk scarf around her neck. The noiseless tread was explained by the expensive pink and powder grey Hogan trainers.

"Are you Jack Shepherd?" she asked, in the husky voice I'd heard down the phone line.

I said I was and motioned her to the client chair in front of my desk. She sat down in it.

"Do you find people?"

"It's part of what I do," I said. "And sometimes, I'm successful."

"Only sometimes?"

The relationship was barely seconds old, so I couldn't tell how serious that question was. I decided we should begin with the conversation as light as possible.

"Well, on a scale of one to ten..."

She interrupted me. "Yes of course. Silly of me. I'm sorry. It's just..."

She stopped talking, sighed, then bit her lower lip. The nervous twenty-five seconds in the corridor hadn't quite done the trick. The confidence displayed on her entrance seemed to have seeped away. We looked at each other, neither of us entirely convinced that she was in the right place. So I offered her an abbreviated CV.

"I was a policeman for twelve years. I couldn't work inside the system, but it seemed churlish to throw away all that training and experience. However, the job opportunities for ex-coppers are limited to the same thing only different. It was either this or the security business... So, I chase up disappeared wives, spy on errant husbands and yes, I find people. I should say however, those who cross this threshold, usually do so as a last resort. *Shepherd Investigations* is the 'go to' place for those who have run out of options."

She considered the summary and stood up again. That appeared to give her some resolve. She swallowed, took a deep breath then exhaled slowly.

"I want you to find someone for me," she said.

"And who would that be?" I asked.

"Me," she said. "I want you to find me."

I stared at her. For what seemed an eternity, she stared obligingly back. And then she conjured up the most extraordinary smile I had ever seen. From nervous to laid back in a moment, the transformation was astonishing. Sparkling white, perfectly even teeth, set like stones in a bracelet. Then suddenly, it was gone, like she had never smiled in her life. I was in turn surprised, transfixed and then distracted. Below us, Patsy Cline had segued into Frank Sinatra and *One For My Baby*.

"You come highly recommended..."

I heard her from miles away. Dragged myself back to the conversation.

"By whom?"

She shook her head. She was nervous again.

"I won't tell you that," she said. "If I do, you'll know where to start."

"And that's a bad idea?"

"Yes."

"So, where can we start?"

She sat down again, arranged herself comfortably in the chair, stretched her long legs out in front of her, pressed the palms of her hands together, raised them to her face as if she was about to pray, then tapped her chin several times. It gave me time to pull myself together and take stock. Tallish – about five ten – shoulder length light brown hair, green eyes, carefully applied makeup. A friendly face, but one, minus the smile, which showed signs of strain. Probably a recent thing. The look in her eyes was resolute enough, there was no fixed expression of worry, no permanent lines of pain. But she was hurting. Something was distressing her.

"Here's the thing," she said. "I have reasoned that if you can't find me, there's a solid chance that others won't either."

"Which others?"

She shook her head. "You mustn't know that. At least, not at this stage and not from me".

"Are you in trouble?"

"I won't answer that sort of question. So don't re-work it and ask again."

Something approaching the truth from a client, or information intriguingly close to the truth, is normally required to kick start any private investigation. Keep information from the police if you must, mislead them, be economical with the truth. But don't lie to your P.I. Defeats the object.

But a job defined by no information at all... Well, that was something else.

"Okay," I said. "We need a base to start from. If I don't know anything about you, I won't be able to find you."

"That's what I'm hoping."

"If that's the result you want, fine. However, if I do manage to find you, starting with no information at all, then the aforementioned 'others' will be able to do so too."

She looked at me in silence.

"And they have a head start. Given that they already know who you are."

She searched for the line she'd rehearsed should this approach come up. I persisted.

"I need to know all that's in the public domain. There is no advantage in me being less informed than the people you're afraid of. I need to know at least as much as they do. You can concede that proposition surely?"

She nodded. "Yes. So if you take this on, I will tell you as much as they know about me and my current situation."

"Why don't you want them to find you?"

"You've just re-phrased the question I told you not to."

"It's difficult to be so non-specific," I suggested.

"If that is so," she said, "then you're not the man I was led to believe you are."

It was difficult not to get irritated with all this. But prospective clients have to be indulged to a degree.

"By whom?" I asked.

She shook her head, then stared across the desk at me.

"Mr Shepherd. I have rehearsed this..." she searched for the right word "... encounter, for some days now. This is neither a game nor a bargain basement intellectual exercise. I haven't created this scenario so that we may walk what is left of our wits. There is no room for error here. I am deadly serious."

The equal emphasis on every word of the last sentence, the body language and the focus of her attention, all combined to reinforce the message. I chose the phrasing of my next question very carefully.

"And so I assume therefore, if whatever this may be is handled wrongly, the consequences could be equally serious."

She nodded once. Her eyes locked onto mine, unblinking.

"Yes. Believe me, yes."

It was hard not to do so. My next ploy, would have been to ask her what else she had rehearsed and how much more she was prepared to divulge. She pre-empted that by slipping into business mode.

"What do I have to pay to retain your services for say, a week?"

"I charge 250 a day, plus expenses," I said. "Seven days for the price of five."

"That's fine."

She dug into the inside pocket of her jacket, produced a money clip, stood up, leaned over my desk, counted out twenty-three £50 notes, placed them on the leather desktop and pushed them towards me. I stared down at the money.

"Do we have a deal?" she asked.

"Do I get to know your name?"

"You get to know the name by which others know me. Not the new name I have just taken."

Then she offered the smile again. A little less lustrous than before, but it was worth the effort.

"You know, that's a good smile," I said. "A little rusty round the edges maybe, but you should let it work for you more."

"My name is Deborah Thorne. Debbie if you wish."

I looked down at the money again.

"Are you going to take it?" she asked.

The question of the day so far. It would be so easy to do that. Then spend a day or two on a minimum amount of sleuthing. Make a couple of phone calls, check the internet, go through something approaching the motions of an investigation and wait for Deborah to call back.

"Have you considered I might take the twelve hundred and fifty pounds," I said, "do absolutely nothing at all, and when you next contact me, simply say I had failed in all my endeavours to trace you?"

"You won't."

"I might."

"No. Not you. I've checked you out remember."

It was immensely gratifying to learn I was a man of such probity. But no one, however quixotic, can accept such glowing references without some response. Between us, we had to be really clear about all this.

"Okay," I said. "We'll leave the money there for the moment. Tell me as much as you can."

That seemed to do it. She leaned back in the chair and returned to the script.

"Deborah Thorne is my real name. It's not the name I'm using now. I'm 36 years old. I was born in the midlands. I've moved around a lot. Until five months ago, I worked at a call centre in Reading."

"Can I know for whom?"

"Yes. It won't help you find me, at least I hope it won't. But significant others know about this, so you should. A company called Home and Domestic Services. Providing insurance for house contents. Electrical appliances, cookers, fridges, dishwashers, that sort of stuff."

She paused, to collate the next bit of information. Now the soundtrack was being provided by Roy Orbison and *Crying'*.

"I came to Bristol in April," she said. "A week after Easter. I bought a house near Victoria Park. Number 15 Grove Road. I dealt directly with the owner and paid cash. So there is no mortgage trail to follow. I am assuming that the people who may be looking for me don't know where I live. I think if they did, they would have found me by this time. But to make sure, I've moved."

There was no point asking her where to. So I contented myself with asking her how long ago.

"Six days," she said.

I decided to move back a few paragraphs. "Why did you leave Reading?"

The change in narrative line didn't faze her a bit.

"Do you mean why did I leave my job? Or do you actually want to know why I moved from London?"

I responded as deftly as I could.

"Okay... Was your move to the Westcountry job related, or was it a personal thing?"

"It was a personal thing. There was no problem with my job. Other than it was unrewarding, boring and frustrating."

"Did you tell anyone at Home and Domestic Services where you were moving to?"

She shook her head. "No."

"Are you working now?"

"No. I don't need to."

I looked down at the money on the desk.

"Because you can afford not to?"

"Yes."

"So where does this money come from?"

There were a couple of beats before she replied.

"Savings."

That was another of the moments she had anticipated and rehearsed. Savings maybe. Money wasn't an issue and she had recently bought a house for cash. I decided to log this topic away for now.

"How much do the 'others' know about West London and Reading?"

"As much as I've told you."

"So if anyone pitches up at Home and Domestic Services?..."

"It will be a waste of time."

We were silent for a while. I looked at her and she looked at me and we stared as if we had forever. Down in Patrick's office, Abba took over with *The Winner Takes It All*. In the torch song hall of fame, Benny and Bjorn's lament for a broken relationship has to be the most revered. Deborah motioned to the desk.

"So will you take the money now?" she asked.

"Maybe," I said and switched topics again.

"Do you have friends in Bristol?"

She took time to go back over the response she'd rehearsed to this question.

"A friend. And half a dozen acquaintances. One person in particular, has been to my house on a number of occasions."

"Someone close?" I asked.

"Close enough," she said. "I won't tell you who the person is."

"Because I would find a way to talk to him..."

"Or her." She smiled again; just enough to acknowledge the ploy. "Please don't assume anything in this matter."

I pondered for a moment or two.

"So... since you moved, the 'friend and acquaintances' no longer know where you are."

She nodded. "That's right."

"Which means you're out of the loop."

She nodded again. "I do hope so."

On a roll now, and ignoring the risk of complicating the dialectic, I ploughed on.

"The reverse may not apply. There is no way you can be sure that the 'others' have not traced the 'friend and acquaintances' in the meantime. Because since you disappeared from their radar, you currently have no idea what's going on. At all. The 'others' may have made progress. Six days is a substantial time, it could be that – "

This was working. Irritating the hell out of her. She held up her hands and shouted at me.

"All right all right…"

I mustered my best injured innocence look and pasted it on to my face. She shook her arms, took a couple of deep breaths and calmed down again.

"That was very clever. And the point is well made," she said. "However, it only serves to show that my position really may be as..." again she searched for the appropriate word, "... compromised, as I believe it is."

I looked at her dead centre. She didn't blink. I reasoned that I'd done as much due diligence as possible under the circumstances. I picked up the £50 notes. She blew out her cheeks and sat back in the client chair.

"Thank you," she said.

"This may be a very bad investment. I can't guarantee anything."

"I appreciate that."

I put the money in the top drawer of the right-hand pedestal of my desk and looked back at her.

"Okay," I said. "A couple more questions. Parents?"

"Yes. Both alive. I won't tell you where."

"Relatives?"

"I have an aunt and uncle in Australia. A sister in Dublin. Her name is Helena. Others know this, but nothing else. She's married."

"So not called Thorne?"

"No."

"Good."

She suddenly remembered something. Took an A5 size envelope out of a jacket pocket and passed it across the desk. I opened it and shook out a photograph. Deborah smiling straight down the lens, apparently happy and relaxed.

"It's a good likeness," I said.

"Others have that photograph, so you qualify also."

I found myself admiring her attention to detail. And her cool. She had gone about this in a highly organised fashion. Presumably spent days covering all the bases. Apart from one moment of confusion, she had stayed on script throughout our conversation. There was just one item that still bothered me.

"I take it you have a passport."

"Yes."

"So you could leave the country."

"I don't want to leave," she said. "This is where I live. I want to hide in plain sight. Not in some cottage on a remote hillside, or some village in the country where people will wonder about the solitary stranger. I need a place where I can get lost in a crowd. And where, if push comes to shove, I can get help."

Deborah hitched at the waistband of her jeans, dug into the right front pocket, produced a set of house keys and held them out to me. She told me the address again.

"Number 15, Grove Road, Windmill Hill," she said. "I would prefer you didn't break in. Keep these until this is..."

I could understand why she was reluctant to finish the sentence with "all over". I held out my left hand, palm upwards. She dropped the keys into it. Then she went into overdrive.

"There is no point in lifting my finger prints from the keys. I know you have a good police connection, but don't waste his time and yours. My prints are not on file anywhere. The money you have in the drawer is in used notes. Three weeks ago, I sold the car I brought down from London. The one I currently drive is registered with the DVLA at that old address – which is of course, the address on my driver's licence. I haven't changed it. Today, I came here in a cab. I shall call another from the lobby downstairs when we have finished. I assume you will make a note of the number, but I'll take several more cabs. I might take some busses. Cross and re-cross the city until I'm sure you're not following me. And now, I have only one more thing to say... I don't want your job to be difficult Mr Shepherd, I want it to be impossible."

So, in a nutshell, my client had handed over twelve hundred and fifty pounds, in the fervent hope I would fail to do what I do.

She stood up.

"Would you like a drink?" I asked. "Coffee, tea? I assume it's a little early for something stronger?"

She smiled the smile again.

"No thank you. But that's genuinely because I don't want one." She nodded at the mugs on the shelf above the sink. "Please don't be disappointed. I'm not on any DNA database either, so I wouldn't leave a trace. You get my admiration for trying however. Goes to show, the right man is on the case."

I stood up too and thanked her for the compliment.

"So I'll leave now," she said, turned and walked out the office door.

I watched her go. Downstairs, George Harrison was singing... *Something in the way she moves...*

Shepherd Investigations may be a one-person operation, but I like to believe that the owner-operator is an honourable and diligent sleuth. I had work to do, but there was no point following Deborah out of the building. Like she said, I would simply lose her somewhere in the city centre. However, I should do the basic stuff.

I called Jason.

"Mr Shepherd..."

"Ms Thorne is on the way out again. She'll call for a taxi. Will you make a note of the operator?"

"I assume it will be City Cabs. That's who she came with."
Jason didn't miss much either.

"And get the cab number if you can."

"Of course."

"Thanks Jason."

The taxi driver would be an unlikely source of information. *I picked her up outside your office and dropped her in the centre.* But following a lead, if no more than half a mile, is a text book requirement. I could find the taxi driver and talk to him later.

I swung my desk chair round to face the window, leant back and started thinking. And suddenly, up from Patrick's office, came Rainbow and *All Night Long*. A quantum leap by any definition.

I listened to Graham Bonnet's soaring vocal for a line or two, then stood up and closed the window. Returned to my desk and sat down again. I took the fifty-pound notes out of the desk drawer and stared at them.

A fistful of money and no leads.

On reflection that wasn't true. Actually, I had two leads. *You come highly recommended*, Deborah had said. And *I know you have a good police connection.* The latter had to be Detective Superintendent Harvey Butler. The straightest of straight arrow coppers, the best that Avon and Somerset Constabulary could boast about. Tough and clever, with an amiability that disguised his thoroughness and his determination. He was a detective sergeant when I first met him; the day after I joined CID some twenty-five years ago. Destined to be the career copper I never could be, he took me under his wing and taught me the ropes. And he supported me through the weeks following the shooting which changed my life. A seventeen-year-old boy, out of his mind on angel dust, came at me in an alleyway with a meat cleaver. I had seconds to make a decision – the one that drove me out of the job. The pictures still come back to me in dreams, in dark moments, and on less successful days.

And suddenly, Harvey wanted to talk to me about Philip Soames.

I put the money back in the desk drawer and locked it.

Deborah's recommendation could only have come from someone I had worked for. Or someone, who knew someone I had worked for. My client list isn't extensive and certainly not blue chip, but the files do fill all three drawers of the filing cabinet. I opened the top drawer and started with A.

I was into the Ds when the phone rang. I picked up the receiver.

"It was City Cabs," Jason said. "Not far from here. Across the river at the bottom of Bedminster Parade. Mrs Thorne was picked up by cab 643."

"Thank you."

"I rang them. The driver's name is Gerry Simpson."

I picked up a pen and wrote the name on a post-it note. Jason appeared to take the momentary silence as some kind of reprimand.

"I'm sorry Mr Shepherd," he said. "I didn't mean to er... I just thought that I could help out."

"No that's fine Jason. Saved me a phone call. Thanks."

I made a mental note to invite Jason to do more legwork for me, then went back to the Ds.

CHAPTER THREE

It was noon by the time I'd read all the files. I concentrated on names going back three years and ended up with a list of twenty-eight. Two, at least, I knew were dead. Ronnie Lister, a one-time short con artist, whose funeral I had been to seven months ago and the recently deceased Philip Soames. Three of them were in prison; more evidence of my lack of top echelon work.

Twenty-eight souls. Most of them had come to me because they were frightened, lonely, desperate, bereaved, sad, angry, or just plain lost. Some of them had gone away feeling better. Like Philip Soames, on reflection perhaps the most well-adjusted person on the list. A few, like Louise earlier in the day, with the result they had fervently sought. But some had lost more than they bargained for. To them I could only apologise. Words that always fell too short of the mark. Some investigations have happy endings. Some don't. I am the keeper of the *Last Chance* saloon.

So what to do? Call all twenty-three still alive or at liberty? Or concentrate on the person whose name I'd heard several times today?

Linda saved me from further contemplation. She arrived in the office posed in the doorway again and beamed at me.

"I got the gig," she announced. "Congratulate me."

"You were a shoe-in," I said.

She stepped into the room.

"It's hot in here," she said. "Mind if I open the window?"

"Help yourself."

Linda crossed the office. Behind me I heard the window catch snap and Guns 'n Roses *Live and Let Die* blast up from downstairs.

"It's a new development," I said.

Linda moved around the desk back into my line of sight and sat down in my client chair.

"An improvement on *Achey Breaky Heart*, don't you think?"

"I don't suppose the two songs are mutually exclusive," I said.

"Everybody's just a little bit country," she said.

I stared at her. She beamed at me again.

"And how was your morning?"

* * *

We sat at a table outside the Nova Scotia pub; on the dockside, in a well of quiet, ringed by the noise of distant traffic. Hotwell Road was a hundred yards away, across the other side of the floating harbour. To our left, the water in the Cumberland Basin was perfectly still. Beyond it, traffic leaving the city eased up the ramp to the swing bridge. To our right looking east, the floating harbour stretched almost a mile towards the city centre. Past the SS Great Britain, the marina the workshops and the ships chandlers; the former industrial museum, now re-born as the hi-tech, interactive M Shed; and on to where the waterfront bars and bistros meet the business of the city.

We had eaten the toasted sandwiches and Linda was drinking a glass of the Nova Scotia house white. I was risking half a pint of Old Ferret, brewed in a back yard a few streets away from the pub. Many people still believe that Bristol is Real Ale Central.

"So?..." Linda broke the silence.

"What?"

"I repeat. How was your morning?"

"Lucrative."

"Really?"

"A little less scorn if you please."

She looked hurt. I swallowed another mouthful of Old Ferret. She waited. I gave up and spilled the beans.

"I have a new client. Deborah Thorne."

"Who is she?"

"I don't know."

I stared at Linda. There was obviously no chance of her bursting into something like "*My God, Debbie. I've known her for years...*"

"Sorry," she said. "I shouldn't ask. Client confidentiality and all that."

She took another sip of the house white.

"No, ask away," I said. "That's what I've got to do. Client confidentiality only matters if there's a pile of secrets to keep. So far in this case, I don't know any. I know my client's name. She gave me twelve hundred and fifty pounds to find her"

Linda swallowed the house white. "Find her?"

"Yes. That's the job."

"Why? Is she going to get lost?"

"She already is, kind of."

"I don't understand."

I gave her a précis of the morning's encounter. She took another drink and looked out across the water.

"No address, place of work, phone number, car registration..."

"I have a photograph," I said.

I fished the picture out of the inside pocket of my jacket. Linda studied it.

"Very attractive," she said. "In a broad-shouldered sort of

a way. So, where are you going to start?"

"Check with the taxi driver for form's sake. Then put on my best smile and go see Harvey Butler."

We walked back to the office building. Linda had emails to check. I picked up my car keys, drove around the office building, onto the ramp up to the swing bridge, across the Cumberland Basin and immediately came to a standstill.

It took the best part of ten minutes to navigate the mile and a half to City Cabs office – a double aspect, ground floor room in Bedminster that had once been the local corner shop. Gerry Simpson, in his mid-20s, with a retro mullet of brown hair and a Zapata moustache, was sitting on a battered sofa waiting for the dispatcher to send him out again. He told me exactly what I had expected to hear.

"I left her in the centre. On the north side. She joined a bus queue. I drove back here."

"Which bus queue?"

"Hell, I don't know." He pondered for a moment or two. "Okay... If you stand in the middle of the pedestrian area, with the fountains on your left and look towards the Hippodrome, there are what... er... three bus stops? She joined the queue on the right. I don't know which buses stop there. You'll have to check."

I got back into the Healey and set off to do that. I left the car in Baldwin Street and walked the couple of hundred yards to the centre. The sun disappeared. A ridge of dark cloud was sprinting from the south west.

Bus numbers 71, 72, 105 and 106 picked up from the queue Deborah had joined. The routes covered huge chunks of the west side of the city. Deborah could be anywhere. I walked back to the Healey. Just as the rain began again.

Sitting in the car, I weighed up the options. I had two

people to see. Philip Soames ran his practise exclusively. No partners, no associates. His secretary was a lady called Sarah. 30 years old, graceful and charming. It would be difficult talking to her, but I had no choice. The difficulty quotient racked up considerably with my second appointment however. He had given me a noon deadline, but I decided to take on George Hood later. I drove round the city centre and up Park Street into Clifton, the rain thudding down on the soft top. Philip Soames' office suite was housed on the second floor of a three-storey regency building in Victoria Square, once the town house of some rich merchant. I found a parking place about fifteen yards from the front door and got into the building relatively dry.

Suite 2A overlooked the square. Sarah's office was part waiting room, part reception space. There were two large sofas set in a L shape in front of the fireplace, a long low coffee table in front of them. A door beyond led to the rest of the suite – a kitchen, bathroom and Philip Soames' consulting room.

Sarah occupied the rest of the space. She was sitting at her desk, in an expensively cut navy suit, designed to be attractive, but business like. Not so today however. Today she looked lost.

She stood up to greet me. I said hello.

"I have cancelled all Philip's appointments," she said. "For this week, that is. I will have to go through the whole of his diary and... well..."

She faltered into silence.

"Sarah..."

She looked down at the desk. "I don't make appointments on Friday afternoons. We use that time for business review. But not last Friday. Philip came back from lunch and said he had something important to do. He picked up his laptop and left. Later in the afternoon, I called his mobile and his home number. There was no answer from either."

"He didn't come back to the office at all?"

Sarah looked up at me and shook her head.

"When he didn't arrive yesterday, I called the police. I spoke to a very polite constable who took a statement and said there was probably a very simple explanation. I called all the clients with appointments and... sat here... waiting for something to happen. Mid-morning, about 11 o'clock, a detective sergeant arrived. He took me to a mortuary in Avonmouth. He asked me to look at three bodies. One of them was Philip."

She sat down again, lowered her head and closed her eyes. There was a long silence, underscored by the sound of rain beating on the window. I waited. Then Sarah raised her head and placed her palms flat on the desk top.

"What is this about Mr Shepherd? What did Philip do to deserve this? What sort of people?..." She left the sentence hanging in the air.

"Can I look at his diary Sarah?"

Her pupils seemed to enlarge, but she didn't look away.

"His diary?"

"Please."

"I'm sorry, the police have it."

Which explained how they knew of my connection to her boss. Presumably he listed his appointments as well as his consultations.

"Why do you want to see Philip's diary?"

"I've been retained by a lady who was recommended to me by a client. That client may have been Philip. If that was the case, then she would have been a client of his. I need to confirm that."

"Do you believe this person may have something to do with his murder?"

"I don't know, but I would like to find out. Name Deborah Thorne. Perhaps you could check Philip's case notes."

There was another moment of silence. Then Sarah stood up, moved around her desk and gestured towards the sofas. We sat down, taking one each. She went on.

"I will not give you access to Philip's case notes, but I don't need to check. I can tell you that Deborah Thorne is a client of his."

"Can you tell me what she is, was, seeing him about?"

"No Mr Shepherd, I can't."

"Is that what you've been saying to the police?"

"I told them I would respect the confidentiality of Philip's clients as long as I could. They are coming back with a court order and a search warrant. Within the hour, I expect."

I looked at the clock on the wall behind Sarah's desk. 2.55. Sarah was displaying extraordinary control, considering the circumstances. She was hurt and devastated, but she was not going to compromise on ethics or procedure. I changed tack.

"Can you tell me when Deborah last saw Philip?"

"Why not ask her yourself? She is your client."

"I can't," I said. "I don't know where she is. That's the problem. I need to find her. Any reference may help."

Sarah got to her feet, moved back to her desk and sat in front of her pc. She tapped a key or two, clicked the mouse, waited a couple of moments, clicked the mouse again, then looked up at me.

"10 o'clock," she said. "Three weeks to the day."

"Was that a routine appointment?" I asked.

Sarah considered the implications before deciding to

reply.

"No. She had a series of appointments over four years. The consultations finished some time ago. But then she rang up out of the blue and asked to see Philip again."

"About what?"

She looked at me with some indulgence. I lifted a hand in apology. She came back to the sofa. Silence descended again, as we both worked out what to say next. The sound of the rain on the window was quieter.

"My investigation has to start somewhere," I said. "As for the police, I don't know where they'll start. But they will dig around until they find something."

"I'm sure there will be nothing to find," Sarah said.

If that was true and the police knew less about Soames than I did, then for the moment at least, I was in the pound seats. I resolved what it was I wanted to say.

"Sarah... Just like this practice, I have a confidential relationship with my clients. I understand the imperative not to divulge privileged information. But I believe Deborah came to see me on a recommendation from Philip. Now Deborah has disappeared. And Philip is dead."

I thought that last sentence was weighty enough and I paused for a reaction. Sarah stared into the fireplace. I pushed a bit harder.

"Sarah, I don't believe in coincidences. Philip's death has something to do with the reason Deborah came to see me."

Sarah turned to look at me.

"All client information and case histories are stored on the office hard drive. Backed up data sticks. And on hard copies in the filing cabinet. Philip's laptop, has his personal correspondence on it and the information he needs to stay current. That's all."

"And the laptop is not in his office?"

"No."

She offered no more. We both knew that I had to propose something. I began with the straight forward bit.

"When CID get back here, co-operate with them right down the line. It will be a serious mistake not to. All the practice paperwork will be seized anyway. They will get phone records and bank statements. They'll turn Philip's office upside down. They'll find his laptop, wherever it is. So give them all the help they ask for."

She nodded. "Very well," she said softly.

That agreed, I proposed the minor conspiracy.

"However, don't volunteer any information. Just answer the questions they ask. They'll be prepared to a degree but they're not known for extemporising."

"Suppose they ask if I have had any visitors."

"Then you will have to tell them I called."

"And what do I say when they ask why?"

"Tell them that Philip was a client of mine," I said. "That much is true. Their reaction will be to ask what I was doing for him. Your reply will be that you do not know. That much is true also."

"And if they ask why you have turned up at such an inappropriate time?"

I took a deep breath.

"Tell them you don't know that either."

"Which will be a lie," she said.

"Just a small one," I said.

"Hardly," she said.

"They won't pursue the matter. At least not with you. Simply say you don't know why and they'll take it up with me."

Once again, she took time to consider her decision.

"Very well. I can do that. 'I don't know' is easily said. But that's not all is it? Please get to the point you have been working towards."

"I need you to copy Deborah files onto a data stick for me," I said. "I don't want you to tell the police you have done this. You won't be deceiving them. At least not in any pro-active sense. You certainly won't be lying to them. Just not telling them something they don't know."

"Something they don't know they would like to know, however," Sarah said.

"Yes, but if they don't know they'd like to know, you can't be blamed for not telling them," I said.

That piece of linguistic hocus-pocus, brought a smile into her eyes. We had debated enough. Sarah went back to her desk, called up Deborah Thorne's files and copied them onto a data stick.

* * *

The carefully constructed subterfuge went to rats out in the street.

The rain had stopped. Detective Sergeant George Hood, a couple of inches shorter than me but wider and tougher, was standing on the wet pavement, staring at the Healey.

"This doesn't have to be my car," I suggested.

"It is nonetheless," he said. "And parked outside the office of a man brutally done away with forty-eight hours ago. I take it you've been in there."

I fished the Healey keys out of my pocket.

"It would be helpful if you could drive straight round to Trinity Road," Hood said. He waved his mobile at me. "I've just been talking with Superintendent Butler."

"I don't suppose there's any element of choice here," I said.

Hood nodded to a uniformed constable, standing by a patrol car, double-parked alongside the Healey.

"I can always get PC Stratton to take you personally. He does need to move that vehicle."

I bowed to the inevitable, climbed into the Healey and fired it up. PC Stratton reversed the patrol car five yards. I turned into the road in front of it and set off for my meeting with Harvey.

Not all coppers are sexist, racist and homophobic. Sometimes they're just not very bright. Harvey Butler is an exception. A perspicacious detective, tough and clever and so straight it hurts. A man with more than his share of insight into the nature of the human condition. And something close to an unshakeable faith in the eventual triumph of good over evil. Thirty years as a detective has not diminished one iota his capacity for seeing though to the heart of a situation and knowing exactly what to do about it. Nor have the years made him cynical. He never takes a short cut, never pursues the line of least resistance, never contrives to make the job easy for himself. The best young coppers in town grew up under Harvey's wing.

His problem however, is that he believes in the system. I don't. Harvey and I are friends, but he regards me at best, as unhelpful. I look at it from a slightly different angle. I am a private investigator, with the emphasis on the first word of the job description.

All of which meant that neither of us brought any baggage to this moment. Harvey granted me the courtesy of saying hello and then waded in without getting up out of his chair.

"How well did you know Philip Soames?" he asked.

"He was a client of mine," I said.

"Is or was?"

"Was"

If Harvey could be succinct, so could I. He stared at me. Then expanded the premise a little.

"Was, in the sense that he's now dead?"

"Also in the sense that it was some time ago."

"What did you do for him?"

"I found his long-lost aunt in Ambleside."

Harvey decided I was trying to be funny. Disbelief morphed into impatience. I ploughed innocently on.

"That's in the Lake District," I said.

"I know where it is," he said. Then, after a beat, "Long lost aunt?"

"I can give you name, address and telephone number."

"And when did you accomplish this essential piece of detective work?"

I ignored the disdain. "November last year."

"Have you seen Philip Soames since?"

"Three or four times."

"Socially, or by way of business?"

"The former," I said.

Harvey didn't blink.

"And you went to his office today because?..."

"It seemed the thing to do."

This conversation was developing a life of its own. It had the propensity to go on for the rest of the morning. Harvey decided enough was enough.

"Here's what we'll do," he said, with all the patience in the world. "I'll start drilling. And you can tell me when it starts to hurt."

He had made his point. So I detailed the number of times Philip Soames' name had come up in conversations over the last twenty-four hours. And I concluded by saying that I went to his office to share a few minutes with Sarah. I omitted the Deborah Thorne stuff.

Harvey sat and listened without interrupting. When I finished, he cleared his throat, swallowed and sucked at his teeth. There were two phones on his desk. He chose the silver one and picked up the receiver. He dialled a number and waited. Then he spoke.

"George, where are you?" He listened for a moment, then spoke again. "Did you ask her why our favourite PI was visiting today?" He listened again. "Is that all?" He listened again. "No, if she's upset, don't do that."

He put the receiver back in its cradle, sat back in his chair, folded his arms across his chest and blew out his cheeks.

"In essence, she says what you say."

"QED."

"So why can't I shake off the notion that it's all bollocks?"

I assumed Harvey wasn't actually expecting a reply, so I said nothing. He unfolded his arms and leaned forward across the desk top.

"I have to tell you that Philip Soames wasn't just sent on the big downer. He was tortured. There are two fingers missing from his left hand. We both know he wasn't supposed to re-surface and I presume we both have theories about that."

He paused. This time he was waiting for me to say something.

"I presume we do," I said. "But I've decided not to dwell on anything."

"Which is the best thing, all in all," he said. "This is an open case Jack. And if I find that you're poking around in it..." He left the sentence unfinished.

"I'm not," I said. Which was true in a way, because I had no idea what I was poking around in.

Harvey got to his feet. I noticed he had lost some weight.

He was still carrying a pound or two more than he should, but he looked fitter than when I last saw him.

"So," he said. "Go now."

I went straight home.

Switched on the pc and plugged in the data stick. And read the story of Deborah Thornton in forensic detail. Two hours later, I was still staring at the monitor screen. Mesmerised.

Deborah Thorne had only been Deborah Thorne for a little over six years. Until then, she had been Daniel Thornton.

I switched off the pc, locked the data stick in a desk drawer and went for a walk in Canford Park.

I knew nothing at all about trans-gender surgery. Only that, despite the now relatively safe surgical procedures, it was a brave, no going back, psychologically dangerous, thing to submit to. Deborah's appointments with Philip Soames covered a three-and-a-half-year period, during which she had begun and completed the whole trans-gender process. Hormone drug treatments, facial hair electrolysis, facial surgery, genital electrolysis followed by genital surgery, breast augmentation, vaginaplasty and finally labiaplasty. Each stage monitored psychologically by counselling sessions with Philip Soames, working in partnership with surgeons in a clinic in Oxfordshire.

One hell of a life changing experience, by anybody's standards.

I came back to reality at the east gate of the park. The front door of the Canford Vaults beckoned from across the road. It was happy hour; the sun was out again and the alfresco drinkers had spilled out of the pub and filled the terrace. Perhaps there was room inside the inn.

I sat in a corner of the lounge with a pint of Butcombe Gold and drank it slowly.

Half an hour later, I was once again, the cool, rational investigator my client was paying for. On reflection, I had made progress in twenty-four hours. The Philip Soames connection to Deborah was clear. The question was, why had he died? For information about Deborah's whereabouts? And did that mean, whoever she was running away from knew her intimately? Knew that she had once been Daniel Thornton? If so, he, she or they, still knew gigabytes more than I did.

I walked home via the Redland Chip Shop and collected cod and chips and mushy peas. At home, I added a bottle of Alsace beer to the feast, sat in the dining room and ate it.

Substantially refreshed, I spent an hour at the pc, writing up my notes on the case so far. I have a safe under the floorboards in the cupboard under the stairs. I locked Sarah's usb stick in it.

Then I switched on the TV, in search of some post watershed entertainment. It was pretty dismal fare. On BBC1, an over-excited presenter was standing in a bog in Wales, amazed by the knowledge that, millions of years ago, dinosaurs had stood in the same spot. BBC2 was ten minutes into a documentary on 'nuclear power reality'. ITV1 was offering a drama series, proudly proclaimed as high concept, about a surgeon who specialises in body part surgery and is an amateur sleuth in his down time. Kirstie Allsop was berating a gloomy Phil Spencer on Channel 4. On Five, there was a UEFA Cup match between two second string European sides. I followed this for a few minutes, but it was difficult to concentrate on the action. The commentator was coping well with the names of twenty-two foreigners, but he was in hyper-drive and constantly in flow. I searched through the rest of the multi-channel stuff, with little reward. Re-runs of re-runs mostly. I settled on Film 4 and *The Day of the Jackal.* Never disappointing, even though we know he's never going to get the job done. But with commercials between every reel, it ran at almost three hours.

I couldn't stay awake, despite Fred Zinnerman's brilliant storytelling. I opted for bed as Edward Fox was going in to the Turkish Bath.

CHAPTER FOUR

I woke up from a dream at 6.30 the next morning, Wednesday, and instantly forgot what I had been dreaming about. I hate that. At the very least, it would be satisfying to know what robbed you of sleep. An hour later, despite my best efforts to relax, I was still awake. I got up and took a shower.

The front doorbell rang as I was contemplating breakfast.

The post person, a soft-spoken lady in her 50s, proffered a large brown cardboard box.

"For me?"

"No, sorry," she said. "For next door. There's nobody in."

"They're on holiday. In Tipperary."

"That's a long way to go," she said.

We both enjoyed the joke.

"Will you take it then?" she asked.

"Yes, of course."

She handed it to me.

"Wait a moment," she said.

From her shoulder bag she fished half a dozen envelopes of assorted sizes and colours wrapped in an elastic band. Dropped them on top of the box.

"Your mail. Looks like a bill or two there. Sorry. Cheerio."

She turned and set off down the path to the gate. I reversed a couple of paces, reached out with my right foot, collected the door and swung it shut. I put the box down at the foot of the stairs and walked back into the kitchen to open my mail.

I support a number of charities on a regular basis, but all of the appeals in the bundle were unsolicited. One of them tugged substantially at my conscience. I kept that and dropped the rest into the bin, then took them out again, looked through them once more and kept another one. At times it's difficult to separate feelings of guilt from notions of responsibility.

The phone bill was enormous. What the hell was I doing? Ringing Australia twice a week? BT were not to be gainsaid however. It was all there. Cheerfully itemised calls, landline, broadband, mobile, plus the preference service. I decided to have my calls screened by BT, after I got sick of people calling at all hours, offering to assist me in claiming money back on payment protection insurance sold to me without my knowledge. I haven't taken out a loan in twenty years. They are a recipe for disaster for the self-employed – there are no guarantees you'll ever pay the money back. Unless you take out payment protection insurance...

From such ramblings do certain basic questions evolve. Like the wisdom of paying two sets of bills. Here and in the office. Spaces I occupy, at least for most of the time, by myself. Maybe I should relocate my business here at home. There was more than enough room to do it.

In the beginning, *Shepherd Investigations* was based in the study; the intention being to cut down overheads and for me to work more user-friendly hours than I had done when I was on the force. The practice proved to be flawed however. There was tension in the house throughout every case I worked on and disharmony when I wasn't working at all. *Shepherd Investigations* moved out of the study after I finally accepted that personal and business affairs needed to be separated. Truthfully, Emily ran out of patience. She decided that separate home and work places, while unlikely to improve relationships or business opportunities, would at least provide definition. Linda announced that the office next door to her was empty. The landlord offered me the first two months rent free and so I moved in. Now I could revise all that.

I set out for the office at 8.30. I walked into the building, said 'hello' to Jason, collected my mail and took the stairs to the third floor.

It was like the great John Fogerty song, 'Deja-vu All Over Again'. Envelopes with windows, one of them a cheerful note from the landlord, proposing a rent increase. Time to do something constructive.

Windmill Hill is in the heart of old town, south Bristol. Streets of Victorian and Edwardian semis and terraced houses, clustered around Victoria Park. A part of the city that keeps a low profile. By no stretch of the imagination the centre of the crime universe. Nonetheless, if I was looking for Deborah, I would have somebody watching the place. Though maybe not after ten days... Still, best to be sure.

Linda found me sitting in the lobby.

"What are you doing?" she asked.

"Waiting for a taxi," I said.

"Something wrong with the Healey?"

"I have to go and look round my client's house. Others may have the same idea. I don't want to announce my arrival."

"I'm on my way out, I'll drive you," she said. "You may need a wing man."

"A what?"

"Someone to watch your back."

"Where do you get this stuff from?"

She shrugged. "Just trying to stay hip."

"If such is the case," I said, "then I don't want others involved. Not you. Not anyone."

That must have sounded harsher than I intended, because Linda looked surprised. I apologised.

"Sorry, I didn't mean to be ungrateful. Thanks for the offer."

A horn sounded outside the door. A taxi U-turned on the tarmac.

"Be careful," Linda said.

The cab driver knew his business and the back streets were empty. Fifteen minutes later we were coasting around the southern boundary of Victoria Park. I stopped the cab, paid off the driver and walked the last two hundred and fifty yards.

There were cars parked, sparsely, on both sides of Grove Road. Maybe a couple of dozen. Presumably, most of the residents were at work. Number 15 was two thirds of the way along on the left. There was space in the road in front of the house and opposite. I chose the right-hand pavement and walked the length of the street. All the cars were empty. No one I could make out lurking in a doorway. I took a deep breath, back-tracked, crossed the road to number 15, unlocked the front door and stepped inside.

I stood silently in the hall and waited. Rooted to the spot for several minutes. No one materialised from anywhere. Onwards then...

The house didn't give much away. It had been searched by experts. Not tossed and ripped up, but carefully and methodically gone over, as though by a scenes of crime team. Stuff had been moved, inspected and put back in place. There were trails in the dust and shapes on shelves and work surfaces with streaks of polish exposed. The visitors had got in via the back door. A window pane was smashed and the mortise lock levered off the door frame.

The house was originally a two up two down, with a washhouse at the back. The kitchen dining room and what would once have been the front parlour, were now one living room, stretching front to rear. Upstairs, a second storey had been added to the wash house, creating a small neat bathroom, leaving the two bedrooms intact. It seemed like all the house was doing, was waiting for its owner to come home from work.

This inspection exercise was a bit like my taxi driver encounter. A detective going through the motions. I couldn't tell if anything was missing. I didn't know what I was looking for, so I was unlikely to find whatever it was. Deborah's desk was tucked away in a corner of the living room. A single pedestal with three drawers, none of them locked. Two were empty, the third contained half a dozen envelopes and a few sheets of A4 copy paper. There was a broadband hub on the desk, plugged into the wall socket but not switched on. No sign of a pc or laptop.

If a coffee pot had been percolating away in the kitchen, the place could have been the *Marie Celeste*.

So, the question... Did anybody miss anything?

I went looking in the cupboard under the stairs. My own version at home is just big enough to step into, as long as you don't straighten up. It's full of stuff, piled in and stored for the duration because it used to be important, although now difficult to recall exactly why. The only thing I take out of the space each week is the vacuum cleaner.

Deborah's cleaner was in her cupboard too. The hose was still attached. It sprang out of the door as I opened it and hit me on the chin. I wrestled with it for a moment or two, then reached into the cupboard, dragged Henry and all his bits out into the hall and stuck my head into the space. There was more room in this hideaway than in mine, but no incentive to pull stuff out and search through it all. Maybe the visitors had decided not to do so. And you have to be in it, to win it...

The space was no more than eight feet wide, the ceiling sloping upwards from left to right as I looked at it. Three feet deep, six feet and a bit at its maximum height. With Henry out in the hall, keeping low I could step in, turn around and step out again, but that was it. There was a pile of boxes directly in front of me, heavy and apparently filled with books. I lifted them out, one at time. Behind them was an old pine chest of drawers. The top drawer was packed with dusters. The middle one housed a collection of 13 amp plugs, plastic wall sockets, light bulbs, curtain rings, a couple of torches and some batteries. The bottom drawer was full of tools. To the left, wedged across the space, were more boxes and a pile of rugs stacked on top of a wooden, ribbed steamer trunk. I got the rugs and the boxes out of the cupboard, but couldn't shift the trunk at all. I stood up and banged my head on a stair beam.

I reversed back into the hall and stared into the space. There was carpet on the floor. An off-cut from the living room, neatly edged and positioned. I had done that as well, at home. I knelt down, reached forward with both hands and lifted the front edge of the chest of drawers. It tilted back enough for the front feet to leave the floor. I shuffled forwards, leaned all my weight against it and pulled the carpet out from under. The exposed floorboards were securely nailed down. But there were two short sections side by side. I raked around in the bottom drawer of the pine chest, found a screwdriver, a hammer and a small cold chisel. It took a couple of minutes to prise the boards up. Wedged in the space between two under-floor beams was a small safe.

All we needed was a safe cracker.

Over fifteen years as a private investigator, I have encountered a Pandora's box of entrepreneurs. Forgers, fraudsters, con-artists and second-storey men; wheeler dealers, blackmailers and bent coppers; and a bunch of people implacably more evil. More personable than all of those put together, a retired safe breaker, appropriately named Joseph Locke – after the Irish tenor his mother adored. Joe is now in his 60s, though you wouldn't know it. Tall, slim and a bit short sighted for a man who does close work, he still referees kids football matches on the Downs on Sunday mornings. He now uses the skills he honed over three decades, as a locksmith, semi-retired.

He was in his workshop when I called.

"I am authorised to hire you to do this," I said.

"On behalf of good people or bad people?" he asked.

"Good people. Scouts honour Joe."

"Your word is good enough."

"Come in the back way, through the garden. There's an alleyway behind the house."

"Give me half an hour," he said and hung up.

I went through the kitchen into the old wash house, now tidied up and re-plastered. A washing machine and a chest freezer shared the space with a small table, a couple of fold away garden chairs, a spade, a fork, a trowel and two pairs of gardening gloves. A tea chest in one corner was stuffed with bits of wood – pieces of batten, short lengths of planed two by one and some squares of three-ply. I collected one of them.

In the chest of drawers, I found an old coffee tin of assorted screws, and a power drill with enough battery life to drill four holes. Back in the kitchen, I screwed the three-ply onto the frame round the broken window. A raw piece of DIY, but probably solid enough.

Five minutes later, Joe came in through the back door. In another ten minutes, the safe was open.

"Worse than useless this model," Joe said. "Anybody could open it."

It seemed superfluous to assure him that I couldn't.

"Do you want me to disable the lock?" he asked. "Will you need to get into the safe again?"

"I might do."

Joe took the lock apart, removed the lever mechanism then put the rest of it back together.

"The handle still works," he said.

He packed his tools. I offered him three of Deborah's £50 notes. He waved the money away.

"Not if it's for good people," he said.

He left the hall, went through the kitchen and back out the way he had come in.

There wasn't much inside the safe. Another bundle of £50 notes. A small pendant on a silver chain, a garnet set in a ring of diamonds. A building society account book. Deborah had £12,000 in an ISA. Two envelopes; a brown one and a white one with a window in it. And two birth certificates.

Daniel Charles Thornton, was born on July 8th 1982, in Northampton. His mother Elizabeth Jane Bassett was a court stenographer, his father William Frederick Thornton was a solicitor. Resolutely white collar. I wondered where they were now. What did they think of Daniel becoming Deborah?

The copy of her birth certificate, with her name registered as Deborah Charlotte Thorne, had been issued in October 2010.

There were two postcard size photographs in the brown envelope, taken on a beach somewhere. In one, a young woman in a red, one-piece swimsuit smiled at me. Streaked blonde hair, green eyes and what looked like a carefully nurtured sun tan. I guessed her age at around 30. The other picture, taken somewhere else, was of a child. A boy, maybe eight or nine years old, with dark wavy hair, brown eyes and freckles. Both pictures had the same hand written notation on the back – 'Devon summer 2010'

There was a bank statement inside the window envelope, dated nine days earlier. Deborah had a special reserve account at the NatWest in Clare Street. In the account, £65,000 plus some small change. I took the bundle of fifties out of the safe and counted them. Another fifteen hundred pounds. I got to my feet again, went into the kitchen, found a wall cupboard with drinks in it and helped myself to a glass of Bowmore. I moved into the living room, sat down on Deborah's large sofa, lay back into the cushions and for two or three minutes enjoyed the malt exclusively.

Why did she leave this stuff behind? Did she really think it would be safe? Well... probably safer than carrying it around with her.

I took the empty glass back into the kitchen, put it in the sink, ran it under the tap, tipped it upside down on the draining board and returned to the hall. I put the birth certificates into the brown envelope, put the envelope into the inside pocket of my jacket and the rest of the stuff back into the safe. Replaced the floor boards and the carpet, put the boxes and rugs and Henry back into the cupboard space.

Then I locked up and left.

I walked back to the office. Across the river, past the old General Hospital and along Cumberland Road. Three miles or thereabouts. It took me forty minutes and I talked to myself all the way. I had discovered a lot about Deborah Thorne in twenty-four hours, but I still didn't know where she was and had no means of contacting her. Philip Soames, the person who knew more about her than anybody else, was dead. But somewhere, maybe, there was a swim-suited blonde and a young boy who had something to do with whatever was going on.

Instead of pondering, I should have enjoyed the walk and kept my eyes peeled.

In the car park behind my office, I caught up with the efforts of the sand blasters. The job was half done. Fifty percent of the wall was now a deeply unattractive sludge brown colour. Hardly an improvement.

Behind me, I heard the man who had been following me say, "It's a bit of a mess."

I turned round to face him. He was taller than me, probably six three or four. He stood upright and straight, but relaxed. Feet slightly apart, his body weight evenly distributed, everything in balance. He was wearing a long grey coat. Unbuttoned. It looked expensive. He obviously didn't shop in high street chain stores; at least not for his clothes.

I had to agree with his assessment regarding the wall.

"Sorry to intrude," he said. "My name is Grant. I would like to talk with you."

The best received pronunciation I had heard outside of re-runs of Pathé News. No accent. Measured vowels, separation of adjoining consonants – *I would like to talk with you...* His words as tailored as his overcoat. He was very impressive. I nodded graciously.

"Talk away," I said.

"What were you doing in Ms Thorne's house?"

I must have looked disappointed, because he went on to explain.

"I wasn't there to see you enter. A colleague of mine failed to do that. But I did get there in time to see you leave."

That was some consolation. If he was at the front of the house, then he couldn't have seen Joe leave at the back.

"Well," he said. "Must I repeat the question?"

That would be a tad unnecessary. The real question was, what was he going to do when I didn't answer him? He provided a little emphasis. He took hold of the left-hand collar of his coat and eased it slightly away from his body. No jacket under the coat, just a five-button velvet waistcoat and a compact automatic, sitting snugly in a holster against the left side of his rib cage.

My heart rate went up and my chest started thumping.

"This is a Glock 357. It fires thirteen rounds," he said.

A very professional piece. Mr Grant was no two-bob hard case.

"I will give you a moment or two," he said.

He dipped his right hand into an interior coat pocket and took out a mobile, thumbed three buttons and put the phone to his ear.

"We are behind the building," he said. "In the car park."

He disconnected the line and put the phone back into his pocket.

"So… You can answer my questions, here, in this place. Or you can come with me to another place and answer them there. I feel obliged to tell you, that option one will be far less painful."

He waited for my response. We stood in silence for a while, the ambient soundtrack provided by traffic circumnavigating the lock basin two hundred yards away. Then the noise of a single car engine seeped through the background. A dark blue Lexus nosed round the side of the office building into the car park and stopped. The driver kept the engine running and stayed inside the car. Grant spoke again.

"The vehicle is for us, should you choose the latter."

The rear access door to the warehouse opened and Jason emerged, out of uniform. He took his lunch early. He stopped and looked round at the car park tableau, then back at me.

"Enjoy your afternoon Ben," I said.

Grant was looking directly at me. He didn't see the momentary confusion on Jason's face.

"Don't forget our 10.30 tomorrow morning," I added.

Jason knew deranged from deliberate, and quickly realised what was going on. A tall man in a long dark coat with eyes locked on one of his tenants, and a Lexus sat with its engine idling. Jason looked back at me.

"Of course not," he said. He fished an ignition key out of a trouser pocket and moved towards the twenty-year-old Defender he off-roads at the weekends.

He climbed in and the engine fired first time. In front of me, Grant took a couple of steps towards me. Rear tyres smoking and squealing, the Defender roared backwards and swung right as Jason spun the driving wheel. The reinforced rear bumper cage hit Grant on the back of his thighs just above his knees. His torso arched up and back, his head slammed against the Defender rear window, then bounced forwards again. His body crescent mooned downwards and his face hit the hardcore in front of my feet.

For a second or two, the Lexus driver contemplated getting out of his car to help. Until Jason selected first gear, floored the accelerator pedal and surged towards him. The driver found reverse and tore backwards along the side of the building, bouncing across the potholes. Jason side-slipped to a halt and let him go. He climbed out of the Defender and walked back towards me.

I knelt down to take a look at Grant and rolled him gently on to his back.

Not surprisingly, he was unconscious. His face was a mess; his nose flattened beyond all recognisable shape, bleeding profusely from a hole where the bridge cartilage used to be. There was a deep jagged cut across his forehead, a length of skin ripped off the bone. Tiny bits of loose gravel, embedded in his face, pocked the skin of his cheeks. I dug the mobile out of my jacket pocket and dialled 999.

I heard Jason say, "AX95 7BT." I looked up at him. "The registration number of the Lexus."

The emergency operator asked for my name and number, then said that both ambulance and police were on the way. She asked if anyone else was hurt. I said no. She said 'thank you' and disconnected the line.

I stood up. Jason seemed remarkably together, considering the violence of the last few moments. Suddenly the colour drained from his face. He swayed on his feet. I reached out to steady him. He said he was all right. He looked anything but.

There was a bottle of water in the driver's door pocket of the Healey. I found it and sat Jason on the front seat, legs outside of the car. He took a drink, then put his head down between his knees.

The police arrived first. Two young constables in a traffic patrol car who had sped the mile or so from Winterstoke Road and seemed to be under the impression they were attending a road accident. I tried to keep the story simple, but as it unravelled, PCs Bullock and Worthington began to view Jason and I with ever increasing suspicion. Hard to blame them really. They weren't sure what kind of felons they had on their hands. They did have time, before the ambulance arrived, to relieve Grant of his holster and gun and search his pockets. Which were empty. No wallet, driving licence, keys or small change. Nothing to identify him.

Grant was still unconscious when the ambulance took him away. By which time, PC Bullock had talked to CID at Trinity Road and was under orders to hold on to the miscreants and seal off the area. Jason and I sat in the Defender and waited.

"What happens now?" Jason asked.

"Our interrogators will believe everything you say and let you go home," I said. "They won't believe a word I tell them and, in all probability, will invite me to spend the night in a police cell."

"What have you been doing Mr Shepherd?"

I was considering whether to tell him, when a black Mondeo swung into the car park. I twisted the Defender rear-view mirror and watched Harvey Butler climb out of the back of the Mondeo. PC Bullock stretched out an arm and pointed at the Defender. Harvey strode across the hardcore.

As I'd expected, Jason was dismissed swiftly, told to leave his vehicle in the car park and handed over to PCs Bullock and Worthington. They escorted him into the office building to take a statement. By which time, another patrol car had arrived. Harvey ordered the area round the Defender and the Healey to be taped off and turned his attention to me.

"It's 12.25. I have a lunch appointment with the ACC. So I won't keep you long. Let's take a walk."

We crossed the old cast iron footbridge, now graffiti free and all spruced up in battleship grey.

"I liked it as it was," Harvey said.

We strolled into the park on the south side of the river.

"Who is he, this Mr Grant?" Harvey asked.

"I don't know," I said.

"Why did he introduce himself to you in the car park?"

"He said he wanted to ask me some questions."

"About what?"

"We didn't get that far."

Harvey motioned to an old wood slatted cast iron bench the urban renewers had repaired and re-painted. We sat down.

There are moments when a private investigator has to bend with the breeze. This was one of them. It would take Harvey no time at all to trace the owner of the Lexus. Which would, in all probability, lead him to the Lexus owner's boss. The person who was looking for Deborah Thorne and who had hired the aforesaid Mr Grant. That done, Harvey would be measurably more well informed than I was. He would know who was looking for me. Which was what I needed to know. We had to make a deal. And as long as I managed to protect my client...

"Yesterday," I said, "I was hired to find someone. It now appears that Mr Grant and the Lexus driver are looking for the same person."

"Why?" Harvey asked.

"I don't know."

He looked at me, suspicion edged deep on his face.

"Slit my throat and hope to die," I said.

"What's the name of the person you're looking for?

"Deborah Thorne."

"Who hired you to find her?"

"Deborah Thorne."

Amazingly, Harvey didn't flinch. He simply stretched out his legs, put his hands into his trouser pockets and stared across the river.

"I should know better," he said after a moment or two.

"Bear with me," I said.

I gave him a précis of Deborah's visit to my office. He listened without interrupting. When I finished, he picked out the piece of core business.

"So it would help your investigation if you were to learn the identity of the people who menaced you today?"

"Yes."

"And you want them, or at least the man in the Lexus, to be free to approach you again?"

"All I'm saying is, that a police investigation will only serve to endanger my client more. I just want to keep her safe."

There was long pause. One of us had to go on. I did.

"Look Harvey, I have absolutely no desire to go up against contractors with automatics. What I want to do, is find my client. Find out why she is so frightened. And get her into police protection. Then leave the rest to you. What I don't want, is to have any of this compromised by a police investigation into what happened half an hour ago. This all needs to stay private, until Deborah is safe."

Harvey batted the proposition back to me.

"That could be considered acceptable, were I reasonably confident that the death of Philip Soames, which is somehow glued to you, was not a significant element in all this."

There was another long pause. Lunch appointment notwithstanding, Harvey sat on the bench like he had all the time in the world. His rules, not mine.

"Deborah was a client of Philip Soames," I said. "Read her case notes."

"Which we will find full of confidential information, potentially helpful to those who killed him."

"My assumption also."

"So how did these villains get from Soames to you?"

I told him about my trip to Deborah's house, omitting the stuff about the cupboard under the stairs.

Harvey got to his feet.

"Okay. I'll find out who owns the Lexus and let you know. I can't stop you working in the best interests of your client. However, the moment your private endeavours collide with those of the public sector..."

I opened my mouth to protest. He waved his hands at me.

"And they will... I will nick you and drop you deep in the clarts." He looked straight into my eyes. "Are we clear?"

"As crystal," I said.

"Then I'm going to lunch."

He led the way back across the bridge.

"It looks like you won't be able to move your car until the SOCO does the necessary. I'll get the team out of the car park as quickly as I can."

CHAPTER FIVE

I walked round to the Nova Scotia, bought a beer and a chicken pesto sandwich and sat on the dockside for a while. I watched the ferry arrive and disgorge a bunch of tourists and floating harbour trippers, then sauntered back to my desk.

I looked again inside the envelopes I had taken from Deborah's safe. I studied the two photographs, but I couldn't see anything other than a woman and a child on a day out. Holiday snaps, like thousands of others. The location was a sandy beach. The woman was sitting on a towel, smiling at something beyond the camera. The background to the shot of the child was a distant wall of rock, out of focus. With a gap sliced out of it on the left-hand side of the picture. A slipway possibly. There was nothing else in the pictures to interpret. I put them back into the envelope.

I had to improve the shining hour somehow. The Northampton Thorntons had to be first up. I called 118 118. The voice down the line told me there was no telephone listing for Thornton at the address on the birth certificate. A long shot anyway.

I tried Chrissie at home. To receive a joyous round of barking when the receiver was picked up and some time before Chrissie was able to speak.

"I'd like you to do something for me," I said. "Have you had cause to log on to the UK Census website?"

"Not much call for that with Russian and French studies."

"Well here's the thing," I said. "The census data is only available to registered users – academic institutions, government departments, selected research centres. Not to individuals and certainly not to self-employed private investigators. You can register through the university."

"Yes I know. All you need is a username and a password," she said. Then a huge dollop of suspicion coated her voice. "What are you up to Dad?"

"Simply working for my client. I have a 1976 birth certificate. The family no longer live at the address on it. I want to find out where they are now."

Chrissie thought for a moment.

"You can do this legitimately," I persisted.

"As you've discovered I'm at home today," she said. "I'll need to find someone who's registered and check if there's anything specific about the username or the password. Give me the details."

I did.

I made some coffee to kill a few minutes. The phone rang as I sat back down at my desk.

"No luck with the Lexus," Harvey said. "The registration number isn't on the DVLA computer."

"Stolen then, and the plates changed."

"No, it's unlikely to be stolen. Probably bought with cash, then registered and insured before the plates were changed. Unless we get hold of the car we'll never know. And it's a safe bet that the plates have been changed again. Or the car's on its way to a scrap yard. We're doing routine checks with car breakers, but don't hold your breath."

"Thanks Harvey."

"Oh... The boffins reckon they'll be out of your car park within the hour. Don't do anything I'm going to be sorry for."

I tried to do some thinking... It was reasonable to assume that Mr Grant and his associate had tortured and killed Philip Soames. And in the process, learned of my client's whereabouts. Whereupon, they had laid siege to the house in Windmill Hill in the hope that Deborah would, at some point, show up. So, considering what had happened to Soames, what was the prognosis for Deborah?

That question frightened the hell out of me. If she was part of this somehow, then the 'significant others' were truly that. And truly dangerous. And if what I was rationalising here was remotely feasible, my client was surely in real and present danger.

The phone rang again. This time it was Chrissie.

"According to the 2011 census, the Thorntons now live in Ringsmere, in Suffolk. She is retired, he works as a solicitor. Do you want the address?"

"Please".

"Easy to remember. Lime Tree House, The Close."

"Where is Ringsmere?"

"Well here's the bonus. About fifteen miles northeast of Auntie Joyce and Uncle Sid. Get your road atlas out of the car and take a look. Later..."

I found an old road atlas in the bottom drawer of the filing cabinet. Auntie Joyce and Uncle Sid live in Broadpole, in the Blyth Valley. A few miles inland from the jewel of the Suffolk coast, the village of Walberswick. Across the river, is another gem, the stunning little town of Southwold. And some dozen or so miles further on, east of the A12, among a cluster of tiny places named after saints, lies the hamlet of Ringsmere.

The Suffolk coast in mid-September... No contest.

Suddenly I had a plan. Go home and pack a bag, come back to the office and, as soon as my car was released, motor east. If the car park was cleared as Harvey had promised, I could be at Auntie Joyce and Uncle Sid's in time for supper. I picked up the phone.

Auntie Joyce was delighted at the plan. She promised to bake a cake.

Jason was, temporarily, away from reception. I left him a note saying I'd be back later and took a taxi home.

* * *

Washed and clothes changed, I was staring into the bedroom wardrobe, considering what to pack, when the telephone rang. I picked up the receiver.

"Jack Shepherd..."

No one responded. There were two or three seconds of line atmos, then a click, followed by the dial buzz. I replaced the receiver and called 1471. There was no number available. Maybe the call was from a mobile, or a public phone box. Or maybe I had been followed home and the caller was just checking I was still here. Whoever he was, he was now assured of my whereabouts. Mr Grant's associate, the Lexus driver – assuming he was still on the case – could be out in the street.

I grabbed my jacket, the envelope with the beach photographs, my wallet and house keys and left by the back door. I closed the garden gate, turned right and headed for the bus stop on the road opposite the lane end.

I attached myself to the back of the bus queue, behind a mother and toddler, an elderly man and his terrier, and two teenagers in tee shirts and baseball caps. The number 128 arrived three minutes later, just as a man in a navy-blue suit, with dark, short cropped hair, joined the queue behind me. I climbed onto the bus, paid the driver £3.15p and sat down in the first seat after the staircase. From here, I could just about use the driver's interior view mirror to look down the length of the bus behind me. The late arrival moved past me along the aisle and sat down three seats further back.

The mirror theory didn't work in practice, the angle wasn't right. The man was sitting on the edge of vision. I couldn't see enough of him to improve on what I had noted so far. He might be the Lexus driver. Could have stationed himself near the lane end, waiting for an escape plan to develop. On the other hand, he could be anybody's bona fide next-door neighbour.

The bus destination was the city centre shopping jungle. In theory, the ideal place to disappear into a crowd. Working on the assumption that I'd get off the bus into a heaving mass of shoppers, I could take a right and then a left, slip into a department store through one door and out through another; double back through Quakers Friars, cross Broad Weir and walk back to the city centre through Castle Park. If the man sitting behind me was an out-of-town contractor, he would simply get lost.

It was a plan, as best laid as I could contrive. In Broadmead, at the end of Penn Street, I got off the bus. The Lexus driver followed me.

In truth, there is nothing special about the Cabot Circus retail experience. It's just another shopping complex, with a long central walkway down the middle, leading towards a huge glass covered atrium which rises up three floors to a multiplex cinema. The place has pretention and ambition, but depends for its existence on the familiar high street names which pack the ground floor – now less of them than there used to be. The middle floor has more interest, with half a dozen local retailers, striving to co-exist alongside small chain shops, alternative therapy outlets and opticians. Cafés, sandwich bars and fast-food restaurants are packed into the food ghetto on the top floor. The signage isn't great and it's easy for first time visitors to get disorientated. The success of my swiftly conjured scheme, depended on the Lexus driver doing just that. But we hit a snag straight away.

There was no great crowd of shoppers to hide in. Instead of the heaving mass I was anticipating, I could count the punters individually. But I was stuck with the modus operandi, and as they say, when plan A fails to work, revert to plan A.

I was saved by a soap star.

Tony Grainger had recently made a sensational exit from his returning drama series after twelve years as the senior villain, when he was shot by a trainee dental nurse he had impregnated one night in the back of his Range Rover. Six months on and times were tougher. He was currently the comedy lead in a series of wallpaper commercials and riding the personal appearances wave to keep his profile up. And here he was, an eight feet cardboard cut-out, in the window of Hartlands department store. The banner above his head said that his wallpaper road show was in full swing in the 'House and Home' department on the lower ground floor.

There were more people at this shindig than outside the door. Gathered three deep in a semi-circle in front of a display area. In effect a three-wall set, with an entrance to the right at the back, built in front of the escalator riding down to the lower ground floor. I squeezed myself into the audience. The Lexus driver stationed himself about a dozen yards behind me, next to a display stand full of food mixers.

Tony was working his celebrity to the max. He was

supported by another actor and between them, they were doing a version of the fifty-year-old Bruce Forsyth Norman Wisdom *Sunday Night at the London Palladium* slapstick turn currently going viral on YouTube – the legendary wallpaper hanging routine.

Not exactly in the same league as Brucie and Norman, but the business did what it was supposed to do. Grabbed the crowd's attention and garnered a hefty round of applause. At which point, Tony the consummate pro, segued into the real work and did his one to one with his audience. No need for paste and mess and mistakes with this revolutionary new wallpaper. Measure, cut, soak the wall and slide into place. His assistant demonstrated briskly and efficiently and everybody applauded again. Whereupon Tony issued an invitation to those who wanted to try this new wallpaper hanging experience themselves. Any volunteers?

I stuck my hand up.

"Yes sir, thank you," Tony crooned. "Step up here sir."

I joined him on the dais and shook his outstretched hand.

"And your name sir?"

I told him and took a step backwards. Tony's assistant grinned at me and began re-arranging the props. Tony stepped to the front of the dais and launched into an explanation of what was to happen next. I took another couple of steps backwards. Over by the food mixers, the Lexus driver took a couple of steps forwards. I turned to my left and dived through the entrance to the set.

It was two strides to the escalator handrail, levelling out at the base of the slope. I vaulted over it, landed on the stairway facing uphill, only to find myself travelling backwards. I began to move forwards, inches before the escalator ran out of track.

Running up a down escalator is a bit tricky. I discovered the principle immediately. You have to hit the steps firmly and accurately. Don't touch the handrail and stay upright. I began one step at a time. I kept upright, but succeeded only in walking on the spot. I tried two steps and began to make progress, then three and moved quickly. Luckily, there was no one on the way down towards me. At the top I turned and looked round. The Lexus driver was at the bottom. He ran at the escalator, got it wrong, tripped before he reached the first step, swayed backwards, shifted his weight forwards and fell to his knees. He drifted backwards in a praying position, ran out of track and was pitched on to the lower ground floor carpet.

The nearest store exit was about fifteen yards to my left. It wasn't the way I would have chosen to leave the building, but it was the quickest. I was through the door, then outside in seconds into a narrow access road. And faced with two choices. Turn right and go back into the main shopping avenue; or go straight ahead, and then left into an alley leading to a multi-storey car park. A maintenance crew had obviously been at work in the alley. There was a red and yellow barrier stretching part way across it. Further back, a ride-on pavement cleaner was parked alongside the wall and behind it a grey circular steel rubbish bin on castors. Between them, they managed to hide the car park entrance from view. Way to go...

I should have thought more about the barrier.

The door to the car park was locked. Sprayed across the door and the wall to its right, was the proclamation – *THE WELSH ARE ALL CUNTS.*

The cleaning crew had made some progress, but had abandoned the work temporarily and gone off to find a stronger cleaning agent. Whether it was the four-letter word or the racism which was considered most offensive, I couldn't imagine. I wasn't sure I was prepared to give the sentiment a ringing endorsement, especially under the circumstances, but I was suddenly angry with myself for getting sucked into a cul de sac.

I turned back into the centre of the alley. The Lexus driver stepped out of Hartlands. He looked left and right and then ahead, straight at me. Then at the sign telling him there was a car park entrance at the end of the alley.

I moved behind the steel bin, out of his line of sight. There was a space between the bin and the wall. I squeezed into it and the bin moved an inch or two. It was empty. I stood stock still, listening to his footsteps on the concrete, the sound growing in volume as he got closer. I had one chance at this.

When I judged he was level, I leaned against the bin and pushed. Then followed on, like a second row forward in a rolling maul. The bin hit the Lexus driver hard enough to knock him sideways. The momentum generated carried the bin across the alleyway and bounced him into the opposite wall.

Everything seemed to stop. Complete silence descended. As if the mute button had been pressed. No sound of people, no rumble from distant traffic.

Then I remembered the last encounter in an alleyway, eleven years ago. A teenager loaded with PCP, gone ballistic with a meat cleaver and a detective sergeant with a .38 Smith and Wesson. The subsequent investigation decided I had no other recourse but to shoot and the killing was declared justified.

Now I had to look at what I had done to another total stranger.

I took several deep breaths, leaned against the bin and rolled it away from the wall. The Lexus driver, until that moment propped upright against the brickwork, dropped to his knees and slumped sideways. Another version of the preying position I'd left him in at the foot of the escalator. What I could see of the right-hand side of his face was skinned almost to the bone. Blood was running from his temple and oozing out of his right ear. He was unconscious.

My stomach heaved. I turned away, crossed the alley and sat down against the opposite wall. I make no secret of the fact that such courage as I possess is severely tested on occasions like this. Something of a handicap you may think, for a person in my line of work. Not so. I regard my affliction as a kind of tolerance indicator; a measuring point beyond which my brain and my guts begin to revolt. I take some satisfaction from this. After twenty plus years working amid foolishness, desperation, cynicism, violence and evil, I still find the propensity to throw up comforting.

Yesterday Grant, today the Lexus driver. One to Jason, one to me. Another broken face. Our signature event it seemed.

Still, opportunity was knocking. The man might have some ID on him. I hauled myself to my feet and stepped back towards him. He was wearing a three-button jacket. The middle button was fastened. I crouched down beside him and reached out with my left hand. I twisted the button with my thumb, hooked two fingers under the jacket seam, and pulled. The jacket unfastened, but disturbed the Lexus driver in the process. He slid forward on to his face. I jerked my hand away like he was red hot. Looked at him again. Still on his knees, but with his forehead now touching the floor, the genuflection seemed to be complete. I'd started this, so I had to finish. I reached out to the man. He sagged sideways and rolled over on to his back. There was a hissing noise from what was left of his nose and blood bubbled from his mouth. I dug into his inside jacket pocket, found his wallet and mobile phone, and stumbled back across the alley. My stomach heaved again. In all my years as an investigator, public and private, I'd never taken to robbing bodies.

But desperation is a miserable bedfellow. I shook my head, took a couple of deep breaths, swapped the Lexus driver's mobile for my own, dialled 999 and asked for an ambulance. I told the operator where I was, the nature of the injuries to the man I had found in the alley, then disconnected the call.

Two minutes later I was sitting in *Costa Coffee* on Broadmead, drinking a large Yorkshire tea and letting my heart rate slow down. I called Jason. He answered after the second ring. Asked me how I was. I told him that, given the circumstances, I was in good shape.

"What circumstances?" he asked.

Car-less and on the run was the best way of describing them, but I managed to deflect his interest and get to the point.

"I need my car," I said.

"It's in the car park," he said. "And the police team has gone."

"That's good."

Jason was confused for a moment.

"Have you lost your keys?" he asked.

"No. I have them with me."

"I don't understand."

"I can't come and get the Healey?"

"Why not? Where are you?"

"Jason listen."

There was a beat.

"Sorry," he said.

"No no, it's me who should apologise," I said. "Suffice it

to say, I need you to drive the Healey to me. Can you get away from the desk?"

"In about five minutes, yes. As soon as Alex gets back. He's collecting some parcels from the top floor. However, you have the keys."

"There is a spare set, locked in the top right-hand drawer of my desk."

"And the key to the desk..."

"I have that as well."

"So how do I? – "

"Just break into it. Find a screwdriver and jemmy the lock open."

"Okay. If you say so."

"You will also find a bundle of £50 notes in the drawer. Put them into an envelope and put the envelope into the glove compartment of the Healey."

I looked at my watch. 3.45.

"Right. In fifteen minutes time, take the Healey to the car park at Ashton Court. Drive around it a couple of times. As if you're looking for the most desirable place to park. If you see me don't acknowledge me. Leave the key in the ignition and walk away. Go straight back to the office. Okay?"

"Yes, of course."

That was it. No more questions asked. I finished my coffee and went out to the Broadmead taxi rank.

* * *

The Healey arrived at Ashton Court dead on time. There was no car following behind. Jason did as instructed, got out of the Healey and walked away. I waited for a while. A silver Audi Estate drove into the car park. A man wearing a flat cap and a tweed jacket got out of the car, walked around to the tail gate and opened it. A Staffordshire Bull Terrier, bounced onto the ground, spun round and sat down waiting for instructions. The man locked the Audi and pointed to a gate in the car park fence.

"Go on," he said.

The dog was at the gate in seconds. The man arrived, opened the gate and the dog hared off across the hillside towards the woods. I watched the man follow him, and waited another couple of minutes. No more arrivals or departures. I walked to the Healey and climbed in.

I called Chrissie at home. Rewarded with the answer mode, I left a message saying I was off to Suffolk for a couple of days. I called Linda and did the same. I found the £50 notes in the glove compartment, put the Lexus driver's wallet and mobile in there too, and turned on the ignition. I drove to Sainsburys on Winterstoke Road, filled the car with petrol, then got on to the ring road ahead of the late afternoon traffic and headed for the M4.

Forty minutes later, I called Jason from the Leigh Delamere services area and thanked him for his efforts. Then I opened the stolen wallet. I found three £50 pound notes, four 20s and two 5s – on this case I was collecting cash like nobody's business – two petrol bills and a receipt for some prescription pain killers from a chemist in Broadmead. And five pieces of plastic; a London Transport Oyster card, a membership card for a drinking club in Soho, a Master Card and a NatWest debit card, both valid until well in to 2017, and a driving licence. All the property of one, Francis Copley.

At least, it did seem that Mr Copley was an out-of-town contractor. I switched on his mobile. It buzzed, the screen turned grey and asked for a pin code. Locked... I decided to consider this problem later.

There was a predictable range of eateries. Burger King, KFC, a Carvery, a sandwich bar and a bunch of coffee franchises. But wonder of wonders, a genuine Harry Ramsdens. I ordered fish and chips and mushy peas, tea and bread and butter and paid the bill with one of Copley's twenties. No need to gripe about motorway prices when a total stranger foots the bill.

Back outside, warmed up and raring to go on, the Healey's engine fired in a second. I drove on eastwards. The sun was shining, the day was warm and my cause was just.

And I had a lead to follow.

CHAPTER SIX

Traffic was light on the M4, relatively user friendly on the M25 and amazingly sparse on the M11. North of Ipswich I decided to take the country route, left the motorway and turned east. Ten minutes after 7 o'clock, I stopped at a pub in Saxted, on the main road through the village.

I sat in the orchard in what was left of the evening sunshine. In front of a half-timbered, flint stoned, thatched cottage. I wasn't exactly on holiday, but I was light years away from Francis Copley. In Suffolk, on a warm evening, in a garden soaked in the scent of lavender.

Twenty minutes later, I was in Halesworth, in the gathering twilight. I turned east and let the Healey roll gently down the Blyth valley to Broadpole.

No one is difficult to find in Broadpole. Everyone lives on The Street. That's all there is to the village. It runs from the parish church on the eastern boundary to the small triangle of village green at the western end. The houses on both sides of the road are a mix of 17th century wattle and daub, small Victorian cottages, early 20th century arts and crafts style villas and a handful of 1950s bungalows. There is a pub, appropriately named the Blyth Arms. The village shop is housed in what used to be the blacksmith's forge. West End House faces the green and looks directly down The Street, back towards the church.

Uncle Sid saw me coming. As I got out of the car, he waved to me and called Auntie Joyce. She came out of the house, the biggest smile on her face. And the years melted away.

This gentle, wise and gracious couple have been my guardians since I was five. Although separated by the width of the country, we are as close as it is possible to be. Bristol to the Suffolk coast is just a matter of geography. No emotional distance at all. We talk every weekend, even if it is only to gossip. Auntie Joyce is lead alto in the Walberswick Choral Society and runs the fiercely outspoken local WI. Uncle Sid worked as a turbine engineer at Sizewell Power Station until eighteen months ago. Now he makes amazing things in his garden shed.

After a glass of wine and an interlude of catch-up chat, Auntie Joyce got straight to the point.

"So…?"

I bowed to the inevitable and answered the question.

"I'm looking for someone."

Uncle Sid asked the next question.

"Around here?"

"A client of mine has gone missing. Her parents live in Ringsmere. I'm hoping they'll be able to help me."

They took this in. The three of us sat in silence for a while. Then Uncle Sid picked up the conversation again.

"Do you know where Ringsmere is?"

"North of here, towards Beccles."

"Do you want me to take you?"

"No. I'll find my way."

Uncle Sid got to his feet.

"Come and see what I'm working on."

He and I adjourned to the shed. It was the size of a single car garage and occupied a huge chunk of the back garden.

"And you actually want a bigger one?"

He pulled the double doors open.

"Ta dah!!"

Inside, on a bench running the width of the shed, was a monster array of woodwork and metal tools. In a corner, an oxyacetylene tank on a sack truck, goggles and a blowtorch hanging over it. And in the middle of the space, a very impressive sculpture. Bent, twisted, corroded bits of scrap metal, welded together with some skill and no less effort. A boat in full sail. Messy, brutalist and formidable. I stared at it. Uncle Sid beamed at me.

"What do you think?"

I found my voice.

"Amazing," I said.

He adjusted the spectacles on his nose and looked at me through the right bit of his varifocals. I stepped into the shed for a close inspection.

"Where do you get the metal?"

"Gently Bentley Murdoch. He has a junkyard down on the estuary."

And junk some of it was. Radiator heating elements, steel chair seats, bits from an old filing cabinet, the top of an engine block, even a dustbin lid. I pointed to some beautifully hammered out metal plates.

"Where are they from?"

"The floor of a low loader."

"And the sail?"

"I made it out of the side panel of a transit van."

I stepped back to get the full picture again.

"Do you know how to unlock a mobile phone?"

Uncle Sid took off his varifocals, put them into the breast pocket of his shirt, cleared a bunch of tools off the saw bench and gestured to it. I sat down. He stood in front of me.

"All right, talk to me," he ordered.

So I did. I told him about Deborah, but not about Daniel. About her empty house, and the photographs I had found there. About the interest from Grant and Copley, but not about what had happened to them. Uncle Sid listened without interrupting. But he had two questions to ask.

"Where are they now? Grant and Copley."

I should have known I couldn't gloss over the ending to the story. Uncle Sid folded his arms across his chest and waited.

"Grant is in police custody," I said. "Copley is probably in hospital. I have his wallet and his mobile phone."

Uncle Sid betrayed no surprise or alarm. Instead, he asked his second question.

"Do you think you'll find Deborah?"

It was the million pounder. And mine alone to answer. I couldn't ask the audience, go 50/50, or phone a friend.

"I believe that Deborah will be found," I said. "Eventually."

The implication was clear enough. Uncle Sid nodded, bowed his head for a second or two, stuffed his hands into his trouser pockets and looked down at the floor. After what seemed an eternity, he lifted his head again.

"Then let's hope and pray you are the first to do so," he said.

Auntie Joyce called from the doorway.

"Sid. Remember you're cooking tonight."

"Yes, coming. The casserole's all done. Just need to put it back into the oven and heat it up." He looked at me. "My signature dish."

Deservedly so. A minor culinary masterpiece, enjoyed by all of us. The rest of the evening sped by. The conversation was warm and relaxed and funny. Full of anecdotes and the best of remembrances. Not one difficult moment.

Afterwards, we cleared the dining table and Uncle Sid announced he was going out for his walk. I looked at the clock on the sideboard. 10.20.

"Walk?"

"Yes, you know, like John Wayne in *Rio Bravo*," Auntie Joyce said. "The Deputy Marshall goes for his late-night patrol."

"I always went out with the dogs at this time," he said. "They're no longer around, but I got into the habit, so..."

He went into the hall, put on a fleece jacket and let himself out the front door. Auntie Joyce and I cleared the dining table and filled the dishwasher. She looked at the dish I was holding.

"That has to be washed by hand."

She took it from me. Then looked straight into my eyes.

"You are a good man Jack. You grew up caring about all sorts of things I barely came into contact with. You invest everything you do with a realism that's... I don't know... tender and hopeful at the same time. We live 250 miles apart, but I swear I know when you're confused, or hurt, or in trouble."

"You always did."

"You're not sentimental. And I suppose that's good in your line of work. But you take a lot of punishment doing what you do. You take on more than you should and you give yourself away by the shovel full. You have been preserved, thus far, because you can give as good as you get, but most importantly, by your sense of honour."

"Have you been saving this up?"

"For the right occasion, yes."

"And this is it?"

"Probably." She put the plate down on the work surface. "I'll do that in the morning."

She closed the dishwasher door and pressed a couple of buttons. The machine hummed, gurgled and then burst into life.

"Let's go into the living room. There's some cognac in the sideboard, if you'd like a nightcap."

We sat down, side by side on the sofa.

"The point I'm trying so clumsily to make, is this," she went on. "I know how important right and wrong is to you. Sid is the same. So was your father. Neither of them ever had to think about the difference between the two. They instinctively knew what it was. You are cast from the same mould. 'He knew the difference between right and wrong', would sit fair on anyone's headstone. But I don't want to see it on yours. And certainly not yet."

She stopped speaking and stared at me. I needed to say something in response. So I tried.

"Firstly, I don't think you said anything clumsily at all. And secondly, I've been preserved thus far because I am careful. I promise you, I will continue so to be."

That seemed to be enough. Her point made and the deal done. Uncle Sid returned five minutes later. Locked the front door behind him and secured the rest of the house. Auntie Joyce said 'goodnight' and Uncle Sid followed her upstairs.

I sat on the sofa for a while longer. Considering. Presumably Grant was still in hospital, with a couple of uniforms stationed outside his door. Copley too. Sooner or later, he was going to get well enough to be able to call his boss. At which point, all hell would break loose. Contracts would be issued to the rest of the associates and then I'd then be on the run as surely as Deborah. I needed to unlock Copley's mobile, get into his contacts list and his mailbox. That required the services of someone cleverer and sneakier than me. Meanwhile, the Thorntons were a priority.

I got up from the sofa and went to bed.

CHAPTER SEVEN

I woke to the sound of banging. My bedroom window was about fifteen feet from the garden shed. And Uncle Sid was hard at work. Thursday morning. At 8.25...

Downstairs in the kitchen, Auntie Joyce apologised.

"He's unstoppable," she said.

"Maybe you should ask yourself what he would be doing otherwise."

"Doesn't bear thinking about," she said.

We had breakfast in the dining room. Uncle Sid joined us. He emptied the cafetière and ate the remaining two slices of toast.

It was time I set about some sleuthing.

Auntie Joyce provided me with the local phone directory. There was only one Thornton listed in Ringsmere. I called the number but a machine answered – apologising that Elizabeth and Bill Thornton weren't in, but giving me a mobile number. I called it and Bill answered from his office in Southwold.

I tried to tell him as little as possible; I needed to give him the whole story face to face. He said he was in his office all morning and would see me as soon as I got there.

"Are you going like that?" Auntie Joyce asked. She looked me up and down and sniffed. "Well?..."

"Well, considering I haven't got a change of clothes..."

"Or the basic requirements for personal grooming."

She set about remedying the situation.

"Sid. Get him a spare toothbrush and razor. And one of your clean shirts. He can't go out looking like he was dragged through a hedge backwards."

"Hardly..."

"I've been trying to make you look respectable for over forty years. I'm not having you disgrace me at this stage."

I looked at Uncle Sid. He shrugged.

"You heard what she said."

Twenty minutes later I looked at myself in the hall mirror. I had to admit to an improvement.

"Now you can go visiting," Auntie Joyce said. And she opened the front door.

* * *

I drove east along the Blyth valley and got to Southwold in fifteen minutes. I found a bank, where I deposited twenty of Deborah's £50 notes to be transferred to Bristol. Then I went for a walk, while I rehearsed what I was going to say to Deborah's father.

It is impossible not to be seduced by Southwold. All the superlatives ever conjured up to describe the quintessential English seaside town are writ large here. Gather up sunshine, stunning coastline, colour washed beach huts, lighthouse, pier; add a touch of picturesque and quaint and a maritime history which goes back to the Domesday Book, then toss them up into the air; and they would come down as Southwold.

Huntley, Rafferty and Thornton sat neatly above a second-hand bookshop at the southern end of the High Street. At least, the latest Thornton did. Huntley and Rafferty were long gone. Deborah's father, a trifle ill at ease, waved me to a chair in his office and explained.

"The original Thornton was my father. He became a partner here thirty years ago, after the grandson of the first Rafferty died. The last of the Huntleys died at his desk in 1996. I joined the firm seven years ago, when my father retired."

This was all stuff I didn't need to know. I took a deep breath.

"Mr Thornton..."

"No no please. Call me Bill. Everybody else does. It's accepted as good form around here. May I call you Jack?"

"Yes of course."

I looked at him. Not tall, maybe five eight. Slim build, grey hair, dark eyes. Pleasant and polite. The potted biography he had just given me, was a way of postponing, at least for a moment or two, the real conversation. He shuffled some papers in front of him, then looked back at me.

"Is Daniel in trouble?"

He shifted in his chair, took hold of the lapels of his jacket, pulled them together and shrugged his shoulders, re-shaping himself into preparedness.

"Elizabeth and I don't really know our son as Deborah," he said. "And we haven't seen him since he moved to Bristol."

"Out of choice?"

"Not entirely. We're trying to work through a... period of adjustment. All three of us." He repeated his question. "Is he, er she, in trouble?"

"Deborah has disappeared," I said. "I'm trying to find her."

"On behalf of whom?"

I decided to be economical with the truth.

"A friend of hers. I'm not at liberty to reveal the name. I'm sure you understand client confidentiality."

There was a desperate hush. I listened to the sound of traffic seeping up from the street. This was the worst opening to any conversation in a long while. Clearly, Bill Thornton hadn't much of a relationship with my client as I knew her.

"This period of adjustment," I said. "Do you see an end to it?"

"We're not making progress."

"Would you like to?"

"Of course."

Then he raised his voice.

"Are you making some kind of judgement here? If so, I don't appreciate it. Am I sad about this? Of course I am. So is Elizabeth. We are confused, desperate, furious. But we have no idea how to proceed. We are waiting for Daniel, Deborah to..."

He stopped. His anger dissolving as quickly as it had materialised.

"That was unpardonable," he said. "I had no reason to shout at you."

"It's okay," I said. "I think you needed to shout at someone. I'm here and I'm not going to take offence."

"Thank you. But I fear that raging is less than productive."

He wanted to go on. I waited.

"Liz and I want to be part of this new world Deborah has created," he said. But for some reason... we haven't been invited into it."

He needed to know why. If only to ease the weight on his shoulders. Of course, he'd then have a whole bunch of other stuff to concern himself with, but that might be easier to process. So I told him about the meeting with Deborah in my office. When I finished he asked a question.

"Are you telling me that nobody knows where Deborah

is?"

"Yes," I said. "At least I hope that's still the case."

"Because she is in danger?"

"Yes."

He sat back in his chair and closed his eyes. Remained frozen in position for several seconds. Then he opened his eyes again.

"Do you think you can find her?"

"The honest answer, Bill, is I have no idea. A lot of people set out to disappear. And they do for a while. Some of them are found. They don't cover their tracks well enough. Deborah has no intention of being found. She has planned, worked and re-worked her disappearance. I'm here because I found it her birth certificate. But I have no idea where to look for her."

"And if you don't find her, the odds are that – "

"I don't know who else is looking for her and what their resources might be. My guess is they're substantial. And these people, whoever they are, won't be inclined to give up. I have no idea how much they know about Daniel Thornton. They don't know about you. If they did, they would have been here by now."

I paused. He nodded, took a deep breath and waited for the coda.

"So I'm hoping you can tell me something about Daniel they don't know, which will help lead me to Deborah."

I took the envelope containing the photographs out of a jacket pocket. I pushed the pictures across the desktop.

"Do you recognise either of them? The woman, or the boy?"

He shook his head. "No. Sorry. Who are they?"

"I don't know. I found the pictures in Deborah's safe."

He passed the photographs back to me. I returned them

to the envelope. And we both sat in silence again. Awkwardness was roaming the office like a caged tiger. Something had to give. Thornton looked at me. Confusion seeped into his eyes.

"I don't know where to begin," he said.

"Begin at the beginning, go on until you come to the end and then stop."

It took him a moment to recognise the quote. "Alice in Wonderland."

I nodded. Thornton rehearsed for a moment or two and then he began.

"When he was young, Daniel had a passion to set the world right. He qualified as a teacher. He got his degree in Bristol. He went on to the Graduate School of Education. Got his PGCE in June 2000. I have to tell you, a one-year post grad course is not for the faint hearted."

"So I understand. My daughter is contemplating the same route."

"Daniel decided to take a year out. He stuck a pin in the map of Europe and hit Switzerland. He went to Geneva. Then two weeks later, he joined *Médecins Sans Frontières*, as a volunteer."

"Without any medical experience?"

"You don't have to be a doctor to work with *MSF*. The organisation needs administrators, fixers, interpreters, drivers... Humanitarian aid is a complicated business these days." He paused for a beat or two. "They sent Daniel to Kosovo."

Not a man for doing things by halves, Daniel. First a Balkan war, then a gender change. Certainly not frightened by challenges.

"We didn't hear from him for almost five months. We just watched the television news and imagined what he was doing. Prayed that he was still alive. Then in May 2000, he called us from an *MSF* aid station in Urosevac province. He had just been to Donjica. Do you remember the place?"

My knowledge of the Kosovan war was sketchy at best, but no one could forget easily the massacre at Donjica. It dominated news headlines for days and almost bounced NATO back into a repeat series of bombing raids.

"Was he there?"

"Yes. God knows what he witnessed. Four months later, after spending some weeks in a place called Lipojane, he was on his way home."

He took a moment, glanced up at the clock on the wall behind me.

"Almost eleven," he said. "Look, you might as well know everything. This is going to take some time. There's a coffee shop in the square."

We re-located to Edna's. A couple of dozen tables with chequered table cloths, in a cosy, sunlit, ground floor room. We sat in the bay window looking across the square. Thornton ordered and I listened while he talked.

"My wife is an American. The daughter of Edward Daley Junior from St Louis. The family firm made a fortune in the 1930s, out of washers and grommets."

"Somebody has to make them," I said.

"Elizabeth was an only child. A true Anglophile, she wanted to go to an English university. Edward decided it should be Cambridge. She accomplished the academic business, he paid for everything. However, as he once told me, he 'cased the joint first'. He bought the Charteris Estate – a Regency mansion and six hundred acres, half a dozen farms and three miles of the River Nene. All of which came with a defunct earldom, and a town house in Wisbech. He became, in essence, the resurrected Lord Charteris."

Which was all very fascinating, but I wondered if perhaps we were wandering off the subject. The coffee arrived. He poured and continued.

"All was going swimmingly until the Haverford scandal. Ever hear of it?"

"No," I said. "Can't say I did."

"The Haverfords were American old money from New Hampshire. One weekend, they were guests at the Daley's summer home in Martha's Vineyard. Charlie Haverford, the favoured son of the family, was found dead in one of the bedrooms. Elizabeth's younger brother, Harry, was arrested, found guilty and despatched to San Quentin. Stock in the family business nose-dived. Harry committed suicide in his cell on Death Row. Edward Daley took to drink and a spectacular bout of gambling. The business was taken over by competitors, broken up and sold off in bits."

He paused and looked at me as if I was dozing off.

"I know this seems as nothing, compared to the accepted excesses of today. But this was uber-respectable, catholic Massachusetts.

"So all this happened when?"

"A year or so before I met Elizabeth. Her father kept the Regency mansion, but he sold off the farms and most of the Charteris Estate to pay the remaining American debts. He sold the Wisbech town house and put the money in trust for Daniel after he was born. He left Elizabeth the mansion and a substantial bill from the taxman. We sold off the rest of the estate to pay HMG. Her father died while Daniel was at university. At which point, I came here and joined the firm. I'm glad I did."

He sipped at his coffee, then looked at me over the rim of

his cup.

"I'm sorry. That's a long story."

And so far, not much about Daniel. Although now it was clear where his money came from. Why he had a mortgage free house in Bristol and cash in the bank, and how he could pay for his gender change. The subject of which however, was rather too personal for Edna's bay window table.

Thornton paid the bill. We left the coffee shop and walked along East Street, towards the promenade and the beach.

"Daniel..." he said. "Where were we?"

"When he came home from Kosovo, did he talk about Donjica?"

"No. He didn't want to. So we never pressed him."

"Did he take a teaching job?"

"No."

"So what did he do?"

"He moved to west London. Bought a flat in Chiswick. He told us at one point that he was going to write about his time in Kosovo. Apparently, he kept a record while he was there."

"Do you know where that is?"

"I have no idea. You obviously didn't find it in his house?"

"No."

He turned away. I moved with him and fell into step as he began walking along the promenade. On our left, the beach huts stretched in line unbroken, towards the north end of the town. All conforming to what seemed the approved style. Grey or brown rooftops over shiplap boarding, seven or eight feet wide, ten feet deep, pediment porches on the front. Painted a base colour white, with highlights in tasteful, bleached-out pastels and occasional Bohemian touches. Horizontal stripes, created by painting every other board in a colour. And flashes of art deco. A silver zigzag here and there, cabin names and numbers in sharp italics.

Thornton stepped onto a porch under a pink and white striped pediment. He took a key from a jacket pocket and opened the cabin doors.

"Welcome," he said. "Make yourself at home"

The pink and white theme continued inside. Pink throws lay across two custom made benches which met in a corner, made an L shaped sofa and served as two day beds. A small sideboard with a pair of binoculars and half a dozen neatly piled magazines on top of it, sat underneath a three-storey tier of bookshelves. A group of small seascape watercolours hung, carefully arranged, on the wall opposite the sideboard. Two wicker armchairs sat looking out to sea, one on each side of the door.

It was a calm, graceful, gently created space

"This is Elizabeth's creation really," Thornton said. As if this kind of quiet accomplishment was beyond him.

We sat down. He looked out to sea, across Southwold Bay and beyond. Then he spoke. In verse.

"Roll on thou deep and dark blue ocean, roll.
Ten thousand fleets sweep over thee in vain.
Man marks the earth with ruin, his control
Stops with the shore."

Lines from a beach hut. Actually, a passable title for a romantic poem.

"Byron," I said.

He looked at me with some respect. "You know it?"

"My wife Emily, was a Byron fan. And over the years, I got seduced into reading him."

"I did too, courtesy of Elizabeth. There's a volume on one of the shelves."

He paused again.

"Deborah..." I said. "We need to talk about the gender change... It may have nothing to do with her disappearance but – "

He nodded. "Yes, of course... Deborah... told us what she was proposing to do in the summer of 2006. Sitting where you are. As you can imagine, it was something of a shock."

"And up to that point?"

"We had no idea what was on her mind. She had never..." He changed the emphasis. "We, had never talked about this. I always reasoned that Daniel had a conventional number of sexual and non-sexual relationships with men and women."

"Do you think that's how this is supposed to be defined?" I asked. "In terms of relationships, sexual or otherwise."

"No I don't. Not now. But at the time... I made a basic mistake. I asked..." He paused to get the definition clear. "I asked Daniel, as he then was, if he was gay."

"And he wasn't."

"No. He just knew, he said, from around the age of twelve, that he was in the wrong body. He grew up with that conviction. Believing that one day, providing he remained balanced and rational and true to himself, he would be able to do something about it. And we're proud of him... her, now. Deborah. Her strength, determination, guts."

"What do you think happened in 2006 that made him want to talk to you. Something to do with his experiences in Kosovo?"

"No. He turned twenty-five. And NatWest sent him a letter asking him to visit the bank and discuss his options. Decide what he might like to do with the £630,000 sitting in his account."

"The Wisbech town house money, plus interest."

"Yes. His 'rainy day' money he called it. He had been talking for a year or so with a clinic in Oxfordshire. Fortunately, the clinic worked closely with someone he knew. A Bristol psychiatrist he had met while he was at university."

We lapsed into silence again. This time comfortable enough. It was simply that neither of us had any more to say. So I suggested lunch.

"No problem," he said. "I have arranged to have it catered. Liz will be on the way right now, with a hamper. I called her mobile after you introduced yourself this morning. She said she would like to meet you, and suggested this rendezvous. A bit Noel Coward perhaps. But it is summer, we are at the seaside and Southwold is famous for its crab sandwiches." He looked at his watch. "She'll be here in about ten minutes."

To fill the interim, I went for a walk along the beach. Daniel's Kosovo adventure strengthened my belief in my client's guts and determination. The latter, she had in spades. Her chances of coming through this were greater than most people you'd meet in the normal run of things. The trouble is, nothing is ever normal in the stuff that I do. The possibilities for error are huge, the margins for a satisfactory outcome are tiny.

I looked back at the promenade. A woman carrying what looked like a picnic hamper was walking swiftly along the row of beach huts. I decided to allow them a few minutes for him to précis our conversation. Maybe Elizabeth would be optimistic enough to see beyond the gloom. If not, then crab sandwiches and an afternoon at the seaside wouldn't amount to much at all. It was possible the Thorntons were on a hiding to nothing.

Bill was waving at me from the promenade. The crab sandwiches and an introduction to Elizabeth beckoned.

CLOSING THE DISTANCE

CHAPTER EIGHT

"What was she like?" Auntie Joyce asked.

It was just after 3.30. We were sitting in the garden in the afternoon sunshine, eating the cake she had baked as promised.

"She is elegant, softly spoken and I suspect, very slow to anger. I liked her. Actually I liked him too."

"So what are you going to do now?

I squinted up at the sky.

"Spend the rest of the day out here in the sunshine. Take you and Uncle Sid to dinner this evening. And go home tomorrow morning."

Auntie Joyce saw straight through that piece of flannel.

"That's a very concise timetable," she said. "But it's not what I meant and you know it."

The honest answer was, I had no long view at all. No scheme, grand or otherwise. In the short term, the best I could do would be to get into Copley's mobile, check his messages and his contact list. Beyond that...

"If I had a halfway sensible plan, I would share it with you," I said. "But the truth is I don't have one."

"Aren't you supposed to be a super sleuth?"

"Yes, well... You've found me out."

"So what do you usually do when you get to this stage?"

I pondered. "I think for a bit. I ask questions. And sometimes the answers lead to more questions. The answers to which, on a good day, lead to me leaping into action. And that action leads to – "

That was enough. Auntie Joyce held up her hands and patted the air.

"All right all right..."

I finished as constructively as possible.

"Look... I poke about, dig into things, hoping I'll unearth something which surprises everyone, particularly the villain of the piece. Who at that point, will be provoked into some action, desperate or foolhardy and hand me something to work on."

I looked straight at Auntie Joyce.

"That's it. I swear."

"Sounds like you haven't a clue," she said.

"Did you hear me say I did?"

Uncle Sid called stepped out of the dining room French windows, carrying a laptop.

"Prepare to be amazed," he announced.

"Where have you been?" Auntie Joyce asked.

"With young Gregory." He turned and looked at me. "He lives two doors along the street. He's fourteen and there's nothing he doesn't know about twenty-first century communication. He sent me a link?"

"To what?" I asked.

"Get that mobile you stole from the man in the shopping centre and come with me."

Uncle Sid went back into the house. I retrieved Copley's mobile from the Healey's glove compartment and joined him in the study. He picked up a USB lead and waved it at me.

"Give me the phone."

I handed it over. He switched the mobile on, connected it to the laptop, double clicked on the link and we waited.

"I may be fifty years older than young Gregory, but never I hope, too old to stay current." He pointed at the laptop. "Look at that."

The screen offered a bunch of alternatives. Uncle Sid followed the instructions young Gregory had written down on a piece of paper. Less than two minutes later, the face of the mobile flashed, the network jingle sang into life and Copley's menu page lit up.

"Bingo," said Uncle Sid.

My Uncle Sid, the silver phone hacker. All I could do was marvel.

He disconnected the mobile from the USB lead and passed it to me. A message in the window said *3 missed calls*. I dialled 121. The response was *you have no messages*. That was either a good thing, or a bad thing. The caller could have been Copley's plumber.

I found my way into the menu and checked the outgoing call box. One call was logged to my home number, timed at 14.56 the previous day – the call I received just before I left the house.

There were fourteen numbers in the contacts box.

"Will you write these names and numbers down," I said.

Uncle Sid fished a sheet of A4 out of a desk drawer and took a carpenter's pencil out of a pot on the desk. I spelled out each name and recited each number. Grant's name was third on the list. Six of the names were solidly English, one was Welsh and one was Irish. Three other persons were listed by the initials 'H', 'M' and 'S'. The remaining two generated a little excitement. They were difficult to spell and impossible to pronounce. Vojislav Dujic and Josip Tudjman.

"Where do you suppose they're from?" Uncle Sid asked.

"Eastern Europe somewhere," I suggested.

"Serbia possibly," Auntie Joyce said, after we had returned to the garden and shared the question with her.

"Is that a guess?" I asked.

"Informed guess," she said. "I have a friend in the WI who is a Bosnian Serb. Mila Bulatovic. She was a librarian in Srebrenica. Survived the massacres and the reprisals of 1995. She escaped into Slovenia and got a boat to Italy. She was given asylum here in England because she had somewhere to stay. Her daughter is married to the carpenter with the workshop at the other end of the street."

"Do you think Mila would be able to locate those names to particular Serb areas?"

"I don't know. She might. I'll call her."

"Invite her to supper," Uncle Sid said.

* * *

On request, Auntie Joyce cooked bangers and mash with onion gravy. Mila's first dining experience on her arrival in Suffolk apparently. Alpha and omega for the rest of us too. Bangers and mash. No contest. Meal over, Uncle Sid organised coffee and cognac.

Mila was as laid back as anyone I've met. Mid 50s, tall and slim, with dark, bubbly hair and green eyes. And with a command of English – as well as Italian and German apparently – which put my meagre French totally into the shade. The names were certainly Serb in origin she said, but locating names to areas was impossible.

"If you're British," Mila said, "You can reasonably expect to have a UK address. Most English people for example, live in England."

"Except for those who live in Europe and the States and far-flung places of the old Empire," I suggested

"That's true," she said. "But most of them are ex-pats, who have chosen to live where they do. Millions of people in eastern Europe have no such opportunity. Ethnic Serbs live all over the Balkans. And there are Albanians, Slovenians, Croats, and Kosovans still living in Serbia.

Uncle Sid passed Mila a cup of coffee.

"So where do these people call home?"

"That's the question that remains, despite years of ethnic cleansing. Do you where Serbia is?"

"In the Balkans."

"Where in the Balkans?"

Uncle Sid thought for a moment or two.

"I see what you mean."

"Serbia is locked in the middle of a European nowhere," Mila said. "Hungary to the north. Romania and Bulgaria to the east. Croatia, Bosnia and Montenegro to the west. Albania and Macedonia to the south. Although that's not strictly accurate. Kosovo borders Albania."

Auntie Joyce took a cup of coffee from Uncle Sid.

"And Kosovo has proclaimed itself a sovereign state," she said. "Because most of its population is Albanian. Right?"

Mila nodded and spooned sugar into her coffee. I summed up.

"We know that Vojislav Dujic and Josip Tudjman have UK mobiles. Which means, they spend a substantial amount of time here."

"So what do you do?" Uncle Sid asked. "Ring them up and ask them where they live?"

"Barmy as that may seem, if I thought they'd give me their addresses, I'd consider it."

"There's always the possibility," Mila said, "that they are living openly somewhere. The internal affairs of Serbia and Kosovo are still a nightmare. Dujic and Tudgman could be living in a penthouse in Belgrade, or in a shithole on the

Macedonia border and be equally invisible in either place."

"But not in neighbouring countries?"

"The reality is, hundreds of thousands of personal records have disappeared from offices all over the former Yugoslavia. And if Dujic and Tudjman have money, they could be living under the radar anywhere."

Which is exactly what my client was attempting to do. Deborah was testing living under the radar to the limit.

Mila raised her brandy glass. "The best of luck with your search."

"Thank you," I said.

She might just as well have been talking about the holy grail. Without breaking cover and mobilising the police forces of six counties I could only work in instalments. It is largely true to say, that everybody trying to keep a low profile breaks cover eventually. Grant and Copley had done that. But as a result, all I had was I list of names and telephone numbers. And considering that was provided by a person with a job description which involved, as a core skill, hurting people, I wasn't exactly in the driving seat.

Uncle Sid escorted Mila home and went on to complete his late-night constitutional. Auntie Joyce and I repeated the previous night's chores and tidied up again.

I remembered that my mobile had been switched off all day. I checked it for messages and immediately regretted doing so. There were two words from a terse and seriously pissed off Harvey Butler.

"Call me."

CHAPTER NINE

I didn't sleep too well. To borrow, from Wordsworth, one of the other pieces of romantic verse I know...
There was a roaring in the wind all night;
The rain came heavily and fell in floods.
There was a similar tempest in the bedroom also. I was still awake and punching the pillow around dawn. At which point I fell asleep and woke three hours later, feeling like someone had been trying to smother me.

Saturday morning. And outside, Wordsworth's day wasn't improving. In fact it was getting worse. The cloud cover was thickening as I looked out of the window, the world was darker than it had been when I went to bed and it was raining pencils. Perfect weather for a five-hour drive home.

"So stay here," Uncle Sid suggested, over coffee, toast and scrambled eggs. "Another day in sleepy Suffolk won't compromise your investigations surely. You're not over-burdened with ideas after all."

I was contemplating how to respond to that vote of confidence, when *BBC Breakfast Time* intervened. Auntie Joyce called to us from the living room.

"Chaps. In here. Quickly." Then she shouted louder. "Come on!!"

We joined her. She pointed at the TV screen.

The studio presenter had swung her chair to face the screen behind her and was introducing a Bristol reporter I recognised. She was standing in front of the 'Out Patients' department at Southmead Hospital. The studio presenter handed over to her and the screen mixed to a full shot. She began to talk.

"The administrators at Southmead Hospital in north Bristol, are launching their own investigation into the circumstances. It appears that a patient, whose name the hospital trust and the police are not prepared to reveal, caused havoc on a ward he was transferred to after receiving medical attention to serious facial injuries. He got of bed intending to leave the hospital. Staff advised him against this. At which point he became violent, assaulted the nurse who was attending him, another nurse who attempted to calm the situation, and the ward duty doctor. Then he made his way to the entrance you can see behind me. He was intercepted just inside the doorway, by a security officer who was punched and thrown against a wall. The man was last seen running across the car park in the direction of Southmead Road. This is as much as we know at the moment. More will emerge as the day goes on."

The studio presenter asked if this sort of incident was rare. Auntie Joyce pressed the mute button on the TV remote.

"I don't suppose that story had — " she began.

"I didn't tell you everything," I said.

"Obviously."

"There was no point in worrying you unduly," I offered, somewhat lamely.

"And now, we're not worried in the slightest," she said.

There was a monster silence. Auntie Joyce and Uncle Sid stared at me, with more menace than I thought the situation warranted. Out in the hall, my mobile began ringing.

The phone was sitting on the table by the door, next to

my wallet, the brown envelope with the photographs inside, my car keys and Copley's mobile. The caller was Jason.

"Superintendent Butler has been chasing you."

"Yes I know," I said.

"He just called," Jason said. "Asked if I knew where you were. I gather he has left messages in the office, at your home and on your mobile."

"Thank you Jason."

He said it was all part of the service and then asked me where I was. I told him I was in Suffolk

"What are you doing there?"

"I'm just about to leave. I'll be back in Bristol late afternoon, weather permitting. It's pissing down here."

"It's great here," he said.

"Keep your own counsel Jason, will you please? Until we can talk."

"Sure. Roger, wilco."

"Later," I said and disconnected the call. I walked back into the living room with the phone in my hand. Whereupon it rang again.

"I told you to fucking call me," Harvey said.

"I was going to."

"Once you had worked out a story you could regale with your face at least half straight."

He took a beat rest, then got to the point.

"So this man who beat up a bunch of hospital staff at Southmead..." He said. "Tell me about him."

This was tricky. I began with, "Why do you assume I? - "

Harvey shut me up.

"Never mind the bollocks. The 999 call was made from your mobile. So, either you stumbled across him and were too busily engaged on some nefarious purpose to wait for the ambulance; or you were responsible for his condition, and suffered an attack of conscience before becoming a fugitive."

"He is the Lexus driver. Name of Francis Copley. He found me."

Harvey heaved a sigh and mumbled something which sounded like 'Jesus Christ'. Then I heard the unmistakable rasp of grinding teeth, followed by a huge intake of breath.

"Where are you?" he asked finally.

"I'm in Suffolk, with my Auntie Joyce and Uncle Sid. Been here for two days. Say hello to Auntie Joyce."

I handed the phone to her.

"Talk to the nice policeman."

She did. Uncle Sid and I listened to her end of the conversation.

"Yes... Making some enquiries into a disappearance... I don't know... He hasn't said... I believe so, yes... Do you want to speak to him?... Yes, I'll tell him... A pleasure"

She switched off.

"He wants to see you as soon as you get back to Bristol."

"He was firm about that was he?"

She nodded. "Seriously."

"I'd better be on my way then."

"Not until you have revealed all," she said. She pointed to the sofa. "Sit down... Now, give."

I did. Told them both everything. They listened. Enraptured, terrified and furious by turns. Auntie Joyce was the first to respond.

"So shall we examine this concept of worrying us?" she asked. "Based on the knowledge we now have at our disposal... You are looking for a lady who was once a man, who is probably in mortal danger, along with you by association. Two enforcers have threatened to kill you. As a result of this encounter, one is, thankfully, in police custody. But the other, is at large in the community, undoubtedly on some vengeance fuelled rampage. And two mysterious Serbian gentlemen, in all probability murderous gangsters, are connected to all this. Now correct me if I'm wrong, but 'worried' would seem a hopelessly inadequate word to describe how we should feel about this... Sid?"

Astonished by her controlled tirade, he cleared his throat and swallowed.

"Absolutely," he said.

When you're on a hiding to nothing it's best to acknowledge so.

"You're right," I said. "And I am not making light of the situation. But my client is in serious trouble. I have to find her and protect her and keep her safe."

"Have you no other choice?" Uncle Sid asked.

"No. At least no other choice I can make."

I looked at them in turn. The two people who had lifted me out of despair in the darkest moment of my young life. Who, with no children of their own, had rescued a frightened little boy, given him solace and care and more love than it was possible to dispose. I owed Auntie Joyce and Uncle Sid more than I could ever repay. And now I was frightening the hell out of them.

"I promise you, all I'm trying to do is find Deborah," I said. "I will not deliberately put myself in harm's way. As soon as I know she is safe, I will go straight to Harvey Butler and tell him everything."

I turned to Auntie Joyce.

"We talked yesterday, about why I do what I do. Well, this is what I do. Though I swear, it's not a prime example of the norm. This case is a bit out of the ordinary. And I have to see it through."

She gave me her open, honest to goodness stare.

"Will you be careful?"

"Scouts honour."

"Then that will have to do."

She opened her arms. I got up from the sofa and stepped into them. She wrapped them around me and held me close. I looked over her shoulder towards Uncle Sid. He smiled and nodded gently.

* * *

I left Broadpole and drove up the Blyth valley towards Halesworth. I stopped in a lay-by, took the sim card out of Copley's mobile and threw the carcass into the river.

An hour later, I was on the A12 and driving south west to the M25.

The rain was relentless. Visibility was down to yards. Overtaking through rooster tails of spray was simply reckless. The M25 was gridlocked, but at least the rain began to ease. By the time I reached the M4, it had stopped altogether and the sky to the west was brightening. It was 1 o'clock and I had been on the road for three and a half hours. I put my foot down. The Healey responded, picked up speed and surged forward. Optimism was short-lived however. A lorry had jack-knifed a mile short of junction 15, ploughed into the central barrier and shed its load of corrugated iron all over the westbound carriageway. I was past junction 14 before I realised. I managed to crawl along to Membury Services and into the rest area, to sit it out.

The restaurant fare wasn't altogether tempting. The tuna sandwich meal deal was a better option. I took the food and a newspaper to a table near the traffic information screen, which was giving updates on the clearing up operation every twenty minutes.

My mobile rang just after 4 o'clock.

Chrissie asked if I was free for dinner. I thought about it. A touch of improvisation was required here. I didn't have a plan for the next few days. All I knew was I should keep a low profile, until I discovered how many Serbs and their accomplices were roaming round Bristol looking for me.

"Love to," I said. "But I don't know what time I'm going to be back."

"You left Suffolk hours ago," she said. "You should be within hailing distance by now."

There was beat. The line crackled.

"I called Auntie Joyce mid-morning," she explained.

Another crackle.

"Dad. Can you hear me?"

"Yes."

"Where are you?"

"Stuck on the motorway," I said. "I expect I'll be here for ages. By the time I get into Bristol, I'll be knackered and useless company. We'll catch up tomorrow."

"Okay. But you're alright?"

"Absolutely."

"Fine. Bye."

The little white lies were mounting up. But so be it. All was for the best in the best of all possible worlds. Still, I had to have a plan, however hastily conceived. I picked up the mobile again and called Jason.

"Are you well?" he asked.

"I'm stuck on the M4, east of Swindon," I said. "I won't get into the office before the end of the day. Enjoy the weekend and we'll have a council of war on Monday."

"Not around," he said. "In Wales from tomorrow, for a week. I'm going up to Snowdonia for some white-water canoeing."

That was good news. A bunch of Serbs and out of town hard cases would be unlikely to find Jason in Snowdonia. And if they did, they'd be easy to spot. Like a privy on the front lawn.

"Have a good time," I said.

"Sure to. Oh and er... Ms Barnes just passed the desk on her way in. Asked if I'd seen you today. Want to talk to her?"

"Yes, okay."

"I'll transfer you. Take care."

Linda asked me where I was. The question of the day, this. I told her I was on my way back from Suffolk. She asked me if I had plans for the evening. Only to rest and relax I said. She asked if I would like to do so at her place.

"Will this be a date?" I asked.

"Sunset with supper and wine," she said. "Would you like anything else?"

I hated to turn her down with white lie number twenty-seven. I gave her an edited version of the story since Wednesday last.

"So?..." was all she said.

"Well, there may be a bunch of evil-doers turning the city upside down for me."

"And there may not."

"There may not. However, I am on the run. And I don't want to collect fellow travellers if I can avoid it."

"So you need to lie low."

"Until I can work something out."

"Then lie low here," she said.

I considered the proposition for a moment or two. Linda supplied the rationalisation.

"You know this house. It's ideal. Out of the way, a tiny road, a cul de sac. And you can hide your not entirely unrecognisable motor car here too. I have a garage."

"So have I."

"Just the place. *Oh, there it is. The man's back in town, clearly.* Let's face it Jack, the Healey is more conspicuous than you are."

She was winning this, hands down. I made one last rearguard effort.

"I do not want to put you in danger," I said, emphasising every word.

"We're both grownups. Well, I'm a bit more grown up than you are. And you need help. Besides, where are you going to stay? Some motel out on the A38?"

"This is a little more serious than being grown up."

"You're big and strong and tough and you'll look out for us both."

"You don't need me, you need Jack Reacher."

"Oh for fuck's sake," she bellowed down the phone. "Just come and stay here."

Even the toughest blow hard should know when he's licked.

"Okay, okay. Thank you."

She took a deep breath. "Good. Straight here."

"I have been summoned to talk with Harvey Butler," I said.

"So call him from my place," she said. "He'll be at home watching Points West by the time you get back into Bristol. Anything else?"

"Ringing off now," I said.

"Later," she said and beat me to it.

CLOSING THE DISTANCE

CHAPTER TEN

At 4.35, the TV monitor told me that westbound traffic was moving again.

I set out for Portishead. A bursting at the seams, old dockside town; now reinvented as a desirable dormitory settlement, complete with Waitrose and executive waterfront homes. The over-hyped centrepiece is Port Marine, newly fashioned out of the old harbour, and for some reason trying to pretend it's a Cornish fishing village.

Linda had moved into the best bit of old Portishead – the Woodhill area – five weeks earlier. I skirted the town centre and found Channel Bank. Drove up the hill and on to Woodlands Road, which runs east, precariously close to the Severn Estuary cliff tops. The entrance to Linda's property is about half way along the road, sharp left through a gateway. I turned into the parking space in front of the two-storey 1920s art deco house, which from this point of view, always seems to be hanging over the cliff edge.

Linda's Golf was parked by the front door. She stepped out of the house, walked to the garage door and heaved it upwards. I drove into the garage.

"Welcome", she said, as I climbed out of the Healey.

She looked terrific. In lightweight, tan chinos and a cream silk shirt, not tucked in, the hem clinging neatly to her hips. The shirt was tailored to fit, the chinos were a bit tighter than chinos should be, but she wasn't making any mistakes. Linda doesn't have to work at being sexy. Dressed up or dressed down, she simply always is. She seems to function by instinct, in a languorous slow motion. Something we'd both acknowledged for years but, somehow, had managed to orbit around. Now there was no need to and we both knew it. But the next step in the relationship was crucial.

She led the way into the house, from the tiny oak front door down half a dozen steps into a living room with a great view.

"Remember that?" she said.

Basically, all of the Bristol Channel. We stood side by side, looking through a twelve-foot square window, at nothing but water below us. The weather was glorious now, and standing close to the glass I could see to the left, as far downstream as the mouth of the estuary and to the right, upstream to the first of the Severn bridges.

"What do you think?"

"I think it looks great now. But what about between the September equinox and mid-April, when the wind is blowing force 8 and the channel is actually whipping up against the window?"

"I'll love it to bits."

"Yes," I said. "I think I would too."

Linda had chosen the furniture carefully, to fit the space. A made to order beechwood framed sofa and two armchairs. A low table, bookshelves and a small sideboard in matching light oak. The dining table sat under a casement window overlooking the small garden at the side of the house, which sloped gently towards a stone wall bordering the edge of the cliff top.

Inland, there was a kitchen to the left of the front door, a walk-in larder next to it and above, a bathroom and two bedrooms, one of which replicated the sensational view below.

"Can you really afford to live here?" I asked.

"Just about," Linda said. "I'll be alright if I find a couple more clients and do less work for you."

I did my best to look hurt. She looked me up and down.

"Is this it?" she asked.

"What?"

"The complete Jack Shepherd? No suitcase and no change of clothes. If only I'd realised..."

"I did leave Bristol in a hurry three days ago."

"Three days in the same clothes?"

"Trousers, yes. This shirt is courtesy of Uncle Sid."

"I suppose he did his best... Oh God no... You haven't been in the same underwear since?..."

I opened my mouth to define the premise a bit. She shuddered.

"No don't answer that. Waitrose. Still open at this hour. Or there's Tesco."

I don't buy my groceries at Tesco. Or anything else for that matter. I certainly can't be persuaded to look upon Tesco as a fashion house. On the other hand, I'm no denizen of the designer outlets. Come to think of it, I don't shop at Waitrose either. But as the high-end grocer has joined its rivals in selling shirts and socks and underwear, I decided that Waitrose it should be.

"Get into the shower," Linda said and pointed along the hall. "I'll sort out your wardrobe and I'll be back in half an hour." She took a long look at my trousers. "They'll have to do."

She went downstairs, found her handbag and car keys, opened the front door, then yelled back up to me.

"There's a dressing gown hanging on the door in the

spare bedroom."

The front door closed. I decided to phone Harvey before I did anything else. I found my mobile and called his. He wasn't best pleased.

"I'm off the clock," he said.

"You told me to call."

"No. I said I wanted to see you. Face to face, in person, in my office."

"Well, that's the point, you see."

I paused. Listened to the buzz on the line until Harvey came back to me.

"Let me guess," he said. "You are hiding from Francis Copley, whose current purpose is your apprehension and the subsequent application of brutal and insensate violence."

"In a nutshell."

"Where are you?

"Not far away."

"Okay. I'll set up a meeting place and call you Monday morning. Stay out of trouble until then, if you can."

He rang off. I got into the shower.

Ten minutes later, dry, pink and shiny, I found the dressing gown on the bedroom door. Actually, a monstrous, fluffy, white bathrobe. Not Linda's surely. For a moment I wondered who it was who last wore this. The secret huge man in her life. No slippers to match however. I put my socks on, immediately appreciated how silly I looked and took them off again. Barefoot, I padded downstairs to the living room.

Sunset, supper and wine, Linda had promised. The premier, heady ingredient was developing outside the window. There was a yellow haze hanging over the Welsh coastline, which deepened into a pale orange as I watched. Sunset over Magor doesn't sound much, but there was a soft edged stripe of gold sliding towards me across the channel, widening as it travelled. As if it would keep on going until the light enveloped me. I re-focussed on my reflection in the window, glowing orange. The room behind me seemed to be glowing too. I heard the front door open and seconds later Linda stepped into the picture. Or rather, she materialised into it. Altogether other-worldly.

"I promised you a sunset," she said.

I turned back into the room. She held up a Waitrose carrier bag.

"Mission accomplished. Make yourself presentable, then come and help me with the stir fry. We're having pork."

She handed me the bag and swayed off towards the kitchen. I adjourned to the bedroom and examined the purchases. Grey socks, blues socks, a choice of briefs or boxers and a couple of soft cotton denim shirts by a young designer who had made the *Observer* colour supplement a couple of weeks earlier. I eschewed the boxers, chose the blue socks and decided on the blue shirt with a signature design on the inside of the collar and the cuffs. I found a clothes brush and spent a couple of minutes attempting to make my trousers presentable. Satisfied that I had done all I could, I reported to the kitchen.

"That's better," Linda said.

She dropped a handful of pork cubes into the wok on the hob. They hissed and sizzled. She picked up a wooden spatula and began to stir.

"So give me something to do," I said.

"This is a double wok operation," she said. "That one..." She nodded to a smaller wok sitting on a chopping board on the worktop in front of me, "has peppers, carrots, broccoli and beansprouts in it. Crush that glove of garlic and mix it in."

I did. The pork fried on for a couple of minutes.

"Okay," Linda said, "Put the wok on the gas and stir away."

We did synchronised stirring for another couple of minutes.

"Add the stir fry sauce," she said.

I poured the sauce over the vegetables.

"Another minute or so," she said.

The aromas were amazing – pork frying in olive oil, vegetables in stir fry sauce and a lingering smell of garlic.

"Going solo now," Linda said. "Let me have your wok."

She poured the vegetables over the pork cubes. The big wok sizzled again and steam hissed upwards into the cooker hood. She picked up a bowl of rice noodles and tipped them into the wok and handed me the spatula."

"Keep going until I tell you to stop."

I stirred for another minute or so. Linda took a couple of warmed plates out of the oven and counted down. Moments later, the stir fry pork, vegetables and noodles were dished up. Along with a bottle of white burgundy

We sat at the dining table to eat.

"Wait," Linda said, "The big finish."

She pressed a tiny rocker switch on the wall to the side of the window looking out into the garden. A row of small dado lights set along the base of the cliff top wall, glowed softly.

"Voila..."

Sunset, supper and wine.

Followed by coffee, conversation and music. Linda held up a bunch of CDs.

"Duffy, Nora Jones or Alison Krause?" she asked. "Or if you like, we can go back a bit. Bonnie Tyler, Bonnie Raitt..."

"Duffy," I said. "What have you got?"

She turned over one of the CDs and began reading the track list.

"Stepping Stone, Mercy, Warwick Avenue..."

I held up my hand. "Okay. No contest."

She put the CD in the player and joined me on the sofa.

"You know, you're really too old for Duffy," she said, as we listened to the title track. "Mid 40s..." She shook her head sadly.

"Just four years older than you."

"It's okay for old broads," she said. "But not for old men."

"You mean, people will point me out in the street? I'll be named and shamed, like some sort of mid-life crisis offender? *You do you realise that he's a big fan of Duffy don't you?"*

"It's a risk, let's not deny it," she said.

"I'm not ashamed of my musical taste. I acknowledge I never embraced Irish folk, punk, or gangsta rap. But I'm not just an ageing rocker. I got heavily into 2-step garage."

It was her turn to stare. "What?"

"2-step," I said, "is the generic name for all kinds of irregular rhythms that cross the beat and don't conform to garage's traditional four on the floor pulse."

I had her complete and undivided attention.

"A typical 2-step drum pattern, features a kick on the first and third beats of the bar and a shuffled rhythm, creating a lurching 'falter-funk' feel... Do you want me to go on?"

"Oh absolutely."

"Resulting in a beat distinctly different from that present in hardcore house or techno."

I beamed at her.

"Where did you pick that up?" she asked.

"Studied it," I said

"Bollocks."

"Abuse is no basis for reasoned argument"

"You got that stuff from the net."

"Er... If pressed..."

She sat back, tilted her head and looked at me suspiciously.

"What else are you getting from the world wide web that I don't know about? I admit I'm genuinely impressed that you remembered all that 2-step stuff, but why the hell go there in the first place?"

"Mentioned in a book I was reading. It was a slow day, so I looked it up."

"And you've immersed yourself in 2-step ever since."

"Not immersed no. But I have listened to Oris Jay and Woody."

"I see..."

"And you should know that 2-step made it into the mainstream in 2000, when Artful Dodger Featuring David Craig, got to number two in the charts with Re-wind. Although that was actually a crossover. 2-step fused with R & B..."

That was as much as I was going to get away with. She waved her hands, like she was swatting wasps away from her face.

"Enough, enough! A girl invites the man in her life to supper, and in return, he takes her on a tour of obscure musical sub-genres."

"Am I?"

She looked at me.

"What?"

"The man in your life."

There was a long silence. Her eyes never left mine.

"Is this the time to confess?" she asked.

"I will if you will," I said.

"Okay..." She took a deep breath. "There is no other."

She waited for me to respond.

"We've shared a lot in the last twelve months," I said.

"You saved my life," she said. "Just a small thing I know but — "

"And you picked me up when I was down. You helped me make sense of the nonsense. I stopped feeling sorry for myself and I focussed. We are close."

"So does that mean?..."

She didn't complete the sentence

"I don't know," I said. "Maybe it does."

"So, what's the worst that can happen? It doesn't work."

"No the worst that can happen, is it does work and then it doesn't."

She took a beat.

"Okay," she said. "One step at a time. Let's see how this works."

She eased a couple of feet towards me, swung her right leg over my knees and sat straddling my lap. She took hold of my face in both hands, pressed my neck gently back against the sofa cushions and leaned into me. She kissed me. I opened my mouth and her tongue found mine. I put my arms round her waist and held on. It was a long time before we started breathing again.

Linda sat back. "Step one," she said. "And that seemed to work."

"How many steps are there to this?"

"I can't imagine."

"We'll know when we get there," I suggested.

"Yes," Linda said. "So let's not rush."

She looked at me for a long, long time. I manage to hold her gaze. Then she straightened up. Raised her arms and linked her hands behind her head. Which meant that all the crucial bits moved in that languorous slow-motion thing that she does. Her breasts strained against the silk shirt as I watched, transfixed.

"I want to enjoy getting there," she said.

I couldn't manage to say anything. She grinned at me.

"Shall I get up now?"

"I think you'd better."

"We've got the rest of the weekend," she said and swung to her feet. "I'm going to clear up."

I got to my feet as well. She held up her right hand.

"It's just a matter of filling the dishwasher. There is brandy in the sideboard. Help yourself."

The rest of the evening passed in a fusion of music, conversation and wine. Just before midnight, I followed Linda upstairs. Escorted her to her bedroom door. I opened the door. She stepped in front of me, then turned and leaned back against the door frame. Graceful, relaxed and sexy.

"I think this next bit should be step two," she said. "And maybe not tonight. If that's alright with you."

I told her it would be.

"Goodnight then," she said.

She straightened up and kissed me. Not like earlier. Not a 'here we go into the relationship' kiss, but a 'this is going to be special, give it time' kiss.

She backed into her bedroom and closed the door.

I looked down at the pattern on the carpet for a while. Then followed it to the spare bedroom. I slept like a man without a care in the world.

CHAPTER ELEVEN

The bedside clock read 9.05 when I woke up, rolled over and looked at it. There was something strange about the face. It was different. Then I realised where I was.

Linda, dressed in light grey track suit trousers and white tee shirt, was sitting in the living room, reading *The Guardian* Saturday review section. There was a cafetière of coffee and a plate of croissants on the dining table.

"Good morning," she said. "Did you sleep well?"

"Careless and dream free."

"That's good."

She stood up, dropped the newspaper onto the sofa, moved into my arms and kissed me. Her hips did a 'meet the day' wiggle, then she towed me across to the table. I sat down. She picked up the cafetière and poured me a cup of coffee. I reached for a croissant

"How long have you been up?"

"Up and out. An hour or so. It's a lovely day."

"So what do you usually do on such a lovely day?"

My mobile rang from somewhere. I tried to locate the source of the sound.

Linda pointed across the room.

"On the window sill," she said.

I picked up the phone. Adam's home number was printed in the window. Chrissie was on the line.

"Good morning," I said.

"Morning Dad. Where are you?"

I looked out of the huge window. The sun was bouncing sky blue light down on to the channel. The surface of the water sparkled.

"Looking at a great view," I said.

"Where?" she persisted.

"Portishead."

"What are you doing in Portishead?"

"I just told you, looking at - "

"Don't be obtuse Dad"

"As in blunt, or as in slow of perception."

"As in dodging the question." There was a pause, then she said, "Oh my God. You're at Linda's."

It was my turn to fall silent. She gave me a second or two then went on.

"Is that where you are?"

"Yes. That's where I am."

"Since yesterday?"

"Yes."

Across the room, Linda was waving at me. I held the phone behind my back and mouthed 'what?' She pointed at the phone, then opened her palms and wiggled her wrists, like a conjuror warming up for a magic trick. I put the phone back to my ear.

"Linda is offering me sanctuary."

Chrissie refrained from the proverbial ironic reply. I took the opportunity to expand.

"I am lying low," I said. "There are some people watching my house."

Chrissie took that seriously enough to stop imagining what Linda and I might be engaging in.

"What people?"

"I don't know."

"Dangerous people?"

"I fear so."

"Oh for Christ's sake..."

She lapsed into silence. Working out all the implications. So I offered a summary of the situation.

"Other people are looking for the person I'm looking for," I said. "They have discovered that I am on the case and consequently, they're trying to find me too. The bonus is, these people don't know what I look like. So, as long as I don't do any recognisably Jack Shepherd things in public – like hang around at home or drive my car to work – I should be safe and relatively free to go about my business."

Chrissie listened to that piece of nonsense with more generosity than it deserved. In times past, she would have run out of patience half way through and given me a bollocking. But now she tends to process my understatements pragmatically. She doesn't approve of what I do, but she is trying to understand why I do it. In return, I am trying to share stuff with her in the way I shared with Emily. Part of Emily's legacy to us was an expectation that we would be honest with each other. Most of the time we manage to achieve this. But Chrissie is no pushover and she doesn't smile sweetly and wave me on regardless.

"And how long will this state of affairs persist?" she asked.

"To be truthful, I don't know. My client paid me for a week's work. I owe her another forty-eight hours. If I don't find her, I'll get help from Harvey Butler. And at that point, this requirement to sneak around should go away."

"Okay," she said. "I'll believe that, for now." Then abruptly, she changed the subject. "Come to lunch."

"May I invite my host?"

"Of course. Put her on."

I held out the mobile to Linda.

"Chrissie wants to talk to you."

Linda put the phone to her ear and said 'hello' to Chrissie. She listened for a moment or two, smiled and said 'thank you'. Then listened some more, nodded, as if in silent agreement to something, closed the call and handed the phone back to me.

"Lunch at 1 o'clock," she said.

"Is that okay with you?"

"Yes of course."

"What else did Chrissie have to say?"

She grinned at me. "Girl talk. Privileged information."

A lazy breakfast segued into a couple of hours with *The Guardian*, punctuated by intermittent cries of scorn, frustration and finally rage, as the paper chronicled the story of yet another government minister outlining the latest Home Office 'big idea' and another desperate opposition spokesperson attempting to ridicule the misbegotten enterprise. Finally, Linda threw the news section across the room.

"It's the same bloody litany of misery every weekend," she said.

"You have to read the *Mail on Saturday* to feel good," I said. "Do you really want to do that?"

She got to her feet. "I'm changing for lunch."

I had nothing to change into, so I skimmed the colour supplement while Linda swopped the track suit trousers for tight blue jeans and added a light weight denim jacket to the tee shirt. I stared in admiration. She acknowledged the attention, stepped into a pair of comparatively low heels and flowed towards the front door. I followed, eyes glued to her backside.

Linda unlocked the Golf and eased herself in behind the steering wheel. I tried to relax in the front passenger seat. But as soon as we got into traffic, I became restless. After a few minutes she got fed up with me.

"Is it my driving?" she asked.

"No," I said. "I just want to be sure we're not being followed."

At 12.45, we drove into Clevedon and parked by the Marine Lake. No one swung into the car park behind us. I got out of the Golf and sauntered on to the promenade, attracting no attention whatsoever. I looked around. Apparently, there was no one remotely interested in me. I sauntered back to the Golf.

We navigated our way along Beach Road, past the entrance to the pier and up to Dial Hill. Linda drove past Chrissie's house, with me searching doorways and parked cars for men with broken noses and wide shoulders. She turned the corner into Vale Drive, stopped and parked under a tree. No one materialised from any direction. I got out of the Golf and walked to the end of the street, crossed over Hill Terrace, sat down on a stone bench and looked out to sea. I sat alone and unmolested for three or four minutes. That was enough rope surely.

I got to my feet and walked back to Linda, who had climbed out of the car.

"Satisfied?"

"Yes."

Together we walked back to Chrissie's house. No car cruised up alongside us, no one stepped out from a gateway. This was the most peaceful street in town. Until we rang the doorbell.

Sam bellowed a greeting from inside the hall. Linda

looked at me. I realised I hadn't told her about the dog.

"That's Sam," I said.

"Don't worry, I like dogs."

Adam swung the front door open and Sam launched himself into the garden. He saw me and leapt across the space between us. We did a reprise of our encounter earlier in the week. I back pedalled onto the lawn.

I heard Adam shout, "Sam! Come here Sam!!"

But Sam was having a great time and oblivious to all exhortation. The wrestling match ended with me grabbing his choke chain and hauling him into a sitting position in front of me.

"Now stay," I ordered.

He stayed. Mouth open, tongue hanging out. He snorted and shook his head. His ears flapped and his dog tags jingled.

"Hello Sam," Linda said.

The dog turned his head and looked at her, for a moment contemplating another round of excitement. Adam beat him to it.

"Sam. Come here."

Without demur, Sam got to his feet, executed a silky 180 and trotted back to the house.

"In you go," Adam said.

I joined Linda by the door. Adam smiled at us.

"Now that's over..." he said, "Welcome."

* * *

The roast beef was terrific. And after lunch we went for a walk. All five of us. Linda borrowed a pair of trainers from Chrissie.

On the sea front, the pier was bustling with visitors,

making the most of the sunshine. The tide was high, leaving little room on the beach for buckets and spades and digging in rock pools, but there was no shortage of kids making the best of it. We walked round the beach, past the re-painted, cast-iron Victorian band stand and on to Marine Lake.

Poet's Walk – named after Coleridge, Wordsworth and Southey – climbs the hillside at the west end of the lake and runs southwest along the cliff tops above the Bristol Channel. It ends by looping round the tiny, ancient church of Saint Andrew and its stunningly set graveyard with widescreen views over the water. If you could choose your last resting place, then surely this would be it.

The channel sparkled silver grey in the sunshine. We stood high on the hill above the church. Sam mooched about on doggie business, sniffing the ground and following tracks; every now and again looking back over his shoulder, to ensure that all of us were still together.

"He likes it up here," Chrissie said.

"Not difficult to see why," I said.

Sam found a stick. He brought it to Adam, put it down on the grass in front of him and looked up, as if butter wouldn't melt. Adam picked up the stick and threw it. Sam hared after the stick and disappeared over the brow of the hill. Adam followed. Linda picked up her cue and chased after him.

Chrissie hooked her left arm into my right, leaned her head against my shoulder and looked out at the horizon.

"How are things with you and Linda?" she asked

"What 'things'?"

I looked down at the top of her head. I shook my shoulder and her head bounced. She straightened up and looked at me, drenched in amazement. Repeated the question.

"You know exactly what I mean," she replied. "What is the

situation?"

"Is that really the sort of question a daughter should ask her father?"

"Then there is something going on."

"There is nothing going on."

"Of course there is," Chrissie said.

She looked at me fiercely, daring me to deny it. So I gave her my best 'I have no intention of dignifying this interrogation with an answer' stare. It wasn't the response of man confident in the unassailability of his position. And Chrissie knew it.

"I'm not asking for chapter and verse," she persisted. "I'd simply like to know the er... current situation."

"When I know what is, you'll be the first I'll call."

She blew out her cheeks in exasperation, freed her arm and thumped my shoulder with it.

"Remember," she said. "We agreed that you would share stuff with me. Like you did with Mum."

"I never shared anything like this with your mother."

She stepped back and gathered herself for a change of tack. She gave me the beautiful, open look that was pure Emily. And now she was serious.

"It's taken a lot of harsh words, months of mending and hard work to get to now… So talk to me and I'll listen. If not about Linda, about the case."

I took some time working out what to say. Chrissie waited. I offered the best explanation I could.

"I've always believed I am sensible enough to know when to keep my own counsel, when to seek advice and when to ask for help. And this sharing thing has to have substance. Your mother and I, always talked when there was something to talk about. Seldom, when there was nothing worth bringing to the table; unless I needed another take on some half-arsed theory I was working on. As to Linda and I, right now, what's going on is..."

I tailed into silence. Chrissie appeared not to be listening. Suddenly she sighed.

"We missed chunks of good stuff, didn't we? You and me. Caught up in missions of our own."

I nodded.

"The sulking and the silences. The arguments. The rows, the fight... and then the storming out. The..." she searched for the right word... "severance. Mum was hurt. Much more than she ever let us know."

"She knew stuff would mend. And it did."

"Thankfully. But too late. There should have been more time for the three of us. Not just eight months. I mean, how long is that?"

"We did the best we could," I said.

"I know," she said. "But with cancer, the best, however good, is never good enough. Is it?"

We stood in silence. Close. Absorbed by the moment.

Sam trundled back across the hilltop, followed by Linda and Adam. He reached us, stood at our feet and stared up at us.

"I think he wants to go home," Chrissie said.

* * *

Linda drove us back to Portishead late afternoon. We climbed out of the Golf in front of her house.

"How about a drink?" she asked. "I don't mean here. You remember the old Royal Hotel at the end of the road.?"

"It's still in business?"

"Yes."

We walked to the pub. The Royal did a roaring trade during the days when the steamers ran a regular service across the channel from Portishead to Barry. Standing just back from the dockside, the pub served food and drink to hundreds of passengers a day, travelling to and from south Wales. The *Balmoral* and the *Waverley* have been refurbished and restored to their late Edwardian glory. And they still visit the channel ports, on both sides, even travelling out to Lundy. But not to the old regular timetable, and no longer in and out of Portishead.

The Royal has a new bunch of regulars from the desirable end of town. No longer hosting the clamour of voices and accents, the agglomeration of day trippers, brothers and sisters, uncles, aunties, in-laws, and even business people who decided they had time to cross the water and could ignore the Severn bridge and the tolls.

I liked the beer on offer, and Linda found a Californian chardonnay that was okay. We sat by a window overlooking the water. The view was great, but the old ambience and the even older landlord, were long gone. Mercifully, the place was quiet; too early for the executive binge drinkers. And the old steamer pictures and histories were still on the walls.

We watched from the lounge as the horizon turned yellow, then orange, then magenta. We finished our drinks and by the time we stepped outside, the world was moonlit. The sky was cloudless, pocked with stars – pin points of sharp, bright light. We walked home, hand in hand, for all the world like new lovers.

"Thank you for the day," Linda said.

Outside her front door she said, "Don't switch any lights on when you get into the house."

I looked around me. "Are we hiding from someone?"

"Indulge me..."

We stepped into the living room and came face to face with what looked like an old 70mm Hollywood movie plate shot. Except that it was beyond the creative talents of even the greatest of the great cinematographers. Framed by the picture window, moonlight bounced off the surface of the channel and lit up the world like it was day. The water was luminous. In the background, lights dotted the Wales coastline like manmade star clusters. We stood, side by side, mesmerised.

"Stunning," Linda breathed. "Happens every full moon, as long as the clouds are high."

There are moments absolutely impossible to ignore. And this was one of them. Linda took the lead.

"Step two," she said. "If that's alright with you?"

I didn't answer the question. I couldn't. Linda decided that meant yes. She lifted the tee shirt over her head and dropped it onto the floor, shook her hair back into place, reached out and began to unfasten the buttons on my shirt. She pulled the shirt out of my trousers reached around my back and drew me into an embrace. I responded and pressed myself against her. She rotated her hips gently. The bedroom was miles away and we were past the point of no return. We made love on the floor, in front of the huge picture window, lit by moonlight.

After it was all over, Linda was the first to speak.

"I love you. You know that. Does it spoil things?"

"No," I said.

"I was so afraid that... when we did this, it wasn't going to work. And I want it to."

"So do I."

And then suddenly it was okay. Everything. She sat up and faced me, her back to the window, silhouetted against the moonlight.

"Then... I want us to be... well us," she said. "But together. I want to be part of you and what you do."

"Okay."

"I've known you a long time. Sharing, isn't something that you're good at."

"You've been talking to Chrissie."

That was a pretty disdainful remark. But Linda surfed it with ease, as if she hadn't expected anything other than such a crass evasion. It behoved me to apologise.

"I'm sorry," I said. "And yes, it is true. I'm not good at sharing."

She looked at me for a long time.

"This isn't a contest," she said finally. "And you're not under siege."

"I know. A question of old habits, I guess. Born out of doing a job in which I spend long periods keeping secrets."

"Did you keep secrets from Emily?" she asked, then suddenly looked startled. "Sorry. My turn to apologise. That was none of my business."

"No, I'll answer," I said. "I tried not to. I shared all the good things and some of the problems, but not always the details. But I never dissembled. At least, not knowingly."

"Can it be like that with us?"

"I think so. Come back here, I can't see your face."

"That's just as well, because I'm going to cry. And it's not a good look. Some people cry beautifully, but I don't."

"Cry away," I said. "Just come here and do it next to me."

She did. And we lay side by side. Then she referred back to the disdainful remark.

"Of course, I did talk with Chrissie. On the phone,

remember?"

"And she said..."

"She said, 'Go ahead, I think it's great.'"

Outside, the moonlight just went on and on.

CHAPTER TWELVE

I woke the following morning in yet another bed. My fourth of the week. Alone. Linda wasn't there. Up and out again apparently. So I had time to rationalise.

I made some coffee and sat down in the living room to think. I swiftly came to the conclusion that there was, after all, no point in keeping a low profile. Everybody involved in this case was hiding from everybody else. Deborah was hiding from Grant and Copley, probably two Serbs, and the person she had hired to find the her. I was hiding from Grant and Copley and probably two Serbs. Copley was somewhere, nursing his broken face and hiding from me and the police and, because he was on a losing streak, possibly two Serbs. The one plus was that Grant was effectively on remand and presumably, as soon as he was well enough to be moved, on his way to the medical wing of Horfield Prison.

So... We could all stay where we were and sit tight. But to what end? None of us was going to make any progress that way. We might as well agree to meet and slug it out.

I resolved to go back home and back to work and advertise that I was back in business.

Linda returned from the Channel Bank Deli with a selection of Danish pastries and pain au chocolat.

"We're going out after breakfast," she said.

"Okay."

"And... I know we have obsessed about you keeping your head down, but I've been thinking about it."

"So have I," I said, and offered her my rationalisation.

"That's substantially how I looked at it," Linda said.

I poured us both some coffee.

"How are you on the countryside?" she asked.

"Terrific on a sunny day. Why?"

"A client has given me two tickets to the Great Western Show."

"That's more than mere countryside," I protested. "It's farmers and prize bulls and tractors and probably morris dancing."

"Members tickets," she said. "Access all areas, including the members bar and restaurant. And a free five course lunch. Which I am assured is very good indeed."

Linda stood up and posed provocatively.

"I'm prepared to take off my clothes, if it helps."

It was a couple of hours before we left the house.

* * *

The showground is in Wraxall Vale, near Tyntesfield House. We were waved into the Members Car Park by a Members Steward and directed to the Members Hospitality Area. We booked a seat for lunch at 1 o'clock and sought out Linda's client, Heather. She was doing duty in the Information Centre, which sat between the First Aid Station and the RSPCA display tent.

"You will have to excuse me," Heather said. "There's a bit of a crisis. A toddler has wandered off somewhere behind the small show ring and we're organising a search party."

"Can we help?" Linda asked.

"Help. Yes, yes of course, indeed you can, thank you so much."

Heather spread a map of the showground in front of us.

"Can you go and have a look in area F?" She pointed to the map. "The little girl was last seen to the east of there. She's likely to be off the beaten track. She would have been found by now if she was wandering around alone in a busy area. She's four years old. Her name's Elaine."

Heather picked up a couple of walkie-talkies and pressed the squawk button on each. She demonstrated one of them.

"That's the talk button. That's the volume control."

She handed them over to us.

"She's been missing about fifteen minutes."

Area F was full of kid's rides and roundabouts. We stood in front of the Teacups and consulted the map. Then Linda looked up and beyond the carousel.

"There seems to be a double row of trailers back there. Generators, exhibitors trucks, that kind of thing. The sort of place where a four-year-old could get lost, don't you think?"

It was worth a try. We took the Teacups as a central reference point, with me working to the right of them and Linda to the left.

I found Elaine three minutes later.

She was standing in the middle of a quadrangle of grass, bordered by trailers and motor homes. Holding a rag doll and a toffee apple, and staring at a huge dog. Some sort of Rottweiler Mastiff cross, tethered to a chrome trailer hitch and asleep on the grass.

I was about twelve feet behind her when she heard me approaching. She turned round and smiled. I nodded at her, trying to stay quiet.

"Big doggie," she said.

She swung back and looked at him.

The walkie-talkie cracked into life. Linda's voice buzzed

out.

"Jack? Nothing this side of the Teacups. I'm working my way —"

I switched off. But too late.

The dog woke up, lifted his head and registered our presence. He was sleepy and he began with a yawn. He rolled onto his belly. His lips slid back across his teeth and the yawn morphed into a snarl. He straightened his back legs and his hind quarters rose up into the air.

The rope tether was longer than the distance between the dog and the girl. I put the walkie-talkie down on the grass and called to her softly.

"Elaine... Can you step back towards me?"

She didn't seem to hear.

The dog transferred his weight forwards and heaved himself upright. He shook his head, like a swimmer with his ears full of water. His muzzle oscillated and sprayed spittle. Then he barked and launched himself at Elaine.

I was closer to her than he was and, mercifully, Elaine's knee jerk reaction was to step backwards. I swept her into my arms and turned away as the dog's jaws opened and then closed on the tail of my jacket. I strained forwards, the dog pulled backwards and ripped a mouthful of jacket away. The onward force pitched Elaine and I forwards onto the grass. I landed on top of her. She shouted in pain and started to cry.

The dog spat out the chunk of jacket and hurled himself at us again. I barrel rolled away from him a split-second before he reached the end of his tether. He was in mid-air as the rope straightened like a steel rod. His neck jerked backwards, his bark turned into a scream then a violent choke. He crashed to the ground and his head bounced a couple of times.

I sat up, hanging on to Elaine, who was crying fit to bust.

She was still clinging on to her doll, the toffee apple had disappeared. She was bleeding from the side of her mouth. She had obviously bitten her lip when I landed on top of her. There was a mud stain stretching across her right cheek from her bleeding lip to her ear. Otherwise, she was okay.

I held her close. She panicked and tried to squeeze out of my grasp. There was nothing I could do but hold her tighter. I got to my feet, my arms wrapped around her and looked for the walkie-talkie. I located it, freed my right arm, picked the handset up and switched it on.

"Linda. This is Jack."

Elaine was still crying and Linda could hear her.

"Is that her? Is everything all right?"

"Fine. Meet me at the Teacups."

Which was also fine, in principle. But I couldn't walk out from behind a row of trailers, in a torn jacket with a squirming, bawling four-year-old in my arms. God knows what the reaction would be. So I sat back down on the grass, released my grip a little and gave Elaine some room to squirm. She responded to the release of pressure and her panic began to subside.

Five or six yards in front of us the dog lay still. Elaine's attention was drawn to it and as she became interested, the crying diminished into a burble and finally into hiccups.

The walkie-talkie burst into life again.

"Jack. Elaine. I'm at the Teacups. Where are you?"

"Doesn't matter, we're alright. Sitting on the grass, waiting for Elaine to calm down. Call Heather. Get Elaine's mother and a First Aider to the Teacups. The girl's okay. A couple of grazes that's all. We'll be with you in a few minutes."

We got to our feet.

"We are going to find your Mum," I said. "Do you want me

to carry you?"

Elaine nodded. "Yes," she said. Then added, "Please."

I picked her up. Sitting in my arms, she swung round and looked back at the dog.

"Is the doggie alright?" she asked.

"We'll see later," I said. "Come on."

The St. John's Ambulance man said that Elaine was none the worse for her adventure. Elaine's mother thanked me for what I had done. Linda said I looked terrific with a chunk missing from the tail of my jacket. I used another £49.95 of Francis Copley's money to buy myself a new one – a dark green lightweight fleece.

I talked for a while with Julia, the Inspector on duty in the RSPCA tent. She agreed to do the paperwork necessary to get an initial investigation into the incident with the dog. I decided to go back to the trailer.

There was a man sitting in a chair on the veranda outside the trailer door. He levered himself upright as I approached. He was wearing a shiny black suit. The jacket was tight around his weight-lifter shoulders and tapered to his hips. His head was shaved. He was big and ugly and he looked bored. Part of his job description however, was to be polite; at least on first acquaintance.

"Can I do something for you?" he asked.

His lips rolled back and a kind of grim, mini smile tried to grow. He looked like he flossed with a tyre lever

"Is this your trailer?"

"No."

"Do you have a dog?"

"No."

"Is the owner in?"

"Yes."

"Do you think I can talk to him?"

"I'll ask."

Without taking his eyes off me, Shoulders stepped back a couple of paces, reached for the trailer door handle, turned it and pull the door ajar. He called inside.

"Mr S. We have a visitor."

There were a few seconds of anticipation, before Lloyd Starratt pushed the door open and stepped on to the veranda. He was mad as hell about something and when he saw me, his mood didn't improve.

"What do you fucking want?" he demanded.

"Where's the dog?"

"What fucking dog?"

"The dog that was tied to the trailer hitch half an hour ago."

"There is no dog."

"Obviously not now," I said. "But there was before."

"Fuck off," Starratt said and went back into the trailer.

Shoulders stepped down from the veranda and stood full square in front of me.

"You heard what Mr S said."

Clearly. And I couldn't misread the vibes coming from Shoulders, silently reinforcing the message.

I said 'goodbye' as politely as I could. Shoulders nodded his thanks. I turned around and walked away from him.

Back at the RSPCA tent I told Julia about Starratt.

"Doesn't surprise me," she said. "We have investigated two incidents in the past eighteen months in which he was involved. Perhaps this time..."

"The dog wasn't there when I went back. It may be dead. I think its neck was broken."

"So, he'll get rid of the body and we won't have any

evidence to go on."

"Isn't there a doggie DNA test? There might be some spit on what's left of my jacket."

"There is a kind of DNA test. But it's basically to determine what breed, or mixed breed, a dog is. It doesn't get much more forensic than that. We might get some sort of classification from spit on your jacket, but not a great deal more. Anyway, without the dog or Starratt's co-operation, we'd get nowhere."

I took that in. She handed me a business card.

"Let's keep in touch anyway," she said. "You never know..."

Linda and I adjourned to the Members Restaurant for lunch.

The soup wasn't great but the other four courses more than made up for the starter. The rioja was good too. All in all, just reward for our efforts earlier in the day. I managed to avoid the morris dancing, although I was introduced to Lucifer, a Highland bull judged the 'Best In Show', who did his lap of honour around the show ring to thunderous applause.

"What a magnificent beast," Linda said.

"This is his third win in a row," Heather whispered with some reverence. "He's worth four thousand five hundred guineas."

Linda spent a little less than that. She bought a Mexican chimera – a clay, tear drop shaped construction on short legs, with a fireplace in the base and a chimney like an upside down funnel.

I stared at it.

"For autumn evenings in the garden," she said.

We got it into the back of the Golf and left the showground

at half four. "It's been a good day," Linda said. "A great lunch, I've bought something for the garden, we have marvelled at Lucifer and you have been heroic."

That was an issue. Heroic or otherwise, my second encounter with Lloyd Starratt within the space of six days was bothering me. It might be argued that the nature of my work makes such rendezvous inevitable. Not so. I never meet scum like the Starratts by coincidence. And certainly not in the course of a Sunday afternoon in the country.

Linda must have noticed me frowning.

"Something bothering you?" she asked. "Jack..."

I realised she was talking to me.

"Sorry."

"Well?..."

"What?"

"I asked if something was bothering you."

"Kind of," I said. "I've had a busy week. One of the most eccentric of my career. With a cast featuring a trans-gender client, a dead psychiatrist, two London enforcers, the Starratt brothers and a couple of unknown Serbs."

She looked across the car at me.

"They are not all connected surely?"

"Everything's connected. Nothing happens out of the blue."

"I don't believe that."

Linda was still looking at me.

"Eyes on the road please."

She looked ahead again.

"So explain," she said.

"I wouldn't have gone to see Auntie Joyce and Uncle Sid three days ago," I said, "if I hadn't discovered my client's parents live in Suffolk. I wouldn't have met Lloyd Starratt's dog today, if we hadn't gone to the show."

"No mystery there surely."

"That's the point. This stuff happens. In sequence. And in context. And therefore, it's not random. My client, the Starratts, Grant and Copley, the Serbs and the death of Philip Soames are all elements in one scenario. All part of the same 'whodunit'."

Linda changed down a couple of gears and turned right. We crossed the M5 and she pointed the Golf in the direction of Portishead. Then she spoke again.

"So..." she said. "We would not have ended up screwing on my living room floor, if you had not agreed to work for Deborah six days ago?"

I looked at her. What could I do but stick to the premise?

"Well... yes." I said. "But we would, I hope, have done something similar at some other time soon." I dug the hole deeper. "As the result of another series of circumstances."

She looked at me.

"How romantic is that?"

"It's not un-romantic," I suggested.

Linda stared ahead again, now concentrating on the traffic approaching the centre of town.

"Look at it this way," I said. "Deborah brought us together."

She didn't say anything.

"Does it matter how it happened?" I asked. "It did. And it was terrific. Wasn't it?"

"Yes. Of course it was. I just didn't expect such a... rationalisation."

The final three minutes of the journey passed in silence. We climbed out of the Golf. She shut the driver's door and stared at me across the car roof. Then led the way into the house.

Inside the living room we faced each other.

"I should go home," I said.

Linda shrugged. "If you wish."

"Tomorrow's Monday. God knows what the week has in store. I have a list of stuff to do. I need a change of clothes..."

"Sure," she said. "Yes, right."

"Linda..."

She held up her hands, palms outwards

"Jack, it's been good. I enjoyed the weekend. We have plenty of time to work on this."

I found my car keys. Linda opened the garage. I kissed her and got into the Healey. The engine fired after a couple of revolutions and I eased the car out on to Woodlands Road.

I was home twenty-five minutes later.

CHAPTER THIRTEEN

Monday morning. 9.15.
The duty PC on the gate at Trinity Road Police Station let me in without a murmur.

"Please park to the right sir," he said. "I'll call reception."

The duty desk Sergeant smiled a welcome.

"You are expected in CID, Mr Shepherd." He pointed across the lobby. "Take the lift. DS Hood will meet you on the third floor."

He did. I stepped out of the lift, almost into his arms.

"Morning Jack," he said.

DC Roberts waved as I walked across the squad room. The politest bunch of coppers you could wish to meet. But that was just the warm up act. Harvey Butler was sitting in his office at the far end of the room. He was the star turn and considerably less affable.

"Ready to co-operate, are you?"

"Since when was it my practice to be difficult?"

George Hood grinned and asked me if I would like some coffee. I looked at him with suspicion

"It's not from the machine in the corridor," he said. "We have a state of the art De Longhi Dulce Gusto. Straight white?"

"Please," I said

"I'll get DC Shackleton on the case."

He left Harvey's office.

"Coppers drinking designer coffee," I said.

"DC Shackleton has an account at John Lewis," Harvey said by way of explanation.

Not entirely explicit, but I assumed the aforementioned DC had bought the coffee maker and presented it to the office."

Harvey motioned me to one of the chairs in front of his desk.

"Sit down," he said. "I take it, you've decided to come out of hiding."

"I reasoned that staying out of circulation was counter-productive."

"You mean you need help."

He stared at me and raised his eyebrows.

I live in the expectation that one day I will get the jump on Harvey, but so far, in the eighteen years I have known him, he had always proved to be the patient, intuitive, detective his rank and reputation merits. I have often been less than truthful with him, I have ignored him, disobeyed him and on occasions come dangerously close to breaking the law, but in the end, I had never been able to out-manoeuvre him. He is quite simply, the cleverest copper I know.

"I have a list of phone numbers I would like you to check for me," I said.

"Being, as we are, at your personal beck and call," he said, without a trace of irony.

I conceded the only way was to be simple and straightforward.

"I should tell you about Francis Copley," I said.

"Indeed you should."

I took a beat. Harvey nodded in encouragement.

"Copley found me. I tried to lose him. I failed to do so. He caught up with me. There was a confrontation. I relieved him of his wallet and his mobile phone."

"You mean you stole them?"

"Yes."

I fished Copley's wallet out of a jacket pocket and passed it across the desk. Harvey looked at it, then back at me.

"Where is the mobile?"

"In a river in Suffolk. I took out the sim card and threw the phone away."

"So we can get Copley's contacts from the sim card?"

"I've already done that."

Harvey held out his hand. I gave him Uncle Sid's A4 sheet with the list on it. He stared at me.

"The sim card?"

"Can I have your agreement that you will trace the numbers for me?"

He looked at the paper and read the list of names.

"Who are these two characters, Dukik and Tugman?"

I corrected his pronunciation. "Dujic and Tudjman. Probably Serbs."

"And what do they have to do with this?"

"I've no idea."

Harvey sighed. I went on.

"Cross my heart and hope to die. Two names in Copley's mobile. That's all I know."

Hood came back with the coffee.

"Better than Starbucks," he said.

Harvey addressed his sergeant.

"George. Our private investigator requires the assistance of the public sector. Do we feel disposed to help him?"

"I would say," Hood said, "that depends on what he is offering in return."

"Not a great deal actually," Harvey said.

"Those phone numbers could be useful to you," I

suggested. "Some of them are listed only by initials because he doesn't want to give away full names. Which may mean they are people of significance."

"By that, you mean of significance to us," Hood said.

"Yes."

"That's your pitch is it?"

"Yes."

"Because you don't really need us to find these people," Hood said. He picked the piece of paper off the desk and looked at it. "Just ring the numbers. And when Messrs 'H' and 'M' and 'S' answer, they will reveal who they are."

"Maybe," I said. "But that won't be enough."

"Harvey waited for me to elaborate. I did.

"I don't want to call any of those people. I just want to know who they are, what they are and if possible, where they are. Then I can figure out what to do next. Grant and Copley began with Soames, for some reason. Then they moved on to me. As to the others, I have no idea who the hell they are, but somehow, they have a connection with my client. I don't mind them coming after me – that's probably what it's going to take – but I don't want them to know I'm on their case. Yet."

I stopped and waited for a response. The detectives stared at me. I continued.

"You can trace every number on that list."

"The trade-off being," Harvey said, "we might discover some major public enemy among Copley's contacts."

"Grant and Copley were hired by someone local, right?"

"That's what we assume."

"So you need to know who he is," I said. "He could be on the list."

"He probably is. Okay George, get it organised."

Hood went out of the office with the list. I took my first sip of coffee. It was very good. I took another. Harvey waited. I put the mug down on his desk. He picked it up and shoved a coaster underneath it.

"Sorry," I said.

"Anything else we can help you with?" he asked.

By which, he meant he had finished buggering around and wanted this conversation to produce something of substance. I asked him if he was looking for Copley. He told me Hood had put DC Shackleton on to it. An important cog in the machinery, DC Shackleton.

"He's young and he's bright," Harvey said. "A bit of routine sleuthing will be good for him. So far, all we have on Copley, is a minor assault charge."

"What about the torture and murder of Philip Soames?"

"Possibly. But in the absence of evidence, all we know is that some person or persons unknown, took Soames out at high tide, presumably in a boat, and dumped him mid channel. Using what kind of boat, from where and from which side of the water, we have yet to discover. We presume Soames was delivered to the boat by vehicle, possibly the Lexus. However, as we have no idea where the Lexus is, we're not on a fast track there either. There's just no trail back from the body."

"Has Grant said anything?"

"His jaw's wired up. Not talking at all."

He changed the subject.

"So, Sherlock... Tell me what you did from the moment you left Copley in Cabot Circus."

I took another drink of coffee then gave him chapter and verse. About Suffolk, the Thorntons, Mila and the Serb names. It took a while. I added the interlude with Starratt for good measure. Harvey picked up a pencil and wrote something on a post-it note as I was talking about the dog. When I finished, he summed up.

"So you are, to all intents and purposes, no further forward than you were when last we met?"

"I have a list of phone numbers," I said.

"And a jacket with a tear in the back."

Hood came back into the room.

"Not exactly names to conjure with," he said. "But interesting."

"You have our complete and undivided attention," Harvey said.

"Okay... Some of them are known to us. Three of the names are from west London. Boasting convictions for activities which include blackmail, extortion, GBH and robbery with violence. The Welshman, Owen Rhys, is a bit of a glory boy from Newport. One conviction for beating up a lady bartender in Bedwas. The Irish connection is another hero, called Michael O'Donnell. He likes to insist that his infamous career is behind him. He now runs a security firm in Lisburn; actually a bunch of doormen and bodyguards. The three names not known to us, belong to Copley's brother-in-law, his sister and his grandma. Again, all in west London."

He paused.

"Which leaves us with?..." Harvey asked.

"The Serb numbers no longer exist. The phones have been ditched. Probably the instant Dujic and Tudjman discovered Copley had mislaid his. They weren't contract numbers anyway. 'H' and 'M' are women. Hilda and Marion. What they and Copley get up to, is open to the floor..."

He paused again. More dramatically this time. Harvey sighed impatiently.

"Which leaves us with 'S'. Get on with it George."

Hood looked straight at me.

"This gives some credence to your theory Jack. 'S' is a man all three of us know and revere. Lloyd Starratt."

I looked at Harvey. He looked at me. We both looked at Hood, who nodded, as if confirmation were needed.

"Lloyd Starratt," he repeated.

"Any more of that coffee George?" Harvey asked.

* * *

Half an hour later, the three of us had shared all we knew about Lloyd Starratt. DC Shackleton had printed out a hard copy of his police record. A bunch of arrests but no convictions. Amazingly. Rancorous and malevolent bastard though he was, constantly in the headlines and on the police radar, nothing criminal had stuck to him in thirty years. He was getting away with it handsomely.

"George," Harvey said. "Assemble a list of all the known associates of every current member of the Starratt clan. Find out where they are and what they're doing."

Then he looked at me.

"I want to know where your client is. I want to talk to her."

I opened my mouth to speak. Harvey raised his right hand and pointed the index finger at me.

"I don't want any bollocks about protection and confidentiality. The lady may have nothing to do with these inglorious people. I fervently hope that's the case. But if she is on the run from the likes of Starratt, Grant and Copley, then she needs more than just your help. Face it Jack."

He waited for a moment.

"Now you may speak."

"A week ago, my client hired me to find her. I've made no

progress in that direction. But she'll contact me again, sometime in the next twenty-four hours."

"Why?"

"Deborah hired me for seven days. The time runs out tomorrow morning. She's organised and methodical. She'll call me."

"So, give us permission to bug your phones," Hood said. "Office, home and mobile."

"Not until I've talked to her again."

"We can link your client to Philip Soames."

"But not to his death."

"You don't believe that and we know you don't," Harvey said.

"He was her shrink. That's all so far. Besides, Soames had seventy something other clients."

"Grant and Copley came looking for Deborah," he said.

"I won't give you permission."

"Then we'll get a warrant."

"You haven't got enough grounds for a warrant."

Harvey ran out of patience. He yelled at me across his desk.

"Don't fuck about with me Jack!"

I got to my feet.

"All I'm doing is protecting my client."

"Obstructing the course of justice is what you're doing. We have a dead body, two assaults, no three if you count the Southmead unpleasantness, and a contractor on the run. Add the Starratt clan to the recipe, along with two mysterious Serbs and your client, who is super-glued to the whole thing… and I have more than enough to take to a judge, the Attorney General and the Home Secretary."

"Okay, so do it."

I turned to leave. Harvey stopped me.

"Wait a minute. Sit down again."

I sat down. Harvey looked at Hood.

"Talk politely to Gloucestershire Constabulary George. Find out how much they'll allow us to do on their patch. Starratt is obviously mis-behaving. He may do something silly and if he does, somebody ought to be around to catch him at it."

Hood left the office. Harvey propped his elbows on the desk, put his hands together as if he was about to pray and tapped the end of his nose with his fingers.

"Are you really going to make this difficult?"

"Afraid so."

"It will end in tears."

"Maybe."

There was a long pause. Time enough to walk twice round the office. I found something to say.

"When Deborah contacts me, I'll do my best to convince her to call you."

Harvey grunted.

"Do more than your best. Because if I have to bug your phones and put a round the clock watch on you, I will."

He meant it. I knew he meant it. He knew that I knew he meant it. We had come to the end of the discussion. Harvey looked at me and held out his hand.

"Give me Copley's sim card."

I handed it over and walked out of the office.

CHAPTER FOURTEEN

Suddenly I couldn't think of anything to do. Out of purpose, out of sorts and out of ideas. An investigator measuring his chances of success in slender degrees of hope. Waiting for his client, whereabouts unknown, to call him and help out.

I drove to my office on automatic pilot. There was a note from Linda, pushed under the door. *There are two transgender help organisations in the city. One in Cotham and one in St Pauls. Why don't you try them? Phone numbers below. Sorry we ended yesterday so stupidly. Love L.*

It was reasonable to assume that, in her five months in Bristol, Deborah had hooked up with other trans-gender people. And on reflection, how many of them could there be? But that was a bargain basement assumption. Maybe it wasn't too patronising, given that it was a rationalisation from a position of some ignorance. But maybe Linda was right. Getting a basic inside track, could help me get closer to the emotional and intellectual responses of my client. And maybe that would help find her. Or at least, give me some confidence to engage with her, if and when, she got back in touch.

A machine answered the first number I called, telling me that Jenny wasn't available, but I should try her mobile; or alternatively, call Sylvia on hers. Both mobiles asked me to leave messages. I decided not to. In this case, introductions should be live. I dialled the second land line number. Annie answered. I introduced myself.

"My name is Jack Shepherd. I am a private investigator. I have a client who has gone missing. I believe she may be in grave danger. I need help to find her."

Annie was less alarmed by this unsolicited call than I feared she might be. She answered directly.

"And how do you think I can do that?" she asked.

"May I give you a name?"

"Yes."

"Deborah Thorne."

There was a long pause before Annie came back to me.

"Tell me a bit more," she said.

I gave her a description of Deborah and a précis of the conversation in my office six days ago. I told her about the trip to Suffolk and the meeting with Deborah's parents. It was enough to convince her I was serious. She asked me about *Shepherd Investigations*. I gave her the office address, phone numbers and a brief biog. She said she would come and see me. I offered to go to her.

"No," she said. "I would rather meet you at your place of work. Later today perhaps. Shall we say mid-afternoon?"

We agreed on 3 o'clock.

"See you then," she said and rang off.

I leaned back in my chair, surveyed the room, then noticed the front of the right-hand desk drawer. Jason had repaired it. The lock wasn't there any longer, but he had refilled and sanded the holes and replaced the handle.

I decided that coffee was a good idea, but there was no milk in the fridge. With Linda absent, I went down a floor to purloin some from Patrick. He was listening to Meatloaf's *Paradise By The Dashboard Light*. I told him I preferred his current hard rock phase. He said he was contemplating a foray into disco. I begged him not to do it. Back in my office,

I made some coffee, filled a mug and drank it, filled the mug again and drifted into consideration of Lloyd Starratt. I needed to know more about him.

I called Adam at the Post.

"Is he part of your investigations?" he asked.

"He might be."

"God, you do pick 'em."

We did a deal. Lunch for information. We met in the Landoger Trow in Queen Street, the literary inspiration of Robert Louis Stevenson, the place he re-created as the Admiral Benbow in *Treasure Island*. It's a long journey from 17th century pirate haunt to 21st century gastro pub, but that's progress for you. Adam was at university with the current manager.

We ordered the Monday house special and sat down with our beers in a corner of the lounge. Adam pushed an envelope file across the table.

"Hard copy of all the *Post* has on Lloyd Starratt and his kith and kin."

I opened the file and read the pages.

The Ma Barker of the outfit was eighty-two-year-old Aurora, the mother of the Starratt boys. She lived with Lloyd in some splendour, in a house he called Southfork, waited on hand and foot by her adoring number one son. Lloyd farmed three hundred and twenty acres north of the village of Parkend, slap bang in the middle of the forest. The youngest Starratt, Ronnie, worked as the farm manager. The only member of the clan not a police database, he was apparently making the place pay. There was money at Southfork and Lloyd was more than happy to wave it about. Starratt Haulage, presided over by the number two brother, Hughie, boasted a warehouse and half a dozen trucks quartered in Cinderford. Never likely to rival Eddie

Stobart, the company did most of its business, trundling around South Wales. Hughie's wife, Brenda, owned a pub in Lydney and ran another in Coleford. Marvin's business, currently being supervised by his cousin Jared, was roof tiling. Jared's cousin Marlene, was married to Ronnie, and ran a low-rent escort agency housed above a bookmaker's in Blakeney, on the eastern edge of the forest.

"It's a glorified knocking shop," Adam said.

Maybe. It was certainly the kind of enterprise that would sit comfortably within the Starratt business portfolio. But nothing to generate the interest of the regional crime squad, or threaten the godfathers of organised crime. The Starratts were as unlovable a bunch of undesirables as you could wish to avoid. But murdering psychiatrists, hooking up with hit men and doing business with mysterious Serbs was substantially out of their league.

Adam had done some thinking.

"This business with Lloyd and his brother and his dog is personal," he suggested. "It's your thing surely, not your client's. Lloyd happened to be at court, circumstances at the showground led you to his trailer. No surprise at all that he was in both places."

"It's not him that's the common denominator," I said. "It's me."

"Okay. But that doesn't mean the events have anything to do with the case you're working on. You were at court supporting a former client. A couple of minutes earlier or later in the lobby and you'd have missed Lloyd. At the show, you went searching for a lost child. If you hadn't pitched up at the Information Tent, you wouldn't have got involved."

"Grant and Copley tortured and murdered Philip Soames," I said. "Lloyd Starratt's phone number is on

Copley's sim card. So are the numbers of two Serbs here in the UK. My client worked in Kosovo, witnessed a massacre and now she's on the run."

"Incidents Jack. Not necessarily co-incidents."

The Monday special arrived. We ate in silence for a while. Then Adam put down his knife and fork.

"Alright... The real problem here may not be who murdered Soames, or why Grant and Copley were looking for Deborah, or what the hell Starratt has to do with anything."

He put his elbows on the table and leaned towards me.

"Focus on the Serbs and ask three questions. Who are they? Where are they? And what are they doing? Then ask yourself another. Given that you're convinced all the aforementioned are connected, who is the person most likely to know the answers to those questions?"

I swallowed the last mouthful of the Monday special.

"Deborah," I said.

Adam nodded. "So your mission Jack..."

* * *

I was back at the office by 2.30. Linda was still out. Or rather she was out again. There was another note, poked under my under my door. *Back around 6. Can we have dinner?*

The phone on my desk rang at precisely 3 o'clock.

Jason's oppo, Alex, said that Annie Marshall was in the lobby. I asked him to send her up and stepped out of the office into the corridor. Twenty yards away, the lift banged, clunked then started to whir. Ten seconds later, there was another clunk and the whirring stopped. The lift doors opened to reveal Annie in a blue summer dress, belted around the waist. I raised my right arm in acknowledgment. She smiled and waved back, stepped out of the lift and walked towards me. Cool, poised and elegant. Tall, like Deborah. Five feet eight or nine.

She held out her right hand.

"Annie Marshall," she said.

I joined her right hand to mine and shook it.

"Jack Shepherd," I said.

I released her hand and waved her into the office. I followed and pointed to one of the client chairs.

"Please sit down."

I took a long look at her from my side of the desk. An important opening survey. I make no apology for this. I do it with every potential client, regardless of sex, race, colour or creed.

She had long streaked blonde hair, blue eyes, mature laughter lines, cheek bones that were more prominent than mine, and a slimline chin. She sat in the chair, crossed her right leg over her left, let the material of her dress settle just above her knee and, totally unabashed by the scrutiny, waited for me to complete the assessment.

I sat down in my chair and then she spoke.

"Do I pass muster?" she asked.

"First impressions count for a lot in my line of work."

"Of course they do. You are an investigator, don't worry. The first time my wife saw me in pearl earrings, she smiled, looked at the wallpaper behind me and asked if she should put the kettle on. I said yes. She walked into the kitchen and made the tea. She spent ages over it, all the time engaged in a huge effort to work out what to say next."

"What did she say?"

"She said, 'From now on, I must think of you as she'."

"And was that okay?"

"Yes it was."

"And was this a genuine trans-gender moment or an early cross-dressing experiment?"

"A trans-gender moment. I never was a transvestite. Not in any demonstrable fashion anyway. Have you heard the joke?"

"Which joke?"

"What's the difference between a transvestite and a trans-sexual?"

I waited for the punchline. She delivered it.

"About three years."

I laughed. She grinned back at me.

"It's a good joke," I said. "But I guess you have to be a trans-sexual to tell it and get away with it.

"Actually," Annie said, "These days there's some debate about 'trans-sexual'. It's not a noun. It's really an adjective."

I considered the proposition for a moment or two.

"You're not a trans-sexual, you're a trans-sexual woman," I said.

"Truly, the words 'sexual' and 'gender' get in the way. They're part of a definition. Not a condition. If the word 'gender' ceases to become the focus and people can stop explaining what it means, then the trans business can be considered over and lives can begin anew. I am a woman. End of story."

She took a deep breath.

"Sorry. I'll climb down from the soap box now. What do you want to know?"

That was a hell of a question. The answer was, anything and everything. Anything that would help me find Deborah and everything that would help to stop me making foolish assumptions.

Annie helped out.

"There is something called a trans road map. Actually the whole process, from the beginning to the end."

"Okay... So where does it begin?"

"It begins with the decision to change gender. You have to know why you want to do this and explain everything to your GP. Then, all being well – by that I mean if the GP believes you – the next step is a referral to a psychiatrist associated with the practice. The psychiatrist has to believe you too. If he does, then he will refer you to a gender assessment clinic or a psychiatrist specialising in gender identity. In my case and in Deborah's, it was Philip Soames, here in Bristol. This is a major examination. If you don't pass, it's the end of the line. A resolute and unchangeable mindset is required. Any display of hesitation, or inconsistency, or recognisable delusion, will bring everything to a grinding halt."

"But if you get through it?..."

"If the psychiatrist believes you, he will diagnose 'gender dysphoria' and prescribe a course of hormone treatment."

"Which begins the physical process of turning you into a woman?"

"Effectively. You combine breast augmentation with electrolysis to get rid of face and body hair. But most importantly, you put on your frock and set about living as a woman."

"And all the while, the psychiatrist monitors the process."

"Yes."

"Then what?"

"Well... that's where some people stop. They decide that passing as a woman is enough."

"But actually being a woman..."

"Is the real issue. You can't be a woman with a penis. To complete the change, it has to go." She let the pause fill. "Shall I go on?".

"We've come this far..."

"Empathy from relatives and friends is an absolute requirement. But this isn't something that can be shared, obviously. What follows immediately is called the Real Life Test. You must live as a woman in every way, for two years. And spend at least half of the period in full time employment or education."

"With no down time as a man?"

"None at all. There are two more psychiatric assessments during this period. If you make it through, you get your surgery. And this is as gruesome as you can imagine."

"Actually I don't think I can imagine it."

And I didn't really want Annie to explain. But she felt she needed to.

"To begin with, it's as basic as you would expect. The removal of the testicles and the erectile tissue of the penis. Obviously, that's not very tricky, it's an amputation. It's the next bit that's clever."

I couldn't believe that Annie was being so matter of fact about all this.

"Clever?..."

"There's a big hole left between the rectum and the prostate. This is lined with the penis skin and the scrotum to make the vagina."

She smiled and turned the palms of her hands upwards.

"That's it really."

Maybe. And having gone through all that, something of a triumph. To know everything about the process and to understand what has to happen, is one thing. But to look forward to it... That takes a special kind of resolve.

"The bonus is," Annie said, "once the surgery is complete, all the bits work."

I stared at her. She grinned back at me.

"Have I embarrassed you?"

"No. I'm just reflecting that if I had said something like that, it would have been deemed smutty."

"Not by present company," Annie said. "Anything else?"

"Your voice."

"Hours of lessons with a voice coach. Contrary to legend, you don't go up two octaves when have your testicles cut off. You have to work at it."

"May I ask you some other stuff?"

"Out of what? Curiosity?"

"Curiosity sounds better than prurience."

"I like a man who suspects his own motives," Annie said.

"It's a side effect of what I do," I said. "Collateral damage."

She smiled again.

"Ask away."

"How long have you been a woman? I mean, how long have you lived as a woman?"

"I'm 49. I had the surgery six years ago."

I must have looked surprised.

"You're wondering why it took so long."

"I think the decision is immensely brave," I said. "At whatever time in life you take it."

"My rationalisation is that, emotionally, I've always been a woman."

"Was that a problem?"

"Weirdly, no. You might assume it would be. You know, a kid on his own, in a corner of the playground, avoiding the rough and tumble contact with others. Interested in art and drama and hopeless at sport."

"It's an archetypal picture."

"Not mine. I played rugby at school. And then at university. I re-built an old Norton motorbike my Dad kept in a shed at the bottom of the garden. Basically, my interests were then as they are now. I didn't give up motorbikes for female pursuits. I was a girl, born into a boy's body, who liked boy's stuff. My early life wasn't beset by demons and dark thoughts. There was never a miserable Alan, desperate to become a re-constituted Annie. My personality hasn't miraculously blossomed since the surgery. But I am a different shape now, which incidentally, I'm rather proud of."

"You have every right to be. You look terrific. Am I allowed to say that?"

"Don't be coy, you're letting yourself down."

"I've only known you twenty minutes."

"I've been propositioned on much shorter acquaintance. I don't mind you, or anyone, inspecting the equipment. I am a woman and my femininity is no more of a mystery than anyone else's."

"You're tall," I said. "Slim hips and long legs."

She nodded in acknowledgement.

"And no cellulite," she said.

Something that hadn't occurred to me. Men don't get cellulite.

"That's a bonus," I said.

"Here's the thing," Annie said. "The bottom line is, no one should worry about their femininity, or their sense of themselves as women. In my case, it just took a while to straighten things out, as it were."

"You got married. To a woman. That's a resolutely male thing to do."

"Yes."

"And you didn't have second thoughts?"

"I was in love with Mel. I still am. We still live together. And we have two children." She gave me an old-fashioned look. "You're trying very hard not to be surprised by all this."

"Sorry."

"Mel claims she knew, long before the pearl earrings moment, that I was trying to work something out. When I finally told her and she got over the immediate shock, she said she was relieved to know what it was."

"What about the kids?"

"Because I did all this so late on, they were grown up and hardly fazed at all. At the time, Charlie was nineteen and at university in the US. He's still there, working in Silicon Valley. Holly was seventeen and doing her 'A' Levels. She's now in Yorkshire, designing wind turbines. We are a very well-adjusted bunch, considering."

Annie was genuinely relaxed. We were both enjoying this conversation. But at some point we had to begin talking about my client. Annie got to it before I did.

"At which point did you realise that Deborah was a woman?"

"Not on first acquaintance."

"So when?"

I took some time over my response. For the first time since we began talking, I struggled to slide into the next chapter. Annie waited.

"You are having trouble with this," she said

"Yes. There's no easy way to say this, so... Do you know that Philip Soames is dead?"

Annie shifted her position in the chair. She put her hands on the arm rests and sat up straighter.

"From what?" she asked. "He wasn't ill, was he?"

"He was murdered."

Annie looked at me without blinking.

"Why?"

"Some people are looking for Deborah."

"People, what people?"

"That's the problem. I think only Deborah knows who they are?"

"Then it follows you should ask."

"Let me tell you the rest of the story," I said.

Annie listened patiently while I did so. Concerned at first about Deborah, then about Sarah, with whom she had become good friends. When I finished, she got to her feet.

"Do you mind if we go for a walk?"

We walked over the re-furbished footbridge and into the park.

"I've known Deborah since she came to Bristol," Annie said. "Which was what?... Four or five months ago?"

"About that. Did you meet up at any time in the years before? When you were both clients of Philip?"

"No."

"In the last four months, have you met any of her friends?"

"No."

"Did she ever talk about anybody?"

"She must have I suppose, but I don't remember who. I don't think I can recall any names."

"A woman in her mid or perhaps late 30s. With a child."

Annie screwed up her face in concentration.

"No. I'm sorry. "I've known her since just before Easter. It has taken me the whole of that time to learn as much about her as you have done in less than a week. I don't think I can add anything."

"I found two photographs in Deborah's house.

Presumably taken by her. The woman and the child are on a beach. In Devon."

Annie stopped walking. I turned to face her. She stared ahead for a moment or two then looked at me again.

"Devon," she said. "Actually south Devon. Once... once Deborah talked about... Oh God what was it?... No, the conversation wasn't about Devon. It was about the surgery. The date of the surgery. We were comparing notes, I guess, about the experience. She mentioned, no more than an aside really, that she had been on holiday in south Devon, just days before going into the clinic... And er..."

She gave up struggling with the story.

"Sorry... I really can't remember any more."

"It may just be enough," I said. "Can I crave your indulgence for another fifteen, twenty minutes."

"Yes of course."

Back in the office, we looked through Philip Soames' notes. Deborah had seen Philip three days after her surgery, on July 25th 2010. So she must have been in south Devon, with her friend and the child, just before that time. Annie agreed with the assessment.

It wasn't much, but it was new information. Not gold maybe, but a little richer than base metal.

"Is it too early for a drink?" I asked.

Annie looked at her watch.

"It's quarter past four," she said.

I fished a bottle of Laphroiag out of the bottom drawer of the filing cabinet.

"Now that is disappointing," Annie said.

"Oh I'm sorry. Don't you like whisky?"

"Yes I like whisky. It's just that the bottom of the filing cabinet is a bit of a cliché."

"It helps with the Philip Marlowe thing I'm trying to get going," I said.

Annie grinned.

I poured the drinks, sat down again and we talked again. About her journey, about her family and about her real happiness with who she is now. About me and what I do and why I do it. About my days in the police force, about Emily and Chrissie. Like we were new best friends. And then about Deborah again. It was Annie's turn to ask the million-pound question.

"Do you really think you can find her?"

"No self-respecting private investigator likes to admit when he's beaten. But I have no idea where she is. Right now, I feel less worried for her than I did. We have a bunch of sensible coppers on the case and they can deal with the UK bad guys. I don't know anything about the Serbs. But the police can put Deborah into protective custody and do something about them. If she'll talk."

"It still bothers the hell out of you."

"I'm making assumption after assumption. All of them ending in the idea that Deborah is hiding from Dujic and Tudjman. The whole business is just plain untidy. I hate it. I need Deborah to come out of the woodwork and talk to me."

"If she does," Annie said, "tell her we have met and talked. Tell her everything we talked about. It may help. God knows you have earned your money. She will recognise that surely and perhaps – "

The phone on my desk rang. I craved Annie's indulgence and picked up the receiver. Linda was calling from next door.

"Am I interrupting?" she asked.

"No no, it's fine," I said. "Come and meet Annie."

I replaced the receiver.

"That was Linda. Next door. My accountant."

Annie wound up. "Ask Deborah to call. She might do so. And, who knows, I might be able to help out."

Linda knocked politely on the door, opened it and stepped into the office.

Annie turned in her chair. I introduced them. Annie looked at her watch and stood up. Linda apologised for interrupting.

"You're not interrupting anything. We have finished. Good to meet you." She turned to me. "Remember. Tell Deborah to call me. See you later, I hope."

She nodded at Linda as she left the office. Linda watched her go.

"Very smart. Is she... a trans-sexual?"

"I have been told that 'trans-sexual' is an adjective," I said.

"I see. She's a trans-sexual woman."

"Just a woman."

"You're being very correct," Linda said.

"I'm learning to be."

It was early, but we were both hungry and there was a Mexican restaurant open on the other side of the Cumberland Basin. We walked to it. On the way, Linda gave me a rundown of her afternoon.

"Lunch in the council chamber. Followed by two hours of hype and nonsense from the directors of a new initiative. More half-arsed proposals for regional expansion. All involving collaborations between the public and private sector, ho ho ho."

"These men are philanthropists," I said. "How can you be so cynical?"

"These men," she countered, "are on the make. Again. More schemes to get local government to pay for their personal aggrandisement."

"Aggrandisement..."

She looked at me, as though disappointed that I wasn't taking this seriously.

"Councillor ShitBrain from Henleaze took centre stage. He came up with a barmy scheme for the redundant electronics factory along the river from here. Another bloody retail outlet. He's even got a name for it. Phoenix Park. And he was supported in his crass proposal, by a group of people who want to build a bunch of starter homes on the brown field site behind."

"Well that's a good thing. Isn't it?"

"You may think so. But there's a reason the site has been derelict for so long. There was a paint and dye factory there for thirty years. The ground is toxic. The developers can't afford to clean it themselves, so they want the council to help out."

"They won't get that surely? I mean nobody's got any money."

"Ah well, that was the point at which the council Finance Director got to his feet and made a speech about promoting growth. And they went on to debate this in all seriousness."

She stared at me, inviting me to say something. So I asked a question.

"Why were you at this gathering?"

"I'm a member of Business West. I get invited to these gigs."

We had reached the door of *Cantina Casita*. I opened it.

"Oh yes," Linda said, "Lloyd Starratt was there."

Leaving me to assimilate that minor bombshell, she swept into the restaurant.

Linda had chicken enchiladas. I had tacos dorados. And we had a couple of bottles of Corona. As we ate, Linda explained that being a substantial local entrepreneur,

Starrrat had been an invited guest. He had shown up in an expensive suit, all swagger and bonhomie, and comprehensively worked the room.

"I have to tell you, he's good at it," she said. "Especially with those who can't distinguish charm from smarm. He announced his whole hearted support for the Phoenix Park scheme. And graciously accepted the applause that followed. The slimey bastard has more front than a row of houses."

I bit into the last taco. Linda changed the subject.

"Did your friend Annie help?"

I swallowed.

"Yes, with lots of background stuff. Thank you for pointing me in her direction. And she knows Deborah. The connection may be enough to persuade Deborah to talk about the stuff she hasn't so far."

"And if it isn't?"

"Then I will admit defeat."

Linda ate her last mouthful of chicken and wiped her lips with her napkin. "Which will leave Deborah where?" she asked.

I picked up the glass of Corona, drained it, put it back on the table cloth.

"I have absolutely no idea," I said.

We walked back to the office and this time talked about us. We came to the decision to let whatever was happening, continue to do so, without questioning and tinkering. It wasn't going to go wrong. We had simply to leave it alone and let it go right.

There were two messages on my answering machine. The first from a man called Leonard Hopkins, asking me if I could call him. The second from Harvey Butler saying he had some information to impart. I called him first. His office phone diverted to his mobile. He was at home.

"We've checked with the Borders Agency," he said. "They have no record of Vojislav Dujic or Josip Tudjman. Neither of them are in the UK as bona fide refugees or would be immigrants. Which means either, they're here illegally, or, they have genuine passports and they're enjoying our hospitality, like every other tourist. Serbs can visit the UK and stay for six months without visas. And if Dujic and Tudjman are Croatian Serbs, they don't need visas at all. They could have driven in through any channel port, waved their passports at the appropriate desk and passed into the UK with no fuss or bother. Sorry Jack."

Dispirited, I called Mr Hopkins. He said he was receiving threatening emails and the police weren't doing anything about it. Could I? I told him it wasn't the sort of work I did. He said something about 'another waste of time' and rang off.

I looked at my watch. 6.25.

Linda materialised in the doorway.

"I've got to go. Homework to do for tomorrow."

She stepped to the desk, leaned over it and kissed me.

"Sleep well," she said.

Then she was gone. Leaving Jack Shepherd, super sleuth and knight errant on his own, with no idea of what to do next.

I decided to go home too.

CHAPTER FIFTEEN

Deborah called at ten minutes past eight. The ensuing conversation had its ups and downs. I went through the investigation so far, day by day and discovery by discovery. Except for one item I reserved for later. The photographs on the beach had to come as a surprise, at the most useful moment.

Deborah reacted like a celebrity whose ghost writer had got all the facts of her biography correct, but given away too many secrets. The news that I had unearthed her gender story shook her up. But the information about Philip Soames generated a brutal despair I could feel at my end of the phone line. She took a long time to recover her composure. Unlike her approach to our original meeting, Deborah hadn't rehearsed this encounter. Or at least, she hadn't allowed for the deluge of stuff I was pouring down the line. I prodded away at the most sensitive element in the story.

"Grant and Copley were hired to persuade Philip to provide information about you," I said. "Somehow, from somewhere, they found out you were a client of his."

"I don't know how," Deborah said.

"Copley is from west London."

"And I used to live there, yes."

"So, it's not unreasonable to ask if you have any previous connection with him."

"I don't know Copley. Or Grant."

"Do you know Lloyd Starratt? It's possible he hired Grant and Copley. Why would he do that?"

"I don't know. I can't answer any of these questions."

"Deborah..."

She was growing impatient. And I was in danger of losing ground. The week's work I had done was being eclipsed by a bunch of 'I don't knows'. And we hadn't got anywhere near Dujic and Tudjman yet. She snapped back at me.

"What have you told the police about me?"

"Very little. Not enough to encourage them to look for you. Although they now have all of Philip's case notes. They know I'm stalling and it won't be long before they run out of patience."

"What happened to your much prized client confidentiality?"

"Philip was tortured and murdered," I said. "Under those circumstances, it took no time at all for the police to get a warrant. They are looking for a motive. You and I both know what that is. It's the search for you."

There was a sustained silence. I counted my way through it, timing the hiatus to my next line.

"We have to meet," I said.

Another pause. This time I waited for Deborah to speak.

"No," she said.

"Then there's nothing more I can do," I said.

And disconnected the call.

And waited.

It was six minutes before Deborah called back.

"I'm sorry," she said.

That was a step forward, so I moved carefully on.

"I need to ask you about Dujic and Tudjman," I said. "Don't say 'I don't know them'. Think for a moment, then tell me why they might know you. Go back to your time in Kosovo. Who might Dujic and Tudjman be?"

That was a useful question. Deborah thought about it.

"Members of some Serbian militia group," she said. "Kosovan vigilantes, ex policemen, criminals, who saw opportunities in the misery and the massacres. There are shed loads of possibilities."

And given what Mila had to say, Dujic and Tudjman weren't necessarily on the run. Whatever they might have been sixteen years ago and whatever they were doing now, they weren't in the UK as political refugees. But their presence and their purpose, directly or indirectly, had dragged a lot of unwholesome stuff into this case.

I asked Deborah if she had been in touch with any Serbs since she came back to the UK. She said 'no'. I asked if she had any residual relationship with anything Kosovan. She said 'no'. I asked her if she was still in contact with Médecins Sans Frontières. She said 'no'. The conversation was hurtling towards a precipice, with huge sign on the edge reading 'Nothing to Learn.'

So I jumped on another bandwagon. I told her about Annie.

"You really have been working for your money," Deborah said.

"Annie said the same thing. And she also suggested you should talk to the police."

"At the risk of sounding like a broken record..." she said.

We were never going to find an ending that would play, so it was time for the photos business. I told Deborah about finding her safe and breaking in to it. I recited a list of the stuff I had found. There was no response from her end of the line.

"Who are the people in the photographs on the beach?" I asked.

"I won't tell you," she said.

"Because, if I can find them, I can find you."

She didn't deny that proposition. She was quiet for a long time. Making her mind up about something. I waited

"I'll call you back in fifteen minutes," she said.

"Okay."

I put the phone receiver back in its cradle. Poured myself a large brandy and sat down on the living room sofa.

I had been making assumptions about Dujic and Tudjman ever since I had discovered their names in Copley's mobile. Because they were Serbs and because Deborah had been in Kosovo. That was all. I had no evidence of any connection between them. The Serbs were probably in the UK on business. And given their association with Copley, their business was probably less than legitimate. So what? Maybe they weren't the issue here at all. It was the woman and the child who were causing Deborah concern.

Speculation is essentially a fruitless exercise. Developing a theory has purpose and direction, pondering is something else entirely. Up to now, this investigation had been a fishing expedition. And I hadn't caught anything of substance. I had driven five hundred miles, asked a lot of questions and assembled skips-full of information. But so far, I had failed to turn lead into gold.

So back to basics. Deborah was frightened, in trouble and in hiding. From some un-detailed menace. If this was represented by the Serbs, the question arose - was this a long-distance menace, or something real and just around the corner? Which in turn begged the question which had haunted this business throughout. Where to begin to look?

The alternative, was simply to leave the stage. Bring down the curtain on the last performance and go on to the next show. I had a week's wages in the bank. There was no need to send my client an invoice. And Copley had covered my expenses. In fact there was enough left for dinner and a bottle of champagne.

But the bottom line was, I had not found my client. And that was the job. Or at least, how it had started. Sure, I had failed in my quests before. I was no stranger to wreckage and unhappy endings. But I had seen all of them through to the end, however bitter.

Impossibilities take a bit longer...

The telephone rang again.

"I want you to stay on the case," Deborah said.

I processed that information. Deborah waited for me to respond. When I didn't, she asked if I was still there. I said I was.

"Use the money in the safe in my house. Take as much you need. You have been brilliant so far. I didn't imagine, for one moment, you would find out so much about me."

"Tell me about the woman and the boy on the beach," I said.

"No."

"Okay, you're trying to protect them. I understand. From what? If it's serious, let's go to the police. Get their help."

"No."

She ordered a change of subject.

"I don't want a conversation about the police. Not now."

"Alright," I said. "So are we going to continue this in the conventional manner? Are you going to tell me where you are and what you're doing?"

"No, the original rules apply. I can't help you with this. That has always been the point. Otherwise, we would not be talking. All this would be at an end."

"At least give me your mobile number."

There was a long exhalation of breath down the line. Then another long pause.

"Deborah?..."

She came back to me.

"I want your word you will not give this number to anyone else."

"You have it."

She gave the number to me. Asked me if I could remember it. I recited it back to her.

"Write it down somewhere if you have to," she said. "But please don't put it into your phone. Or anywhere it can be traced."

She rang off before anything else could be discussed. I went into the kitchen and made some coffee, wandered back into the living room, poured some more brandy and returned to the sofa.

* * *

I talked with myself for an hour or so. Having resolved to see this through to a conclusion, I ought to have a plan. However optimistic.

Lloyd Starratt was the most accessible character in this drama. At least, in the sense that I could find him. I decided to believe my supposition that he had hired Grant and Copley. That being the case, his best laid plans had failed so far. He hadn't found Deborah, Grant was under arrest, Copley was in hiding and Starratt himself was on the police radar. I could take some measure of credit for the scenario and that helped me feel better.

Feeling positive was next up. And that came with the plan. Which could work, if I stayed in one piece and avoided getting stomped on by people such as the man outside Lloyd's trailer.

A trip to the Forest of Dean was required.

I hadn't been in the forest for years. Bristolians don't have it high on their list of places to frequent. Like Londoners don't visit the Tower of London – they live next door to it, they know it's there and not going away. This corner of Gloucestershire is more tatty than romantic. What remains of the forest itself, almost fifty square miles of dense woodland on the banks of the River Wye, is magical. But the 21st century has imposed itself resolutely on the rest of the region. Local industries have died and jobs along with them. People born and bred in the forest, stay because it's all they know and join the dole queues and live on benefit. Long established, ancient communities have withered away. While, in contrast, the wild boar continue to flourish. The sitting Tory MP doubled his majority at the last election. Add to that, a bunch of in-breds like the Starratts, who all have the same chin and who have survived by shortening the odds and playing the percentages, and the history comes up to date.

Tomorrow's job, was to beard the lion in his den.

CHAPTER SIXTEEN

Tuesday morning. The second Tuesday on the case.

I decided I didn't need to burgle Deborah's safe again and spent a couple of hours with Adam's notes and the road atlas. Trying to pinpoint the locations in the Starratt empire. I found all the places listed. But there had to be more. The Starratts flourished, in all their tainted glory, like feudal barons in a medieval kingdom.

I crossed the Severn Bridge just before 10 o'clock, in glorious sunshine. Drove in Wales, and then drove north, back into England. Through Chepstow and on up the A48 towards Lydney. Turned northeast into the forest and headed for Parkend.

A couple of miles later, I pulled into a lay-by, screened from the road by a fringe of trees and lined on the other side by a farmer's hedge. I climbed out of the Healey and looked around. The day was warm and the lay-by buzzed with activity. There was a hum from insects in the nettles. Bees were busy, darting in and out of a bunch of wild roses, their heads open to the sunshine. A butterfly settled on the Healey's driver side wing mirror. I watched her open her wings in slow motion, then dip from side to side like a fighter pilot saluting. She was light grey and blue and white and luminous in the sunshine. Her wings flapped twice, she rose, then dipped, turned and flew into the trees by the road.

I found a gap in the hedge, stepped into it and took time out for a pee. I heard a car pull up behind me. I ignored it, finished what I had started, zipped up and stepped back. The barrel of a hand gun was poked into my right kidney.

A voice, thick and nasal spoke into my right ear.

"Don't turn around until I say so."

The owner of the voice sucked in breath, then spoke again. I waited.

"Now. Turn around now."

I did. Francis Copley stood stock still, bloodshot eyes looking at me from behind a nose like Charlie Caroli's. Worth a huge laugh and a round of applause, if it wasn't for the 9mm Browning automatic he was pointing at me. He sucked in breath once more, through thick, bruised lips. He let it out again, slowly and gently. His nose currently wasn't up to the job.

The Lexus was parked behind him, engine idling.

Copley eased the Browning's safety catch off.

"I knew if I hung around your place long enough, we'd eventually get to be alone somewhere," he said.

He sounded like Melvin Bragg with a bad cold. With his left hand, he pointed to the offending proboscis.

"This hurts like hell and the painkillers don't help."

"Just reward for your misdeeds."

Copley grimaced. At least I think he did. Difficult to tell in the mess of nose and lips. Maybe it was a smile.

"Be cheerful as long as you can," he said.

"I try to stay bright," I said, "Whatever the company."

Copley ignored the jibe.

"We have things to talk about before... well, before what happens after that," he said. "But not here."

He waved the Browning in the direction of the Lexus. I looked at the car. It had a new registration number.

"Go on," he said. "You first."

I led the way to the Lexus and stopped, facing the radiator grill. Copley moved to my left and opened the driver's door. He took a couple of steps back and opened the passenger door behind it.

"Come round here and get into the front," he ordered.

We climbed into the Lexus, in formation, like dance partners. The moment I landed in the driving seat, I felt the Browning in the back of my neck, pointing at me over the head rest. We closed the car doors on the same beat. The pressure of the gun barrel went away, as Copley slid to his left and positioned himself in the middle of the rear seat. Then I felt the gun once more, against my left cheek.

"Now then," he wheezed. "I'm going to sit back a little and let you drive. But I can't miss from half a yard. So take it easy and we'll get this first bit done without mishap. Alright?"

"Yes."

It was all I could manage to say. He was a few lines of dialogue away from shooting me, at least, but my mouth was dry and my heart rate up thirty or forty beats.

"So off you go. Slow and sedate. It's a lovely day and we're in no hurry. Out of the lay-by and turn left."

It was an automatic gearbox. I slipped the lever into drive, eased the Lexus out of the lay-by and onto the road. Half a mile later, I was ordered right, then in a mile or so, left onto a narrow lane with grass growing along the middle. The lane crumbled into a track, the grass grew longer and a minute later I drove the Lexus into a farmyard. Copley told me to switch off the engine.

"Leave the key in the ignition," he said.

He moved across the seat and opened his door.

"Okay, your turn."

I opened the driver's door and we slid out like we got in, synchronised, one behind the other.

"Take a couple of paces forward," Copley said.

I did. There were two big stone barns in front of me. The one to the left had holes in the roof and no doors and windows. Inside it, I could see an old John Deere tractor with no wheels, sitting on its springs and a collection of pieces of knackered and rusting farm machinery. The barn to the right was in better condition. A restored roof and windows and big double doors. And it was being extended. The foundations of an adjoining building to the right, about the same size as the existing one, had been completed.

Copley noticed me looking at the work.

"Eighteen inches of hardcore in the bottom," he said. "Easy enough to scoop out six feet of it. And when it's back in place and level... who's going to know. There's a team coming to pour the concrete later in the week. The weather forecast is bright and sunny."

He stopped talking, to let the information sink in.

"Now turn around."

He was about eight feet away, still pointing the Browning at me. He couldn't miss from there.

"That's fine," Copley said. "Let's talk."

He backed up to the Lexus driver's door, still open. He eased himself onto the seat, his feet on the ground outside the car.

"I'll sit, if you don't mind," he said. "I have moments when I get a bit dizzy."

He had added another couple of yards to the distance between us.

"Whose place is this?" I asked him.

He didn't reply. I persisted.

"Belongs to Lloyd Starratt, doesn't it?"

He still didn't reply.

"He hired you to find my client. Why?"

Now he replied.

"He hired Grant. Grant hired me."

"Why?"

"I don't know. He didn't say."

"How did you get to Philip Soames?"

He waggled the Browning at me.

"Enough of this," he said. "Where is your client?"

"I have no idea," I said. "One of the conditions of the engagement."

He grimaced again. I decided it was supposed to be a smile. I let it subside, then went on.

"You have a 9mm automatic and you'd have to be the worst contractor in the business, to miss from there. I have no wish to become part of the foundations behind me. Deborah is hiding out somewhere. She hired me to find her, working on the assumption that if I could do that, then so could you. I haven't found her. And it's what I do. I'm good at it. So..."

There was a pause. Copley raised his left hand and gingerly pressed what was left of the bridge of his nose. He tried to sniff. It hurt and something rattled. Then he took his hand away and re-focussed on me.

"Is that it?"

"Let me sum this up for you," I said. "Yes. Absolutely. Yes."

Copley stood up. Obviously in pain. He closed his eyes, dipped his head, lifted it and opened his eyes again. Anger blazed across the yard. He bellowed at me.

"Don't fuck me about!!".

He raised the Browning and fired a shot over my right shoulder. The bullet hit the wall of the barn behind me and ricocheted off somewhere into the distance. I held up my arms and patted the air in front of me.

"Hang on, hang on..."

He extended his right arm and aimed at the gun at my forehead.

"This can be so simple," Copley said. "Just tell me where your client is. Then we'll get the unpleasantness over with."

Then he swayed on his feet and lifted his left hand to his head again.

"Oh Christ," he said.

I launched myself across the space between us, dipped my shoulder and slammed into his chest. He went backwards like he was being pulled on a bungy rope. Into the car and onto the driver's seat, still hanging on to the Browning. The back of his head bounced off the steering wheel. He straightened up and looked me.

I balled my fist and hit him hard on the nose.

There was no resistance. What I hit disintegrated with a soft, squelching sound. I drew my fist back, covered in blood and bits of broken nose. Copley screamed in pain, turned ashen in an instant, passed out and fell towards me. I caught him, straightened him up again and pushed him back into the seat. I grabbed his legs and swung them into the seat well and leant his neck back into the head rest.

He had dropped the Browning. I picked it up, ejected the clip and stowed it in the inside pocket of my jacket. I checked the glove box, empty except for the car manual. I went through all Copley's pockets - a grim reprise of the last time I did this. I looked under the seats, in the compartment between the seats, and the door storage spaces. There were no more clips to find.

Copley came to, threw up down the front of his jacket, then passed out again.

I found my mobile and dialled 999. Explained that the man I was with had serious facial injuries and was drifting in and out of consciousness. I gave the best directions I could to wherever the hell we were.

There was a dismal pattern emerging here. Hitting people in the face, then phoning policemen and paramedics. I stood and waited, holding the Browning and staring at Copley.

He woke up once more. I shifted into his line of sight and told him an ambulance was on its way. He tried to say something, but words wouldn't form. Blood burbled out of his mouth. Then he passed out again. I put the Browning into a jacket pocket.

It was a desperately long twelve minutes, before the ambulance arrived. The paramedics took one look at Copley and set to work immediately. He was ready to leave for the hospital as a local police patrol car turned into the yard.

PC Renshaw was in her late 20s. Slim, faired haired and around five feet six. Her partner PC Walton was slim and fair haired too, a bit older I guessed and the same height as me. Both were concerned and keen to work by the book, anxious that their approach should be user friendly and on message. All was going swimmingly, until I explained that the man the paramedics had just rushed away had tried to kill me. And not just today, on a previous occasion also. User friendly turned to suspicious, then to genuine alarm as I produced the magazine clip and the Browning.

"Have you got an evidence bag?"

PC Walton ducked into the patrol car, fished about and found one. He held the bag open and offered it to me. I dropped the Browning and the clip into it.

"That may have been used in the murder of man called Philip Soames, in Bristol last week. The policeman in charge of the case is Superintendent Harvey Butler. I'll happily go with you to the nearest police station. We can sort out things from there."

PC Walton sealed the bag and stared at the contents. PC Renshaw coughed politely. I looked at her.

"Is the Lexus yours?"

"No. It belongs to Mr Copley."

"Did you come here with him?"

"Some of the way, yes."

PC Walton had recovered his composure. He joined in the discussion.

"What do you mean by that?"

"My car is in a lay-by a couple of miles away. I stopped there. Mr Copley appeared, waved the Browning at me, made me get into the Lexus and drive it here."

"Why?"

I went through the whole chain of events, the conversation and Copley's offer to plant me in the foundations of the barn extension. I stopped when I got to the end of the story. PC Renshaw and PC Walton stared at me for ages. Directly above our heads, I could hear a skylark.

"You come with me," PC Renshaw finally instructed. "PC Walton will drive the Lexus."

* * *

Twenty-five minutes later, we were all sitting in the canteen at Lydney police station; PC Renshaw staring at me across a plastic topped table, PC Walton fetching the tea. Harvey had been informed of my escapade and George Hood was on his way from Trinity Road. PC Renshaw's radio crackled into life. She answered it. Where I was sitting, it was impossible to distinguish what was coming from the other end. So I waited. PC Walton arrived with the tea. PC Renshaw ended the call and looked at me.

"Mr Copley will be alright. Once they've mended his nose again."

"Make sure you hang on to him this time."

PC Walton snorted into his tea. I couldn't tell if he was disgusted by the sarcasm, or thought it was funny.

PC Renshaw's radio burst into life again. She nodded her way through more incomprehensible stuff, then switched off and got to her feet. PC Walton looked at her.

"We have to go," she said to him. Then turned to me. "May I respectfully request you stay here in this room until Detective Sergeant Hood arrives."

"You may," I said. "And I will."

The young coppers left me to myself. I waited, as patiently as I could. Not something I'm good at. The clock on the wall said five minutes to noon when Hood and the indispensable DC Shackleton walked into the canteen.

Hood introduced him. 30 years old or thereabouts, curly brown hair and hands the size of goalkeepers' gloves. I stood up. Shackleton offered me his right hand, clamped it around mine and shook. I got pins and needles in my fingers.

"Pleased to meet you," he said. "You're a bit of a legend at Trinity Road."

"And you're the coffee king," I said.

I freed my hand from his, trying to smile. Hood noticed and grinned.

We all sat down. Under the table, I clenched and unclenched my fist and waited for the feeling to come back.

"So..." Hood began, "I hear you have re-arranged Francis Copley's face once again. I appreciate he was no oil painting to begin with, but A and E has enough to do, without you persistently adding to the load."

"He started it," I said.

Hood sighed.

"Come on. Show us this place of Starratt's."

We all stood up again.

"Can we pick up my car on the way?"

We called at the lay-by, picked up the Healey and I led the way back to the farmyard. We gathered in front of the barns. Shackleton stared for a long time at the restored building. He walked up to one of the windows, pressed his face against it and looked inside. I watched, intrigued. Hood looked at me nodding approvingly, like a fond parent watching his child do his party trick. Shackleton turned back to face us.

"Hay bales up against the windows. Blocking out the light. Why would someone do that after he had put new windows in?"

"He wouldn't," I said.

"Unless he had something to hide," Hood said.

"It fits with what we know," Shackleton said.

Hood nodded.

"What do we know?" I asked.

Neither of them responded. Hood moved to the barn. He and Shackleton inspected the big double doors, chained together and padlocked.

"Question," Shackleton said. "How to get in without the owner knowing."

"Let's take a look around the back," Hood said. He called to me. "Are you coming?"

"What, stay here and miss all the fun?"

Shackleton led the way. He chose the left-hand side and walked through the passageway between the two buildings. Hood and I followed.

The area behind the barns looked just like another piece of farmyard. Except that it wasn't. It was tidy. And empty. No bits and pieces, none of the usual farm yard detritus and no machinery. Except for a red, two wheeled cart, parked tight against the wall, in front of a door. It was a big metal beast. Eight feet high, ten feet long and six feet wide. Resting at the front on its tow hitch.

Freshly laid concrete stretched from the back of the barns for about fifteen yards, to a tall thick hedge, which actually bordered the whole chunk of land. The hedge stretched from left to right as we looked at it, then back on both sides, past the barns, to the entrance yard. The entire site was enclosed and camouflaged from the outside world. And there were a couple of other structures. To the left, behind the un-restored barn, two steel ship containers, re-painted green. Presumably used for storage.

Hood consulted Shackleton.

"What's beyond the hedge?" he asked.

"Hang on," Shackleton said.

He dug into the inside pocket of his police jacket and took out his smart phone. He pressed buttons for fifteen seconds or so. The gadget sang and bleeped. Shackleton flicked his right index finger across the face of the screen, stopped, looked at the result, then showed the screen to Hood.

"Two fields," Shackleton said. "Starratt rents them for grazing. They run directly up to his own land." He pointed over the hedge. "Southfork is about three quarters of a mile, as the crow flies."

Hood looked around him.

"How many vehicles can you get in this space do you think?" he asked.

Shackleton put the smart phone back in his pocket.

"Twenty, maybe twenty-five," he said. "Depending on the size."

Hood nodded, looked round the whole area again, then focussed on the piece of engineering.

"It's a Grain Cart," I suggested.

"Proper name, Chaser Bin," said Shackleton.

Hood and I looked at him. He shrugged.

"My uncle's a farmer," he said.

"Can we move it?" Hood asked him.

"We'll never manage to drag it," Shackleton said. "But the Volvo's got a tow hitch. If I drive and you two push, we may get it clear of the door."

DC Shackleton was the Man, so neither Hood nor I could gainsay. He skirted the extension and went to fetch the Volvo.

"He's got a degree in communications sciences," Hood said. "Being fast-tracked. Word is, he's been watched by HO15. A bunch of funny people at the Home Office."

Shackleton drove the Volvo into the yard, U turned and backed up to the chaser bin tow hitch. Hood grabbed the handle of the turning bolt and began spinning it clockwise. The cup on the chaser bin hitch rose. Shackleton backed the Volvo tow hitch ball under the cup. Hood turned the handle anti-clockwise and the cup dropped neatly onto the ball. Shackleton unlocked the tow hitch brake. Hood and I got into position behind the bin.

"I'll hit the horn when I want you to push," Shackleton said and got into the car.

He gently revved the two and a half litre engine, the horn barked, Hood and I pushed and moments later the chaser bin was clear of the re-conditioned door. Shackleton locked the tow hitch brake again and we gathered in front of the door. There was a long steel bolt bar across it, pushed into the wall on the right-hand side of the door frame. Hood hauled it backwards and the door swung open towards him.

Shackleton and I followed him into the barn. And found ourselves standing in what looked like a circus ring.

We stood in the centre of the barn, in the shaft of daylight which lanced in from outside and looked round three hundred and sixty degrees. We were inside a circle of hay bales, about fifteen or sixteen feet in diameter. Complete except for two gaps – in front of the doorway we had just come through and the padlocked double doors in front of us. They led out of the circle like exits from an arena. Behind the hay bales, there was a ring of chain link fence, three feet high. And behind the fence, space where the audience bleachers would be if this was a circus ring. More hay bales were piled in the corners of the barn and up against all the windows.

"What the hell is this place?" Hood asked.

Shackleton was thinking. Hood and I waited.

"I think it's a dog fighting ring," Shackleton said. He looked at me. "You know Starratt. et one of his dogs. What do you think?"

I thought it was the most frightening proposal I'd heard in a long time. But I did know somebody who could give us a second opinion. I found my mobile and called Julia, the RSPCA Inspector I'd met at the Great Western Show.

She was in her office. I described the mis-en-scene and its location on Starratt land. There was a couple of seconds pause when I finished, then she spoke.

"Hang on a minute."

She put down her phone receiver and moved away from it. I heard her voice again, distant, talking to someone else in the office. Meanwhile, Shackleton was taking pictures with his smart phone. Julia came back to me.

"We think your DC Shackleton is right. It is a dog fighting ring. And we have some new information here that may lead to something. Will you and your two policemen come in to see us?"

I relayed the request to Hood. He nodded.

"We'll be there within the hour," I said.

I ended the call. Once Shackleton had completed his photographic essay, we moved out of the barn and locked the door. Hood stared at the chaser bin.

"Can we get it back into the same position?" he asked. Then he looked at Shackleton in apology. "Sorry..."

The bin was reversed back across the doorway. Almost inch perfect. Leaving no sign, at all, of the barn invasion.

A couple of minutes later, I got into the Healey and followed the Volvo out of the yard.

CHAPTER SEVENTEEN

The Bristol RSPCA headquarters is south of the city centre, in St Phillips. Julia met us in the lobby and took us up a flight of stairs to a large open plan office. She introduced us to Chief Inspector, Andrew Overton, who ushered us into a smaller office by the head of the stairs. The five of us sat round a table and filled the rest of the space in the room. There was a laptop, a blue folder and a couple of DVDs on the table.

Overton picked up one of them.

"This was sent to us three weeks ago. Anonymously. In a padded envelope, post-marked in Newport. See if you recognise anything."

He slid the DVD into the drive slot of the laptop.

"The pictures have been transferred from phone footage."

We all watched the laptop screen. The pictures were shot from distance, and from some very odd angles. From behind cars and behind people's backs. Presumably the operator was being careful. But there was no mistaking the location. The farmyard, the restored barn, a digger to the side of it, the car park behind it, crammed with expensive metal. I looked at Hood and Shackleton. They nodded in agreement. We continued to watch as people got out of their vehicles and moved into the barn. The pictures ran out and the DVD froze.

"Nothing from inside the barn?" Hood asked.

Overton shook his head.

"No phones, cameras, recorders of any kind allowed into one of these events. Everyone is body searched at the door."

He waited for one of us to say something else. Julia prompted Hood.

"Is that where you have just been?" she asked.

"Yes," Hood said.

"Is it Lloyd Starratt's place?"

"We believe so."

"Tell me about the interior again. Does it look as if it's ready for business?" She turned to me. "Jack?"

"I don't know," I said. "I mean, what state of readiness does it have to be in?"

"Was the ring set up?"

Shackleton freed the phone from his uniform pocket and looked at Hood.

"Sure," Hood said. "Go on."

Shackleton showed his pictures to Julia and Overton. When they had scrutinised the folder, Overton talked to all of us again.

"Looks to me like it's ready for action. We don't know how long ago the DVD footage was taken. Whoever sent the picture didn't say. But he, or she, did say, that there was another event planned. There was a hand written note in the envelope."

"Have you still got it?" Hood asked.

Overton opened the blue folder and pushed it across the table. The note was in ink and written in neat, capital letters – *THIS WILL HAPPEN AGAIN SOON*. Hood leaned forward and read it. Then looked across at Overton.

"That was all?"

"Yes. Which is why we have kept it to ourselves so far. You know how investigations have to be conducted Sergeant. It takes a long time to gather enough evidence to get to the stage when we can ask you for help. We can't steam in mob handed like the police, if you'll forgive me.

However, it looks like you have just found what we need. Thank you."

Julia took up the story.

"We have all been on Lloyd Starratt's case for a long time. We know he keeps a number of dogs which only just avoid infringing the Dangerous Dogs Act. None of them makes the banned breeds list. And that's the problem. He doesn't keep American Pit Bulls, Blue Nose Pitbulls, Japanese Tosas – there's a dozen or so. Any of his dogs walking down the High Street on a lead would pass for anybody's family pet."

DC Shackleton interrupted.

"But surely, the act deals with more than just a list of breeds. The legislation covers any dog, which in the opinion of the Home Secretary, is bred for fighting."

Overton re-joined into the discussion.

"Or has the appearance of a dog bred for fighting."

"So..." Shackleton said, "That gives you room doesn't it?"

"No. You can train any breed of dog to fight. But do you think anyone is going to look at a Cocker Spaniel and say he looks the part? The law should be based on deeds, not breeds. When a house is burgled, you arrest the burglar. Not the crow bar he jemmied the door with."

"Okay," I said. "We all know who's to blame here. It's the Lloyd Starratts of the world."

Overton went on.

"Absolutely. No legislation will keep any animal or person safe from dogs with irresponsible owners."

He got out of his chair, walked to the office door, opened it and called out.

"Rufus..."

Moments later a huge, bronze German Shepherd trotted into the room, stopped, looked at Overton and sat down.

"Good boy," Overton said. "Lie down."

Rufus stretched out flat on the carpet.

"He comes to work with me every day. Sits by my desk while I work. Goes out with me on calls. Does he look dangerous?"

"No of course not," Hood said.

"Are the German Shepherds your Dog Unit works with dangerous?"

"No. But, hopefully, to malefactors, they can appear dangerous."

"So there you are," Overton said. "Don't blame the breed. The hard cases and thugs involved in dog fighting can trash the reputation of any dog. Rottweillers were bred as sled dogs. They have immense strength, they can pull carts. They have beautiful faces and instinctively beautiful manners. But at some point, some arsehole with a tattoo starved one, stuck it outside in a kennel, threatened it and turned it mean. So the Rottweiller isn't trusted. Like a bunch of other genuinely friendly dogs. But you can't take Bull Terriers and Doberman Pinschers away from responsible owners."

"Did you get a good look at that dog outside Starratt's trailer?" Julia asked me.

"Yes. But all I can tell you is I thought it was some kind of Mastiff. I don't know if I was anywhere near any kind of breed recognition. Elaine wasn't frightened of it."

"Her family has two Collies. Of course she's not frightened of dogs. She is used to well socialised animals. So she didn't understand the danger. Didn't recognise the threat signals given out when the dog woke up. The dog on the other hand, knew that aggression was the way to get what it wanted. When Elaine didn't back off, it attacked her. That wasn't the dog working on instinct, whatever breed it was. The sad, bloody beast was taught that."

"So what do we have to do?" I asked.

"Change the legislation," Julia said. "Make it tougher. And give us more powers to nail people like Lloyd Starratt."

There was a long pause. Julia sighed.

"Yes, this is old ground I know."

Down at my feet, Rufus started to snore gently. Overton grinned.

"Have you got another five minutes?" he asked Hood. "I'd like to show you something else. I think it's part of this investigation."

Hood said we had all the time in the world. Overton took the DVD out of the laptop and replaced it with the other one from the table.

I wasn't prepared for what I was about to see. And it turned my stomach over.

The pictures were taken in the Forest of Dean. RSPCA Inspectors digging soil out of two shallow graves. Uncovering the corpses of three dogs. Gaping wounds on their necks and shoulders. Fur and skin ripped from their chests and flanks. Brutal, sickening and finally, impossible to watch. I got up and left the room, found my way to a toilet and threw up.

A couple of minutes later, as I was washing my face, Julia found me and apologised.

"But I can't say I'm sorry we made you look at that stuff," she said. "Now you know what we're up against."

"Why were they buried? Surely it would have been sensible to burn the corpses."

"Usually they are. We suspect that on this occasion, the dogs died on the way home from a fight. So they were dumped."

"How did you find them?"

"Straight out of *Midsomer Murders*. You know, the scene.

The one where the local shopkeeper's dog finds something half buried on his morning walk through the woods." Her voice softened. "Are you okay? You look a bit green."

I pulled a paper towel out of the wall dispenser and dried my face.

"You know, our main purpose isn't to save animals – although that's what we are forced to try and do. Our job is to find the people who do these barbaric things and prosecute them. In essence, it's so simple. Stop them doing what they're doing and the problem will go away. I can tell you, hand on heart, that I would joyfully embrace not having to do this job. If overnight, it was rendered unnecessary and I found myself out of work, I would raise the biggest cheer ever heard on God's green earth."

I dropped the paper towel in the plastic bin under the dispenser. Julia held the door open for me.

"But then, all of us in the charity business have the same unredeemable mantra. 'If only we didn't have to do it'. I apologise again, for the outburst. We get too involved sometimes."

We went back to the office. Shackleton was sitting on the floor with Rufus. Overton was talking to Hood.

"In the past, we've assisted on raids by officers at Trinity Road from a unit called ST5."

"Yes, I know it. I'll talk to them."

"Can they get some surveillance in place quickly? This next event may be in a couple of days."

"The sooner the better I should imagine," Hood said. "Less expensive if we don't have to hang around."

The two men shook hands.

"Thank you," Overton said. He looked round the office. "All of you."

Shackleton got to his feet. Rufus looked up at him.

"Bye Rufus," he said.

"Say goodbye Rufus," Overton ordered.

Rufus barked once and got to his feet. We filed out into the main office. The dog escorted us to the head of the stairs.

* * *

I drove across town. Realised I hadn't had any lunch and picked up a tuna sandwich and a salad. I was back in my office at 3.15. Linda was out on business again. There were no messages on the answering machine. I made some coffee and pondered. I couldn't finish the sandwich.

It was obvious I had to suspend operations on Lloyd Starratt. We all had to let this planned dog fight go ahead. And if Starratt was caught in flagrante, so much the better. He would have the guardians of law and order swarming all over him, like flies on the dog turd that he was. And that could only enhance investigations into the whereabouts of Dujic and Tudjman.

So, what else to do?... I locked on to a revolutionary idea. Call my client. I did, got the default message from the service provider and rang off. I called again, this time checking the display on the handset, to make sure I wasn't hitting the wrong buttons and leaving a message for a stranger. I told Deborah that Francis Copley was out of the picture, that we were making progress with Lloyd Starratt, and that I would get back to her in due course.

A minute's work done and I was back in limbo again. Which led me to further contemplation and to considerations of south Devon. I needed a new road atlas for the office. As big a scale as possible.

I decided to avoid the miseries of the approaching late

afternoon traffic, walked round to the Nova Scotia and took the harbour Ferry into the city centre. I paid £3.50 and we chugged gracefully through the sunshine. Giving me time to work out what I was really after. Twenty minutes later, I disembarked at Castle Park, crossed the kids playground and walked into Broadmead.

In W H Smith, I bought the three ordinance survey maps which cover the south coast of Devon.

OS maps are brilliant for beaches. Cliff faces, shale, shingle, pebbles, and what I was looking for, sand. There's actually not much of that in south Devon. A spectacular coastline it is, but not the first choice for a bucket and spade holiday. Apart from Seaton and Sidmouth, west of Lyme Regis it's mostly pebbles all the way to the English Riviera. Torbay has a sandy beach. But that gives way to shingle and the rocky bays and soaring cliffs round Brixham. On past Dartmouth and all the way round Start Bay it's the same. No sand. And from Start Point, westwards, there is only one real sandy beach. Or rather a cluster of them, around the gloriously named Bigbury-on-Sea.

I had maps spread over the floor and across the top of my desk, when Chrissie arrived. With Sam. He bounced into the office and Chrissie called for him to 'Sit'. He did. On Totnes. Which didn't matter much, because Totnes doesn't have a beach.

"Not barging in are way?" Chrissie asked.

"No, you're not. Great to see you."

"We've just spent an hour running round the Ashton Court estate."

I tried to gather up the maps on the floor; at least those Sam wasn't sitting on. As every activity in his life equates to play, he thought this was some new game and it was ages before any semblance of order was restored.

"Are you thinking of buying a boat?" Chrissie asked.

I looked at her. She went on.

"Or a cottage by the sea perhaps?"

Sam slid into the seat well under my desk and lay down.

"This is research," I said. "Into the sandy beaches of south Devon."

"There aren't many of those."

"So I've discovered."

"And the best is at Bigbury-on-Sea."

"Do you know it?"

"I've been there. With Adam. He knows the place really well. He's at the paper. Do you want me to call him?"

Chrissie caught Adam in the lobby of the *Post* building, on his way out of the door.

"I'll be with you in fifteen minutes," he said.

I took the beach photographs out of the desk drawer and passed them to Chrissie. She studied them.

"Could be," she said. She gave the picture of the boy back to me. "Look at the sand."

There was a lot of it. The boy was surrounded by sand. Firm dark sand. The sort of sand that is regularly covered by the incoming tide. Chrissie handed me the other photograph.

"Now look at that one again."

The woman was sitting on her beach towel on different sand. Soft, light coloured, lie down in and sunbathe sand. Inshore sand, beyond the high tide line. Behind her the shoreline cliffs. I looked at the picture of the boy again.

"Notice," Chrissie said. "No sea anywhere. In either picture."

"Well there wouldn't be in the photograph of the women," I said.

"Absolutely. But what about the boy? Where is he standing?"

"The background's different. And the tide's out. So he's

on another part of the beach. At a different time of day."

"Supposing he isn't?"

"But he is. Obviously."

Chrissie grinned at me.

"I don't want to say any more. I might be wrong. When Adam arrives, show him the pictures cold. Don't give him any clues. Just tell him south Devon. Let him come up with his own assessment."

I stared at the pictures again.

* * *

"They're not taken in different places," Adam said. "They're reverse points of view. The one of the woman is shot looking up the beach, the one of the boy looking out to sea."

"Can't be," I said. "There's a wall or a cliff behind him."

"It's an island," Adam said.

I looked at the picture again.

"Behind the kid. Bright Island." He pointed at the desk top. "Look at the OS map again. The Torbay and Salcombe one."

All three of us gathered round my desk. Sam shuffled forwards and poked his head out of the seat well, decided that nothing interesting was happening after all and dropped his head back on to his paws.

On the map, Adam traced the coastline westwards from Start Point.

"No sandy beaches until you get to Bigbury. And there, out at sea, across two hundred yards of beach, is Bright Island. Just a big rock really. With a hotel on it."

He picked up the photograph of the boy.

"The background's out of focus, but... Behind him, is the

base rock. To his left, is the slipway up from the beach. Can I use your PC?"

"Sure."

Moments later Bright Island was on the screen. A stunning shot, taken at high tide, from the hillside above Bigbury beach. The island was just that. Two hundred yards from the shore and surrounded by water.

"For a couple of hours, twice a day," Adam informed us.

He tapped the keyboard and the picture was replaced by another, taken from the same place, at low tide. And we were looking at the beach. Unbroken, rich, bronze sand.

On the island, just above the slipway, the Bright Island Hotel sat in restored art deco splendour. Adam gave us a potted history.

"The original house was built in the 1920s. By an Edwardian captain of industry, for his Bohemian wife and her friends. Almost as far west as you could get from London. A luxury gaff, away from the prying eyes of his business competitors. A bolt hole for the artistic and the extra-ordinary. A place where it didn't matter who your companion was, or what their sexual preferences were. Flappers and bright young things, played and drank and danced to swing bands from London clubs."

I looked at the screen for a long time. They must have had great parties.

"It's a mega exclusive hotel now, of course. And everyone dresses for dinner."

"How do you know this place?" I asked.

"We ate there once upon a time," Chrissie said, "A couple of summers ago. No more than lunch, I hasten to add." She nodded at Adam. "He has occupied a suite there however."

"Back in 2012," Adam said. "A weekend bash, at the

invitation of the only truly rich person I know. Hamilton Bainbridge. Known as Hammy to his friends. He's a broker. Sort of. He fiddles with money."

"The appropriate choice of word," I said.

"I shared a room with him, first year at university. I saved his life."

"What?"

Adam looked at me and grinned.

"That's how he's always looked at it. We were both on the swimming team. He turned up for training one day, pissed. Dived into the shallow end of the pool, hit his head on the bottom and floated back to the surface. Unconscious, face down in the water, blood pouring from his forehead. I got him out of the pool, woke him up and staunched the bleeding. He has cherished that moment. He emails me a couple of times a year. And we catch up at places like Simpsons and the Savoy. He's actually one hundred and fourteenth in line to the throne."

"Why haven't I heard this story before?"

"Just a bygone deed of heroism I never talk about." He looked at the photographs again. "So who are these two?"

"I don't know," I said. "But suddenly, I'm getting closer. I think the pictures were taken by my client. On holiday." I pointed to the PC screen. "There, at Bright Island, maybe."

Expensive it may have been, but it was the sort of place Deborah could afford. Exclusive. Well that was good too, given the date. Deborah had been living as a woman for eighteen months at that point. Coping with all the complications and the uncertainties, and the terrifying prospect of the surgery she was about to undergo.

"So," Chrissie said, "If you want peace, tranquillity and uncomplicated days, Bright Island is the place."

"And if the three of them did stay there," Adam said, "the

hotel will have names and addresses. Information they may pass on to you... If you give them reason enough."

We all sat in silence for while. Then Adam spoke again.

"Okay," he said. "Who's for something to eat and a night on the town?" He looked at me. "Jack?"

"Even if I thought you were being remotely serious I'd still say no. A takeaway, home, bath and early bed for me."

Adam called to the dog.

"What do you think Sam?"

There was a grunt, a rustling and a scraping and Sam came out from under the desk. Tail wagging, ready for anything. Chrissie told me to sleep well and the three of them left the office.

I tidied up the maps and sat at my desk for ages, suddenly overwhelmed by tiredness. Nine hours ago, I had driven over the Severn bridge to find Lloyd Starratt. Instead, I had met Francis Copley, two paramedics, a bunch of Gloucestershire coppers, Bristol coppers, RSPCA inspectors and a German Shepherd called Rufus. Along with Chrissie, Adam and Sam. The most beings I had ever encountered in the course of one working day.

And now Linda. There was a gentle knock on the office door. I invited her in. She was wearing another stunning business suit, this time a navy-blue number.

"Have you been out impressing people again?"

"I guess some of us can afford to sit at a desk all day."

She took a step forward and tilted her head to one side.

"You look terrible," she said. "Are you alright?"

"I will be. Given a little TLC."

"Oh dear," she said. "That's a little un-subtle. You must be desperate."

She stood in front of my desk. I got to my feet, moved

round to join her. She swung to face me, leaned her backside against the desk and let it take her weight.

"So?..."

I kissed her. She opened her mouth, arched her back and gently rotated her hips. It was a while before we finished. I stepped back.

"Better?" she asked.

"All the difference in the world."

"So where have you been all day?"

I told her. She grew more astonished as the tale progressed. I finished by promising her it had not been an example of an average day. Simply a little over-worked.

"I have a drinks date with a client in a few minutes," she said. "But we can meet later."

I shook my head. "I need a few hours to myself. And a bit of thinking time. Do you mind?"

"Of course not." Linda opened the office door. "See you tomorrow."

She glided out into the corridor. I picked up the laptop and the OS maps, found my car keys and moved to the door.

The phone on my desk rang. I turned and stared accusingly at it for a couple of seconds. Yes or no? Had to be yes. There's always the possibility that the call at the end of the day will be the one which breaks the case. I put the laptop down on the desk and picked up the receiver. Some manic tosser in a call centre asked me if I was aware that sixty-five percent of small business persons were under insured.

As the song says – *There's a fool on every corner, when you're trying to make it home.* But make it home I did. Up through Clifton away from the traffic and then east into Redland from the Downs. With a short stop at the Shing To

Takeaway, to pick up beef in black bean sauce, fried rice and vegetables.

While I was eating, I watched a double bill of *Dads Army*. The immortally funny episode with the grenade down Jones' trousers and the heart breaking 'brief encounter' story. That was the highlight of an 85 channel choice. I tried to get interested in the new ITV, post watershed, dystopian thriller; but lost interest during the first commercial break, which arrived less than eight minutes in.

I called Chrissie and we talked for half an hour or so. Then Auntie Joyce rang moments later. She sounded relieved to find me still in one piece. I told her that all was well and all the bad guys, save the two Serbian gentlemen, had been dealt with. Had I found Deborah? Not exactly, but we were now communicating by phone. Auntie Joyce suggested I might consider updating the Thorntons. So when she rang off, I did. At least I spoke to Elizabeth. Bill was out at some local business do. 'Supernaturally boring' was Elizabeth's take on it. She thanked me for all that I was doing. Deborah had called. Once and briefly, but it was enough to know she was well. I told her I was pleased. She thanked me again.

I was in bed before 10 o'clock.

CHAPTER EIGHTEEN

Over breakfast, I made a decision about south Devon. On offer, was a two-and-a-half hour drive, to persuade a bunch of people who didn't know me from a hole in the ground, to talk to me. The hotel staff might not fess up. But they would have to respond to the police. So, breakfast over, I drove to Trinity Road to talk with Harvey.

He made a massive effort to suppress his amusement when I asked for his help. He almost managed to keep his face straight. We sat in his office, drinking more cups of DC Shackleton's freshly brewed coffee. If attention could ever be assessed as both rapt and ironical at the same time, then Harvey was accomplishing it. When I finished pleading, he sat up straight and looked me right in the eyes.

"Are you not at risk of betraying client confidentiality here? Personally I don't give a toss. 'Information information information' is my motto. But with you, it's a matter of integrity, embedded deep. You'd better be careful this doesn't get out. All the people queuing up to offer you work will lose confidence."

He was really enjoying this. He had an axe buried in my head and he was managing to grind it at the same time.

"Are you making progress on the Philip Soames business?" I asked.

My attempt to deflect his purpose didn't bother him at all.

"Are you offering to help?"

"How? I don't know any more than you do."

"So what are you offering? In return for the favour you're asking."

"I've done my best to give you Lloyd Starratt." I said "I've hoovered up a couple of west London enforcers..."

"Indirectly..."

"And now, finding my client will help with everything else. In particular, the Philip Soames murder."

"We don't know that."

"Jesus Christ Harvey!..."

He stared at me. Then down at his desk, then out of the window, then back at me. He blew out his cheeks. I pressed on.

"I need your help," I said. "That's all. I'm not asking you to break any rules. It's a genuine, routine piece of police work. You can do it in moments."

Harvey folded his arms across his chest and nodded his head.

"Go and see DC Shackleton. Tell him I said it was okay."

He un-folded his arms, sat back in his chair and waited for me to leave. But I had to establish something else.

"Can I have your assurance that you won't act on the information DC Shackleton will gather? At least, not before I can."

"Why would we waste police time and resources looking for someone who, currently, is of no direct interest to our investigations?"

"Thanks," I said and got to my feet.

"However," Harvey said, "If, at some time in the near future, we deem the information useful to us..."

He gave me his best 'understand what I mean' stare. I left the office and went in search of DC Shackleton.

I showed him the photographs and told him the story. He called the Bright Island Hotel and talked to the manager, who passed him on to the owner, who consulted his wife, the co-owner, who agreed they should all help. As soon as they could, but not immediately. There were two weddings and an evening function to get through today.

"We'll do this by email," Shackleton said. "Give them twenty-four hours. Don't worry. We'll get you what you want to know."

He scanned the beach photographs and Deborah's picture into his computer. I gave him a list of questions to ask the hotel staff.

I was back in my office by 11 o'clock. The phone began ringing as I opened the door.

"I'm working up a story about the Starratt clan," Adam said. "I cast the net a bit wider than the bounds of the Post archive. And I found something which might give you pause. Latterly, Lloyd Starratt has been given to good works."

I sat down in my chair.

"Difficult to imagine I know, but his deeds are writ large."

"Where?" I asked.

"In the Chepstow and Wye Valley Gazette ."

"So not that large then."

"Nonetheless, worthy of note," Adam said. "I'll email you a folder. Take a look at it."

I switched the laptop on and set about making coffee. Not up to DC Shackleton's mucho gusto standard, but drinkable enough. I took the mug back to my desk, sat down, called up my email inbox and downloaded Adam's file.

And worthy of note it was.

The South Wye Valley Academy sits on rising land north of Chepstow. Separated from a 60s built council estate and its primary school on the outskirts of the town, by what was once an acre and a half of meadow. Owned by Lloyd Starratt. And now transformed, through the generosity of its benefactor, into a playing field, to be shared by both schools. A cricket square in the middle, a four hundred metre running track, two football pitches, showers and changing rooms.

The inaugural football fixtures were scheduled for the first Saturday of the autumn term, but meanwhile, midway through the previous summer term, there had been a bit of a do. A marquee, a barbecue and *Ballistic* – the band from South Wye Valley Year Twelve. Children, parents, local dignitaries, teachers, and school governors, celebrating the completion of the work, with a cricket match between parents and the South Wye Valley First Eleven.

A reporter and photographer from the Gazette had chronicled the event. The article glowed with praise for the project. An album of pictures were taken. And there was Lloyd, posing and posturing and milking the occasion for all it was worth. He had even made a speech, thanking all those who had come together to make it all possible.

Albeit coming from Lloyd, the un-knowing reader would have given way to emotion and felt a lump in his throat. However, the more cynical among us could be forgiven for feeling their gorges rising and searching for the sick bag. Lloyd was at it. In spades.

The phone rang again.

"Have you got the stuff?" Adam asked.

"Only Lloyd Starratt could morph from philanthropist into dogfight promoter."

"And I've just discovered something else. The primary school, Meadow Estate, has been in 'special measures' for three consecutive Ofsted inspections and is now deemed a failing school. The local education authority, in cahoots with the Minister for Education, has informed the governors they intend to turn it into an Academy. Do you know how academies work?"

"They're self-governing yes?"

"Essentially. Most are taken under the wing of already existing charitable organisations. There's a bunch of those around the country, running groups of academies. This, that and the other trust. Academies operate independently of the local education authority. They're usually funded by some version of a public private partnership. These private sponsors are charged with bringing, and here I quote... *qualities of success to academies, to be creative and innovative, and change the long-term trend of failure in the schools they replace.* That's the mission."

"So the story with Meadow Estate is?..."

"The governors feel they're being bullied by the Education Department. The teachers think they're going to lose their jobs. And a group of parents have got together to oppose it. But here's the thing. One of the putative investors in the Meadow Academy Charitable Trust, is Forest Holdings. Whose CEO is? One guess only..."

"Lloyd Starratt."

"Every egg a bird."

"So what does he get out of the deal? I mean, he can't claim to have a track record in educational reform."

"Apparently, in return for a minimum investment of ten per cent of the academy's capital costs, the sponsor is able to... *influence the process of establishing the school, its curriculum, ethos, and any specialisation.*"

"Such as?..."

"Take your pick. Science, business and enterprise, sport, technology, the performing arts. You remember Sir Reginald Verrell? The evangelical Christian car salesman."

"Boss of the Reg Verrell Dealership. He got into trouble didn't he?"

"He was accused of promoting the teaching of creationism and something called macro-evolution, in his Genesis Schools Foundation academies."

"Leaves the field wide open for Lloyd," I said.

"It's all glorious bollocks," Adam said. "But more than likely to happen. Think about it Jack. Lloyd Starratt running a school."

I couldn't bear to think about it. It was unimaginable, untrammelled absurdity.

"So are we on a crusade to put a stop to this foolishness?" Adam asked.

"Absolutely," I said.

"I'll keep digging," he said. "In the meantime, I'm going to talk with the parents action group. Write something about them. Big them up a bit. Talk to you later..."

He rang off.

I shook my head. Tried to clear it of all thoughts of Lloyd Starratt the educator. I was having no success, when the phone rang again. It was Julia.

"We have just heard from ST5," she said. "Their intelligence leads them to believe the dog fight is happening tomorrow afternoon."

"They got on to that quickly."

"They were most of the way there apparently. They have people under cover among Lloyd Starratt's cronies. They just weren't sure about the location. You gave it to them."

Suddenly I felt five hundred per cent better. I must have been deep in thought for a while, because Julia asked me if I was still there. I asked her what the next step was.

"ST5 organise the raid. We support them with our own inspectors."

"Can I be there?"

"Officially, ST5 won't let you go along. It's a police operation after all. But we can. As a support investigator. Maybe with the video team."

"You record the raid?"

"In all its hideous drama. We have to have evidence."

I began thinking about this. Julia came back to me.

"Do you have a strong stomach?"

"No. You saw yesterday. I'm one of the great throwers-up."

"You don't have to be there," she suggested.

"Yes I do. What's the schedule?"

"There will be a briefing tomorrow morning. Andy Overton will describe what we think is likely to happen in the barn. The DI heading the ST5 team will then go through the whole operation in detail. The police team will include two marksmen with rifles and tranquiliser darts. We will have two vets with us. The problem is, nobody can move in until the whole gruesome business is under way. If we move before it begins and put a stop to it, we will save the dogs, but that's all. We might be able to pin something on the organisers, but we want to be able to prosecute everyone there, including the punters. If there is nothing happening, we won't be able to. It's not against the law for a bunch of people to gather in the country for some private doggie celebration."

"How many are there likely to be? Do you know?"

"Twenty-five or thirty. And there may be a number of fights on the bill"

"So what is the main attraction. The fighting? Or the betting?"

"The betting is as ferocious as the action. Bets can be huge. Two or three thousand on a dog. This is a business Jack. And it turns over a small fortune for the promoter."

In this case Lloyd Starrat and his cronies.

Julia asked me, once again, if I wanted to be involved in this. I assured her I did. She asked me to be in her office at 10.30 tomorrow morning and ended the call.

The euphoria of five minutes ago had evaporated. Suddenly I was thinking of Sam and Rufus and the joy they bring to all of us. Dogs give unconditionally. Sure, they expect to have a roof over their heads. To be fed and played with and exercised and allowed to sleep soundly and unafraid. But for that small outlay, the humans get massive returns. Friendship, love and a relationship which last the dog's lifetime. We bring dogs into our world and they live with us on trust. It's a very simple deal. The minimum requirement is that we return the love they inspire.

I needed a distraction. Some entertainment.

Considering an early afternoon screening at one of the multiplexes, I went out and bought the lunchtime addition of the *Post*. But the movies on offer failed to excite. It was mostly franchise fair. More of the *Twilight* saga, the latest Jason Statham violence fest, a new vehicle for Justin Beiber which had bored the critics comatose and a romcom starring Adam Sandler, Sarah Jessica Parker and a quartet of meerkats.

But there was an invitation to excitement on page three of the paper. A four-column ad for the annual September Fair, up and running on the Downs. The Waltzer, the Dodgems, the white-knuckle Bomber, carousels and candyfloss, hot dogs and fried onions. Just what the doctor ordered. I knocked on Linda's office door.

"Are you busy?"

"I'm devoting the rest of the day to making phone calls and emailing client invoices," she said.

"Take a break," I said. "Come with me to the fair."

She stared at me.

"On the Downs," I said. "When were you last on the Helter Skelter?"

"Probably when I was twelve."

"Far too long ago. Come on. I'll buy you a toffee apple."

"Irresistible," she said. "How can a girl turn down a toffee apple?"

And with that, we were under way.

* * *

We had a terrific two hours. Excited as we could only remember being. Daft as a couple of kids.

The Downs Fair has been running for generations. With a license from the city council to return every autumn. It was the highlight of the year for Chrissie, until she decided she was too grown up to be out having fun in the company of her parents. So the visits stopped. And today, it was great to be back.

Getting in to the Healey, mid-afternoon, I asked Linda if she had to go back to the office.

"Afraid so," she said.

"Can't the invoices wait?"

"Not if I want the books to balance at the end of the month

"I was just thinking..."

I put the key into the ignition. When I looked up again, Linda was glaring at me. She looked like she was about to say something, so I waited.

"Okay," she said. "What have you been thinking Jack?"

I stared at her. She elaborated a little.

"You know what you did? You thought us into this

relationship. Then you thought us on to hold. Then you changed your mind. So what are you doing now? Thinking us into an interim tea time fuck?"

"I thought some candyfloss and a toffee apple..."

It wouldn't have been an award-winning joke, even if I had managed to get to the punch line. As it was, I comprehensively ruined the day. Linda spoke quietly, but seemed to emphasis every word.

"It's bloody simple, Jack. Or it should be. You and me and no thinking. It's either the best idea in the world, or it isn't. As far as I'm concerned..."

She stopped mid-sentence. She shook her head.

"Never mind..."

"What?"

"Just that. The office. Please."

The Healey engine turned over and fired. I backed out of the avenue of parked cars and turned onto Downs Road. We drove back to the office in silence. I stopped at the front of the building. Linda climbed out of the car and went into the lobby. I watched her go. Like an alchemist who was seeing his gold bars turn back into lead in front of his eyes.

I didn't need to go back to my office. I U-turned the Healey, drove round the Cumberland Basin and headed for home. I switched on the radio. Trisha Yearwood was singing *Two Days From Knowing.*

A prime candidate for Patrick in his torch song mode.

As for me?... Stupidly, I was complicating something which should be dead simple.

CHAPTER NINETEEN

There were twelve of us sitting in a meeting room at Trinity Road. DCI Maynard and DS Brown from ST5; Hood and Shackleton; Andy Overton, Julia, Tony the video technician and me; two vets and two police marksmen. One of them, DS Allen. was explaining how the tranquilliser gun operated.

"The rifle shoots darts by compressed gas. As we presume there will be two dogs fighting when we get into the barn, a sedative will be no use. We will have to use a paralysing agent."

He held a dart up for us all to see. It was about half an inch long.

"Actually 13mm," Allen said. "Basically, it's a ballistic syringe, with the drug loaded in a hypodermic needle. The needle has a barbed collar on it, to ensure the dart stays in the dog and the full dose is administered. There is a steel ball at the back of the dart and on impact, the momentum of the ball pushes the syringe plunger and injects the drug into the dog."

He gave us a couple of moments to absorb all that, then continued.

"As soon as the dogs are shot, the vets and the RSPCA inspectors must move quickly to protect the animals and monitor their vital signs. If, as a result of the fighting, the dogs are deemed to be too badly injured, the vets will destroy them immediately."

DCI Maynard took over. Gestured to DS Brown, Overton

and Julia.

"We've done this sort of operation before," he said. "Alas, too often. But it does mean we can predict how the people in the barn will react. Some of them, instinctively, try to leave. But most of them accept they're in trouble and behave. If we manage to get in immediately the first fight starts, there should only be two dogs to deal with. Leave that in the hands of the marksmen and the vets. When we get to Chepstow we will be joined by local police officers, who along with myself, DS Brown, DS Hood and DC Shackleton will deal with the guests."

He now included Tony and me.

"Concentrate on taking pictures of the dogs. Ignore the people. We will deal with them as soon as everything calms down."

Then he surveyed the whole room again.

"Any questions?"

There was complete silence in the room. DCI Maynard looked at the clock on the wall at the far end of the room. 11.45.

"We leave at high noon," he said.

* * *

We left Trinity Road in two vehicles. The four detectives, looking every inch a Countryside Alliance quartet, in a silver-grey Range Rover; the rest of us in a dark blue Mercedes minibus. We picked up another Mercedes in Chepstow, then drove to the now familiar lay-by.

We assembled in front of Maynard. He completed the briefing.

"There will be a couple of men stationed at the lane end

leading to the farm. The two buses will pull up a quarter of a mile short, while we go on with the Range Rover. Hopefully, they will think we're late arrivals, at least long enough for us to surprise them. Once we have dealt with them, we'll radio back to the rest of you and you will come on. Follow the Range Rover up the lane, stop with fifty yards to spare and let us drive into the farmyard. Again, we'll deal with any security problems in the yard, then ask you to join us."

He pointed at the line of uniformed coppers and counted to twelve.

"There are barn entrances back and front. You will go around the back. On my signal open the door and go in. And hold your positions. Don't wade into anything, just don't let anybody out. The rest of us will go in the front door. The dogs are a priority. Let the marksmen and the vets go to work. Once that's accomplished, you can then set about anybody who's misbehaving. You have my permission to be a pro-active as you feel is necessary."

He took a brown A4 envelope from Hood and handed out copies of a photograph.

"Keep a sharp lookout for him. That's Lloyd Starratt. He is the chief malefactor. Grab him, any of you; sit on him and don't let him go. I don't care how many size twelve boots have to stand on his neck."

Maynard looked at his watch.

"It's now 1.30. Festivities begin in half an hour."

At just before 2 o'clock, we parked up again. From the front seat of the Mercedes, I watched the Range Rover disappear around the bend in the road ahead. The second Mercedes pulled in behind us. The walkie talkie on the shoulder of the cop sitting next to me crackled into life.

"Complete radio silence," Maynard ordered. "We'll get

back to you."

Three minutes later he did.

"Come on now," he said.

A couple of heavyweights were sitting side by side on the grass with their feet in a ditch, about twenty yards along the lane. They were dragged to their feet, dumped into our empty bus and handcuffed into a couple of seats. Two of the local uniforms joined them. The rest climbed out of the second bus. The driver U turned the bus, parked it across the lane and blocked it.

The Range Rover went on ahead and the four detectives did their routine again. Then the rest of us were called into the yard. Two more of Lloyd's associates were in handcuffs. Chained to the wheel spokes of a hay baler.

Maynard gave his final instructions to the police who were headed for the door on the other side of the barn.

"Apparently, the door isn't locked," he said. Then he included all of us. "According to Dumb and Dumber, there are twenty-eight punters inside."

"The door opens outwards into the yard," Hood said.

A huge roar of noise erupted inside the barn. Maynard yelled out.

"Thirty seconds from... Now."

We all started counting. Brown and the back door cops set off at a run and disappeared around the side of the building. Maynard, Hood and Shackleton stepped towards the double doors. The rest of us closed up behind. Hood took hold of the right-hand door hook, Shackleton the left. Everybody counted down. Maynard yelled at Hood and Shackleton and they heaved. The doors swung open. The wall of noise spilled out into the yard. Flanked by the marksmen, Maynard led the way into the barn. The rest of us moved in behind them and fanned out left and right. Across the floor, the rear door opened. Brown and his band of locals dived in from the car park.

That's all I could take in, before the reality of the carnage in the middle of the ring hit home. Tony began filming. I could only watch, rooted to the spot. One of the dogs, dark grey in colour, bleeding from a hole where the flesh had been ripped from its left flank, had its teeth deep into the neck of the other – a huge white beast, which was shaking its head from side to side, desperate to dislodge its opponent's jaws. The dogs rose up on to their hind legs, lost balance and thumped to the ground. The grey dog's head hit the barn floor with a crunch like a hammer splintering wood. It lost grip on the white dog. The white dog rolled over, then stood up, blood streaming out of the wound in its neck. The two were separated by about eight feet. And it was enough for the marksmen. The white dog was hit in mid-air as it launched itself across the space. A shock wave rippled from its head to its flanks and it lost all control of the attack. It hit the ground inches short of the grey dog; which got to its feet as the dart went into its shoulder, spun around, staggered a couple of paces, fell onto its belly, got to its feet and fell again.

By which time, chaos was reigning supreme among the punters, although the noise level had fallen considerably. Maynard took a police .38 out of a shoulder holster and fired twice into a pile of straw bales to his left. On the other side of the barn, Brown did the same. Three of the punters made the mistake of trying to get through the police lining the main doors. The first was felled by a kick in the groin. Another was punched in his adam's apple; he grabbed at it and fell to his knees choking. The third was lifted off his feet by two cops, up-ended and dropped face down on to the floor.

Suddenly everything was quiet. The two vets, Julia and Andy were inside the ring.

George Hood had Lloyd Starratt in a half nelson, his face buried in a straw bale. Lloyd was struggling and yelling something indistinguishable. Hood pulled his head up. With his face full of straw, Lloyd looked like Worzel Gummidge.

"What was that?" Hood asked.

"You have no right to – " was all Lloyd managed to get out. Hood shoved his face back into the hay bale.

Maynard addressed everyone else in the barn.

"Where are the rest of the dogs?... Come on... Somebody..."

There was no response. Maynard called across to Brown

"Take a couple of officers and go look in the car park. And while you're out there, take a note of all the registration numbers."

Brown and two of the local cops went outside. Hood collected a pair of handcuffs from another cop and clamped them on Lloyd's wrists. He turned Lloyd round, then pushed him back down onto the bales.

"Don't move a fucking inch," Hood said.

Maynard walked into the centre of the ring. He knelt down beside the white dog, still bleeding from its neck. He looked at the vet tending to the dog. "He's going to die, he's lost two much blood," the vet said. "I'll put him out of his misery."

He took a hypodermic of pentobarbital out of the brief case on the floor next to him and injected the beast. Julia stepped over to the dog and watched. Maynard turned away and gave orders to the police officers.

"Get all these people over there next to Starratt. Sit them down. Names and addresses and car registration numbers. Check with the officers in the car park. When you match owners to any dogs outside, arrest them. Find out who's holding the betting money and arrest him too."

He looked around at all the cops now busy doing stuff.

"Where's the officer who drove the Mercedes down the track?"

One of the local cops answered him.

"He's outside, Sir."

"Okay you'll do. And you are?"

"Dobson, Sir."

"Right Dobson. Go and get the bus, bring it up here. And when you've weeded out the hard cases, get a couple of other officers to help you. Shove the rest of the bastards into the bus, lock it and stand guard over it."

Dobson left the barn.

I moved into the ring and stood at Julia's shoulder. The vet dealing with the white dog got to his feet.

"He's gone," he said.

A couple of yards away, Overton was discussing the grey dog's prospects with the other vet.

"He has skull damage," the vet said. "I don't know how bad it is. X-rays will tell us, but even if the poor bloody creature survives..."

He couldn't finish the sentence.

"Put him down," Overton said.

Julia asked me if I was alright. I couldn't speak. I shook my head and walked out into the sunshine of the farmyard.

* * *

The next half hour or so, was a haze of discomfort and misery. I was sick down a drain in the yard. I found a bottle of water under a seat of the Mercedes I had travelled in.

Maynard came out into the sunshine and talked into his mobile. I watched as a crocodile of punters was escorted across the yard and on to the other bus. The two men handcuffed to the hay baler looked on, helpless and pissed off. Two more police vans, one of them a Ford Transit with grills on the windows, drove into the yard. Maynard now had a sizeable chunk of the Gloucestershire Constabulary's police fleet at his disposal.

As I dragged myself back into a reasonable state, I got fed up with sitting in the yard. I had no desire to go back into the barn, so I took a walk around the real estate.

In the car park, Overton, Julia, Tony and the vets were dealing with the other four dogs on the afternoon's bill. Something else I didn't want to see. Which left me with no choice other than to inspect the green painted ship containers.

The doors on both containers were closed and padlocked. I walked around them. First one, then the other. They were as boring as big steel boxes can be. But the padlocks were brand new, big silver heavy duty items. By no means your average, across the counter, hardware store kind.

I went looking for a sledgehammer and found one in the un-restored barn; behind an old workbench, amongst the wooden crates, the engine blocks the broken machinery and the tractor bits.

Despite its weight, the lock on the first container bolt, broke at the second blow of the sledge. I swung the doors open.

And out of nowhere, the day offered up a truck load of brand-new possibilities.

Inside the container, there were two battered sofas, a couple of old armchairs, a cheap chain store dining table with half a dozen wooden chairs around it. There was a double door kitchen unit standing in the down right corner, with a two-bar electric fire alongside it. And lying on the floor was a metal inspection lamp, the kind a car mechanic uses to hang above a car engine when he's working under the bonnet.

Heat and light. Sort of. The left- hand wall was lined with bright red, metal framed, bunk beds – eight of them, stretching four by two, along the wall from the doors to the rear of the container. And in the extreme right-hand corner, was an area fringed by a plastic shower curtain. There was even a carpet on the floor. Not Axminster by any means, but somebody's careless attempt to turn a crap steel box into a crap steel box with a carpet.

Even with the doors open, the container smelled like a locked-up fish and chip shop. With a combination of other odours attached, like damp and sweat and the faint smell of shit.

I stepped inside and walked to the shower curtain. It was hanging from a track drilled into the roof above it. The shit smell intensified as I got closer. I opened my mouth, sucked in air, blew it out and pulled the curtain aside. There was a portable plastic toilet in one corner of the space and a plastic topped table filling much of the rest of it. There were buckets under the table with large bars of cheap soap in them.

Enough was enough.

I pulled the curtain back across the space and turned round. George Hood was standing outside the container, looking in.

"Jesus Christ," he said. "What the hell have you found?"

I joined him. Shoulder to shoulder, we stared at the second container. Hood nodded at the sledgehammer. Then at me.

"You don't need a search warrant."

I picked up the sledge. Hood gestured to the padlock.

"Go on. The last thing we want is for Lloyd Starratt to accuse the police of breaking and entering."

I smashed the lock on the second container door. The interior design concept was a replica of the first. But the carpet was thicker and the furniture a bit less tatty. This was the deluxe version.

Hood called Shackleton on his mobile and told him to join us. He looked at me.

"Don't touch a thing," he said and stepped into the container.

We had just seen a demonstration of how much Lloyd Starratt cared about animals. Now we were being offered his opinion on how human beings should be looked after. These two containers represented his version of a halfway house. Presumably for immigrants. Probably illegal.

Assuming the latter, it wasn't difficult to work out for whom Lloyd was running this gruesome B & B. And if Dujic and Tudjman were in the people trafficking business, then I had stumbled into something way beyond anything I had experienced.

"Take a look at this," I heard Hood say.

He was standing in the nearest right-hand corner of the container, looking at the floor. I moved to him and looked down too. There was a double plug, plastic electrical socket lying on the floor, with what looked like a two-kilowatt cable stretching out of the back of it. Running behind the kitchen unit and up the wall to a junction box, a couple of feet short of the roof. And beyond the box, a yard or so in from the corner, a grill, about a foot square had been cut into the roof.

"That's how the air, such as it is, gets in," Hood said. "And the mains power cable. Seems to have some sort of hat over the top. You know, like a chimney pot cover. To stop the rain seeping in. Or at least some of it. There's one in each corner."

Shackleton arrived and stood staring into the containers, as gobsmacked as Hood and I had been. Hood pulled him out of his reverie.

"How's it going back there?

"Almost done. The punters are in the buses. The dog owners and Starratt's four guards are in the Transit. All the registration plates in the car park have been logged. The camera guy has photographed the dead dogs. They're in body bags and another couple of local vets have been called in to take them away. The RSPCA inspectors are discussing what to do with the dogs that didn't get to fight."

"Where's Starratt?"

"There are four of our men superglued to him in the barn."

"Right. Keep him there for now. Give my compliments to DCI Maynard and ask him to come round here. And get somebody to find a ladder." He pointed to the grill. "I want to take a look at that from the roof."

Shackleton set about the business. Hood finished his inspection of the inside of the container. I waited in the sunshine.

One of the uniforms came back with a ladder, as amazed as the rest of us had been about what he was looking at. Hood propped the ladder against the container and climbed up on to the roof. Examined one of the corner holes. He called down to me.

"The cover's like a coolie hat," he said. "Raised a few inches above the hole. Un-noticable from down there I'd guess."

I backed away, towards the un-restored barn, then up to

Hood.

"You're right, I can't see it."

Maynard arrived at my side.

"What the hell is he doing up there?"

Hood climbed back down the ladder while Maynard took in the scene. After which, they discussed how to wind up the day. Hood explained that he and his boss needed to talk with Lloyd Starratt about a whole bunch of stuff besides the dog fighting and asked for time to do it. Maynard agreed. He wouldn't be persuaded into letting me talk to Starratt, but he did agree to hand him over to Hood.

Back in the farmyard, the local buses were full of punters and police. All the leading miscreants, save for Lloyd were in the Transit. The rest of the local cops piled into the van that had arrived with it. The three vehicles left for Chepstow. Tony completed his work, photographing the empty barn and the bloody evidence of the fight. It was decided that the four dogs which didn't get into the fray, should be destroyed also. The local vets did the work. The six bodies were loaded into their ambulance and driven away. I joined the Bristol party as they were climbing into the remaining bus. Shackleton, smart phone in hand, walked across the yard towards me.

"I've just checked my emails," he said. "The Bright Island Hotel manager has sent us the info you wanted. You've got it now. Check your inbox when you get back to Bristol."

In the Mercedes, I sat down next to a window and looked out as the bus pulled away. We left the Range Rover, the four detectives and Lloyd Starratt in the yard.

CHAPTER TWENTY

Back in my office, I read DC Shackleton's email.

The three guests who had stayed in the *Rennie Mackintosh Suite* at the Bright Island Hotel, during the second week in July 2010, had signed in as Sofie Thornton, Daniel Thornton and Deborah Thorne. The bill had been paid by Deborah. The family were all listed at the same address. In the village of Woodcroft Dean, Chepstow.

There was an email from Linda also. Saying she had a client to see in Southampton. A couple of days work to do. She was driving down and staying over and would be back on Sunday. There was no suggestion as to any prospect that Sunday might hold.

I emailed a note to DC Shackleton, thanking him for his help, then sat back in my chair to consider the next move. A drive back across the Severn bridge seemed to be it. On the other hand, a call to 118 118 might be a sensible interim endeavour.

Which was a good decision, given the result. There was no listing for Deborah Thorne, but there was for Sofie Thornton. Only, when I rang the number, I discovered Sofie Thornton didn't live there anymore. Alfie Betts did. He was renting the property.

"From Sofie Thornton?" I asked.

"From Ashdown and Noakes," Alfie said.

"How long have you been renting the house?"

"Since the beginning of July."

The pattern was just too bloody familiar. Every time I got near to closing the distance between a discovery and what should then prove to be a result, the whole narrative broke down. And I was left with a big hole where there should have been progress. I slammed the phone receiver back into the base. On reflection, Alfie must have considered that seriously rude.

So another drive across the bridge was necessary. With a cast iron ploy to prise Sofie's current address out of Ashdown and Noakes.

But that was tomorrow's task. The clock on the office wall said 5.45. I was out of all sympathy with the day and I had no plans for what was left of it, except to go home. Or maybe go to see Chrissie and Adam. And Sam.

I called the number in Clevedon. I got Adam's recorded message. I said hello and goodbye. I dialled Chrissie's mobile and received her apology too. Finally, I tried Adam's mobile. He wasn't answering that in person either.

A quarter to six was late enough for a drink. I fished the bottle of malt out of the filing cabinet and looked at it. Thought for a moment or two about Annie Marshall. Then put the bottle away. Drinking in the office was one thing. Drinking alone in the office with nothing to do, was something else. I recalled the brilliant Tony Hancock solo episode where he spent the whole day on his own, trying to find stuff to do. A tour de force. But he was a lot funnier than me...

I was saved from further introspection by the phone ringing.

"Sorry, Dad," Chrissie said. "Sam and I were out for our tea time walk. Come for supper. Adam will be home soon."

"I'd like that."

"Bring red wine. Oh, and bring Linda."

"She's in Southampton."

"That's a pity."

* * *

An hour later, I was rolling around the hall floor, locked in a wrestling match with Sam. I finally got the better of him. He lay on his side panting. I patted him on the shoulder and got to my feet. He turned his head and looked up at me, thought about getting up, then decided to stay where he was.

Adam had cooked. He delivered his terrine to the dining table and we sat down to eat. Sam strolled into the dining room and sat down to watch.

After a couple of minutes, Chrissie got to the point.

"How are things with you and Linda?" she asked.

"I think we're on a break."

"Already? What did you do?"

"Why are you assuming it's my fault?"

"Because it probably is."

I looked to Adam for support.

"Don't involve me in this," he said and began clearing away the first course.

"Seriously Dad..." Chrissie went on.

"I had one relationship for twenty-three years," I said. "Exclusively. Through all the great bits and the good bits and even the best forgotten bits, Emily and I stayed close. It seemed that, no matter how tough it got, there was never space between us. Even when she was having to do the patching up and the healing. Right now, I really have no idea how to begin again."

"Do you want to? With Linda?"

Yes I did and no I didn't. Linda was right about that. It was as though I had done all the commitment I could possibly do, with Emily. Which, if I thought about it, was nonsense. Just lame and final. Nobody should close down in that way. Yes, you should be positive and selective about the stuff you don't want to repeat. Like open heart surgery or the deepest of sorrows. But relationships ought to be able to start out well, at least. Linda and I had been involved for a week. And considering we had known each other for fifteen years, I owed the positives on offer, a little more effort.

I don't know how much time that rationalisation took, but Chrissie waited. We looked at each other, wondering which one of us should speak first. Adam came in with the beef stroganoff and the conversation was put on hold. Sam got to his feet and waggled his nose, padded around the table and sat slap bang underneath the casserole pot.

"Lie down Sam," Adam ordered.

Sam considered for a moment, then did as he was bidden. Put his head down on his front paws and sulked.

The stroganoff was terrific. I stopped thinking and gave myself up to enjoying it. Adam appreciated that.

"You may now re-convene," he said, as he began clearing the table once again.

"Well?..." Chrissie asked.

"Must try harder," I said.

"Indeed you must. When is Linda back from the south coast?"

"Sunday, she said."

"Then make the most of it. And that's an order."

Adam put a large plate in the middle of the table. On it, a gorgeous, pink wigwam of a desert.

"Summer pudding," he said with pride. "Strawberries, blackberries, raspberries and redcurrants."

He sat down, picked up a knife, sliced it open and the

delicious fruit came tumbling out.

We finished the second bottle of red wine and Chrissie made coffee. When that was mostly done, she gave me the considered, old fashioned, sideways look that was pure Emily.

"Why did you call?" Chrissie asked. "I sensed you weren't on top form when you did."

"I thought that too," Adam said.

"I'm sorry. I shouldn't have allowed my misery to seep down the line."

"Yes, you should. Especially if it was misery."

"Don't worry, I'm not going to whinge. In fact, this is something I think you ought to hear. More ammunition for your crusade against Lloyd Starratt."

I looked at both of them, across the table, then for some reason, down at Sam.

"I went to a dog fight this afternoon."

They both stared at me in horror.

"A what?" Chrissie asked. As if she needed to be sure she had heard me correctly.

I told them the story. Précised the violent stuff. There were pauses and astonished silences, but I got to the end. Chrissie called to Sam. He got to his feet and moved round to her chair. He looked up at her. Chrissie began to stroke him. He responded and leaned his body against her knees.

Adam slipped resolutely into work mode.

"Will anyone object if I write this story?"

"I'm sure the RSPCA would love you to write it. As far as they're concerned, all intelligent advocates for their cause are welcome. Talk to Julia. And Tony, the video man, he has pictures."

Chrissie looked up and across the table.

"Pictures?"

"Evidence," I said. "He recorded the events of the afternoon." I looked back at Adam. "And talk to DCI Maynard at ST5."

Chrissie and I took Sam for his late-night walk.

"How are you? Really?" she asked.

"I'm okay. A bit shell shocked that's all." I looked at Sam, on the end of the lead, nose down and sniffing. "I wonder if he knows how lucky he is."

Sam responded by lifting his right leg against a lamppost. We waited for him to finish his business, then moved on.

"What about Deborah? Are you any closer to finding her?"

"No."

"And the Serbs?"

"No."

"What about the people on the beach in Devon?"

"For a while, I was doing well with that."

"Until?"

"I hit another dead end. Messrs Ashdown and Noakes."

"The estate agents?"

Sam stopped to sniff at a car wheel. I told Chrissie about finding the Chepstow address and then finding her tenant.

"So if Ashdown and Noakes are acting for Deborah, they will have her current address," Chrissie said. "Problem solved."

Not exactly. But Chrissie went on to explain.

"I help out in the student union accommodation office. Just about every estate agent and landlord in the area is listed. Names, addresses emails. Ashdown and Noakes have a place in Clifton and another one in Bath. If Deborah approached them in something of a panic because she wanted to get out of her house quickly, they probably asked if she'd be okay with students in the place. Usually the guarantee of a quick let. So, she says yes, gives the estate agents her new address, drops off the keys and moves to... wherever. Obviously they lucked out with Mr Betts. But if he's got a short lease and Messrs Ashdown and Noakes want the business ongoing, the owner's contacts will be in the system. Maybe I can find them."

"Won't they be confidential?"

"This is the internet we're talking about. Confidentiality is a long-forgotten concept." She grinned. "Leave it with me."

Sam seemed to be finished doing what a dog has to do late night. We reversed course and headed back to the house.

Chrissie took off Sam's choke chain in the hall. He sped into the kitchen, sat down and waited for his supper biscuits to materialise. He ate them, slurped away in his water bowl, lifted his head and dripped all over the kitchen tiles. I wiped his beard, he padded back into the hall, did his customary double 360 and sank to the carpet.

"Do you want to stay over?" Chrissie asked.

CHAPTER TWENTY-ONE

I fell asleep as soon as my head hit the pillow. With no thoughts of my client, Lloyd Starratt, or Serbs to keep me awake. But I ended up in a nightmare world of ferocious four-legged creatures with night vision sites for eyes and relentless stamina.

I woke to find Sam staring at me from six inches away, his head resting on the duvet, his beard flattened under his chin, ears cascading down each side of his face. The moment I opened my eyes he was on his feet. He stretched out his front paws, bowed his head, lifted his bum, hoisted his tail like a flagpole and stretched. That done, he grabbed the duvet in his jaws and hauled it off the bed.

I looked at the bedside clock. 7.40. There were no sounds from the direction of Chrissie and Adam, so I reported for duty. When I got downstairs, Sam was sitting by the front door, on his best behaviour.

The walk down to the sea front was most enjoyable. The sun was up and the tide was high. Sam may behave like a maniac while at home, but in public, butter wouldn't melt. He doesn't molest pedestrians or chase cyclists; he backs his bum into hedges to do what a dog has to do and shows off disgracefully when anyone takes the slightest notice of him. Which is, of course, an ongoing routine, because he's such a stunner.

A shaven headed teenager was sitting on a bench with a girl. She was wearing a ring in her nose and a series of them in her left ear lobe. They were drinking coffee and eating doughnuts. Sam ambled up to the bench, sat down on the path in front of the couple and, a moment later, raised his right front paw. The act was shameful, brilliant and irresistible. The two kids were seduced in an instant. Two bites of the second doughnut went into Sam.

Back home, he belted round the garden while I made his breakfast.

Adam had gone into Bristol. Chrissie occupied his desk in the study and googled the student accommodation website. Breakfast eaten, Sam settled down in the hall and went to sleep.

The website gave up the information I needed. Sofie Thornton was living at an address on Thackeray Road, in Horfield.

North of Bristol city centre, Horfield straddles Gloucester Road and spreads east a couple of miles towards the M32. It's a busy, organised, self-contained part of town. Away from the centre and the big chain stores, it still boasts local shops and trades. I scrutinised the A to Z. Thackeray Road sits in an enclave of terraces inspired by giants of literature. There is also a Shelley Way, a Dickens Close and a Shakespeare Avenue. The houses are tightly packed together. They have tiny gardens, a few paces deep, between their front doors and the road.

* * *

Just before 10 o'clock, I parked the Healey a dozen car lengths from Sofie's house. The doorbell rang inside the hall when I pressed the button, but no one answered. I went back to the Healey to wait.

Forty minutes later, Sofie and Daniel walked towards me from the direction of Gloucester Road, carrying bags of shopping. He was a young teenager, almost as tall as she was. They were both dressed in blue jeans and white tee shirts. I got out of the car as they reached the front door of the house. Sofie put down the shopping, swung her bag off her shoulder, dug into it and searched for her house keys. Daniel waited at her side. I stepped into the garden behind them. Fiddling around in her bag, Sofie failed to hear me arrive. Daniel did and swung round to face me.

"Hello," he said.

"What?" Sofie asked, over her shoulder.

"He was talking to me," I said.

Sofie, right hand still in her bag, turned and stared at me. I introduced myself. Sofie continued staring at me; the question 'So?' etched across her face.

"I'm a private investigator," I said. "Deborah came to see me last week. Now she has disappeared and I need to find her."

Sofie seemed glued to the doorstep. Eventually produced her house key. Spent another moment or two on scrutiny.

"You had better come in," she said. With a trace of an accent. Probably eastern European.

Inside the house, Sofie and Daniel led the way along the hall and into the kitchen. The shopping bags were dumped on to the table, then Sofie surveyed us both.

"Daniel," she said. "Take Mr Shepherd into the living room and keep him company while I make some coffee." She looked at me. "Or would you prefer tea?"

"Coffee will be fine, thank you."

Daniel and I sat down in the front room. Me in one of two small armchairs, him in the other. Between us there was a mahogany coffee table about eighteen inches square. A two-seater sofa sat against the wall which separated us from the entrance hall. And a fat, analogue television set with a digi-box on top of it, was squeezed into a corner, to the left of the window facing the street. A cosy room, but not one for running around in.

"Who are you Mr Shepherd?" Daniel asked.

I compared him to the photograph. He was six years older and six years taller. He had his mother's eyes and nose. And he was, apparently, totally unimpressed by the man who had invaded his house. He had a picture of Kristen Stewart printed on his tee shirt.

"I am a friend of your friend Deborah," I said.

"Oh," he said. "Do you know where she is?"

That question again. Now coming from a fifteen-year- old.

"She's supposed to be here, you see," he went on. "But she isn't."

"Does she live here?"

"Yes. We were all here, together, for a bit. Then she left. Mum says that as soon as we see her again, we can all go back to Chepstow. If she doesn't come back, I have to go to school in Lockleaze next week."

Suddenly he looked depressed.

"And you don't want to?"

"I want to go back to Chepstow."

Sofie came into the room carrying a tray with two mugs of coffee, a milk jug and a can of Sprite.

"We will," she said. "I promise. But while we are here..." She put the tray down on the coffee table. "You must go to school here."

She handed the Sprite to him.

"Can you leave us alone for a few minutes Dan? You can have your X Box in your room."

"Okay," he said, cheered up at a stroke.

He left the room. Sofie called after him.

"Just while Mr Shepherd is here." She turned back to me. "He's not usually allowed to play during the mornings. I try to get him out of the house as much as I can... Milk?"

"Thank you. Do you know where Deborah is?"

Sofie put down the milk jug and passed me the mug of coffee.

"No. She left here 8 days ago. She won't tell me where she is."

"Do you speak to her?"

"Yes. On her mobile."

Sofie leaned back into the sofa cushion and sipped her coffee. I watched. She was as relaxed as any tense and suspicious person could be and there was a stillness about her. The beach photograph didn't do her justice. It was a 2D holiday snap. In 3D she was both graceful and beautiful.

I decided to concentrate on stuff she could tell me. On her, rather than on Deborah.

"Your accent," I said, "Is it eastern European?"

"Yes," she said.

"Are you from Kosovo?"

"Yes."

"Which is where you met Deborah, when she was Daniel?"

Sofie swallowed a mouthful of coffee, leaned forward and put the mug back down on the table. Slowly and carefully. Then she looked up at me.

"How do you know this?"

I told her the whole story; everything I had learned about Daniel Thornton and Deborah Thorne. The information about Deborah's parents astonished her.

"Didn't she tell you about them?" I asked.

"No."

I explained there were other characters in this story. Offered her the names of Starratt, Dujic and Tudjman. She grew more and more uneasy. She wrapped her arms across her breasts and around her shoulders, hugging herself tightly. As if trying to contain some kind of panic attack. I got out of my chair to move to her. She shook her head fiercely and unwrapped her arms.

"No no," she said. "Stay there."

I sat back down in the armchair and waited. With an immense effort, she regained control of her runaway emotions, dropped her hands to her thighs, leaned back into the sofa again and closed her eyes.

"My father is Serbian. My mother was Albanian. That would not happen now of course. But I was born in 1981, in Mitrovica. We were all Yugoslavs then. Tito was still alive. Now, my birthplace is a symbol of all the wrong that has been done. The River Ibar divides the city in two. The Serbs live north of it, the Albanians to the south. It is madness. But generations will have to die before anything can change."

"Tell me about Donjica," I said.

"Thirty-six Albanians were murdered by the Serbs in April 2000. It is a tiny place. Insignificant. Its misfortune was that the Kosovo Liberation Army had a base in the hills. Without that, only those who lived there and a handful of other people, would know of it."

"Were you there?"

"No. I was never in Donjica. Daniel was. Two days after the massacre. By accident. His truck broke down as he was driving north from the Macedonian border."

"So where did you meet him?"

"In Pec. It's in north eastern Kosovo. Médecins San Frontières had a base there. I was working as an interpreter.

Daniel arrived from Donjica. I had never seen someone so shocked and so angry. But that was nothing, compared to what was to come."

She drifted into silence. Seemed to be miles away. I waited. Her eyes misted. She blinked. Tears rolled down her cheeks. She sniffed, wiped her eyes with the back of her right hand, then looked at me again.

"We were sent a few miles south, to Lipojane. Have you heard of it?"

"Of it, yes."

"Another place of no significance. In May 2000, Serb police and para-militaries entered the village. They rounded up everyone who had not managed to escape. They took the women and children away and assembled the men in the main street. Twenty-two of them were machine gunned to death. Then the Serbs burned the village and forced the women and children to travel south, eventually to the Albanian border. Most of them walked all the way. Word got to Pec from the people who returned to the village. Daniel and I went into Lipojane three days later with an OSCE Team. I talked with a man who had survived. He was not hit by machine gun fire. He lay under some corpses for three hours and crawled out after the Serbs had gone."

She looked at me, dead centre, now making no attempt to control the tears.

"This happened in my country. My home. I was there. And I still do not understand how ordinary people can turn into butchers."

"The people who do this are not ordinary," I said. "They are criminals, feeding on a residue of centuries of fear and hate. Like you said before. Even after you eliminate them, the situation will take generations to mend."

"Dujic and Tudjman were in Lipojane," Sofie said. "The OSCE Team had photographs of men they suspected of war atrocities. They were passed around the village. Seven people identified Dujic and nine picked out Tudjman."

"So, who are they?"

"They were policemen. Who saw opportunities. Who rode on waves of prejudice and advanced politically, stole property, made money. All they had to do was learn to kill. I suppose that came easy."

"Tell me about your relationship with them."

"I do not have one."

"Yes, you have," I said. "And it's frightening you to death. Deborah too."

I let the pause fill, then tried again.

"Talk to me. Please. Otherwise I can't help."

She took a deep breath.

"I saw Dujic and Tudjman again in September 2001. In Pec. I was in a Serb area, for some reason I can't remember. I went into a café. I was drinking coffee when they came in. I could not help it, I stared at them. Once, or perhaps twice, Dujic saw me looking at him. He smiled. And he thought... well you can imagine. I went home, to the apartment Daniel and I shared. They must have followed me. A few minutes after I got there, they knocked on the door. I opened it, then tried to close it again, but Dujic kicked his way in."

Sofie had come to the difficult bit. I was about to tell her not to go on, but she held up a hand.

"No. I will tell you," she said. "Tudjman held me down while Dujic raped me. Then they changed over. And then again. And once more. When they had finished, they left. Daniel came home half an hour later. He got into a rage and then he went quiet. He stayed in his room for maybe an hour.

Then he came out and said we had to leave. We did. We packed and we left the apartment. That evening we got a ride on an *MSF* truck into Croatia. We took a boat from Dubrovnik to Pescara in Italy. Two days later we were in London."

"When did you come down to the west country?"

"A few weeks later. We rented a cottage in the village of Aust. Do you know it?"

"Yes. Just this side of the bridge."

"Then I discovered I was pregnant. I hated it. I was sick with misery. Two possible fathers. Both of them murderers and rapists. But Daniel was wonderful. He kept me focussed and together and gradually I began to look forward to being a mother. Then he asked me to marry him. I could not be an illegal immigrant if I was his wife. He did not ask anything from me in return. I realise now, that he was already planning his gender change. Young Daniel was born in May 2002."

"So you were now Sofie Thornton, wife and mother?"

"A single mother it came to be. Daniel moved into Bristol. She began living as Deborah."

"Why did she move?"

"She had no doubts about what she was going to do. She knew that the next few years were going to be immensely hard. She did not want to draw Daniel and me into what must happen. And in her future relationship with him, she just wanted to be Deborah. She did not want him to know her as anybody else. Daniel and I moved into the Forest of Dean house when he was three. And regularly, this wonderful lady came to visit us. Daniel fell in love with her. We had lots of holidays together. Not just the one on Bright Island."

"So when did Deborah move to Chiswick?"

"After the surgery."

"Why?"

"She wanted to start over. Somewhere new. Away from the support system she had built up. To really be an independent woman. The call centre job was good for her. A work place she could control. She did not have to present to the public at large. It gave her confidence."

So the question begging to be asked was, what happened to threaten this carefully constructed new order?

The answer, was a trip from the Forest of Dean to Bristol's retail Mecca, the Mall at Cribbs Causeway, north of the city. A delight to retail junkies, an abomination to those to whom shopping is less than pure joy. Several square miles of retail sprawl, with pubs, restaurants, cinemas and enough parking spaces for a football stadium crowd. Host to pop concerts and flash mobs.

"Back in April," Sofie said, "the week after Easter, Daniel and I were at the Mall. And I saw Dujic and Tudjman, coming out of *Hugo Boss*. All these years later. For a moment, I was convinced I was wrong. How could they be here? These criminals. Dressed in Boss suits. But it was them."

"So you called Deborah. She left London and came to Bristol."

"Yes."

"And you moved here."

"Not at first. It seemed best to stay where we were. Out of the way. But things got more complicated."

Sofie sat upright in the sofa and leaned towards me.

"Daniel should be starting his GSCE year at Wye Valley Comprehensive School," Sofie explained.

Connection made.

"Which has a brand-new sports field, courtesy of Lloyd Starratt." I said. "There was a cricket match to celebrate his generosity, back in May."

"Yes," Sofie said, "And Mr Starratt was there."

I nodded. She looked at me for a long time, then dropped bombshell two. "So were Dujic and Tudjman. Large as life. Standing among the parents and the teachers and the guests. Joining in the applause for Lloyd Starratt."

"Did they see you?"

"Perhaps. But why would they recognise me? A nameless rape victim, long forgotten among countless others. I thought Daniel and I would be safe. Deborah did not agree."

"So it was then that you moved."

"Yes. I took Daniel away from his home and his school and his friends. He has been very good about it, but he does not want to be here. I have managed to persuade him this is only temporary. I hope it proves to be so. I only wish I knew what Deborah was doing?"

A consideration which had obsessed me for twelve days.

"Mr Shepherd, if you can accomplish what you have to do, as soon as you can, I would be delighted."

"So would I," I said. "But, in truth, I've run out of plans and purpose."

"We should be at home," Sofie said. "Daniel should be getting into his new year at school. But we must wait here."

Out of nowhere, I remembered something Bill Thornton had talked about.

"Daniel kept a journal during his time in Kosovo," I said. "Do you know where it is?"

Sofie looked concerned. She shifted her position on the sofa.

"Do you have it?"

She made a decision and nodded.

"Yes."

"May I read it?"

She stood up.

"It is in my bedroom. I will get it."

I followed her into the hall and waited at the bottom of the stairs. She came back down with a brown, leather-bound notebook. She handed it to me.

"Please take care of it Mr Shepherd."

"Of course."

I turned to go.

"I will call Daniel," Sofie said.

"No leave him. Tell him I'll see him again soon."

"Is that a promise."

"Yes."

"You did not say 'If I can'."

"It's a real promise," I said. "And they come without 'If I cans'."

She smiled.

"Thank you."

Back in the street, I sat in the Healey and talked to myself for a while. In spite of all the work I had done during this investigation, the good people were still losing. This had to be put right. Giving up, wasn't an option. Deborah and the Serbs were around, somewhere. And if Lloyd Starratt was the only lead left, then he would have to do.

My mobile rang. I fished it out of the glove compartment.

Harvey wanted to talk to me.

"Do you fancy a trip to the seaside?" he asked. "Seriously. A walk along the beach at Weston, followed by fish and chips. I want to help you Jack. We have some talking to do, but not at Trinity Road. Somewhere out of the way. How about it? I'll drive."

"I never turn down fish and chips at Weston," I said.

"Where are you?"

"On my way back to the office."
"I'll pick you up in half an hour," Harvey said.

CHAPTER TWENTY-TWO

I like Weston-Super-Mare, even if its baron incumbent is Jeffrey Archer. Happily, it's more famous for its donkeys, which have graced the beach since 1886 and have been worked for the whole of that time, by generations of the Mager family. It's an impressive job record, but then the Weston donkeys are legendary. The quintessence of the British seaside holiday. And a symbol of continuity, like the apes on Gibraltar and the ravens at the Tower of London. If ever the donkeys were to leave the beach...

Harvey parked the Vauxhall at the south end of Marine Parade and we stepped on to the sand, stretching unbroken for a mile and a half, along the front and round the curve of rock at Knightstone. Past the town landmark, the magnificently re-imagined and re-built pier pavilion, now defiantly back in business after the violent destruction of the fire.

The sky was cloudless. The donkeys were about their business, the beach was dotted with kids, parents and grandparents engaged in sandcastle engineering and games of cricket. Weston in the sunshine. Unbeatable.

We hadn't talked about anything in particular during the drive from my office and Harvey was in no hurry to launch into anything now. We walked for a while before he got round to explaining what this excursion was all about.

"The conversation we're about to have," he said, "must stay on this beach. I'm breaking a lifetime rule here, because

I want to see justice done. And because I'm pissed off that I can't be in charge of doing so."

I didn't say anything.

"You know me, Jack. I don't believe private enterprise has any place in the day-to-day business of law and order. At best, you're what I can't be – Don Quixote. But mostly, you're just a vigilante, albeit with some moral purpose."

"Well at least there's that," I said.

"Let me finish this," he said. "We don't have Lloyd Starratt anymore."

I stopped walking. So did Harvey, a step ahead of me. He turned to face me.

"What do you mean you don't have him," I asked. "Where is he?"

"Back at Southfork I imagine."

"Jesus Christ Harvey, how did that happen?"

"DCI Benjamin happened. The star of Gloucestershire Constabulary's Major Crimes Unit. He's claimed the people trafficking case. Southfork is on his manor, not mine. And Starratt's done a deal with him. To roll over on the Serbs, if he's not prosecuted for dog fighting and only for housing illegal immigrants, rather than for running them into the UK."

"But you had him, at Trinity Road. All you had to do was put the thumbscrews on him."

"I'll ignore that attempt at levity."

"So how did this DCI get him?"

"Maynard and George had him for three hours. Starratt admitted he was at the dog fight. He couldn't do otherwise. But he said the organisation of the gig had nothing to do with him. The barn wasn't his to control. He had temporarily leased the place to a company in the Cotswolds, as a storage facility."

"So how did he explain all the work going on?"

"He said he was in the process of restoring all the buildings, with the intention of creating up market, country holiday accommodation. Currently, suffering a minor cash flow problem, he had suspended building operations and let the place."

"Then why was he spectating?"

"He claimed, he had developed concerns about what the facilities were really being used for and had turned up to investigate. He had not promoted the event. He wasn't the banker. And of course, he was horrified by what he had encountered and hoped we would prosecute everyone involved, with all the machinery of law at our disposal."

"What does Maynard think?"

"He's pleased. He has busted the ring. Nailed everybody else involved, including the banker and the bookie. Starratt is out of the dog fighting business. The RSPCA has permission to examine all his animals and they will conduct their own prosecution regardless. It's not a total bust by any means."

"Did you get anything else out of him?"

"The interview was suspended and Maynard left. I joined George and we started again. Getting into the stuff about ship containers and suspected links with Serb people traffickers. Starratt had figured out what he wanted to say. But he got very jumpy and lost track of what he'd rehearsed. We had him scared. We were miles away from dangerous dogs and he knew he was in the mire. Steadfastness isn't one of his qualities. He started to panic. Then there was a knock on the interview room door. I took a phone call from the ACC, who had just taken a call from Gloucester HQ. We were ordered to render the utmost courtesy to a DCI who was, at that moment, speeding down the M5. Clowns to the left, jokers to the right. We got glued, screwed and papered over. There was some sort of deal done and Starratt went home. Bailed to appear before Chepstow magistrates, on the charge of allowing his premises to be used for illegal purposes."

"So we're bolloxed."

"Well... Not altogether."

He looked out to sea, lifted his face to the breeze and allowed it to caress his cheeks. Then he turned back to me.

"Words of one syllable," he said. "I am, but you're not. I can't go looking for the Serbs. But you... You can feel free to pursue enquiries in your independently resolute fashion. I can't stop you."

"But DCI Benjamin can."

"That's your problem. However, your presence in this endeavour so far, is not recorded. DCI Benjamin doesn't know you from a hole in the ground. That's the advantage you have. Use it."

We started walking again.

"By the way, did you find the woman and child you were looking for?"

"Yes, I did."

"Do they know where your client is?"

"No."

"Still not getting any closer?"

Harvey looked across Marine Parade, towards Beach Road. We had walked as far as the Grand Atlantic Hotel.

"I think we deserve superior fish and chips," he said. "I hear the chef at the Grand Atlantic is from Newcastle. He cooks them in dripping."

"I won't eat them any other way," I said.

* * *

Friday night at home.

I settled down in the living room, with Daniel's journal and a large glass of twelve-year-old malt.

And I read his words about Donjica.

Kosovo is land of mortar holes and rubble. Donjica is a prime example. Blasted and broken down. A year ago, the place flourished as best it could, in this wasteland. Close to 1600 people lived in and around here. A woman I spoke to today told me, that at the last count, there were now barely 350.

Today, 36 of those are bodies. Men women and children, some of them mutilated beyond all recognition. There was a line of bodies in the village square, in front of the mosque. In a gully, on rising ground above the village, I saw another one, covered with a dusty blanket. When the doctor who was with me, pulled it back, we saw there was no head on the corpse. Just a sickening bloody mess on the neck. I don't know where the man's left arm was... is... we couldn't find it. Further up the gully we found a head. A woman's head, with silver grey hair. The doctor said she was probably in her mid-60s. Then another group of bodies. I didn't count them. I just looked and saw holes in their twisted shapes and dismembered limbs. A man came down the gully towards us and said there were other bodies, further up the hillside.

If the people who did this, truly believe that the butchery of farmers, labourers and villagers, in this nowhere corner of Stimlje province, is the way to the creation of Milosevic's 'Greater Serbia', then may this reality burn their lousy souls.

I walked back to our truck in the village square and went searching for the driver.

The journal chronicled a story of organised violence and

brutality. And in trying to act as witness, Daniel had descended into hell. As events unfolded and the pages went by, his notes became less and less structured. The writing more and more distraught. Sentences turned into phrases, then into roars of rage and finally into incoherent, unfinished, distracted, segments of words. Shortly after his visit to Lipojane, Daniel stopped trying to write altogether.

I closed the book and poured another glass of whisky.

So how was Deborah, right now? That was the question. It had been twelve days since she had walked into my office. And I had spent most of that time working in instalments. Going along with ideas as they materialised and leads as they came up. Deborah was so determined to protect Sofie and Daniel, she had achieved what she said she would. Made my job impossible. I was overloaded with information, but it was all sound and fury. Finding some direction out of the noise, had always been the problem. And one that I hadn't been able to solve.

My client was hiding in the city, somewhere. But from what? Or rather, from what now? Dujic and Tudjman couldn't possibly recognise her as Deborah. Could they? And Starratt was now in cahoots with Gloucestershire Constabulary.

And that, was personal. Everybody I had encountered on this case, fervently wanted Lloyd Starratt's bollocks on a skewer. Which certainly wouldn't happen if he gave DCI Benjamin all he needed. Apart from a couple of overnights – at times when he had been brought into a police station for questioning – Lloyd had not spent a single day of his fifty-six years on this planet, behind bars. Which had to rate as a monumental judicial oversight.

The phone rang. Deborah was angry.

"Why the hell are you bothering Sofie and Daniel?"

"Doing what you hired me to do."

"You are supposed to be looking for me."

"And that's what I'm trying to do," I said. "The fact that you're ringing me in such a rage means I'm close. Now I know your connection to Dujic and Tudjman. And a team of Gloucester coppers is investigating their UK operation."

"What operation?"

I ignored her question and ploughed on.

"And that they're using Lloyd Starratt as a conduit. I've seen his five-star hospitality suites."

"This operation, whatever it is," Deborah insisted, "has nothing to do with Sofie and Daniel."

"Do you have anything to do with Lloyd Starratt?"

There was a pause. The mobile connection started to hiss.

"What sort of question is that?"

"Just answer it."

"No."

The line interference grew. Deborah raised her voice and shouted above the noise.

"Consider your job over. Take what you feel you're owed out of the safe at Windmill Hill and stop what you're doing. I mean it. No more."

She disconnected. The line hiss oscillated in my ear. I pressed the off button and threw the phone receiver across the hall. It smashed into the wall, gouged a chunk out of the wallpaper and dropped to the floor, the casing in three bits.

Over and out.

CHAPTER TWENTY-THREE

When you're fired by your client, usually the best thing to do is accept defeat and quit the field. But some cases require more backbone. This was one of them. I contemplated driving over to Windmill Hill and collecting a thousand pounds from the safe, but this next move had to be on my money.

Sunday morning, I was on my way to Southfork at 7.45. I crossed the Severn Bridge twenty-five minutes later and by half eight I was on Starratt land. Given his deal with the police, it was safe to assume Lloyd would be at home.

Southfork was a monstrous piece of self-indulgence. *Footballers' Wives* meets *Dallas*. Clearly a big fan, Lloyd had commissioned his own version of the Ewing mansion. Huge was a fair description, extravagant certainly; but the building had not so much as one ounce of class. The panelled front door was six feet wide and ten feet high, painted white and studded with bolts.

I knocked and waited. Nothing happened. I knocked again. Still no response. No one at home. No servant, no mother Aurora, no Lloyd. I took hold of the ornamental cast iron door ring and turned it. The door swung open. That meant Lloyd had to be around somewhere.

I stepped into the hall. It didn't disappoint. It was octagonal and dominated by a circular staircase, sitting bang in the middle. There were eight doors, one in each straight of the octagon. The floor was tiled black and white. He had obviously paid the tiler a fortune, but I wondered what the artisan had thought about the commission.

"Anyone at home?"

Discounting the front door, there were seven others to choose from. One of them opened in to a storage room, piled with tea chests and cardboard boxes. Another revealed the downstairs loo, again an example of impeccable taste. Black tiles, a gold bath and gold, swan necked taps. Deeply disturbed, I closed the door quickly. Five rooms to go.

One was the door to the study, with of course, the biggest desk Lloyd could have found anywhere. It looked like it was real mahogany at least. Next to the study, was some kind of glory room. Full of pennants, rosettes, and king size trophies for macho sports like 4 by 4 off-roading, truck racing and tractor pulling. That left the kitchen, the dining room and to the extreme left, the door to the living room. I chose to start there.

The white shag pile closed round my shoes and reached up to my ankles. The tan leather furniture suite consisted of a sofa and four armchairs with over-stuffed cushions and big, fan-shaped, shell backs. At the far end of the room, two high backed, wicker chairs sat in front of the French windows looking out across the lawn at the rear of the house.

There was somebody sitting in the chair on the right. At least, there was an arm, hanging over the arm rest and dangling down to the floor. Below the arm, there was a dark stain on the carpet. The stain was dried blood and the hand at the end of the arm was minus two fingers.

Lloyd was roped into the chair, eyes closed; his face as white as the shag pile. And there was more blood, which had seeped out of the bullet hole in his forehead, dribbled down his face and his shirt front. There were bits of skull and skin and brain, sprayed across the chair back behind his head.

I opened the French windows and stepped out onto the lawn, gasping for breath. I bent forward, put my hands on my thighs, dropped my head between my knees and looked down at the grass for a while. The waves of nausea began to wash away.

Lloyd had been tortured and then executed in the same way as Philip Soames. Obviously not by Grant and Copley. This time, the fingers were somebody else's signature. Maybe those whose idea this kind of exercise was originally. Dujic and Tudjman. Who had ultimately decided that Lloyd was a liability? I could see their point. Lloyd had stirred up so much interest in the last few days, he was no longer any use - a low-profile associate.

Fortified, I stood in the doorway and looked at the man again. If this was the work of the Serbs, there must be clues to their whereabouts somewhere in this house.

I stepped around Lloyd, crossed the living room and the octagonal madness of the hall towards the study. Five minutes ago, I had poked my head round the door and noticed the desk. Now, inside it, I discovered something else.

The room was a shrine to Deborah.

There were at least a couple of dozen pictures of her. On the office walls and on the desk. Looking stunning in frocks and heels. At parties and functions. In many of them, on Lloyd Starratt's arm.

I swear I felt my blood run cold. Deborah and Lloyd? In a relationship? No, that was impossible. Surely...

Two photographs set the seal on my minor bout of turbulence. In one, a quartet of people, dressed to the nines were smiling into the camera lens. Deborah, Lloyd, Philip Soames and his partner. In the other, Deborah was pictured, flanked by Philip and Lloyd. I looked at the pictures closely.

In the bottom left-hand corner of both, someone, presumably Lloyd, had scrawled *Mind Care Charity Ball.* The occasion may have been a one-off encounter, but it would have been enough. Even assuming Lloyd knew nothing of Deborah's past, he couldn't have failed to notice that she and Philip had some kind of connection. So later, when Deborah dropped out of sight...

As satisfying as this rationalisation was, it still left me tired and desperate.

The mobile on Lloyd's desk began to ring. I rehearsed my best, gruff Forest of Dean 'yes', then picked up the phone and hit the green button.

The 121 service played a message left three minutes earlier. A strongly accented male voice said, "We are here, as you asked. Where are you? We give you another fifteen minutes."

I pressed the red button.

Dujic or Tudjman? Fifteen minutes to get where?

I put the mobile back on the desk, left the study and went up the staircase, as fast as going round in circles would allow. At the head of the stairs, I took stock. Which bloody direction was I facing?

The first door I tried, opened into the main bathroom. The second, into a pink bedroom with a massive en-suite. A big bath with a door in the side, so there was no necessity to climb up and over and a seat to sit on. Aurora's room obviously. For a moment I wondered where she was, then swiftly dismissed the consideration and went back on to the landing. The next door I opened was the one to Lloyd's bedroom. An inferno, in shades of red and bronze. I don't think I have stood in the middle of anything so gross.

Still, this was no time to diss the design concept. I crossed the room to the huge double casement window and looked out. Dead ahead, beyond the garden, a field with half a dozen horses in it, a stream and another couple of hundred yards of grazing land, was the hedge camouflaging the dog fighting barn. Three quarters of a mile as the crow flies, according to DC Shackleton's smart phone. And from here in Lloyd's bedroom, I could see over the top of the hedge into the car park.

There was a pair of binoculars on the window sill. Big and black, with sixteen times magnification, like the those used by battleship officers in 1950s British war films. Powerful enough to make out the craters on the moon.

I put the binoculars to my eyes and re-focussed them. It took up precious time, but it yielded a result. There was a car in the car park. An ostentatious, designer 4 by 4. The kind of vehicle it is always assumed pimps and hit men drive. And in European movies, ex-Soviet bloc gangsters.

Whatever, the car park was where I needed to be. And there was a gate at the end of the garden.

When I was running seriously every day, I could do a mile in six minutes, on tracks around the Ashton Court estate. Farmland was another proposition altogether. And the stream wasn't user friendly. I took me ten minutes to get to the hedge behind the car park. I arrived, gasping for air, shirt sticking to my back, socks squelching in my shoes.

The foliage was so dense I could barely see through it. So I stood and listened. Tried to imagine the lie of the land in front of me from this direction. The restored barn and its extension was to my left, the ruin and the containers to my right. I chose the latter and began to crab my way around the hedge. Bits of the ruin came in to focus, then dissolved again into a haze of leaves and branches. I came up against the boundary of the field; another hedgerow running back towards Southfork. And there was a gap here, the branches forced apart by the run of some animal. A deer perhaps.

Through the gap, I could see I was right behind one of the containers. In fact that was all I could see. A corrugated steel wall. I ducked, squeezed through the hedge, stood upright and listened. To what passes for silence in the country. The swish of the breeze in the leaves behind me, a cow mooing a couple of fields away, a confused chattering of birdsong and the buzz of a chainsaw somewhere to my right.

Now what?

I didn't want to blunder into the arms of a couple of angry Serbs. On the other hand, there was obviously no mileage in skulking behind a big steel box. So, up and at 'em then...

I shifted to my left, still squelching in my socks and found myself looking across the yard towards the chaser bin door. To the left of the bin, sat the 4 by 4; big and black, with tinted windows. There was no response from inside it. I walked quietly along the length of the container towards the ruined barn and into the space in front of it.

I was alone in the yard. Or so it seemed, from the direction I was looking. I swung round and looked back at the container. It was closed up and locked. The door to the other box was open. I squelched towards it.

Two of the dining chairs inside the container were occupied. Two men were roped into the chairs and their mouths were sealed with gaffer tape. The man on my right, had a bloody hole in his left thigh. He was unconscious. The other man was awake. As soon as he saw me, he began groaning and shaking his head and bouncing in his chair.

Behind me, a husky voice called out, "I was under the impression you had been sacked."

I turned round. Deborah was standing about ten feet away. She pointed over my shoulder, into the container.

"I'd like you to meet Vojislav Dujic and Josip Tudjman."

There was a gun in the hand she was pointing with.

"A Russian Makarov M57," she explained. "Supplied to Serb security forces by the Chinese. I picked it up in Kosovo. It fires eight rounds. There is one in Starratt's head. And one in Tudjman's leg. As you can see, he's the bastard on the right."

For a moment or two I wondered how Deborah had managed to subdue the pair of them. She read my mind.

"I shot him, Dujic tied him into the chair, then sat in that one and did as he was told."

She was calm and cool and as collected as anyone I've met. But there was something wrong about her.

About the way she was dressed, about the way she stood, about the pitch of her voice. There was no carefully applied makeup, the shoulder length hair was now cut short, her breasts were barely noticeable, obviously strapped up. The pink scarf she was wearing when we first met was gone, no longer in place to disguise her adam's apple. Her tight Wranglers had been replaced by workaday men's jeans, the Hogan trainers by soft soled, brown shoes.

She wasn't Deborah. She was Daniel again.

Daniel, steely eyed and concentrated. Taking revenge on behalf of Sofie and her son and the butchery he had witnessed in Kosovo. Because it was he, Daniel, who been there at the time. Deborah was later. A new life, a new person. Light years away from the brutal realities of 2000.

I couldn't begin to guess what sort of psychological state Deborah/Daniel was in. But right now, Daniel was cold as ice.

I heard him from miles away.

"Of course, you know what they've been doing?"

I nodded. Came back to the present.

"I'd be interested in knowing how," I said.

Daniel grinned.

"It's very simple. They are using a route that *MSF* knew all about back in 2000. It's essentially the way Sofie and I came to England. The difference then, was that Sofie had a Croatian passport. She was travelling with a UK citizen. And once into Italy and the EU, we just climbed on a train. The people Dujic and Tudjman are smuggling into the country, begin with Serb passports, at best, and can't get visas because they're on the run. These days, being smuggled into the EU can be less of a risk than waving a forged passport, or being searched, at a European border control."

Daniel pointed the Makarov at the container.

"Trafficking, as well as smuggling."

"There's a difference?"

"Trafficking, is a much more evil business altogether. The end of the journey isn't the end of the story. At best, the immigrants go underground and are left to struggle on as well as they can, without papers or work permits, living with relatives. That's a happy ending of sorts. The unhappy ending is, as you'd expect, much worse. Some illegals never get out of the clutches of the people who got them into the UK. They end up living in shitholes, four or five to a room, working as prostitutes, or rent boys, or worse."

Daniel paused to give all that an opportunity to sink in.

"But it's a risky business to be involved in," he went on. "Too many people on the books, as it were. Plain straight forward smuggling is relatively low risk by comparison. The tricky bit is the journey into an EU country. Once that's accomplished, it's a lorry drive to northern France or the low countries, followed by a short, if uncomfortable, ferry crossing. The current Brexiter crusade this. Border agencies aren't too inquisitive about UK road haulage contractors working inside the EU, if the paperwork is in order. And searching a lorry load of fridge freezers is nobody's idea of preferred work. Smuggling is the high end of this business. And much more lucrative."

He pointed at the Serbs again.

"According to Starratt, he came across them when they switched their UK entry operation from Folkestone to Avonmouth. They changed the MO, began smuggling in fellow Serbs from Brest, instead of desperate Bosniaks and Albanians. Their new clients are one-time members of Molosevic's police and security services, who have decided they're no longer altogether bullet proof. Most of them have money. And Dujic and Tudjman are only two happy to take it away from them. Once they get into the UK, they spend two or three days in a halfway house like this, after which they're delivered into an established Serb community. Where only cream and bastards rise. And where they become the pimps and the drug dealers and the enforcers."

"Lloyd told you all that did he?"

"And then some."

"But only after you had taken the tin snips to his fingers."

"That's what Grant and Copley did to Philip."

"At which point, he agreed to set up this encounter?"

"He called the Serbs from his mobile. I told him to tell Dujic there was a serious problem and they had to talk."

"About what?"

"His percentage. That he wanted a bigger cut. I knew that was sure to bring them here. Starratt was getting ten per cent, by the way. Of ten thousand per head. A lot of money."

The sums weren't difficult to do. Eight beds in each container. At one hundred percent occupancy, that was sixteen thousand for three days hospitality, each time around.

"He said they'd had three successful runs. And they were working on a fourth. Well now, I've put a stop to it."

"You could have helped the Gloucestershire police to do that."

"I could have, yes. And those two might have been caught. And then what? Held in detention for a while perhaps, then deported. Back to Serbia. Where's the justice in that?"

"Is that what you're after?"

"Natural justice is what I'm after, Jack. For Donjica and Lipojane. And for Sofie. Those monsters don't deserve to live. So I'm going to make sure they don't get a chance to."

Daniel swung round, aimed the M57 and fired. A hole appeared in Dujic's forehead. He screamed, jerked in his chair, fell onto his back and died. Daniel fired again. Tudjman's left eye socket blew out. It didn't bother him. He just didn't wake up.

It was over, in the time it took to pull the trigger, re-sight and do it again. Daniel was a hell of a marksman. He swung back to face me.

"Mission accomplished," he said.

I stared at him. Then eventually found my voice.

"Now what?"

Daniel sighed. "It's all done now."

"Not quite," I said. "Tell me about Lloyd Starratt."

Daniel nodded.

"Okay. You deserve an explanation," he said. "Deborah came to Bristol, as she told you, back in April."

Suddenly, Deborah was somebody else.

"Because Sofie had seen Dujic and Tudjman at Cribbs Causeway. It was after she saw them again, with Starratt, at the cricket match, that Deborah figured out what to do. She asked around about Starratt. Then decided he was her way to the Serbs."

I stared at Daniel, astonished at his segue into this third person narrative.

"She got an invitation to a charity dinner at a dinner at the Swallow Hotel. Introduced herself to Lloyd Starratt. And seduced him."

He looked at the expression on my face.

"Why are you surprised? She's a very sexy lady."

I dredged up a response. "That's not why I'm surprised."

Daniel continued as if he hadn't heard me.

"The trouble was, Starratt had no intention of giving anything away. And the longer the relationship went on, the more degenerate and brutal it became. From blow jobs, it was downhill all the way. Into games with ropes and handcuffs and just enough violence to get him excited. That's why it was easy to get him into that wicker chair. A promise of sex with him tied up in it. His mouth watered at the prospect, the fucking degenerate bastard."

I didn't want to hear any more of this. I wanted Daniel to stop talking and give me the gun. Instead, he waved it around in the air, as though he was amazed at the absurdity of everything.

"In the end, Starratt decided he would get even more aroused if Deborah attempted to strangle him."

He stopped waving the gun and looked back at me.

"It's called erotic asphyxiation."

"I know what it's called."

"He told Deborah he had heard that doing this during orgasm, produced a bigger rush than cocaine."

"On occasion, it also produces death," I said.

"Oh yes. And Deborah was seriously tempted. Especially at the moment when Starratt produced his home-made ligature. 'End the bastard's life' she thought. How easier was it ever going to get? The problem was, she still did not know the whereabouts of Dujic and Tudjman. Lloyd Starratt was a pig. A sex addict. A vicious, masochistic deviant. But he never talked about his business. Not once."

"So what did Deborah do?"

"She tried to get out of the relationship. But Starratt was obsessed with her. He went looking for her. Eventually, he remembered the night he had met Philip Soames."

Fine. But Lloyd was in no position to hire Grant and Copley. Way out of his league surely. Lloyd was big fish in a very small pond. Head of the clan sure, but not even a wannabe gangster. With absolutely no track record as a major criminal.

"He simply wouldn't let Deborah go," Daniel went on. "And he was also intoxicated by the cash he was making from his deal with the Serbs. He was beginning to feel like a player. Earning huge sums of money and getting sex the way he liked it. Both were driving him to places he'd never been before. So when Deborah disappeared, he moved heaven and earth to get her back."

He pointed the M57 at the Serbs.

"He took his problem to those two. They introduced Grant and Copley to him."

Who, in all probability, uncovered the scope of their new associate's sexual proclivities and the unpredictability of the rest of the family. And, under orders from the Serbs, monitored Lloyd's progress. All the while encouraging him to believe he was in the driving seat, as the godfather of organised crime in these parts.

Daniel summed up the final chapter.

"In the end, when the Serbs realised that Deborah was impossible to find, they began to imagine all sorts of risks and complications. Which left them with two choices. Either pull out of their arrangement with Lloyd, or slip Grant and Copley's leash. They chose the latter."

"Let's talk about that," I said.

Daniel shook his head and looked away across the yard.

"Philip Soames' torture and murder was a direct result of the course Deborah set herself on," I said. "Therefore, she is responsible. Does she realise that?"

Daniel didn't respond. I insisted he did.

"Does she?"

Daniel turned back to me, eyes blazing; in a moment overwhelmingly angry. He pointed the Makarov at Dujic and Tudjman again and yelled at me.

"Those two sub-humans tortured, raped and butchered their way around the former Yugoslavia. Donji Vragovac, Glavicica, Pocesce, Babic. Tiny places, dots on the map. People blown out of their homes, survivors dragged from the ruins and force-marched to the Albanian border. Then the villages put to the torch. All of this inspired and excused by the most monstrous ideological nonsense since the Third Reich. Milosevic gave them means, motive and opportunity. And left a legacy so out of control, we have come down to this. A couple of ship containers in Gloucestershire,"

Daniel stabbed the machine pistol at them, like he was using a pointing stick.

"Those bastards gloried in the whole murderous business. Well, the glory days are over."

He fired again. The bodies of Dujic and Tudjman jerked in response. I took a step towards him. But too slowly. Daniel squared up to me once more and raised the M57.

"No no. Not yet. I haven't finished."

"Philip's death," I said, going back a few moments, "was more than just an acceptable piece of collateral damage."

Daniel nodded in acceptance.

"Yes... You will never know how sorry Deborah is about the death of her friend. Without Philip, she would not have made it through transition. She would not be a woman. She would not be herself."

"But the decisions she made —"

"All she wanted was to protect Sofie and her son."

"So why didn't she tell me that? Tell me she was really looking for Dujic and Tudjman. Hire me to find them. Not give me all the nonsense about finding her."

"Sofie and Daniel, Sofie and Daniel," he said. "Nothing, no one, is more important."

"Philip Soames sent Deborah to me. She trusted Philip and therefore she should have trusted me. With the whole story."

"No. That would have meant risking the security of Sofie and Daniel."

"But I found them anyway."

"It was not supposed to happen," he shouted.

I raised the volume level too.

"Deborah lied to me!"

Daniel stared at me. We were both silent. I could hear both of us breathing. I broke the silence.

"Deborah set me up," I said. "To do the work she couldn't accomplish. Always intending to exact her own revenge, given the opportunity."

Daniel was struggling with the reasoning here.

"No... The revenge... was my responsibility... Deborah, you see, was in no position to trust anybody."

I counted back over the days. And the timeline made

sense. Philip disappeared on the Friday. On the following Monday, he failed to turn up at his office. His murder hit the news-stands on Monday evening. The next morning, Deborah called me. No longer capable of pursuing her vengeance without help. And she presented one hell of a challenge. Find her. She must have been convinced I would take that on. A much safer bet than trying to talk me into searching for a couple of Serb rapists and murderers."

"All along, she wanted me to flush out Dujic and Tudjman," I said.

Daniel nodded.

"And did she always intend to kill them?"

Daniel shook his head.

"No no. It was me who had to do that. Deborah was never in Kosovo. I was the one, the only one, who could dispense justice."

This was his ultimate rationalisation. And I couldn't find anything to say. Daniel wound the business up.

"Now it's done," he said. "And so am I."

He raised the automatic, pressed the barrel into his right temple, and fired. The left-hand side of his head exploded outwards and he fell to his knees. He looked up at me in mute apology and dropped onto his face.

CHAPTER TWENTY-FOUR

I spent five hours in Lydney, with the Gloucestershire constabulary and a way beyond furious DCI Benjamin.

He didn't believe a word I said. About anything. You know the old saying about banging your head against a brick wall? The best thing about it is when you stop. So I stopped trying to explain and that only made matters worse. In the end however, he had to admit that I wasn't responsible for the collapse of his gold medal bust and grilling me wasn't going to improve the shining hour.

I drove back across the Severn Bridge late afternoon.

First to Clevedon, where I told the story of the last two days to Chrissie and Adam. He listened with his sub-editor's hat on and went into his study to think. From Clevedon I drove to my office, where I worked out what I was going to say to Sofie. I picked up the phone, told her I would be with her in half an hour, ran through what I had devised one more time, then drove across town to talk with her. I kept the explanation simple. Sofie cried, softly and gently, weeping for a dear friend, rather than raging at the absurdity of it all. I sat next to her as she told Daniel that Deborah was dead. He cried too and Sofie held him tight. I stood up to go. I dropped the keys to 15 Grove Road and the envelope containing the Bright Island photographs on the coffee table, and let myself out of the house.

From the Healey, I called Annie Marshall. We met in the *Clifton Coffee House*. She struggled, as I had done, with the re-appearance of Daniel.

"Deborah was not suffering any gender change complications at all," Annie said. "She had done all the hard work. Daniel was way back in the past. She had stopped explaining herself to herself. During the beginning of your new life as a woman, the knee jerk reaction is to try and forget that you have ever lived as a man. And if you persist with that, you struggle. Best to acknowledge the past and move on. Deborah had done that. She had made the biggest decision of her life. One that was physically and psychologically irreversible. She was over it and she was thriving."

Until a fifteen-year-old atrocity came back to haunt her. And hammered into her, a deep-seated fear of what would happen if she ignored it. To deal with it, she chose the worst thing she could possibly do. Go back into the past and confront her demons. And to kill, she chose to pass as Daniel. Deborah was now. The best time in her life. Kosovo was then, the worst time in Daniel's life and it was he who had to deal with the sequel.

Annie picked up the teaspoon in the saucer in front of her and scooped sugar into her coffee. She stirred the coffee. Almost an absent-minded action.

"It was a complicated scheme she worked out," Annie said. "And supposing you hadn't found them..."

"I was bound to do that, eventually. Deborah knew that Lloyd Starratt's contractors would find me if I went to Windmill Hill. And once that happened, I would have something to work on."

"Providing you stayed alive."

"A risk she was prepared to accept."

"She could have gone to the police. After Philip's murder."

"Then she would have lost control of the situation. A

police investigation would have spooked Dujic and Tudjman into disappearing. And that wasn't the desired end result. Everything worked out as planned. Until I found Sofie and her son."

"Which forced Deborah out into the open," Annie said. "And back to Lloyd Starratt."

"As Daniel," I said.

Annie sipped her coffee, then cradled the cup in both hands. "God know what courage, or madness, it took to do that."

I drained my cup of coffee and asked a passing waitress for the bill. Outside the *Coffee House* we shook hands.

"Take care Jack," Annie said. "And call me. Soon."

I promised her I would. She turned away from me, crossed the road and set off along Victoria Street. I watched her until she disappeared into the throng of Clifton village shoppers, then I walked to where I had parked the Healey.

Back in my office, I put all my notes on the case into a buff folder, labelled it 'Thornton' and filed it in the middle drawer of my filing cabinet under 'T'. Actually, straight after the last 'S' – Philip Soames.

The phone on the desk rang.

"I'll be back in Bristol in time for brunch tomorrow," Linda said.

"It's a date," I said.

"A date? You sweet old-fashioned thing."

* * *

There's always a story which comes after the end of a story. Events and their consequences, roll on into sequels. Life doesn't wrap stuff up in tidy conclusions.

The Gloucestershire Constabulary held on to Deborah's body for three days. Bill and Elizabeth Thornton were informed of the death of their daughter. I remembered, like it was yesterday, every occasion during my years on the force, when I had to stand on someone's doorstep, ring their doorbell and ask "May I come in?" Breaking the worst news of all, is never routine, even to the toughest case-hardened investigators.

I called the Thorntons myself to offer my condolences, which were received with grace. And Sofie, the daughter-in-law they had never met, called them. She and Daniel went to visit and Deborah's funeral service was held in Ringsmere.

Adam, Chrissie, Sam, Linda and I headed east too. We loaded ourselves into Adam's Espace and took a charabanc trip to Suffolk a few days later. The welcome was wonderful. Auntie Joyce baked. And Uncle Sid unveiled his latest piece of work.

Changing the Odds

The Jack Shepherd Collection
Volume One

JEFF DOWSON

CHAPTER ONE

The woman I hit turning the car into the lane behind my house, died three quarters of an hour into Sunday April 16th.

"Mr Shepherd..."

I was leaning forwards in the blue plastic chair, elbows on my knees, staring down at the threadbare carpet in the A&E waiting room. I sat up straight, lifted my head and looked into the face of the man standing in front of me.

"I'm David Young," he said. He stretched out his right arm. I stood up and shook his hand. "Supervising doctor this evening." He looked at his watch. "Actually, this morning."

I checked my watch, too.

"I understand you rode here in the ambulance with the lady."

"Yes."

"We had to inform the police, obviously, and there is a Detective Constable on his way here to talk to you. He asked if you would wait." He pointed to his left. "Consulting Room 4 is free. You can talk there."

DC Reynolds arrived ten minutes later. A straight forward sort of copper; brisk and efficient. He asked if I had been drinking. I told him I hadn't but blew into his breathalyser anyway. He looked at the read-out.

"Well that's okay then," he said.

I had spent the last six days checking beaches on the Cornish coast, trying to find a client's seventeen-year-old surfer daughter. Without much success. I decided not to spend another night in another cheap hotel and left Newquay to drive home. The traffic came to a standstill on Bodmin Moor. Up ahead, there was some commotion I couldn't see. I managed to get off the A30, threaded my way through a tangle of B roads to Jamaica Inn, and sat in the Smugglers Bar for an hour drinking orange juice. At half nine, a uniformed PC in bike leathers came into the bar and announced that the road to Launceston was now clear.

It was five minutes to midnight when I swung the Healey into the lane leading to my garage. The headlights panned across the woman a nano-second before she was felled by the front bumper. I got out of the car. She was unconscious and bleeding from a deep cut in her forehead. Her shoulders were corkscrewed to the right and she seemed to be imprisoned under the chassis.

The medics said I had been right not to move the woman. However, as they couldn't work on her where she was, reversing the car clear of her body was actually the thing to do. I did so. The medic kneeling down, looking under the car and lit by the headlights, grimaced.

I took a long look at the woman during the ambulance ride to Southmead Hospital. Mid 50s maybe, her face tired, creased and beaten. She was wearing a long, black woollen coat which looked as worn out as she did. She survived the journey, but died in A&E with multiple fractures and a ruptured spleen.

DC Reynolds apologised for detaining me, and gave me a ride home. He examined the scene of the accident while I stowed the Healey in my garage. He said I should go to the nearest police station when I got up the next morning and make a statement for the record. We shook hands. He watched as I crossed the garden and went into the house via the back door.

I didn't sleep. Or rather, I had short, fractured bouts of sleep, and re-runs of the accident while awake.

After breakfast I walked the few hundred yards to Redland Police Station and explained all to PC Knowles. He gave me my statement to check and asked me to sign it. He told me to expect an interview with the Coroner sometime soon.

I spent the rest of the day trying to concentrate on the surfer daughter case, without coming to any helpful conclusion. I called my clients, carefully suggesting there was no point spending more money. They thanked me for being courteous – I thought I was stumbling a bit – and told me to send them a bill. They were a gracious and gentle middle-aged couple, baffled by the situation they found themselves in, but trying to look ahead in expectation rather than hope. I always feel I'm selling cheap tickets at an inflated price at times like these.

DC Reynolds rang just after 4 o'clock.

"Just a courtesy call, Mr Shepherd," he said. "Apparently, the lady you knocked down was called Lily. She had a silver-plated name tag chain around her neck. The sort of trinket you can buy in any souvenir shop on the sea front at Weston. I thought you might want to know."

"Why was she wandering around Redland at midnight?"

"No explanations yet. The pervading theory is that she was homeless. The case has been passed to Missing Persons. It's no longer the concern of Traffic, but in matters like this, I try to wrap things up as best I can." He apologised for troubling me and then remembered something else. "Oh yes. The lady was missing a kidney."

* * *

Two days later, I had my date with the Coroner. She mentioned the kidney too. The Forensic Pathologist said the extraction had been a skilful piece of surgery. The Coroner's Court recorded a verdict of 'Death by Misadventure'.

The only detective I knew in Missing Persons, was a dedicated misogynist called Hitchens. We had growled at each other a couple of times. He was where he was, because he couldn't hack it in any other department. And he wasn't helpful. He did confirm that Lily was a vagrant of no fixed abode. Not much detective work needed for that analysis.

So I called somebody who knew a lot more about street people than both Hitchens and me.

May Marsh was in her mid-60s and a force of nature. I'd known her husband Bill a long time. May was the patron of several local charities, a thorn in the flesh of committees, city councillors, desk jockeys, time servers, the faint hearted and the poor in spirit. A constant lobbyist on behalf of the homeless and the forgotten. She ran a second-hand furniture shop and a Drop-In Centre in east Bedminster.

A week ago, she had been on *Points West* mixing it with a property developer who wanted to pull down an empty block of flats over a boarded- up pub. The developer insisted that part of town needed a mini shopping mall. May maintained that a community centre and a children's playground was a much better idea. The developer said this was a great opportunity to earn much needed revenue. May asked for whom? The developer side-stepped that and said the site was an eyesore. May agreed, and said that a community centre with a garden on the roof and a playground built out of user-friendly materials would solve that issue. The developer said she was talking nonsense. May asked him if he intended to shop in this proposed mini-mall of his. The developer said he didn't live in the area. May suggested that his only intention was to line his pockets. The developer was outraged at the idea and began to bluster. The beaming news presenter ended the conversation there and handed over to his colleague, who led into the next item.

Two days after the confrontation, the BBC asked May if she'd be the subject of a local documentary. She said no. The astonished twenty-two-year-old researcher asked why. May's response was typically forthright. Not the thing to do. The researcher should have left it at that, but instead suggested that the 'homeless issue' needed to be aired. May said no, it needed to be dealt with; which wasn't the same thing.

The depressed researcher was left trying to think up another 'appointment to view' TV idea.

I told May about Lily. She shared the information with the Drop-In Centre volunteers. None of them knew her, or had heard anything about her. She suggested a couple of other places to try and wished me the best of luck.

Lizzie, the administrator of a Night Shelter in St Werburgh's, greeted me affably enough, but had some questions to ask. On hearing the answers, she phoned May. She sat with the receiver at her ear for a minute or so, then scrutinised me from across her desk.

"Around six feet, I estimate," she said.

"Five eleven," I said.

"Grey eyes, dark hair," she went on.

I helped out. "Forty-seven years old, just under twelve stone, collar size – "

Lizzie raised her hand and went on. "Light brown blouson

jacket, dark trousers, pale blue shirt, no tie."

She listened to the response, thanked May, put the phone receiver back in its base, and smiled at me. It was a great smile and genuinely offered.

"You may not be on the side of the angels, but May says you're alright."

Good to hear, although the rest of the story wasn't. Lily had been a regular visitor to the Night Shelter until four weeks ago. No one had seen her since early March.

Lizzie looked at me, dead centre. "Why are you doing this, Jack?"

"Because I killed her," I said.

She nodded at the phone. "That's not the way I heard it."

"That's the way it was."

"It was an accident," she said.

I was the last person to slip into Lily's broken-down world. Tired and short on concentration. Less than a hundred yards from my garage and counting the seconds to home.

"My job is finding missing people," I said. "Not running them over."

"I'm sorry I can't help you more," Lizzie said. "The Salvation Army might be able to."

I paid a visit to the East City Corps and talked with Captain Rachel Maitland. She listened to the story.

"I know the work you do with street people," I said. "Can you help me with this?"

"We'll do our best."

I thanked her.

"You seem to be on something of a mission," she said.

"It appears to be that way."

"Do you get sentimental, Jack?" she asked.

I shook my head. "I get involved in stuff. I get frustrated

when I can't make sense of what I'm trying to do. My daughter says I get angry at injustice and inequality, both perceived and real, too easily. But sentimental... not usually."

She smiled.

"I suppose you can't afford sentimentality in your line of work. We'll spread the word. Do all we can. Give me your phone numbers and I'll call you. Whatever the outcome."

I walked back to the Healey, wondering if I really was on a mission.

* * *

Four days later, Rachel called me at home.

"No luck so far," she said. "No one we have talked with has any recollection of Lily. I am sorry, Jack. We'll keep asking however."

I spent the next couple of weeks doing pretty much as I usually do when out of work. Gardening, which I'm not crazy about, but which I do because Emily liked the back garden looking the way she had planned and created it – I often feel she's at my shoulder, checking that I'm taking the proper horticultural care. I caught up with Chrissie and Adam, dog sat with Sam, spent time with Linda, watched films on TV, vowed to clear out the cupboard under the stairs but lost enthusiasm for the task the moment I began.

Then Rachel called again.

"We have found a lady who knew Lily. She won't talk to you, but she has given us some information. Lily's full name was Lillian Margaret Barrett. She has a married sister living in Sutton Berkeley."

"By that do you mean the Sutton Berkeley on the old

A420?"

"Yes. The sister's name is Marshall, or Maxwell. That's as close as we got. Apparently, Lily told all one night after she had begged enough money to buy a bottle of vodka. The street person we know said that Lily became falling down drunk and raged about her sister for a long time. Until they both fell asleep in a shop doorway. Does that help?"

"I hope so. Thank you, Rachel."

The Bristol Public Mortuary is southwest of the city, on the old road to Weston. I rang and got hold of a pathology technologist called Irving. He was polite and helpful. And as soon as he realised who I was talking about, deeply sorry.

"The lady was cremated yesterday," he said. "The police and the coroner had ruled that all efforts to find a next of kin had been exhausted."

"After four weeks?"

"I'm sorry, Mr Shepherd," he said. "I will inform the coroner's office of this new development. Perhaps you'll give me the information you have and —"

I disconnected the call, went out to the garage, and took the road atlas out of the Healey.

Sutton Berkeley. One of the richest little enclaves in northwest Wiltshire, just south of the M4. I drove into the village three quarters of an hour later. Called at the village shop and introduced myself to the lady behind the counter. She said there was no Mrs Marshall or Maxwell, but there was a Mrs Maxted. She gave me directions to an imposing three storey house, set back from the road behind a regency red bricked wall. I tugged the bell pull. The bell jangled somewhere way inside the house.

After some time, the door was opened by a tall, attractive woman in her late 40s. She smiled at me. I asked her if she was Mrs Maxted. She confirmed that she was. I introduced myself.

"What can I do for you, Mr Shepherd?"

One of the worst jobs in the world becomes part of a policeman's skillset almost from the moment he joins the force. But no copper, however experienced, takes it in his stride. I can remember every second of the first time I rang a doorstep bell and asked if I could come into the house. And telling a nineteen-year-old girl and her sixteen-year-old sister that their mother had been bludgeoned to death by a crack addict, for the money in her purse.

I asked Mrs Maxted if she had a sister called Lily. She became agitated for a moment or two. Then she nodded without saying anything and beckoned me into the house. We sat down in the living room, or the drawing room, or whatever the fancy name was.

"I haven't seen my sister for twelve years, Mr Shepherd. I have no idea where she is."

"She died four weeks ago. Late at night. She stepped into a lane in front of my car. I couldn't stop. I didn't see her in time."

"Where was this?"

"In Bristol."

Mrs Maxted stared at me for a long time, before she spoke again.

"So close," she said. "Oh God, so close." She sat up straight. "I searched for years. I've lost count of the police officers I talked with, the agencies I employed… And in the end… she was living barely thirty miles away." She stood up. "Excuse me a minute, Mr Shepherd."

She left the room. I stayed in the armchair, not quite sure what I was supposed to do. I looked around the room. The fireplace was white veined marble, the porcelain was expensive and the grand piano was a Steinway.

Mrs Maxted came back with a photograph. She handed it to me.

"The only picture of Lily and me together. Taken fourteen years ago in Westonbirt Arboretum. Before everything began to go wrong. I was thirty-two. She was thirty. And so, so beautiful. She was engaged to Raymond, loved him to distraction, but they had a huge row."

"Raymond?

"My husband."

"What did they row about?"

"To this day, I don't know. He never spoke about it. Neither did Lily. She just grew to hate me. It made things easier for her I guess. She disappeared the day before the wedding and I haven't seen her since. Raymond died last year, after nine months of heart trouble." She looked around the room. "You see how well I live? All the money in the world is not enough, if it can't get you what you need the most."

A little of it might have helped Lily, I thought.

Mrs Maxted apologised. "I'm sorry, Mr Shepherd. You don't want to listen to all this."

Listening was easier then talking.

"How was Lily?" she asked "Did she have friends? A family of her own?"

There were two choices by way of an answer. I opted for the truth.

"She was homeless," I said. "Living on the streets, sleeping in a Night Shelter."

"Oh Lily... Is it possible to see her? No, I suppose it's too late... Is it too late?"

"I'm afraid it is," I said. "She was cremated yesterday."

Mrs Maxted nodded. "I see." She stared across the room. Then turned back to me. "Oh, I'm losing my manners. Would you like some tea?"

I said yes, for some reason. Politeness probably.

"My name is Elaine. I should have said before."

I drank my tea and left an uncomfortable ten minutes later, the last words Elaine said ringing in my ears.

"Thank you, Mr Shepherd."

CHAPTER TWO

At exactly 5.30 on the morning of July 4th, Three Fingers Banducci took a .38 slug in the back of his neck and a nose dive off Pier 13. The receding tide dragged him way out to sea. Four days later, what was left of him washed up on the beach in Summerville, fourteen miles to the south. His funeral was a low-key affair by gangster standards - two cars, half a dozen wreaths, the heads of the three families, and Rocco Gianelli, boss of the Stevedore and Longshore Men's Union, who had set up the hit. His relationship with Banducci was history.

So was my interest in *The Family Affair*. Banducci should have smelled the set up from the other side of the bay. He was huge and slow witted, with an IQ that barely made double figures; but he'd been the Spitaleri family enforcer long enough to be able to put two and two together.

My own fault. I should have stayed with ITV's new 'cutting edge' drama about a murderer out on parole 17 years after chopping up his wife; and now a qualified solicitor, thanks to years studying in the prison library. I didn't mind the premise – as rehabilitation stories go it was promising – it was just that the actor's mannerisms irritated the hell out of me.

I leaned back into the cushions and stared up at the ceiling. The phone rang out in the hall. I levered myself upright.

"Jack, it's May. I need your help. Something's happened to Bill," she said. "Can you come round?"

"Yes, of course."

"Thanks."

She rang off. I listened to the buzz on the line for a moment or two, then disconnected my end. I looked at my watch. 9.25.

I hadn't seen Bill Marsh for five months or so. I liked him. He was sixty-nine. A retired turf accountant. He had been in the betting business since the age of eight, long before the days of legal high street emporia. He worked as a bookie's runner for his Uncle Jimmy; who was run down by a Ford Consul in 1976, after consistently refusing to hand over protection money to a latter-day re-creation of Pinkie Brown. The driver, in turn, suffered the same fate as Three Fingers Banducci. Bill always denied any association with the event. 'The man was foolish', was all that he said. At the age of twenty-seven he took over Uncle Jimmy's business and prospered. I met him and May for the first time, during my days on the force; not long after I made Detective Sergeant.

Bill and May lived in Syme Park on the edge of Clifton Down – home to big mansions and bank accounts. Bel Air in the Westcountry. The uber-expensive domain of the great and not so good. Situated above the Avon Gorge, close enough to the city for residents to eavesdrop on the world below, but far enough away for them not to have to care about it. It has great views, lots of money and its own private police force. I was offered a job, the day after I resigned from Avon and Somerset Constabulary; as Liaison Commander, Street Section B. I thought about it. Emily didn't. She turned it down without a moment's hesitation. She didn't agree with my resignation either, but she accepted the why. I didn't join the police force to shoot anyone. Certainly not a seventeen-year-old out of his mind on angel dust. She said the resignation had substance. Therefore what followed, must have so too. And there was none in spending my time protecting the insurance payments of those who never strove as much as one day for a just cause or the common weal. A private eye could choose which side he was on, and down which streets he should go.

The streets in Syme Park had laburnum hedges, gated security systems and manicured lawns. Downs Avenue was truly exclusive and ran for a hundred and fifty yards to the cliffs overlooking the Avon Gorge.

A pair of stone lions flanked the gate to number 15. The house was set well back from the road and occupied more ground space than the average football pitch. Bill never ceased to enjoy the fact that a man resolutely old-time working class, was living between a High Court Judge and some sort of money juggler, in a house bigger than both of theirs.

I rang the doorbell. Heard footsteps inside the hall.

May called out. "Is that you, Jack?"

"Yes."

She opened the door as far as the chain would allow. Smiling in apology, but frightened nonetheless. She closed the door, unhooked the chain, opened the door again, and took a step backwards.

"Be careful."

I stepped into the hall. And almost into a pool of blood on the parquet floor. I stared down at it. Then up again at May. She breathed deeply, and blinked a number of times.

"Bill's not here," she said.

"Is he expected to be?"

May nodded. "Monday is his night in, my night out. I've been to a meeting in the Council Chamber."

"What time did you go out?"

"Just after 7 o'clock. I got back a few minutes before I called you."

I toured the house. Checked all the bedrooms, dressing rooms and bathrooms. The living room, dining room, library, billiard room, and kitchen. A door in the utility room opened into the garage. The British racing green Jaguar XKR sat serene and quiet and locked. The bonnet was cold.

I found May in the kitchen, looking out of the window into the night. To her right the kettle was hissing and boiling. I moved to it and switched it off.

May turned to me. "Sorry, Jack. I was miles away."

"We should call the police," I said.

"Yes," she said, distracted and unfocused. "I'll make some tea."

Detective Sergeant George Hood was working late. A tough and quick-witted DS on the Murder Investigations Team, run by an old friend of mine, Superintendent Harvey Butler.

"This might turn out to be way below the MIT remit," I said. "But there's a big pool of blood, and Bill Marsh isn't here."

"I'll come and take a look," Hood said. "It's a slow night. And this is something of a novelty. You calling in the police to investigate a crime."

He arrived, wearing a suit that clearly hadn't come from a High Street chain store, with a SOCO, a photographer and PC Eve Laker. She joined May. They drank tea and talked in the kitchen. The photographer and the SOCO went about their business. Hood and I sat, side by side, at the foot of the stairs.

"Have you looked around?" he asked.

"Yes."

"Touched anything?"

I stared at him. He apologised.

"Sorry..."

We both looked at the pool of blood once more, silent for a long time. Holding station like two of the three wise monkeys. Then Hood spoke again.

"I like Bill, he's got style. And his word means something. That's unique in these days of wannabes and second-string crime lords. Pygmies by comparison with Bill, all of them."

That was some tribute coming from George Hood, the 'by the book' copper.

"However..." He turned and looked at me. "I hope you have no intention of getting involved in this."

"I don't know what 'this' is," I said. "No more than a missing persons case maybe. And finding people is what I do."

Although my recent track record was a bit below par. I hadn't unearthed the surfer daughter, and the Salvation Army had found Lily.

The SOCO called from the living room doorway.

"There's something in here you ought to see."

Hood stood up. "Don't move. We have to discuss your concept of private sector involvement a bit more."

He walked across the hall and disappeared into the living room. I got to my feet and walked into the kitchen. PC Laker stood up and moved into the hall. I sat down at the breakfast bar, opposite May. She was silent, a cup cradled in her hands. Two or three months younger than Bill, five feet four, with dark blue eyes, natural fly-away dark hair, and the sunniest disposition anyone was ever likely to encounter. Not so, at this moment, but she was holding on.

"That might not be Bill's blood in the hall," I said.

"Okay, Jack," she said. "But where the hell is he?"

Hood walked into the kitchen. May smiled a greeting and put the cup down in front of her.

"Will you come into the living room?" he asked. "There's something I'd like you to see."

May and I followed Hood out of the kitchen and across the hall, both of us unable to resist a glance down at the blood pool. May paused in the living room doorway. I stepped to her side. Hood moved to the SOCO who was standing by the fireplace. He looked down into the fire grate.

"Will we get anything out of those?"

The SOCO shook her head. "Unlikely."

"What?" May asked. "Those what?"

She moved to the fireplace. Hood gave me his best 'stay where you are' look. I stayed.

"Why did he light a fire?" May said softly. "We never have this fire on," she said. "Bill likes the temperature a couple of degrees lower than most people. So we set the thermostat over there and leave it. Bill never lights this fire..."

The SOCO spoke again.

"Somebody burned something tonight. Letters, notes, something like that." She pointed to the tiny flecks of blackened paper in the grate. "Not exactly a novel. But maybe twenty, twenty-five sheets, at a guess."

I asked if I could step into the room. Hood said that would be okay. I moved to May's side. She took my hand. Hood asked if there was anything out of place. May shook her head. Pointed to the sofa beside her.

"May I sit down?"

"Yes, of course," Hood said.

I sat next to her. The SOCO picked up the conversation.

"Mrs Marsh... Can you tell me your husband's blood group?"

"AB Negative. It's rare."

Hood looked at the SOCO, who nodded in confirmation.

"So how soon can we get an analysis of the stuff in the hall?" Hood asked.

"If I take it into the lab myself, wake up some technician and stand over him while he analyses the stuff, I can let you know within a couple of hours."

Hood nodded his thanks. "Call me on my mobile."

The SOCO and the photographer went into the hall and out of the front door. Hood turned his attention back to May.

"Is there somewhere else you can stay?"

"Why? Can't I stay here?"

Hood chose his next words carefully.

"We're in a bit of a quandary... If the blood in the hall isn't Bill's, it can be cleaned up and Missing Persons will take over the investigation. If it is his blood, then we have to consider more serious matters. And we'll have to do a full forensic sweep of the house before anything is touched. In either case, we'd rather you weren't here. At least until lunchtime tomorrow."

May listened to Hood without a trace of emotion in her face. I suggested she stay with me.

"Yes," she said. "That will be fine. Thank you, Jack." She looked at Hood. "And thank you, Detective Sergeant, for your consideration."

"We'll do everything we can, May," he said.

May stood up. "I'll just get a few things."

"Okay. But PC Laker will have to go with you." He looked at her and raised his hands. "Sorry..."

She left the room, picking up PC Laker along the way. Leaving two detectives, public and private, staring at one another.

* * *

I live in an Edwardian semi in a quiet road in Redland. The first and only house I ever bought. I mean, we bought, Emily and me. I ushered May into the hall.

"This is a comfortable house," she said. "Welcoming."

I hung her coat in the hall and took her suitcase upstairs to the guest bedroom. Downstairs again, I asked May if she wanted a drink. She said no and we sat down on the living room sofa.

"Our first house was half this size," May said.

The remembrance seemed to catch her by surprise. She scrolled back through the years.

"A two up two down, in Bedminster," she said. "We didn't have a bean. Bill had just started working for his Uncle Jimmy – officially that is. And he gave us the deposit."

She breathed in and out. Lost in days gone by and once upon a times. She shivered back into the present.

"I heard the Salvation Army found someone who knew Lily."

It was a useful change of subject for May, so I took up the cudgel. I asked her the question no one had been able to answer so far.

"Why would she be wandering around a well-heeled suburb like Redland?"

"She might have had nowhere to sleep. Or she might not have slept much. Many homeless people spend nights on the move. Some of them have the stamina to walk miles."

"She was a regular in a night shelter," I said. "But she hadn't been there for a while."

"Then something out of the ordinary must have happened in her life," May said. "Sometimes people disappear and we hear no more about them. That's not always bad news. So we hope for the best and try to believe they have had a change of fortune."

The handset rang on the coffee table. I picked it up.

"The blood is AB negative," Hood said. "I'm sending a full team back to the house first thing. I'll have someone clean up the blood, then call you when May can go home. This looks like it might be an MIT matter. I can't stop you working for your client, but be careful that nothing you do ends up with both of us regretting it. In return, I'll keep you in the loop as much as I can."

"Thanks, George."

I relayed the information to May. She looked down at her hands resting on her knees. We sat as though we had settled on this forever. Then May lifted her head.

"Will you try and find him, Jack?"

"Of course."

"Thank you."

I looked at the clock above the fireplace. 10.45.

"You should get some sleep," I suggested.

May stood up, moved to the living room door, then stopped and turned back to face me. It seemed she had something important to say but couldn't recall what it was. I tried to help out.

"May," I said. "At the moment, Bill is simply not at home. Hang on to that. Don't start imagining 'what ifs?' And remember, he's a tough old bugger. Not easily fooled and well capable of taking care of himself."

"All that sounds like you believe he'll walk in through the door at any moment," she said.

"Why not? He might do just that."

May stared at me. Like an illusionist's assistant who knows the trick is a stinker and the audience will see right through it.

"Goodnight, Jack," she said.

I watched her leave the room. Listened to her footsteps as she climbed the stairs. Waited for her to reach the guest bedroom.

And I pondered... Bill was an uncomplicated, sensible man. Not one to disappear taking nothing with him and leaving behind his blood on the floor. So what sort of state was he in? He hadn't packed anything or taken his car. He walked somewhere? No, he was driven somewhere. And then what?

I decided to go to bed too. Picked up the phone, intending to return it to the hall. It began ringing in my hand. I pressed the call button and put the receiver to my ear. May appeared at the head of the stairs, still dressed.

Chrissie asked me how I was. I looked up at May and shook my head. She moved out of sight again. I talked to Chrissie.

"I'm er... doing something?" A faintly ridiculous thing to say.

"What?" Chrissie asked. "Something fun, something good?" Then a little alarmed, she asked. "Something dangerous?... Dad?"

"No no no. May Marsh is here. It looks like Bill has disappeared."

"Looks like? Don't you know?"

I told her the story of the evening. She asked how May was.

"She's scared to death."

"Would you like me to come round?"

"No, don't do that. She's gone to bed. Best to leave her trying to sleep."

"Okay. Call me in the morning," she said. "Goodnight, Dad."

I switched the phone base to silent, took the receiver upstairs with me and put it on a bedside table. The phone trembled and buzzed.

"I'm not calling too late am I?" Linda asked.

"No not at all," I said.

Linda is the sexiest accountant I have ever met. Five feet six, long brown hair, dark blue eyes and great legs. She has the office next to mine; on the third floor of a red brick converted tobacco warehouse by the river. Linda's fellow accountants work in the city's business quarter in serviced executive suites and hold conferences in well upholstered meeting rooms. Linda is smart and funny and constantly being head-hunted, but she is comfortable with her surroundings, has an appreciative client list, and no desire to labour among the denizens of tofu Bristol. She was, before Emily died, one of her closest friends. It took eighteen months for us to acknowledge the relationship that was growing between us. Currently, we were still exploring the possibilities.

I asked her if she was at home.

"No, I'm still in London. Meetings went on all day. I'm going to stay here tonight, with my brother. Just wanted to hear your voice before I go to bed."

"That's good to know."

"How was your day?"

"The day was alright. The evening's been something of a kicker."

"Why?"

I told Linda all I had told Chrissie.

"And you're going to help, of course," she said.

"Of course."

"Okay. But at least, contrive to stay in one piece until I get back."

"Will do."

"I love you," she said. "Goodnight."

I lay awake for an hour or so, listening to the sounds of the house. On the other side of the wall, I heard May crying. Eventually I slept.

CHAPTER THREE

I woke up at ten minutes to eight. Miserable and uneasy. I usually manage to park such first moments in the section of my brain which doesn't keep nagging at me. Not so this morning. I got out of bed, showered, which helped a bit, but not much, and met May in the kitchen. She was boiling an egg.

"I hope that's okay," she said.

I laid another place on the kitchen table. She took a long look at me and asked if I was alright. I reflected that under the circumstances the counsellor in this situation ought to be me. I tried to brighten up.

"Yes," I said. "Coffee or tea?"

"Is the coffee real?"

"Absolutely."

The egg timer buzzed. May scooped the egg out of the pan and into an egg cup. Transferred the egg cup to the table, then sat down. I sat down opposite her. She picked up the tea spoon and tapped the top of her egg, levered it off, and looked at the yolk inside the shell.

"It's a bit runny. I should have left it boiling a few seconds longer."

We finished breakfast. I went out and bought a newspaper. May found a copy of Kate Atkinson's *Case Histories.*

"Is this a good read?" she asked when I got back.

"Yes," I said. "It's about a private detective. I like to keep an eye on the competition."

May smiled. She sat on the sofa. I occupied an armchair. Began with the sports section of the *Guardian*, which seemed the lightest read to concentrate on. I read and re-read the headlines, but didn't get into the copy. On the sofa, May shuffled and changed position a number of times.

I thought about Mrs Maxted. I picked up the phone and dialled Irving. Apologised to him for rudely ending the conversation last time we talked. He said that was alright. He had discovered that Lily's ashes had been scattered in the Garden of Rest at South Bristol Crematorium. I rang Mrs Maxted and gave her the information. She thanked me.

George Hood called just after 11.30.

"The team is finished here," he said.

"Find anything?"

"Nothing out of the ordinary. A series of finger prints. Two sets all over the place, which must be from Bill and May. And odd ones, here and there, we could pick up somebody known to us."

"What odds would Bill give you on that?"

"Let's hope we get to ask him," Hood said. "The bloodstain has been scrubbed out of the parquet. May can go home now. And tell her, we have a lot of people working on this."

* * *

We stepped, somewhat nervously, into May's house. Both of us looked at the place where we thought the bloodstain had been. A kind of memory reflex. There was nothing at all to see. George Hood's cleaner was someone to be recommended. The house was exactly as it should have been. Except that Bill wasn't there.

May took her suitcase upstairs. I took a look in Bill's office.

It was clearly signposted 'this is Bill's space'. As ordered, neat and tidy as his range of bespoke suits. With a huge modern lacquered desk, matching two-drawer filing cabinets each side of it, a big swivel chair behind it and five grand's worth of leather corner sofas with a lacquered low table inside the L. On his desk was a fabulous Victorian silver and glass standish and a Versace crystal Medusa paperweight. Christ knows what Bill had shelled out for those.

In my twenty-one years as a detective, public and private, I have encountered a boat load of premiership hard cases; rich beyond the dreams of avarice, living in staggeringly expensive faux mansions with a conspicuous lack of style. But not Bill. He may have started his working life as a bookie's runner, but no one could deny he had class.

The desk drawers weren't locked, because there was nothing personal or secret in them.

The filing cabinets were unlocked too. Names and addresses, letters and faxes and email print-outs, went back ten years in some cases, basically covering the decade since Bill sold his business. But there were no secrets, no diaries, no hidden agendas. Except for a note, paper-clipped into the Y folder behind half a dozen sheets of Y business. A list of nine or ten digit numbers and letters. Passwords probably. There was no trace of a laptop or a mobile. With Bill somewhere, I presumed. Unless...

I walked back into the hall. Above me, May arrived on the landing, clothes changed and considerably refreshed. She moved on down the stairs, a new resolution in her body language. I asked if she had a spare key to the Jaguar. She collected it from a small wooden box, on the wall by the front door.

I found Bill's mobile in the arm rest console between the

front seats of the Jaguar, and his laptop under the passenger seat. I took both pieces of hardware into the office and returned to the kitchen. May was making a second round of breakfast coffee. She had also written me a cheque. She slid it along the work surface.

"I want to retain your services for a few days."

I picked up the cheque and looked at it. A thousand pounds.

"I'm not taking this."

"Yes you are," May insisted. "You charge 250 a day, don't you?"

"Not to you," I said. "This is too much."

"Not for Bill," she said.

I slid the cheque back along the work surface. May shook her head fiercely.

"I want you to work on this, to the exclusion of all else. So take that cheque. Go on. Put it in your wallet." She looked straight into my eyes. Her voice dropped almost to a whisper. "Please, Jack…"

I reached out and gathered up the cheque again. I asked her if she knew the lock code for Bill's mobile.

"3344," she said.

"Is Bill in good health?"

"A slight blood pressure problem, but that's all?"

"And he hasn't appeared worried or stressed recently?"

"No. I would have known if he was."

I unlocked the mobile. It offered two voice messages from Len somebody. 'Call me, it's urgent,' he said. The first time at 4.20 yesterday afternoon, the second at 5.35. I asked May if she knew who Len was.

"No idea," she said. "Sorry."

I found the outgoing calls log. One only. The previous

evening to a mobile; timed at 6.54. If there were others, they had been deleted. May peered at the phone display.

"So is that this Len bloke's number?"

"The timing's right," I said. "Could be that Bill called him back after the second message."

I pressed the recall button. The line was live, but Len didn't answer. I heard the first eight bars of *The Magnificent Seven* title theme, before his voice interrupted.

This is Len Coleman. Leave a message. Short and sweet.

"Now what?" May asked.

"I think you should invite to someone to stay with you."

She nodded. "My friend, Helen. She likes Bill and we get on well enough when we're together."

I had met Helen half a dozen times. She was five years younger than May. Widowed eighteen months earlier, having already won her own battle against breast cancer. Her terrific sense of humour had survived the surgery and the long nine months she spent nursing her husband. Like May, she had truckloads of passion and determination. She lived on her own in Bedminster; three streets away from the house she was born in.

"I'll call you regularly," I said.

"Thank you, Jack."

Armed with Bill's mobile, laptop and list of passwords, I set off sleuthing. In the direction of Trinity Road Police Station and Detective Superintendent Harvey Butler.

* * *

Harvey was coming along the corridor to my left as I stepped into the building. The slow, rolling gait is deceptive. Although he carries a kilo or two more than he should, he's lighter on his feet than any man I know. Harvey is probably the best copper in town. Tough and clever and so straight it hurts. He was a dead ringer for head of the Murder Investigations Team when it was re-structured four years ago. The drawback was having to report, more often than he wished, to a group of uniformed officers with scrambled egg on their caps. As to private investigators... he regards them mostly as vigilantes, and at best, wayward knights errant. We have remained friends however down the years – since the shooting and my acknowledgement that I was never going to be a career copper.

We shook hands, but he was grumpy. I asked him what was wrong. He led me along the corridor.

"I am a man under siege, Jack. The new ACC has an obsession with high profile policing. You've probably seen him on TV recently, speaking on behalf of the new order. Two days ago, he stole my top inspector to head up his new Task Force. Squeezed the budgets of every department in the building to pay for these buggers. And for some reason, he keeps inviting me to attend meetings about 'the challenges of a new age of policing' - whatever they fucking are."

He reached out and opened the door into the MIT squad room.

"Meanwhile the members of this elite mob are charging around my manor like a bunch of designer commandoes."

He led the way across the room to his office at the far end. We sat on opposite sides of his desk, drinking coffee. Eventually, he leant back in his chair and asked me what I was after this time. I looked as hurt as I could. Harvey pointed at the carpet with his right hand and traced the distance between me and the door.

"A well-trodden path, Jack."

I decided it would be best to get straight to the point.

"Len Coleman..."

"Never heard of him."

"He may be on your database nonetheless."

"What does he do?"

"I've no idea."

Harvey sat up in his chair and placed his elbows on the desk.

"Is that the sum of your rehearsed plea? Or do I get to know anything else?"

"He might have been the last person to speak to Bill Marsh last night."

"Ah... You want the public purse to pay for part of your current investigation."

This was another well-trodden path.

"I just need his address, Harvey."

He looked me straight in the eyes. Hood walked into the office, picked up the vibe, turned and walked out again. Harvey called him back.

"Len Coleman, George?"

Hood doubled the length of the pause, before he responded.

"Never heard of him."

Harvey beamed at Hood, then at me. "There you have it. We know not the man."

I decided getting thrown out was better than getting nowhere.

"Come on, both of you. This tired routine is all bollocks." I pointed at the screen on Harvey's desk. "PC, keyboard, tap tap, database. The work of moments. I'm simply asking the guardians of law and order to help a council tax payer."

Harvey looked across the office to Hood. "Fun this, isn't

it?"

"Unhelpful is what it is," I said.

Harvey grinned. "What the hell... Find out what you can, George."

Hood left the office. Harvey changed the subject.

"How's Chrissie? Did she decide to do her PGCE?"

"Yes, she did. Two thirds of the way through it now. Bloody hard work."

"She'll make it," Harvey said. "She's got the genes. Stubbornness, persistence, grit, bare-faced cheek... Want some more coffee?"

Five minutes later, Harvey, Hood and I knew as much as the police computer. Len Coleman, aka Leslie Chisholm, aka Laurence Charlton, was a con artist with a Maths degree. Since achieving his majority, he had done three stretches at Her Majesty's pleasure, totalling seven years. He was now in his 60s, and free and clear since 2008. The database said he was living in a garden flat in Bishopsworth.

CHAPTER FOUR

That was bigging it up somewhat. It was a two-room basement with a bit of lawn out the back.

I rounded the corner of the house as a man a couple of inches taller than me, stepped out of the flat doorway. Long grey coat, fair hair, dark eyes, slim straight nose. He wiggled the 9mm automatic he produced from inside his jacket, advising me to get out of his way. I was about six feet from him. I dropped my head, lunged forward and met him hard at the base of his ribcage. The breath left him in a mighty rasping wheeze. Back-pedalling furiously, he came up against a big stone planter with some sort of mini tree in it. He fell backwards but managed to swing his body away from the planter. I landed on top of it, chest first. The tree collapsed, my ribs made contact with the rim of the planter and I slid head first into a big green plastic bin.

For a nano-second I felt okay. Then the pain arrived and washed all over me. My heart began thumping and breathing was agony. I rolled onto the lawn, taking a long time to focus. By the time I got to my knees my assailant was hovering over me, a chunk of stone in his hand. He smashed the automatic down on the back of my neck, the pain switched to the base of my skull and I slumped face down into the grass.

The man slipped away.

I rolled onto my back, stared up at the sky and waited for my heart rate to slow down. My ears were ringing, and what vision I'd had a few seconds ago, was lost in a haze. My back, neck and shoulders hurt like nobody's business. There was a pain under my left eye. I probed gently at the spot. No injury, no torn skin, but I could feel a bruise already under way. I closed my eyes and lay still for a while. When I opened them again, the view out of my left eye was in cinemascope.

I turned my head and squinted towards the garden flat door. It was open and glass seemed to be missing from the top half of it. A few moments staring, gave rise to the conclusion that, as I was here, and not responsible for the breaking and entering, I might as well go into the place and explore.

I got to my feet, swayed, regained my balance, and aimed myself in the direction of the door. The glass from the top half of the door was lying in segments and shards on the hall carpet. The far end of the hall opened into the living room. There was one door on the left-hand side of the hall, the bedroom maybe, and two doors on the opposite wall – kitchen and bathroom, if I was right with the first assumption. I stepped into the hall, my shoes crunching the glass into smaller bits.

In the kitchen, I turned on the cold tap stuck my mouth under the spout and sucked in gulps of water. I straightened up, breathed deeply, and looked around. The kitchen was small, but graced with furniture and appliances way above the price range of B&Q.

The bathroom was actually a mosaic tiled wet room, with an expensive German shower system. I ran some water into the wash basin and splashed my face.

The bedroom was a small slice of Arts and Crafts style. William Morris was undoubtedly the inspiration for the wallpaper. An iron framed bed with a gleaming brass headboard sat between two oak bedside tables with a leaf design carved across the faces of the drawers. The same design was matched by the doors of the wardrobe standing against the wall opposite the foot of the bed.

The living room was clean and tidy. Oak floorboards, and minimalist modern furniture ordered from one of the weekend colour supplements. Unlike the others, this room was totally without character. No personal stamp anywhere. No pc, no personal papers on the desk in the window alcove. Nothing declaring that the place was the home of Len Coleman.

Other than his body lying on the floor, in front of the fireplace.

I crossed the room and looked down at Coleman, flat on his back on the hearth rug. His head lay on one side, a lumpy, bloody mess where his left ear should have been, holes gouged out of his cheek. In spite of the damage done to him, he was still recognisable from the picture on the police computer.

I groped for the mobile in my jacket pocket, found it, and called George Hood.

My head was beginning to clear. So, Len Coleman... Hardly a major villain, judging by his criminal history. Living low profile at an address which would attract no attention, although furnished with a serious amount of money. Clever. I sat down in an armchair by the window. Felt better staring at Len from a distance. There was a single, heavy, brass candlestick sitting on the left end of the mantelpiece. No companion piece on the right – the murder weapon maybe. If so, it was sensible of Coleman's killer to take it away with him. Better than washing it in the kitchen sink and leaving it here. I gave up thinking about it, leaned my head back and closed my eyes.

Hood, a female DC, and two uniforms, arrived ten

minutes later.

"This is more like it," Hood said. "Us finding you with a corpse at your feet. Did you do this?"

I stared at him. He grinned, and introduced the woman standing next to him.

"This is DC Holmes."

There was moment of silence. As if we were all on QI and trying not to say the obvious. I thought what the hell…

"I suppose everybody calls you Sherlock," I said.

Holmes looked at me as if she had a headache.

"My friends do, Mr Shepherd."

Hood grinned again. He pointed at my face.

"You're getting a bruise there," he said.

He handed me over to DC Holmes and went for a prowl around the rest of the flat. She looked into my eyes. Hers were green.

"Do you know Len Coleman?"

"Only as a corpse. We haven't actually met."

"But you had arranged a rendezvous?"

"No."

Holmes squinted at me. "I've been told about you, Mr Shepherd. A fully paid-up member of the awkward squad."

I decided as she was on Harvey Butler's team, and therefore a smart copper, I'd help all I could. Which wasn't much, unhappily.

"All I know about Len Coleman is what the police database kicked out." I looked across the room. "I came here hoping to talk to him."

"About what?"

"A friend of mine." I gestured towards the hall. "Your boss will tell you about him."

My jacket pocket began ringing. I looked at Holmes. She nodded at me and turned back to Coleman. I thumbed the mobile receive button and raised the phone to my right ear.

"Have you had lunch?" Chrissie asked.

"Not yet."

I looked at my watch. Just after 1 o'clock. Chrissie issued an invitation.

"We're all here. Adam's working at home this afternoon."

Adam is a senior journalist on the Bristol Evening Post. He is twelve years older than Chrissie, who was nineteen at the time she informed Emily and me she was moving into Adam's house. I made my position clear. A rushed and ill-considered response, which sparked a series of family rows and ended up with Chrissie moving anyway. Throughout the nonsense, Adam sensibly stayed in the background and let us get on with it. Within days, Emily was diagnosed with cancer, whereupon all the wasted energy of the previous weeks paled into insignificance. It was clear Adam would run into an inferno for Chrissie if he had to. And he was at her side during the eight months it took Emily to die. There had been some talk recently of getting married as soon as Chrissie left university.

"I'm just finishing up here," I said. "I'll get to you as soon as I can."

I spent another fifteen minutes answering questions about the tall man and the assault. Holmes looked aggrieved when Hood dismissed me.

"Mr Shepherd will make a statement at Trinity Road later," Hood said. Then looking at me, he stressed every syllable in his next sentence. "He can be trusted to do that."

* * *

I discovered more bits that were hurting as I eased myself

into the Healey. Everything above my waist basically.

Forty minutes later, I pulled up outside Adam and Chrissie's house – one of twenty in an impressive Victorian terrace on Dial Hill in Clevedon. I had stiffened up during the journey. Getting out of the car proved to be as painful as getting in. Upright I was okay. I walked slowly up the garden path.

The house greeter is hairy, a little over two feet high, with four legs, matchless enthusiasm and boundless energy. Sam the Bearded Collie is five years old and a stunner. He began barking when I rang the bell and didn't finish until we were lying on the carpet in the hall and I had him imprisoned in a head lock. I let him go. He reversed away from me and sat down, panting like an idling traction engine, delighted with the tussle we had just had.

Which was more than I could claim. Getting up from the floor was no easier than getting out of the Healey. Chrissie watched this manoeuvre, then studied the bruise developing nicely below my left eye.

"What have you been doing?"

I told her. About the tall man, but not about the corpse.

"Jesus Christ, Dad!"

She shook her head and retreated to the kitchen. Sam followed her.

Adam ushered me into the living room. He is always the perfect host; welcoming and disarmingly urbane – qualities I don't readily associate with journalists. The three of us concentrated on the meal. I had no clue as to the assault that was to follow. I was enjoying Adam's cognac when he volunteered to make the coffee and disappeared into the kitchen.

Chrissie was up to speed in seconds. "Are you ever going

to learn?"

I stared at her. "The risotto was terrific," I said.

She grimaced, opened her mouth to go on. I beat her to it.

"May and Bill are old friends. I have to find out where he is, and if he is alive."

"Which entails, of course, fighting with strangers on garden flat patios."

"Not necessarily..."

Her exasperation boiled over. "I mean, look at the state of you."

"Late 40s, straight backed, all my own teeth..."

"Shit, Dad. You look like you've just done two rounds with Joe Calzaghe."

No argument there, but logic has no emotion. And emotion was driving this discussion. Both sides of it. We were stamping on old ground, and dangerously close to the kind of face-off we thought was consigned to history.

"Finding people is what I do," I said. "And May and Bill are almost family."

"No. You and me and Adam and Sam are family." She stared straight into my eyes. "Please stop this. You are an investigator, not a brawler."

"Oh come on, Chrissie, it doesn't happen every day."

"No, but it happens. You take on too much, Dad. You shoulder other people's burdens and you give yourself away by the shovel full. Are your clients really so deserving?"

"If we waited until people were deserving, the world would go to hell."

A needlessly smart remark, and with reason, not well received. The cushion from the chair next to her frizbee'd its way across the room. I caught it.

"Howzat?" I appealed.

Chrissie yelled in frustration and began throwing at me everything she could reach. I raised my arms to my head. Three magazines and a paperback from the coffee table bounced off my elbows. I was trying to make myself as small as possible in the chair, when she picked up the glass paperweight which had slid off the table and onto the carpet. I looked up at her.

"The proverbial blunt instrument."

Chrissie looked at the paperweight and then at me.

"One day," she muttered. "One day…"

Adam came into the room as if nothing was going on, put down a tray of cups, nodded cheerily at me, and reversed into the hall. Chrissie retrieved the book and the magazines, picked up the cushions one by one, then sat down again and glared at me. I felt I ought to respond to all this. Chrissie intercepted the move.

"Don't. Not a word. Clever or otherwise. Give May her money back and leave this to the police."

I shook my head. "I can't do that."

Adam arrived with the coffee. He sat down at the table and grinned at us.

"Help yourselves," he said.

Chrissie picked up the coffee pot. Put it down again and left the room.

"Do you take sugar?" Adam asked. "I never can remember."

* * *

Chrissie and Sam went out for a walk. I finished my coffee, thanked Adam for his hospitality and left too. The argument with Chrissie had been all too familiar. We should have moved on. I should have moved on. Emily had got us back together. She would have despaired had she witnessed that re-run after lunch. Must do better Shepherd…

I slid into the Healey and drove to my office on automatic pilot.

CHAPTER FIVE

The building, a one-time tobacco warehouse, has five floors and sits on the north side of the Avon, facing the river and backing on to the Cumberland Basin. Inside, the bricks have been steam-cleaned. The reception space is friendly. There are big sofas and low tables sitting on the re-constituted flagstone floor. And the inevitable huge Yuccas to give the place a sense of 'green'.

Jason was on duty at the security desk. Recently a sports student at Bath University and a brilliant kayaker, he missed qualification for the 2014 World Championships by eight-tenths of a second. He joined *Harbour Security* to help pay off his student loan, while he figured out what to do next. He started training three hours a day alongside his eight-hour shift. Then his employers woke up to the possibilities. Bought Jason a Renault Espace with piles of interior space for his kit, and a roof rack big enough to carry two kayaks. He went to north Wales and trained six hours a day. In Rio, he aced the prelims and missed silver by just 2.65 seconds. The European Championships were eleven months away, so he was currently in light training and back at reception. Unfailingly polite, smart and funny, he was a real asset.

He handed me three white envelopes with windows in them.

"Have a nice day, Mr Shepherd," he said.

I took the lift up to the third floor. The doors opened in front of me like a pair of curtains doing a reveal. Once again, I slid into discussion with myself about the sense in having some place to work I didn't really need. When Emily was alive and Chrissie was living at home, *Shepherd Investigations* was evicted from the spare bedroom. Linda announced that the office next door was empty, so I moved in. An arrangement no longer necessary, now that I had the house to myself.

I unlocked the office door. It was a good shift psychologically. The place looked, felt, and smelled like a workspace. Therefore, as I said to myself the last time we shared this dialogue, *Shepherd Investigations* operated better from here.

Which in turn led me back to the current commission. This case had all the ingredients for a grade A unhappy ending. Often, missing persons don't stay missing for long. They turn up again within days. Sometimes they just want to say "I'm fine I don't need you anymore." Or worse, "I've found someone else." Sometimes they turn up dead however, having left a pool of blood on the parquet floor.

I put Bill's laptop on my desk and switched it on. It fired up and demanded a password. As the first one needed each day, maybe it was top of the list on the Y file notes... The desktop opened. In seconds the laptop was mine to play with.

I spent a couple of hours going through Bill's files.

There seemed to be no direct line to anything remotely nefarious. No names of hard-line villains I had heard of, although there was a character or two I wouldn't spend time with by choice. I got the impression that a lot of stuff in these files had been deleted and the hard copy shredded. Or burnt maybe, in the living room fireplace.

I opened the envelopes in my post and threw the contents into the waste paper bin at the side of the desk. I checked my own laptop. Nine emails, none of them to do with work of any sort. I created a new file and labelled it Bill Marsh. I made some notes on the day so far, and saved them on a data stick.

* * *

I have a place to go when I can't make sense of anything.

Emily's memorial stone lies in a quiet corner of St Edward's churchyard, underneath a three-hundred-year-old yew. I coasted to a stop by the lych gate, at the end of a lane lined with beech trees, slid out of the Healey and looked around. In the stunning peace and quiet, it was hard to believe that the clamour of the north end of the city was only a few hundred yards away. I opened the lych gate. The daffodils were over and the tulips were clinging on to another day's welcome sunshine. There was the rich, sharp smell of new mown grass.

In memory of Emily 1969 to 2015.

I looked at the stone, fringed with grass cuttings. I knelt down and brushed them away. Emily was my life and my strength and my motivation for twenty-three years. When the cancer took her, I was totally lost. What saved me was her voice. Telling me I had things ahead of me I had to do. She was the love of my life; still in my heart and head, chastising me every time I appeared ready to give up.

We talked for a while. Then I said goodbye.

I stepped through the lych gate again, and got back into the Healey. I glanced in the rear-view mirror. A sporty looking silver Audi nosed into the lane and glided up behind me.

I stayed in my seat and watched the driver climb out. He was big. Bigger than he had seemed in Len Coleman's garden. He moved alongside the Healey passenger door and in the process, blocked out the light. I waited to see what would happen next. He opened the door, bent down a couple of feet and looked into the car.

"May I speak with you, Mr Shepherd?"

"About what?"

"Please get out of the car."

Behind me the Healey sagged on its springs as something weighty dumped itself onto the boot. My interlocutor spoke again.

"Pretty please…"

I opened the driver's door and slid out of the car. When I stood up, I was able to confirm the man was three or four inches taller than me, and considerably wider. I looked back to the rear of the car. His associate, who appeared to have no neck, grinned at me from a face which sat on his shoulders like a beach ball in a trough in the sea.

The man at the passenger door asked for my attention again.

"Mr Shepherd..."

I turned back to him. His neck was solid, like a racing driver's. But then, he looked strong all over. And his smile was a revelation. He beamed at me, by way of some truly expensive dental work.

In return, I tried to be gracious.

"We didn't have time for introductions last time we met," I said.

He smiled again. "My name is Smith."

I turned to the man sitting on the boot lid. "And you must be Mr Jones."

By the passenger door Smith said, "He's called Smith, too."

"Ah," I said. "The Smith brothers."

"You're obviously going to keep us in stitches," Smith Two said.

"I'll try."

I turned to face Smith One. He reached inside his jacket. I froze. He produced a large white envelope and passed it across the roof of the car. He didn't have to stretch at all. It seemed he had long arms too.

"What's this?" I asked.

"Ten thousand pounds," he said.

I took some time over the next sentence.

"And what do I have to do for this ten thousand pounds?"

He smiled again. The sunlight flashed on his teeth.

"Nothing," he said. "My employer simply requests you do absolutely nothing."

"And who is he?"

Smith One gave a shrug of regret. I looked at the envelope in my hand. Time to be resolute.

"Well, 'nothing' is a problem," I said. "You have to be careful with 'nothing'. 'Nothing' can take you over. Then where are you?"

To my left, Smith Two sighed deeply.

I looked at him. "Difficult, is it? This concept?"

He pulled a .45 automatic out from under his armpit. Obviously…

He stood up and the car rose on its rear springs. He stepped back, took his time, aimed the .45 at the rear window in the soft top and pulled the trigger. The roar was deafening, even in the open air. The bullet went into the car through the plastic rear window and out again through the windscreen; leaving a hole in the centre of it and the rest of the screen opaque, a web of jagged lines barely holding it together.

Smith One spoke. "My apologies…"

He took a couple of steps to his left, bent down and retrieved the spent cartridge case. Experienced and careful.

"Mine too," I said. Stretched over the top of the car and handed the envelope back to him. He shrugged once more and returned it to his pocket.

"The offer won't be made again," he said, emphasising every word, and slammed the Healey passenger door.

The damaged windscreen disintegrated, showering glass over the front seats. The Smiths walked back to the Audi. The car reversed along the lane, swung to the right, disappeared for a moment or two, re-appeared, drove past the lane end and out of sight again. I cleared the driving seat of as much glass as I could, eased myself carefully into the Healey, turned on the ignition, and looked into the rear-view mirror. There was a neat, round hole in the plastic, about half an inch in diameter and right in my eye line.

I drove home with the wind stinging my face. In the house, I called *Autoglass*, ran a bath and eased myself into it. The bruises from my first encounter with Smith One were now well established. But the twenty-minute soak helped a bit. The man from *Autoglass* arrived half an hour later, apologised for being so tardy, and explained it had taken a while to find a match for a Healey windscreen. He nodded at my face and asked if I had walked into something. I thanked him for his concern, guided him through the house, out of the back door, and pointed him in the direction of the garage. Where he installed himself and set about his business.

At 4.15, I was sitting in my living room contemplating the latest turn of events. After not coming up with ideas on how to improve the day, I decided I'd had enough of it.

I made some coffee and switched on the TV. It came into life tuned to Film 4. The afternoon western was into its fifth reel and too confusing for me to pick up. On BBC1, a middle-aged couple from Rotherham, in search of a haven by the sea, were failing to get interested in an 80s built bungalow in south Devon. On BBC2, a man in the Methodist Hall in Ely, was offering the *Flog It* porcelain expert a hideous piece of Moorcroft for his assessment. I left them to it and looked elsewhere; and realised that people were dealing all over the medium. Antiques dealing, *Dickinson's Real Deal, Deal or No Deal...* I tried Five. Another film was on offer. A US made for TV movie, about a woman trying to drive her stepson insane – for some reason I failed to grasp – underscored scene after scene, by a relentless music track. In the meantime, ITV1 had changed programmes. But sticking firmly to the demographic, the channel was now re-running a fifteen-year-old episode of *Poirot*. I've never been a fan, so I went back to the western a second time. The hero was dying of his wounds on a dusty street, while the mayor was making the townsfolk ashamed of what they had let happen.

I was contemplating diving into the mire of cable offerings, when the man from *Autoglass* called to me from the kitchen. He said the screen was now fine, but there was nothing he could do about the rear window. He scrutinised my insurance certificate and agreed all was in order. I wrote him a cheque for £55 and he took his leave.

I called Mr Earl.

His grandfather had arrived in England on the *Empire Windrush* in 1948. So two generations later, Mr Earl is now twenty-five percent Jamaican and seventy-five percent south Bristol. Laid back and totally unfazed by the complexities of the world around him, he lives above his car workshop in a cul-de-sac in Southville, with his wife Alesha and his son Hamilton. Each time he presents me a bill, Mr Earl shakes his head sadly. But I've had the car fifteen years. Too late to chastise myself for holding on to it.

"Hi there, Shepherd Bra," he said. "Healey broken down again?"

I described the hole in the soft top rear window and asked if he could repair it.

"It needs mending with a new one," was his deadpan response.

"But in the meantime...?" I asked.

"Stick a piece of Sellotape over the hole," he said, in all seriousness.

"Can't you accomplish something a little more robust than that?"

"Hang on," he said.

There was a clunk as he put the phone receiver down. Somebody was banging something in the background and I could hear Bob Marley singing *No Woman No Cry*.

Mr Earl came back on the line.

"I've got some toughened plastic here, and some heavy-duty adhesive. Bring the Healey in first thing."

"Thank you," I said.

"You're welcome," he said and rang off.

I switched on the 6 o'clock news and found myself plugged into an ongoing litany of misery. The top story was hard to watch; another scenario from central Africa, which was unfixable because nobody but Bob Geldof and Richard Curtis and their friends cared enough to tackle the problem. An all too familiar sight of young children dying because adults put greed, crossing the road to the other side, and 'why the hell do I have to care?' before simple compassion. By contrast, the second item bordered on farce; a cabal of UKIP leaders, broken down MEPs and a gathering of right-wing Hungarians, with yet another reason why Europe wasn't working.

I went into the kitchen to find something to cook. I looked across the garden into the gathering dusk. The clocks had embraced British Summer Time three weeks ago. It had been a bright, sunny afternoon and dusk was only now making an effort to close down the day. I trawled the fridge and the kitchen cupboards and decided on chilli.

My mobile rang. I found it in the inside pocket of my jacket, draped over the newel post at the foot of the stairs.

"Where are you?" Linda asked.

"Home."

"I've got one chore to do here in the office," she said. "I'll be with you in the next half hour."

The bath earlier, may have improved how I felt, but not the impression I was giving. I stared at my reflection in the hall mirror. The bruises on my face were livid enough to frighten a class of mixed infants. I put the thoughts of chilli to the back of my mind and made some more tea.

The front doorbell rang. Linda greeted me with a smile as I opened the door.

"I left my key at home, not used to the..." The smile morphed into a grimace. "My God! What have you been doing?"

I moved to one side. Linda stepped into the hall and I closed the front door. She pointed at the bruises.

"I've got them round my ribs too," I said. "Mr Smith did that. And his friend, also called Mr Smith, shot a hole in my car."

"He did what?"

"Well actually, he shot a hole in the back window, but the bullet went straight on and -"

Linda interrupted me. "Stop. Stop... Somebody shot at you?"

"Not me, the car. Smith Two did it, because I turned down an offer of ten thousand pounds from Smith One."

"I don't believe this."

"That's probably best."

"No, Jack. I mean that you – "

"Yes. I know what you mean. It was just a warning shot."

"Who from?"

I told her I had no idea, and regaled her with the events of the day. She stepped forward and wrapped her arms around me. I winced. She unwound herself and stepped back.

"I came here for a bout of un-bridled sex," she said. "And I find you in no fit state to join in."

"I'll be alright lying down," I suggested. "If you do all the work."

"How many times have the sisters heard that, I wonder?"

CHAPTER SIX

I woke just before 8 o'clock with a twenty-four carat headache. The bruises on my cheek and across the left side of my ribcage were now glowing yellow and purple. I found some codeine in the bathroom cabinet, took as big a dose as the bottle label would allow and stepped into the shower.

As I emerged from the steam, the sun came out. I gingerly towelled myself down in the warm light refracted through the bathroom window.

Linda was still asleep. I unhooked a pair of jeans and a shirt from their coat hangers in the wardrobe, picked up a pair of socks and my gardening trainers, and left the room, avoiding the creaky floorboard in the doorway. I dressed in the kitchen, opened the back door and walked into the sunshine. I sat down on the garden bench, raised my arms and looped them over the back rest, lifted my head into the sunshine and closed my eyes. The lead in the morning chorus was a blackbird, singing the sweetest heart stopping song.

Somewhere in the distance a phone rang.

I slipped into another 'how far have we got?' moment and struggled a bit with it. There was no answer in the discovery department; although some ground had been covered in the menacing and beating up departments. While Len Coleman was dead, and no help at all.

Linda's voice rescued me. I looked towards the house. She was standing in the kitchen doorway, dressed in blue jeans and matching shirt. She called to me.

"Adam rang a couple of minutes ago."

I got up off the bench and walked towards her. She looked terrific and I told her so. She said 'thank you'. I took the phone receiver out of its cradle on the kitchen wall and called Adam's mobile.

"I'm at the *Post*," he said. "Got your pc switched on?"

"No. Why?"

"Get to it. Google newspost dot local dot co dot uk slash Bristol. You're the headline this morning."

"What?"

"You, and Bill Marsh. Take a look. I'll stay on the line."

I went upstairs to the PC on a desk in the small bedroom. A minute later I was reading the post. *Prominent Syme Park Millionaire Disappears*, the headline yelled, *Private Eye Discovers Blood In Empty House*. And there were pictures. A recent one of Bill at a charity function and lower down the page, a grainy blow up of me, taken God knows where and when.

"Where the hell did they get all this from?"

"Don't know. No one here has a clue as to the source."

"Will newspost dot whatever know who is responsible?"

"Probably not."

"Will they care?"

"No. They cherry-pick from thousands of emails they collect, then upload them. No names no pack drill, no editorial, no taste, no concern for the truth."

Adam paused. I was thinking. He continued.

"I expect the paps will get onto this soon. Stay at home until you work something out. Then call me. I'm not doing this story, but I'm about to be swamped by scribblers asking questions about you."

"Where's Chrissie?"

"She's in some school somewhere, on a teaching placement. I'm going home around 1 o'clock to spend the afternoon with Sam. Talk to you later."

The doorbell rang. It was Angela, the post person. She took a step backwards as I opened the door. My bruises and I must have been lunging with intent. I apologised for surprising her. She recovered, stretched out an arm and offered me a padded envelope.

"Too big to go through the letter box," she said.

I took it from her, backed into the hall and closed the door.

Linda made toast and scrambled eggs. I opened the envelope. Dug out four catalogues, courtesy of a group of companies I had indicated an interest in receiving mail from, apparently.

"Did you?" Linda asked. "Indicate an interest."

"Not that I recall."

"That's the problem," she said. "You respond to some deal from somewhere, and then it begins. You surface on some supplier's database. And within days, the whole bloody retail world assails you with offers you can't refuse. And you can't stop the bastards. Because the manufacturers are based in Holland, the stuff is made in the Philippines, the telesales department is in Minnesota and the customer services department is in another fucking inaccessible place altogether."

I stared at her.

"I've never heard you rant first thing in the morning. Should I log this away and beware?"

"Oh yes…"

I examined the paperwork. There was a country clothes catalogue; full of hunting and fishing garments with special pockets for gun cartridges and tins of bait. Introductory offers on garden rotavators, strimmers and chainsaws from *Great*

Country Gardens. And two holiday brochures, with the strap line *Sensational Singles Holidays in Thailand and Malaysia.* Basically, for sex tourists. A cut price opportunity to exploit young women, young men, poverty and moral misery without any noticeable attack of conscience.

Linda asked me if I was going into the office.

"I'm going to see Mr Earl first," I said.

I escorted her to the front door. She leaned into me, let me take her weight and enjoy the smell of her.

"Later," she said.

I opened the door. She glided out of the house and swayed down the path to the front gate. Fabulous...

* * *

"That's a bullet hole," Mr Earl said.

I couldn't deny it. He shook his head sadly.

"Go and get some coffee. Come back in half an hour."

Alesha was behind the counter of the *Soul Food Café* across the road. Like Earl, born and brought up in south Bristol; mother to their son Hamilton and the beating heart of the family engine. She was known by everyone within a half mile radius, and no one spoke ill of her. Tall and slim and darker skinned than Mr Earl, everything she did seemed to have a purpose. And you couldn't see the joins. She went about her daily business seamlessly, through excitement and joys and crises. She handled those imposters all the same. And she brewed the best pot of coffee in the city.

Labi Siffre's *Something Inside So Strong* was playing on the café CD player.

Alesha smiled, stepped out from behind the counter, embraced me, and sat me down in the window facing the street. Labi Siffre segued into Jimmy Cliff and *You Can Get It If You Really Want*. The man at the next table tapped the soles of a pair of battered Hush Puppies on the laminate floor. He nodded at me and smiled. I had a second cup of coffee. The man swayed in his chair along with *The Harder They Come*.

Back in the workshop. Mr Earl told me the repair would last for a while, but I ought to consider saving up for a new hood. I dug my wallet out of my jacket. He waved it away.

"Not worth opening the till for," he said. "Next time will do."

There was a message on my mobile. May asking me to call her. I did that when I got to the office. She told me she had found Bill's wallet.

"In the pocket of an old blue fleece he wears every morning when he walks into Stoke Bishop for his newspaper. Sergeant Hood's team missed it."

I asked what was in it.

"Sixty pounds in notes," she said. "Co-op Bank debit and credit cards, his bus pass, his Senior Rail card, and his *Silver Star Casino* card. He's been a member for years. Some of his old mates are too. He's there twice, maybe three times a month. Could this help?"

"It could, yes. Are you okay?"

"Fine. Helen's here. She just supplied the journalists at the gate with tea."

She ended the call.

There was something about the *Silver Star* that rang a bell. I'd never been in the place, but now the name was in my head. I googled the casino. Moments later, the website sprang into life. And so did the hairs on the back of my neck. The owner operator of the establishment was Frederick Arthur Settle.

Not one of nature's noblemen, Freddy. A genuine south

Bristol hard case. An expert in all aspects of law breaking, menace and violence. With a deft side-line in jury tampering. I arrested him, in the days when I was a DS, for extortion and aggravated assault. The trial lasted three days. The jury was out for all of thirty-five minutes. Settle walked and the CPS got a bollocking from the judge.

What the hell was Bill doing in such company? He was once in the gambling business himself, and he could afford to lose a little here and there. But I could feel a stirring of panic, mixed with a dose of anger. Those moments happened, usually under stress. And Freddy Settle could manufacture other people's stress in his sleep.

Whatever... All conjecture was ludicrous. I would have to pay him a visit. Freddy Settle. Christ... Why would any person in his right mind, regardless of his profession, bravery or foolishness want to confront Freddy Settle? The outcome of any direct encounter was pre-ordained. But forewarned is forearmed, and other platitudes – how the hell was I was convincing myself of this? Surely, if I was polite and didn't diss his soft furnishings….

For some reason, I showered, changed into lightweight trousers, put on a clean white shirt and a cream linen jacket. Maybe because I was calling on money. Maybe because I was a hell of a detective and cool as Sonny Crockett. Or maybe because, in lightweight clothing I was less likely to sweat.

CHAPTER SEVEN

The Silver Star, converted from a row of two storey quayside workshops, sits on Welsh Back.

The place looked very ordinary in the afternoon sunlight. A man in jeans was waving a wash leather at the street level windows. I asked him if the Boss was in. A pair of watery blue eyes looked at me from each side of a broken nose. He grunted and said he thought I might find her in the office.

Her...?

I was still distracted by this revelation when I bumped into an old acquaintance inside the foyer. Smith One. The bearer of ten thousand pounds, on behalf, it was now clear, of Freddy Settle. My heart rate began to soar.

"Mr Shepherd..." Smith One smiled graciously. "I'm sorry, but we are not open for business this early in the day."

"I appreciate that. But I would like to talk with the Boss if I may."

He considered the proposition. Decided it might be possible, and moved to a phone on the wall to the right of a pair of huge padded doors.

"This is Gareth," he said. "Shepherd is here."

I left him to his conversation and looked round as he talked. The foyer was a handsome art deco statement and designed with some imagination. The door to my left opened. A cleaner pushed a trolley full of brushes, cloths and cleaning materials over the threshold. I had time to look into the room behind her. The bar, as sumptuously art deco as the foyer.

The cleaner pushed her tools across the floor. I opened the door she was heading for, stepped into the gaming room and waited for her to pass by. She thanked me. I surveyed the room. More art deco.

I heard Gareth speak to me. "This way, Mr Shepherd..."

He beckoned me back into the foyer and pointed up the staircase. A polished wooden handrail swept round the white walled curve, supported all the way up, by a series of interlocking art deco motifs. The stairwell was lit by an oval skylight in the ceiling at the head of the stairs.

"Gareth what?" I asked.

"Thomas," he said.

"And your partner?"

"He really does have the same surname. We call him Dylan. He doesn't get the joke and we haven't explained."

He waved me on up the staircase. Dylan appeared on the landing and waited as I climbed up to him.

"Good afternoon, Shepherd," he kind of grunted.

It was a few steps to a walnut, zigzag patterned door, with the name 'Settle' on it. Dylan knocked on the door, opened it and ushered me into a large sitting room. A redhead, wearing a dark blue silk shirt and designer jeans flowed towards me. She held out her right hand.

"Frederica Settle," she said. "You can call me Freddie." She shot a look over my shoulder. "Thank you, Dylan."

I heard the door close behind me. I couldn't take my eyes off the hostess. The coolest of cool elegance. Mid 30s, five feet nine, long legs and sensational dark eyes. She turned her attention to me.

"I know. Dylan doesn't ring out 'enforcer' does it? But he likes it. So we all refrain from taking the piss."

She smiled. I smiled back.

"It's a pleasure to meet you, Mr Shepherd."

"You can call me Jack," I said. It seemed best to enjoy the informality while I was still in a position to do so.

There were two sofas in the centre of the room, with a low satinwood table between them. She waved me to one of them. I sat down, lower than I had anticipated, and was embraced by the soft cushions. Getting up out of the sofa again swiftly, should the need arise, would be difficult.

"Can I get you a drink?" Freddie asked.

"No, thank you."

She moved to the other side of the table, dropped into the sofa, relaxed, raised her right arm and rested it on the top of the cushion behind her. Crossed her left leg over her right and waited while I looked around me. This room was the best of the recce so far. I'd always believed that Freddy Settle wouldn't recognise taste if it wrote him a cheque for a million pounds. It looked however, like he'd spent close to that in here.

"It's not exactly my style," Freddie said. "I prefer lean looks and clean lines. But Dad likes it."

"Where is he?"

"He's retired. I'm the Boss now. You're surprised of course."

I had to admit I was. But pulled myself together sufficiently to qualify the consideration.

"Not that you're in the job, specifically. Rather, that Freddy has managed to produce such style and refinement. I include you in that assessment of course."

"Benenden and the LSE," she said. "I was born into this business and groomed to run it. It's not about threats, broken kneecaps and protection any more, Jack. Those days are consigned to retro TV. This is a motivated, creative, high investment company. Dad's money wasn't wasted. This is where we both want me to be."

I couldn't think of anything to say. Freddie moved things along.

"Now what can I do for you? I was given to understand that you and my associates failed to get on."

"A question of ethics, Freddie."

"That's how I heard it. Still, you're here now."

"Why did you offer me ten thousand pounds?"

Freddie pasted the smile back on her face and crossed her right leg over her left.

"Do you really expect me to answer that?"

"I guess not, but I am a detective. I'd fall short of my job description if I didn't ask."

"And you'll also understand why I don't feel disposed to explain. Suffice to say, I'd hoped you'd look upon it as a windfall and accept."

'Less is more', is an often-tested concept. This lady was the best at it I'd ever come across. So, clinging on, I changed the subject.

"How are you on other information?" I asked.

"Okay, probably."

I tried the intro I had rehearsed.

"Len Coleman," I said.

"Who?"

"Len Coleman," I repeated. "He was a member here."

"Was he?"

Freddie stared at me. I managed not to blink.

"Okay," she said. "Let's see..."

She stood up. Moved to her desk and reached for the phone. Pressed the speaker button on the base. Then a couple of numbers. Somewhere in the building, a man called Cyril answered the call.

"Yes, Ms Settle..."

"Cyril, do we have a member called Len Coleman?"

"Give me a moment."

"Of course."

A moment later, Cyril came back with the answer.

"We did. He's no longer with us."

That was open to many an interpretation. Freddie also in the moment, grinned at me.

"Since when, Cyril?"

There was a beat. Which turned into several bars rest. Freddie and I waited. Cyril came back to us.

"He was invited to renew his membership last month. As yet, he hasn't done so."

Freddie looked up at me. "Do you want to ask him anything else?"

I talked to the speaker. "No. Thank you, Cyril."

"Is that all, Ms Settle?"

"Yes, Cyril. Apologies for disturbing you."

She ended the call. "There you have it."

I managed to get to my feet, squeezing out of the sofa's embrace. Freddie had all the time in the world to stretch a restraining arm.

"Is that all?" she asked. "Surely not. There must be something else we can help you with."

She said that with consummate seriousness. I couldn't help but stare. Then she smiled again. She was really good at this stuff. I allowed myself to assume she was unlikely to summon Gareth and Dylan to rough me up in her office, and risked one more question.

"Why was Gareth at Len Coleman's house?" I asked

"Was he?"

For a moment, it looked like she was about to do another

phone check. But no. If ever there was a dead horse getting a good kicking, this was it. The interview was officially over. She crossed the room, pressed a button on the wall beside a chunky sideboard with overlaid swirls on the doors.

"Any time you want to risk a few notes come back and see us. Free membership for you of course."

"Thank you. But I can't afford the losses."

"The downside of the detecting business," she said. "Prospects few and far between."

The Settle firm knew all about prospects. There were people propping up motorway intersections who did too. The door opened and Dylan came back in.

"Please see that Mr Shepherd is escorted off the premises."

Dylan nodded, stepped to one side and motioned me to the door. Freddie, now once again uber-gracious, bade me farewell.

"I'll give your regards to my father," she said. "I'm sure he will be interested in how you are. Take care now."

An image of her father grinning at me from the dock in Bristol Crown Court, was seared onto my retina.

"I'll do my best, Freddie," I said.

Dylan escorted me back to the head of the stairs, where he pointed to Gareth waiting for me at the bottom.

I stepped out into the sunlit street, shaking from head to toe. I walked to the Healey, fished the keys out of my pocket and dropped them on the pavement. I picked them up again. Fumbled them into the door lock, got the door open, climbed in and sat behind the steering wheel, my heart thumping.

CHAPTER EIGHT

I drove to the office, picking up a sandwich and a salad on the way. In the lobby, Jason handed me an envelope with a note in it.

"Ms Barnes said you were not answering your mobile," he offered, by way of explanation.

I read the note. Linda was off to Plymouth, not likely to be back until late evening. She suggested I meet her at home in Portishead. For which, I now had a door key, and about which, I wondered from time to time.

I was married to Emily for twenty-two years. The relationship was exclusive from the day we met. Emily was... Emily. Unique. Linda was altogether different. She was taking time and care to build the relationship we were currently embarking on. But I was still dithering.

I took the stairs up to my office. Made some coffee in the kitchen along the landing, ate the food and fell to talking the situation over with myself.

Bill had disappeared without his car and his wallet. The plan Bill and Len had worked out, had gone to rat shit in the face of intervention by a person or persons unknown. The musing was interrupted when the phone on my desk rang.

"What do you know about Walter Cobb?" Adam asked.

Walter Cobb... Entrepreneur, impresario, football club director, and scrap metal merchant. Alleged to owe money all over the county in guise number one, implicated in a series of concert ticket scams in the second, derided in equal measure as idiot and buffoon in the third, and richer than Bernie Ecclestone courtesy of the fourth. Bristol's original kipper-tied wide-boy. More old-fashioned chancer than serious villain. Something of a poker player however. Legend has it he won the scrap business in a game of five card draw one night, in a motel out on the A38. There is a stonking caricature of him, complete with medallion and chest wig, adorning one side of the only gentlemen's public convenience still functioning in Southville. His sworn enemy on the city council fought for years to prevent the cleansing department clearing it up. Now the work of art is something of a landmark. *"How do I get to Ashton Gate?" "Second left and straight on past Walter Cobb."*

"I know as much about the man as anyone else," I said.

"Can you meet me?"

"Haven't you got to get home?"

"No. Chrissie and Sam are doing their weekly hospital visit. This evening, it's the Oncology department at the BRI. Sam's a star. Shows off like the clappers and the patients and staff love him to bits. I'll meet you at the Nova Scotia in fifteen minutes."

The pub is a short walk from my office. It sits on the Cumberland Basin dockside at the western end of the floating harbour. It's a place to drink and eat, a rendezvous, and a harbour ferry stop. Old and comfortable inside, with tables and seating on the dockside for summer days and lazy afternoons. The sun was warm enough to sit outside. Adam bought the tea. I thanked him and opened the conversation.

"So… The local hero we were talking of earlier."

"Indeed," Adam said. He raised his cup, took his first sip of tea and went on. "Walter Cobb is about to go broke. Spectacularly. No business, no dosh, and soon, in all probability, no roof over his head."

"Refreshing to know, but er..."

"Indulge me for a minute. Tomorrow morning, everything he owns is being taken away from him. The Bailiffs will be in by noon."

"How do you know all this?"

"I've seen the paperwork. Courtesy of his PA. A lady called Bridget Dean, who by all accounts has kept Cobb's business afloat almost singlehanded in recent years. He owes her four months' wages. Which in itself is not the problem, Cobb has been short of readies before. But this time, he's been paying his personal bills, with money Bridget put into the company. So, understandably, she's mad at him."

"Okay…"

"Yes, sorry. I'll get to the point. A swift eye cast across the paperwork reveals the list of major creditors. Among them, Bill Marsh."

"How much is he owed?"

"A little short of fifty-two thousand."

"Christ…"

"And meanwhile, according to Bridget, Walter was in hock for a time to the *Silver Star Casino*. The owner-operator of which, is the one and only Freddy Settle."

He waited for me to respond to the last sentence. Expecting me to turn a whiter shade of pale and shift in my seat. But I had already done that bit.

"No it's not," I said. "The place is now in the hands of his daughter, Frederica." Adam stared at me. "She says I can call her Freddie."

Adam struggled to find something to say. I moved the conversation along.

"Bill is a *Silver Star* member," I said. "I went there earlier today."

Adam, amazed at the idiocy of such a move, managed one word. "Why?" Then added another four. "For God's sake why?"

"I wanted to get a feel of the place," I said.

"Feel of the…"

He lapsed back into speechless. Took in air and blew out his cheeks.

"I know it was a little ill-advised," I said.

"Actually, not to be advised at all," he said.

We both took time to contemplate that. Adam spoke again.

"So come on. Explain."

I gave him chapter and verse. He listened without interrupting. At the end of the story he went back to the subplot.

"Well, Walter ought to be a breeze after Freddie," he suggested. "There should be no threats, real or implied, from a man who glories to such an extent in the image he pedals, that he's happy to allow himself to decorate a bog wall."

"How bright is he?" I asked. "Really."

"Bright enough at poker. Bright enough to get by, until now. What I mean is, he's not a total buffoon."

I must have looked at Adam in disbelief, because he elaborated.

"Just don't think he's a pushover. His hyper-opinionated, on the edge of foolishness schtick, hides a devious, lying get. Think Boris Johnson."

* * *

The headquarters of Cobb Business Ltd was situated in Whiteladies Court, a four-storey building of serviced offices across the road from the BBC. Inside the entrance hall, a man behind a marble desk pointed me at the doors of an exclusive lift. Inside, there was one button only. Top Floor.

I stepped out of the lift into the top floor lobby. A blonde with blue eyes and a brunette with hazel eyes were stationed behind a huge walnut desk. Hazel Eyes was wearing a telephone head set and attempting to pour oil on troubled waters.

"I'm sorry, Mr Satchell. Would you like to speak to Bridget?"

Blue Eyes smiled at me. "Can I help you, Sir?"

"I want to see Mr Cobb," I said.

"I'm afraid he's just gone out," she said.

"How long will he be?" I asked.

She looked to her left for assistance. Hazel Eyes wound up her conversation.

"No… I'm very sorry… Please do. Goodbye, Mr Satchell."

She pulled off the head set. "Dear God!" Then she registered my presence and apologised. "I beg your pardon."

I told her not to worry. Blue Eyes helped out.

"This gentleman wants to know when Mr Cobb will be back."

The brunette sighed. "I'm sorry, Sir. I'm afraid I have no idea."

"Then I'll pop in and see Bridget," I said.

Hazel Eyes pointed across the lobby. "First left along that corridor, Sir."

A brass plate on a walnut door said *Bridget Dean*. I knocked on the door. There was no response from the other side. I opened the door and stepped into an office about fifteen feet square, with a suspended ceiling, hidden lighting and more walnut furniture. There was no sign of Bridget. The door which I assumed to be her access to Cobb was closed. I walked across some extremely expensive carpet and opened the door. Something weighty zoomed past my head and on into Bridget's office. A second later it hit something which crashed to the floor.

"Oh God I'm sorry," Bridget said. "I could have killed you."

Five feet two or three, with cropped auburn hair, she was wearing a white tee shirt, blue jeans and trainers. She was breathing heavily and she looked fierce in spite of the apology. She was standing behind Cobb's desk; a monster piece of walnut like the desk in reception, in front of a huge window with a view across Whiteladies Road. Bridget seemed to be ransacking the place.

"Forgive me. I thought he was back."

"You should have taken a moment to check," I suggested.

"Yes, I'm really sorry."

"Where is he?"

"He's gone out, the fucking shit."

That assessment chimed with all that was known about him.

"He just sacked me. Do you know that?"

It seemed discourteous not to ask why. So I did. Bridget shook her head ferociously then stepped back and slumped down into the chair behind the desk.

"None of your business," she said.

I took time to look round the office. It was a bit of a mess. I asked Bridget if this was her work. She confessed it was. I asked her what she was looking for.

"Something expensive. He owes me something expensive?"

"Did you find anything?"

"I think the bronze I threw at you was it. Do you fancy a drink?"

"What has he got?"

"No not here," Bridget said. "I wouldn't drink his whisky if I was dying of thirst. Over the road."

She led the way out of Cobb's office.

The franchisees of the eateries, bistros and bars on Whiteladies Road change often these days. We sat facing each other across a table in a window booth in *Brunel's Bar* – all velour covered foam and laminated surfaces. A couple of months ago, the place was an overpriced restaurant called *Filippo's*. When I used to spend money here, three or four years ago, it was a pub called *The Engineer.*

Bridget had downed her first house cocktail, now she sipped at her second. I was drinking a glass of beer and taking a long look at her. She knew I was doing so but she was clearly confident enough to let that sort of thing happen. I guessed she was around the same age as me. Her hair colour came out of a bottle but the rest of her looked absolutely genuine.

"Is there a Mr Dean?" I asked.

"No," she said. Sipped at her cocktail again. "Okay… Who are you?"

"Jack Shepherd," I said. "I come to you via Adam Leslie. He's my daughter's partner. I'm a private detective, looking for a friend. He may have got involved in some deal with Walter."

"Presumably Walter owes him money."

"Yes."

"And his name? A straight swop. In complete confidence," she said.

"Bill Marsh."

Bridget sighed and sat back in her chair. "I remember. Fifty something thousand pounds."

"Yes. That's what Adam said."

"I like Bill," she said. "I've known him since he took over his Uncle Jimmy's business. He gave me a job when I desperately needed one. A bit of a wide boy, not entirely straight, but proper south Bristol."

"How long have you worked for Walter Cobb?"

"Almost ten years."

"That's long enough to get close."

"Close...?" She looked as if I'd just asked her to eat something foul. "If by that you mean close enough to second guess his every move, to tidy up the wreckage he leaves behind him, to smile at the people he needs to impress, to side track the people he needs to dodge. I know the business version of him inside out. But close? Nobody gets close to a man like Walter Cobb. His daughters knew that better than anyone."

"Where are they?"

"Lauri is dead. The other two are in New Zealand. That's the farthest away you can get, before you start coming back."

"So what's going on over the road?" I asked.

"Nobody was paid last month," Bridget said. "Walter's broke."

"That's just relative," I said. "There's a difference between broke and over-extended. People like him are always short of cash."

"No, really. He's flat broke. Bust. Down and out. He owes money all over the city and beyond."

"How much money?"

"A few hundred thousand."

"Is he going to survive?"

She snorted. "*Cobb Business Ltd* isn't. But there's no doubt Walter will get by. There'll be something stashed away somewhere."

I asked Bridget where Walter lived. She gave me an

address north of the city, near the M4. I asked for his telephone number. She recited it to me. I logged it.

"Aren't you going to write it down?" Bridget asked.

"I don't need to. I remember numbers."

"Just in case however…"

She called a waiter over, borrowed his pen, asked for a page from his order pad and wrote on it. She passed it to me.

"Mine. And my mobile," she said, looking me straight in the eyes.

"Thank you," I said.

There was a pause. Then Bridget wound things up.

"Just remember this. Walter fucking Cobb is as cold as the Russian Steppes in February, and slippery as a boatload of eels. Be careful."

She downed the rest of her drink and stood up to leave. I let her go and watched through the window as she crossed Whiteladies Road.

CHAPTER NINE

Late afternoon now. Whiteladies Road was gridlocked. And there was only one way to go; onwards and up to the Downs. It was twenty minutes before I cleared the traffic, and 6.30 by the time I turned the Healey into Smallwood Avenue. The lane was two hundred yards long or thereabouts and led straight onto Cobb's front drive. The black and gold painted cast iron gates were open, so I drove on through and parked the Healey behind the Bentley in front of Cobb's garage doors. The house was a mock Tudor affair; half-timbered and hideous.

Cobb had seen me arrive. He opened the front door before I reached it. He was shorter than me, but heavier. Late 50s maybe, greying hair, dark eyes, and a moustache which would have looked better on just about anybody else. He wasn't in a good mood.

"Who the hell are you?" he asked.

I told him.

"A journalist?"

"No."

"I mean, look," he said. "The fucking excitement's over. I'm going broke and that's it. End of."

"Maybe not," I suggested.

He ignored that and asked what I was doing on his doorstep. I told him I wanted to talk with him about a mutual friend.

"Who?"

"May I come in?"

He must have decided he wasn't over-burdened with things to do. He stepped back and waved me into the hall. Floor to ceiling dark oak panelling. And a misguided attempt at a country house staircase, which began on the left and wrapped itself around the hall as it rose upwards. Cobb ushered me into what he must have considered the drawing room. It looked just like the hall, the mock Tudor motif continuing to run riot. The fireplace took up most of one wall. Somebody had made a list of period features and installed them in all the wrong places.

"So... The money's all gone," he said.

"Do you care?"

He glared at me. "What the hell is that supposed to mean?"

"Simple question," I said. "Are you upset?"

"Of course I'm fucking upset."

"I ask that, because you may also be taking the friend I mentioned with you."

"Yeah? Who?"

"Bill Marsh."

Cobb grinned at me. "Dear oh fucking dear... Hardly. Bill Marsh could buy my debts three or four times over."

He looked for a moment, as if he was weighing up the pros and cons of throwing me out. Instead, he asked if I wanted a drink. I told him 'no thank you'. There were two padded armchairs facing each other in front of the fireplace. He sat down in one and pointed me to the chair facing him. I chose to stay on my feet. He shrugged, settled back in the chair cushions and stared up at me. There was a long pause. He gave up first.

"So... How is Bill?"

"I'm not sure," I said. "He's disappeared."

He looked blank. Scrunched up his face, like a child making a big show of thinking. I asked him where he was on the previous Monday night.

He smoothed his face out. "Can't remember."

"Try."

He sniffed. "Alright, I was here."

"Were you alone?"

"Unfortunately."

He waited for me to go on. Looked confused when I didn't. Then the phoney politeness suddenly evaporated. Cobb stood up and pointed at the living room door.

"Right, that's it. I've had enough. Get out of my fucking house."

I did. As I walked to the Healey, Cobb yelled at me from the doorway.

"And fucking stay away!"

I reversed through the gateway, U-turned, coasted a few yards along the lane and stopped. I took my mobile out of the glove box, called Adam and relayed the conversation to him.

"I don't know what the score is. Cobb didn't act like the man with brains you suggested he was."

"I told you, that's his schtick. You're supposed to fall for it."

On the road back into the city, I wondered if Linda had begun her journey back from Plymouth. Probably not yet. I could spend the time making some notes on what this case had yielded so far. And even if I ended up with more questions than currently in the log, something might surface.

Or I could worry about my relationship with Freddie. I'd get shorter odds on surviving it than an apprentice wire walker's first attempt to cross the Avon Gorge. Thanks to newspost dot whatever, Freddie could now monitor my progress, pop up every now and again to enquire about my health. Confident that the time would arrive when frustration would drive me to tell her what she wanted to know – whatever that was – or do something foolish.

Walking from the garage across the back lawn, I had a minor brainwave. I poured a generous double malt, sat down in the living room and phoned Adam again.

"Accepting that Bill Marsh is at the top of Freddie Settle's 'Things to Do' list," I said. "Do you think we could use the newspost blog to confuse things?"

"Blogs are always good for that."

"Could we concoct some story, outrageous enough to appear to be true?"

"Such as…?"

"Something that implicates me in Bill's disappearance."

"Why? Bloody hell, Jack…"

"See if we can drag something wicked out of the woodwork."

Adam was quiet for a few seconds. I listened to the buzz on the line.

"We'll need a laptop," he said. "Can't use yours or mine." There was time to draw breath, then he went on. "Chris Gould's the man. He sells re-conditioned pcs from a workshop in Bedminster. I'll call him."

I sat for a couple of minutes wondering how this mad scheme might play out. Then fell to considering how long it was likely to take Linda to get home. I called her mobile. She didn't answer. I left a message, turned on the TV and discovered a re-run of Dennis Potter's *The Singing Detective* on BBC4.

Linda called at 9.20.

"I thought we were going to meet here," she said. "Are we

not spending the night together?"

"I called earlier," was all I could think of saying. "Your mobile. I left a message."

"Ah right... But you're still not here."

That was clearly the case.

"Shit, Jack... I was stationary on the M5 for the best part of an hour. Then on the A38, dribbling along for another hour and a half. Looking forward to being greeted by you, holding out a glass of chilled something or other."

Any response I could offer was going to be a mistake. I was indisputably at home on my own sofa. The fact I had been side-tracked by the genius of Dennis Potter, and assumed that Linda would call me from somewhere along the way, was probably no basis for negotiation.

"I did ring…"

Her voice went up a couple of notes, which is what happens when she is being severe. Only she was about to be more than that.

"The battery was dead actually. Because I had left it in my briefcase, switched on, all day." She took all the full stops out of the next sentences. "I appreciate how stupid that was I know it's not your fault but I'm stressed and hot and tired and all the way up the fucking A38 I was ticking off the miles thinking about later expecting you to be here and you weren't and that pissed me off."

She stopped. There was a weary sigh. Followed by a lengthy silence.

"I'll come over now," I suggested. But the night was lost to us.

"Best not," Linda said. "I'll have a bath and a drink and find a movie to watch in bed. I'll see you tomorrow. Goodnight."

"Goodnight."

Linda ended the call. I was left listening to the dial tone. Another rousing hit, Shepherd…

CHAPTER TEN

Adam rang at quarter past eight the following morning. I rolled over in bed and reached for the phone.

"We're up and running," he said.

I was still not fully awake. "With what?"

"Chris Gould has an old laptop, with the absolute minimum of software; no games no apps, no shit like that. We're going to use a no-reply address. He suggests we work from his place."

"Which is where?"

"The old trading estate off Bedminster Parade. I'll email you the address and Chris's phone number. Meanwhile, we need to think about the tone of this diatribe."

"Come round for breakfast," I suggested. "We can talk across the coffee and doughnuts."

"Doughnuts?"

"Fresh from the baker on the corner."

* * *

We were eating the custard filled doughnuts thirty-five minutes later.

"Did you see Linda last night?" Adam asked.

"It's considered not done to speak with your mouth full," I said.

"That's obviously a 'no'."

I glared at him. He swallowed and put down the doughnut he was working on.

"I've been thinking of something along the lines of… *Bristol PI, Jack Shepherd, appears to have solved the mystery of the disappeared bookie. His investigations led him to a one hundred percent reliable source of information. And Shepherd is now in the process of liaising between this source and police officers involved in the case…* What do you think?"

"I think we'll get arrested for attempting to pervert the course of justice," I said.

"What justice? No copper is actually on the case. You won't get anything approaching justice at the hands of Freddie Settle. And the conspiracy, if there is such in this case, begins with Bill Marsh and his mate Len Coleman. We, or rather you, are simply after the truth. And along the way, unfortunately, a serious bollocking from the women in your life."

I offered him a look I hoped defined the stress I was feeling.

"Okay, let's really examine this," Adam said. "What, do you think, is the accepted credibility rating of the newspost site?"

"I guess not much."

"Exactly. And as such, it will be devoured by all the people who actually want the story to be true. Around here, that could amount to tens of thousands. You will be hot news for days, if we can keep it up."

"Or on the run, like Bill," I suggested.

"Yes, well, let's not go there right now," Adam said. "We have three sets of people whose interest we need to retain. Bill, Freddie Settle, and the Murder Investigations Team."

"Actually four," I said. "Walter Cobb is in play."

"Four then," Adam said. "Bottom line is, we don't care whether any of these people believe us, so long as the post creates an itch irritating enough for them to scratch. Freddie might just believe this scurrilous shit to be true. In which case, she will upgrade her interest in your welfare."

"Something to cherish."

"I guess Harvey Butler might ring up and ask a question or two. You will of course berate him for doing so, and tell him in no uncertain terms, that none of it is true. The ideal phone call will come from Bill, concerned that increased public interest in whatever he's doing, will be no help to… well whatever he is doing."

None of the possible reactions to this nonsense was comforting. But desperate though this endeavour was, it was plan A.

Adam looked at his watch. "I've got to go." He stood up. "I'll call you as soon as Chris calls me."

I was left alone to consider the day's schedule. Going into the office might give rise to the opportunity to apologise to Linda. The phone rang again, as I reached the back door. I took the receiver off the wall phone.

"Jack, it's May. We have a bit of trouble here. The Drop In Centre. We seem to have had a break in."

"Are you alright?"

"Yes, I wasn't here. No one was. It happened sometime overnight."

"Have you called the police?"

She said she didn't wish to do that. "If you come down here, I'll explain."

The Drop-In Centre used to be shoe shop – a three storey, terrace building in Bedminster, sitting between an electrical chain store and a local bakery. I drove around the back, parked the Healey and found the door to the tiny back yard. The brick outhouse to my left, was originally the outside loo. To the right of the rear door was a window with very little of the bobbled opaque glass left in the frame. May was on the other side of it, sweeping the floor. She looked up, disappeared, and the door opened a few seconds later. I stepped into the narrow corridor which opened up and led into the old shop space. I looked into the room May had been sweeping. There was glass all over the floor.

"Just a store room," she said.

"Anything missing?" I asked.

May shook her head. "Not from in here."

"And this door to the left?"

"It's a shower room and a toilet."

I looked in the direction of the shop space. "And in there?"

"Come and see," she said.

It was the first time I'd been in the place. The old shop floor was fifteen feet wide, and maybe twenty-five feet deep. It was mainly a seating area, with four old, re-conditioned sofas, a dozen armchairs and some low tables. There was a reception space to the left of the front door. An old civil service desk with pedestals and a plastic inlaid top, had chairs both sides. A staircase led up to the next floor.

I turned to May. Dealt first with the elephant in the room. Told her I'd made no progress with the search for Bill. I asked her how she was getting on. She said she was keeping busy and that helped. This morning's discovery however…

She gave me a tour. The first floor housed a dining area the same size as the main room downstairs, and a kitchen behind it.

"There's not much room to swing the centre's cat," May said. "But running at full steam, we can cook lunch and an evening meal for sixty-five. Sometimes we have more guests than that. We don't turn anyone away, but the hospitality suffers a little. We're open from 11 o'clock in the morning until nine at night."

There was another bathroom directly above the one downstairs, and at the back, a small office. The door was open. The architrave around the lock catch was splintered.

"Did you come up here earlier?"

"Yes, but I didn't go into the office. I called you downstairs from my mobile."

There were four rooms on the top floor. The smallest housed two desks and two chairs; the room next to it, a couple of football tables; the other two, some floor cushions and shelves with small collections of books. I asked May why she hadn't called the police.

"That's the last option, Jack. We have a lease from the city council. It's renewed every year. Some people would be delighted to see the back of us."

"And it's time to talk about the lease?"

"Yes. Another six weeks until we sign again. We have always kept a low profile. A Drop-In Centre in this street is a problem for some of the rate payers and their customers. Although, our adjoining neighbours don't seem to mind. Others however, live uneasily with the idea that this place is undesirable at best. A break in would give them a chance to take the moral high ground. And a police investigation would trigger that."

"So what do you want me to do?" I asked.

"I don't know really," she confessed.

Downstairs again, I looked at the alarm sensor above the front door and along the corridor to the one above the back door.

"These are triggered if the doors are forced?"

"Yes. One of the bakery employees lives in the flat above

the shop. He used to be a visitor here, when he was on methadone. He went through the misery with a crushing amount of hard work. And he made it. Got his job, and volunteered as unofficial caretaker here. He has a key and the alarm code."

"So what happened last night? Did the alarm go off?"

"Yes. But there is no sensor in the store room. A major error, as I now appreciate. When the baker got down here, the back door was open and… whoever… had gone."

I walked to the back door. May followed. We stepped into the yard. I looked towards the old privy.

"Do you keep anything in there?"

"Stuff to be re-cycled, that's all. Take a look."

I opened the outhouse door.

There was a man, 40 something maybe, wearing an old brown woollen coat, lying on a pile of flattened boxes. The coat seemed too big for him, the cloth cap on his head, too small. He might have been taller once, but I guessed if we pulled him upright, he would fold like an old concertina. I got closer. He smelled of booze and damp and loneliness.

"May…"

She stepped into the doorway. "Oh God…"

"Do you know him?"

She took a while to reply. "Martin. He visits often. Sleeps a couple of streets away."

"Not last night." I spoke to him. "Martin…" Then a little louder. "Martin…"

His head was tilted towards his right shoulder. I felt for the carotid artery on the left-hand side of his neck. No pulse. I checked for a second time. Nothing. Behind me, May let out a long quiet sigh.

"He's dead, isn't he?"

"I'm afraid so." I stood up. "You can't keep this from the police."

* * *

"Was Martin a regular visitor?" George Hood asked May.

We were sitting in the main room. The venetian blinds over the windows were closed. The blind on the door, was pulled down. The SOCO and his associates were out in the yard. A Forensics Officer was in the store room.

"Yes, he was."

"Do you know much about him?"

"No."

"His second name?"

"No. That's the case with a most of our visitors. And we don't insist they tell us."

In spite of being detectives and, by definition, people alleged to have a grasp on the world most ordinary mortals don't, Hood and I were listening to stuff new to us.

"Many of the people who walk, and sometimes stagger, through these doors have no recorded history," May went on. "Whatever name they offer us, we accept. Unreservedly. This place is just a step away from the end of their world. We try to make it as welcoming as possible. For drinkers, drug addicts, street people, the shoeless, the unknown, the beaten, the lost…" She stopped talking. "Sorry I'm on my soap box." She went on. "Like Martin, many of them drop in regularly. But we rarely learn anything more about them, regardless of the number of times they visit."

"Has Martin ever spent a night in the shed out there?" Hood asked.

"Not that I know of."

"Would you? Know I mean."

May nodded. "I think I would, yes." She blinked furiously as tears built up in her eyes. "What is going on here, gentlemen?"

"The break in might be the only issue to address," Hood offered. "We won't know anything about the death of Martin until the post mortem is done. There is no obvious link between the two situations."

May looked at Hood again. "But there might be, you mean?"

"It's something we might have to take a view on later."

I changed the subject. "Can we look in the office now?"

May led the way upstairs. The room housed a desk with a keyboard and a screen, and a telephone. A three-drawer metal filing cabinet stood in a corner, by the window which overlooked the yard.

"And are you sure you were the last person in here yesterday?" Hood asked.

"Yes, I locked up. And I still have the key."

"Are there any copies?"

"The volunteers have one each."

"So is that how you left the desk last night?"

"What do you mean?"

"The papers, the pencil pot, the phone, the mouse... Is anything in the wrong place?"

Hood asked her to sit in her chair. She did. And the inspection directly from her point of view worked.

"The mouse pad," she said. "And the mouse. They are not the way I left them. When I finish with the pc, I push the pad away to the right. And I always leave the mouse on top of it. The pad and the mouse have been moved."

"Someone used the pc after you closed up and left." Hood

said.

"But that person would have to know the password," May said.

"Where do you keep the piece of paper you wrote it on?" She looked at Hood sheepishly. "Everybody does the same thing," he said.

May bent down, opened the bottom drawer in the desk pedestal and dug a small piece of paper out from under all the other papers. Then looked down at the pc.

"There are no real secrets in here. Just stuff on how the Centre works. Records of donations and finances, lists of people who support us… well some of them. And of course, the meagre knowledge we have managed to assemble on our visitors."

She was close to tears again.

Hood ordered us out of the way while he looked around. I made coffee in the kitchen below. May sat at one of the dining tables, staring out of the window, occasionally shifting in her chair.

Fifteen minutes later Hood walked into the room. He said 'no thanks' to coffee, and the three of us moved to the ground floor. We met the FO, who delivered his verdict on the storeroom.

"The place is covered in prints," he said. "And some glove smudges. Left by the last night's visitors, I guess. If you're serious, we ought to print everyone who has a connection with this place."

"No no," May said. "I appreciate that you must discover the cause of Martin's death and investigate whatever turns up. But please, make as little fuss as possible."

The FO looked hurt.

"We think someone has used the office pc," Hood said. "Print the desk, the mouse pad and the mouse. Write your report and give it to me. No one else."

The FO shrugged. "You're the boss."

He turned and walked towards the staircase. Hood said 'goodbye' to us and moved out into the yard. May watched him go, then waved me to one of the sofas.

"Is our relationship confidential?" she asked. "I mean between client and investigator?"

"Absolutely. Except perhaps under torture."

She smiled and sat down next to me.

"Since the Lily business, I've been doing some checking. Looking at faces, counting heads. Visitor numbers have dropped, in ones and twos, during the last nine months or so."

"And what's the problem with that?"

"No problem at all, if the missing people have moved on to other places, and, hopefully, better things. Doesn't make any difference to us in organisation terms. Actually, it helps to make the money go further."

"Will your donors approve of that?"

"Of course. They give us what they do without conditions. We have some still with us after almost twenty years. One of whom, has a considerable personal fortune. In the end, unfortunately, those who stop coming here, will be replaced by others. The current estimate is there may be close to four hundred people living rough in Bristol."

The locking gizmo outside the front door buzzed; then beeped as a series of buttons was pressed. The door opened and a lady with shoulder length silver hair, stepped over the threshold. Monica, one of the volunteers. May introduced us, before regaling her with the events of the day so far.

I spent the next half hour at the Centre, as the volunteers arrived and prepared to open for business. May and I talked in one of the top floor rooms for a while, sitting on the floor cushions.

"Why do you do what you do?" she asked

"It's my day job," I said. "If I don't do it, I don't eat."

"There are other endeavours which could probably deal with that."

"I don't know how to do anything else."

"Oh come on, Jack. You do what you do because you believe in it."

"Not to the superhuman extent that you do," I said. "You fight the good fight on a daily basis, it seems to me."

"Okay. Why did you spend all those days on Lily's behalf? And don't offer me any guff about knocking her down."

I thought about it for a while. May waited.

"Recently, I saw a film called *Life And Nothing But*. The story of a French officer in the aftermath of the Great War, charged with establishing the names and histories of thousands of dead soldiers. His job as he saw it, was not to find the Unknown Soldier, but to make sure he didn't." May was looking straight into my eyes. "It made an extraordinary impression on me. Hell, I can't claim to have done anything close to one percent as important. But even in the small things, somebody has to care."

She shuffled into another position on the bean bag.

"You agreed to try and find Bill because I asked you to. You didn't believe you could do that. You don't believe it now."

"Actually, I don't believe it's a lost cause at all. Yes, Bill has disappeared. I've no idea where he has gone, or why. But others are looking for him too. People who wouldn't be doing that if they thought he was dead."

May opened her mouth to say something. I beat her to it.

"Dangerous though these people might be, they are no more clued up than I am. I just have to stay one step ahead and find Bill before they do."

There seemed sense in that. May nodded her head

"And his mobile," I said. "There are no numbers in his contacts box. No one in crisis, spends time deleting phone numbers, unless he's working to some agenda."

May processed all that. I wound up.

"The odds are long I know. To be honest, I think Bill might give us a hundred to one. However, Adam and I have a plan for changing the odds. Not tried and tested I have to admit, but it might just work."

There was a call from below. The chef had arrived to begin preparing lunch. May led the way downstairs.

My mobile rang as I crossed the courtyard. Adam said that Chris Gould wanted us to meet him at 2.30.

CHAPTER ELEVEN

The room behind Chris Gould's shop was packed with used hardware. There was a work bench against one wall and racks along all four, built with Dexion and shelved with plywood. A wooden table with an old laptop on it, sat in the middle of the floor with bentwood chairs on opposite sides.

Chris was probably around the same age as Adam, five eight or nine, thin as a barber's pole, with sparse, light curly hair. He shook my hand and explained that most of the hardware was in the process of being renovated, before being shipped to schools in Malawi.

He pointed at the laptop. "A no-reply email address. Nothing else. No files no folders and no frills. Difficult to trace."

He left the room and went into the shop. Adam sat down in front of the laptop and began to type.

The story of the Bristol PI and the blood-stained parquet floor grows curiouser and curiouser. The man he is seeking, is now hiding from him, the police, and a city crime boss. It's only a matter of time, surely, before the investigator's client is caught by one team or another. The blood on the floor was just the prelude to something more brutal. Fascinating though it is to speculate on which way this will go, my money is on the crime boss.

Adam typed the newspost email address into the box and pressed send.

"Bingo," he said and swung round in his chair.

"Do you really think that Bill or Freddie will read that?" I asked.

"If they're keeping an eye on the local news."

We thanked Chris. Adam went back to the *Post*. I went to my office.

Linda was in her office too. I stood outside the door rehearsing what I hoped would be an acceptable apology. It just sounded puny. I knocked on the door. I heard her say 'Come in'.

She looked up at me from behind her pc screen. "Hi…"

"I'm sorry," I said. Seemed simpler than beating round the bush.

She nodded. "Okay…"

I sat in the chair in front of her desk. She waited for me to go on.

"Yesterday was a bit confusing," I said, lamely.

"Okay…"

"I got involved in stuff."

"Really? What sort of stuff? And how would you rate the involvement level? It's clearly pretty low in our thing. Or rather, in your section of it."

"I have your front door key."

That provoked the response it deserved.

"So why didn't you use it last night? Christ, Jack. All you had to do was take a twenty-minute drive, make yourself at home and pour me a drink when I arrived. Which I did, knackered, pissed off and hungry, only to find the significant other in my life conspicuous by his absence."

"I er…"

"Don't bother, Jack. I don't want to hear the explanation. I lost several hours of working time yesterday, which I'm now trying to catch up on."

I went back to my office. I remembered Chrissie once telling me how useless I was at this stuff. "You mean well, Dad," she said. "But you've got a pretty small skills base to work from." This from a fifteen-year-old. I thought it way off the mark at the time. I talked to Emily who was clearly at one with our daughter. At which point, I began to appreciate that Emily was the driver of the family engine and I was just the fireman. And not truly successful at that. I mastered the major tasks but failed to keep up with the small things. I realised how important they were when Chrissie and I started to fight. By the time she moved out of the house I was up to speed, but of course it was too late. We had lost years of precious time.

And now Linda was suffering from my lack of input.

I had nothing else to do but wait out the day. I caught up with emails. I made some coffee, drank it, typed and sent half a dozen in return. Then I waited for something to happen, like the refugees in *Casablanca*.

At 5 o'clock I rang Adam.

"Nil desperandum, old man," he said. "We've held on to the idea that Bill is alive, and making a serious attempt to convince the rest of us he may not be. So, let's be patient. I'm going home. I'll call you tomorrow."

"Yes, thanks. Give Chrissie my love."

"Sleep well, Jack."

"And you."

I pressed the red button and put the phone receiver back in its base. I decided to get my notes up to date. A couple of hours later, the last four days were chronicled on six sheets of notepaper. Including one whole sheet of questions. About the blood on the parquet, the papers in the fire grate, Bill and Len, Walter Cobb and Freddie Settle, and was this all some bloody conspiracy?

It was at this point I came up with a scheme to move things along. I called Harvey Butler with a proposition.

"You want me to do what?" he asked, incredulity hurtling down the phone line.

"Bug my phones," I repeated. "All three of them. Home, office and mobile."

"Why?"

"Well…" I began.

Harvey interrupted. "I know. You want me to agree to this exploitation of the public purse, without asking too many questions and not getting involved in whatever it is you're doing."

"Yes. But it's likely to work for both of us," I insisted.

"Okay, one question only, Jack," he said. "What has provoked this request? No flannel or bullshit. Just a direct answer."

"I'm hoping Bill Marsh will call me during the next twenty-four hours. And whatever I can prise out of him, might lead to some real evidence gathering. I know this is not a Murder Team case. Not yet. But it might turn out that way."

Harvey was silent again. I pressed him.

"I'm not suggesting anything unofficial or off the books here. Just what you do all the time. These are my phones we're talking about and I agree to it. I'll sign whatever piece of paper I have to."

Harvey responded. "Okay. Come round here now, and we'll set it up."

I left my office. Linda's door was locked. I was in Harvey's office twenty minutes later.

"What's the matter with your face?" he asked.

"I tripped on the hall stairs and made contact with the top step."

Harvey shrugged and didn't pursue the matter. He offered me some forms to sign. He counter-signed them, and I was out of his office five minutes later. Home at 7 o'clock.

Waiting again. Just like earlier.

My mobile rang. It was Bob Carlton, from Tech-Surveillance.

"Just making sure that everything works at both ends," he said.

The background office volume rose as he took the receiver away from his face. He shared a sentence or two with somebody else, then talked to me again.

"I guess you know the drill. Keep the miscreant on the line. Don't make him nervous. And we'll pinpoint him."

There was another moment of background ambience then Carlton spoke again.

"We are in business," he said. "Good luck."

How many clichés can you muster to reference how time passes? Stuff about waiting for trains, watched kettles, paint drying, grass growing, and of course waiting for some bugger to call. To avoid interruptions, I switched the landline into answer mode; ready to pounce and go live if it did so. Chrissie rang a few minutes after nine, leaving a message. Linda called just before ten, wanting to talk. I listened to her, weirdly at odds with myself and counting the seconds, until she stopped abruptly and said, "Hell I'm just rambling, talk tomorrow." and rang off.

Carlton and I spoke again at 10 o'clock, before he went off duty. He was surprisingly upbeat about the whole business.

"Your man will call the moment you stop looking at your watch and pacing up and down. I suggest you go to bed, Mr Shepherd."

That seemed like sensible advice, so I did. And instead of sitting on the sofa wide awake, I lay in bed wide awake. The last time I looked at the bedside clock, it said 2.56.

CHAPTER TWELVE

The front doorbell woke me up. Or rather, the persistent knocking which followed. The clock on the bedside table said 7.15. Dressing gown wrapped around me, I yelled to whoever was out there that I was on my way.

The milkman was standing on the doorstep. He handed me a pint of milk and a bill for £65.42p.

"Three months," he said, with some menace.

I promised to give him a cheque the following day. He said that wasn't the way it worked if I remembered. The billing was all done on line. Before I could ask him why he was, therefore, standing on my doorstep, he said that in extreme cases, it fell to him to act personally to collect money owing. An enforcer driving an electric milk float. No getting away from that combo. He ordered me to log in and pay *Milk Direct* before noon.

I made some coffee. Poured milk into the mug from my brand-new pint. Drank the coffee, went back upstairs, and took a shower. Minutes later, soaking wet and reaching for the towel rack, I heard the phone ringing in the bedroom. I grabbed the towel and dripped swiftly from shower to bedside, to answer the call.

George Hood asked me what I was doing. It told him I was soaking the bedroom carpet. He said that was the mistake he had made. Using *DriFoam* was the best way to clean a carpet. No water and no shrinkage. I laid the towel on the duvet and sat down on it. And immediately began to feel cold. Mercifully Hood moved on quickly.

"Do you know the burger van parked on Durdham Down?"

"Yes."

"How long will it take you to get here?"

"Once I'm dressed, ten minutes."

"I'll buy you breakfast."

* * *

The sun was up and awake. Hood was sitting at a plastic garden table, eating a bacon sandwich.

"What can I get you?" he asked.

"Just coffee thanks."

I sat down while he organised that. He put the mug in front of me and returned to his sandwich. He finished eating. I waited. He wiped his lips with a paper serviette.

"The mouse we took from the Drop-In Centre didn't give us anything," he said. "But I have some news about the man in the outhouse. The pathologist reckons he died around twelve hours before you found him."

"Died of what?"

"Heart attack. At least, his heart stopped." Hood sat up straight in his chair. "But here's the thing. Martin whoever he is, is missing a lung."

He paused long enough to let that sink in. In return, I stared at him. Then found a question to ask.

"Can you live with only one lung?"

"Apparently. As long as everything else works and you look after yourself. Take it easy, walk don't run. Sport is out of the question. In fact anything which makes you breathe heavily. Although Martin was never going to make it in any case. The remaining lung is in very good health, according to the pathologist. But the same can't be said for his liver and his kidneys. Somebody relieved him of one of the few major organs in good nick."

"Somebody qualified to do it presumably."

"The pathologist said it was a truly professional job."

"So what did Martin do?" I asked. "Did he sell it?"

Hood shrugged. "I've been pondering on that."

"What's the going rate for a healthy lung?" I asked.

"Under the counter... anything up to twenty thousand pounds, to buyers in wealthy circles. Maybe Martin was paid a few hundred. Not much, but a lot to someone with no money and no roof over his head."

Hood swallowed a mouthful of coffee.

"So if this theory stands up," I said, "someone picked him off the street, examined him, found out what was working and relieved him of it?"

Hood put his mug down. "Improbable though it may seem..."

"In which case, that person has an operating theatre at his disposal."

"And facilities to keep the lung alive between harvesting and transplanting," Hood said."

"And how wide is that window? A few hours?"

"Sometimes longer than that. Nonetheless, it means the harvesting was done to order and they lucked out with Martin. They were looking for a lung in working order. And he had two of them."

I took a drink of coffee. Hood went on to explain all he had discovered about body part surgery.

"At your demise, with permission, any hospital can harvest all organs that are useful. At any time in your life, you can donate a kidney or bone marrow to a relative or friend, providing you are a match. Along with your blood, skin, and hair. Actually the law allows you to sell those bits if you can. But nothing else."

"And there's a black market for the big stuff."

"People like Martin could be prime targets for those engaged in the trade," Hood said. "No addresses, therefore no records. Few people who know who they are. And those who do, with rare exceptions like May and her friends at the Drop-In Centre, don't give a toss. The Martins of this world are multiple losers."

"So what do you do now?"

"Nothing," Hood said. "Not in the Murder Team's purview, street people. Unless they die unlawfully. More your line of work, I'd say."

He looked at me steadfastly.

"Should I take that look to be one of some significance?" I asked.

Hood changed the subject. "Len Coleman, however, he's definitely my pay grade." His eyes remained glued to mine. "So what is it you know about him that I don't?"

That was easy to answer. With the whole unvarnished truth.

"Absolutely nothing," I said.

Hood grinned in disbelief.

"Slit my throat and hope to die, George. Someone else was looking for Coleman and got to him before I did, obviously. Why are you asking this now?"

Hood sat back in the chair. "Someone else is in the loop, Jack. Who is it?" He beamed at me across the table. "There's a gang of people working on this now. I can sit here all day. Actually I wouldn't mind another mug of coffee. Your shout."

In this mode, George Hood is like Banquo's ghost. He won't go away.

I ordered two more mugs and took them back to the table. Hood looked around Durdham Down. At the joggers, the women with kids in pushchairs, the dog walkers. The sun was now beginning to warm the day. Hood looked at his watch. He said the morning was flying by. Clearly, he was able to cultivate an immensely high boredom threshold when required. Not one of my accomplishments however. My resistance was disintegrating like a beach sandcastle overrun by the incoming tide. Hood calculated we had farted around enough.

"Jack… Who did you go and see concerning the whereabouts of Len Coleman? Give. Or I'll take you to Trinity Road and get the Boss to work you over."

I looked at him. He sat forward in the chair and began to count on the fingers of his right hand.

"Obstructing the police, interfering in the course of an investigation, conspiring to pervert the – "

"Ah come on, George…"

"Who is it, Jack? Who did you talk to?"

I took a couple of beats. Then I told him. He stared at me, gobsmacked.

"Not the Freddy Settle we have grown to despise," I added. "He's retired. Daughter Freddie has taken over the family business."

Hood breathed in and out. "Right…" He looked at me again and waited for the whole explanation.

"Bill is a member of the Silver Star Casino. Len Coleman used to be, until a fortnight ago. Freddie told me she had no idea as to his whereabouts."

We sat in silence for some time, each of us considering the problem from opposite ends. Clearly confronting Freddie Settle would yield absolutely nothing. Visited by the police or the private eye, the outcome was likely to be the same. A display of cool but outraged innocence, and all the time she needed to check that everything was locked down tight.

Hood spoke as though he had been reading my mind.

"Okay," he said. "Assuming Freddie ordered the Coleman killing, she might have over-cooked this a bit. Coleman dead is a statement of intent. Crystal clear. He's out of the way and you're in the clarts. But the rest of us public servants are in this too. She must know that. And it may be the one thing that keeps you out of her clutches."

That was kind of comforting.

"But it might be best to stop the bollocks you're pedalling on the net. That will swiftly irritate your allies as well as your targets."

"I don't know what you're talking about George."

"DC Holmes reads everything. And she's known for her imaginative leaps."

He drained his mug and got up out of his chair.

"As to Ms Settle," he said. "No point poking a hornet's nest with a stick, unless you have everything ready to control the outcome. But should we unearth something solid, it will give me the greatest pleasure to steam in and put the cuffs on her. In the meantime, Jack, stay out of trouble."

He turned and walked to his car. I watched him get in and drive away.

The trail to Bill was getting colder with every ongoing event. Following it was leading me nowhere. And Martin was just another lost soul. No family, no friends, no life. He was what he was.

I am. Yet what I am, none cares or knows
My friends forsake me like a memory lost.
I am the self-consumer of my woes...

I first read that poem by John Clare when I was a young copper, during an investigation into a teacher's suicide. I was searching his bedroom, and there was a copy of Clare's collected works on the bedside table. I'd never heard of him, but I opened the book and was drawn into his personal darkness. His poetry is heart breaking stuff. And it echoes down the years to me, still. John Clare knew more about loneliness, loss and despair than most. Like Martin, and somehow my teacher suicide case, he lived among the forsaken.

I drained the coffee mug, stood up, waved my thanks to the burger van proprietor and walked to my car.

CHAPTER THIRTEEN

Detective. The job description couldn't be clearer. The work is all in the name. But with it, comes a host of unpredictable elements. So when the going gets tough, do something easy...

Back home, I sat down in front of the pc, googled *Milk Direct* and paid my bill. I could look the milkman in the eyes next time we met.

I drove to the office, thinking about Freddie. I had said no to the largesse she had offered. So she had simply reversed her strategy. Instead of receiving money for doing nothing, I was now going to get nothing for doing all the work. The odds on a successful outcome were risible. Every sensible bone in my body said, 'Go on holiday and send Freddie Settle a postcard to show how far away you are.' It was just plain daft to upset her.

By comparison, Walter Cobb seemed no more than a minor sub plot. He was under siege from bailiffs, the Inland Revenue and the VAT Man. He was broke and desperate, but he had no reason I could see for being involved with Bill's disappearance. Fifty-two thousand pounds was a lot of money, but not enough, surely, to risk the consequences of doing away with his major creditor.

Jason was off the clock. His oppo, Eric, was an efficient though charmless character. He liked the uniform he wore, and on quiet afternoons, was given to walking the floors like Mr Mackay in *Porridge* – slow and straight backed, checking that the cleaners' work was up to par.

Right now though, he was dealing with an unwanted visitor.

It was difficult to guess how old the man was. Somewhere between thirty and forty maybe. Tallish. Long hair and a moustache which made him look like Frank Zappa. Wearing a blue anorak over a woolly shirt, battered corduroy trousers, and on his feet, brown shoes with thick soles. He was begging for money. Eric dragged the man past me and shoved him out of the door. I watched the man swing round, trip, stagger a few yards, then regain his balance and move slowly across the turning circle in front of the building. Beyond that, he disappeared into the gloom and the maze of concrete pillars supporting the road which funnelled traffic onto the bridge over the Cumberland Basin.

"Filthy, useless git," Eric muttered. "There's a bunch of them living over there."

He moved back to the reception desk, brushing imagined dirt and disease off his uniform jacket. Suddenly I had an idea. From my office, I phoned George Hood.

"Can I have a copy of the photograph your man took of Martin?"

"Er… Why?"

"No concern of the Murder Team you said. Come on George, speed is of the essence."

"I'll email it to you," he said.

I was printing out copies when Linda knocked on the office door and stepped over the threshold.

"Have you time to talk?"

I should have said, 'of course, sit down', and made her welcome. I should have said I was truly glad to see her. I should have poured oil on trouble waters. I should have said anything but the sentence I did say.

"Not right now. Sorry. There's something I have to do. We can talk as soon as I get back. Yes?" I gathered up the copies of the picture. "I have to chase up someone. It might be important."

"Of course," she said, without a trace of emotion in her voice.

She stepped into the corridor. I apologised again, closed the office door and set off towards the lift. I pressed the call button and looked behind me. Linda had gone into her office.

In the foyer, back from his lunch, Jason waved at me as I followed the steps of the man Eric had thrown out. Across the turning circle, over a wide pavement backed by a low concrete wall, and into the cavern under the flyover. A huge space, supporting double-lane roads into and out of the city over the Cumberland Basin Swing Bridge; with lines of concrete pillars growing from short props to twenty feet columns as the road rose up to bridge level. Way beyond, the river flowed westwards under Brunel's suspension bridge. I walked towards the view. In front of me the space opened out. I was now directly underneath the traffic, the noise magnified by the concrete echo chamber around me.

There was a grubby makeshift village built under the flyover. Put together from wood, cardboard boxes, chicken wire, blankets and old tarpaulins. The remains of a fire smoking on a metal grill, rested on a circle of bricks. Two broken armchairs, one on three feet so it leant over at an angle, the other on no feet at all, a couple of empty fruit boxes and a wooden stool, sat on the concrete surrounding the fire. It was a dismal and desperate place. The kind of alfresco shithole most of us don't want to think about.

I counted seven people. Three men and two women who looked like they might be inhabitants of this place. And two men who were clearly visitors, standing at the rear of a Transit van which had backed into the space from the access road.

There was a discussion going on, mostly drowned out by the noise of the traffic, and accompanied by lots of arm waving. They were all too busy to notice me. One of the visitors opened the Transit rear doors. Visitor Two, reached out to the tallest man in the group and gripped his arm. The man tried to shake him off. At which point, one of the women detached herself from the rest of the group, picked up a length of timber and launched herself at Visitor Two. He turned back to face the group and failed to dodge the piece of 2 by 2 as it swung towards him. It thumped into his shoulder. The tall man shook himself free from Visitor One, who grabbed him again, pointed him at the nearby concrete pillar and shoved him at it head first. The man crunched into the pillar, staggered back a step or two and sank to his knees. Visitor Two, meanwhile had wrenched the piece of 2 by 2 from the woman. He pushed her away from him. She staggered, over balanced and fell back onto the concrete.

I fished the mobile out of my jacket, thumbed the office reception number, and got Jason. Visitor One saw me as I dropped the mobile back into my pocket. He called out to his associate, who swung to face me, still holding the chunk of wood. He shifted the timber from his left hand to his right and re-arranged his grip.

I stepped forwards slowly, counting the time I figured Jason would take to materialise behind us. Six seconds to cross the lobby and get out of the door, five seconds to cross the turning circle, another five to cross the low wall, another six or seven to arrive on the scene...

Visitor Two nodded at his partner. Twenty yards behind us, Jason hove into view. It was now two against two. And the visitors had to decide how important their mission was. They decided to tough it out.

It was a mistake.

Jason was at my side moments later. Standing straight and tall, he was an imposing presence. He crabbed to his left, taking with him the attention of a suddenly much less confident Visitor Two. I crabbed the other way and inched towards Visitor One. No weapon appeared from anywhere; obviously no hardware was required for a trip to a group of down and outs under a flyover. Taking comfortable strides, I closed the space between myself and Visitor One. He wasn't sure what to do. He swayed from left to right and bounced a couple of times, like a goalkeeper preparing to face a penalty. He allowed me to walk straight at him, concentrating on my face. He raised his arms and took up the stance of a nervous southpaw. I swung my right leg and kicked him in the crotch. He yelled in pain and sank to his knees.

There was a roar of agony to my left. The piece of timber was on the ground. Jason had Visitor Two in a half nelson, his right arm under the man's chin. He heaved his arm upwards, pushing the man's face up and back. The man started to choke. Jason released his grip. Visitor Two staggered forwards grabbing at his throat. Jason picked up the length of 2 by 2, raised it and thumped it down on the back of the man's head. The man yelled, raised his arms to the source of the pain, and keeled over.

There was a ragged cheer from the village inhabitants. Eric's evictee moved towards the injured man. Another man found some rope. We sat the visitors down, tied them together back-to-back, and with the amount of rope left, tethered them to the Transit trailer hitch.

I asked the villagers if they objected to me phoning the police. This was greeted, not un-naturally, with some suspicion. They had all been demoted to an un-fixable underclass and none of them expected to receive anything but trouble from those who didn't give a toss about them. The woman who had brandished the 2 by 2 was nominated spokesperson. As she moved towards me, I had time to notice how she looked. Short brown hair, closely cropped; dark eyes, cheeks more hollow than they should have been. She was wearing a dark blue boiler suit and a scruffy denim cap. She looked every inch like a Brecht heroine.

"We would rather not have anything to do with the police," she said.

I looked at the Transit and the trussed-up visitors. I asked Jason to go back to the office, and drive my car round to the front of the building. I gave him the keys.

"Leave them in the ignition," I said. "And wait for me to arrive."

He didn't object or ask any questions; simply nodded yes. He said a genuinely felt 'goodbye' to the villagers and moved away. I watched him until he was out of sight, then gathered the villagers around me. The injured man had stopped bleeding from his forehead and insisted he was okay.

I showed them the police photograph. The lady with the piece of 2 by 2 shivered.

"That's Martin," she said.

"What do you know about him?" I asked.

There was some discussion; followed by some whispered moments I couldn't hear under the traffic noise. The 2 by 2 lady spoke to me again.

"Martin didn't live here. Do you know the old engineering factory off Parsons Street in Bedminster? That's where he was sleeping. Under some boxes at the back of the car park. The other people there might help you."

She gave the photograph back to me. I talked to the group again.

"One more thing," I said and pointed at the Transit. "Help me to untie those two and we'll let them leave."

The villagers set about the business. The 2 by 2 lady produced another blunt instrument – a length of metal gas piping – and offered it to me. We stood shoulder to shoulder, acting as menacingly as we could, while two of the men released the visitors. Number one was tallish and wearing a cheap, black suit. His associate was shorter, shaven headed, clad in jeans and a blouson jacket, trainers on his feet. A pair of cut-price heavies. They did as instructed. I committed the registration number to memory. Gave the metal pipe back to my new friend and wished her luck.

"My name's Molly," she said.

The Transit doors slammed and I set off like Dwain Chambers. Across the open space, over the low wall, and out into the daylight. The Healey was parked, engine idling, driver's door open. About fifty yards to my left, the Transit drove out into the sunshine. I reached the Healey, yelled my thanks to Jason, slid into the car, found first gear and pulled away.

Ahead of me, the Transit was turning on to the road which fed traffic up and round and onto the swing bridge. I slid into the traffic three cars later. The roof of the Transit was clearly visible and easy to follow. We drove over the bridge, kept to the left and slipped down the ramp onto the Portway – the route to the M5 and Wales and all points west.

The thickening traffic was never going to allow the Transit to reach enough miles per hour to break the speed limit. We trundled underneath the suspension bridge and cruised along the Avon Gorge. Five minutes later we reached the sprawling M5 motorway junction in Shirehampton. The Transit drove straight on into Avonmouth.

No place to visit for an afternoon out. Fuel depots, a massive container terminal and cold storage warehouses line the dockside. Inland of the dock complex, the industrial estate creeps northeast from the mouth of the Avon for a mile and a half and spreads eastwards back to the M5. There's a huge chemical plant in the middle of the acreage, and alongside that a sewage treatment works. Around these places, occupying a series of industrial zones, is the mandatory gathering of DIY centres, furniture outlets, electrical stores, car parts distributors and storage facilities.

We turned north into the trading estate which runs parallel to the dockside. I dropped back and let the Transit open up space between us. It turned left into a cul de sac of small warehouses, swung into the car park in front of one with number 9 above the roll up door and stopped. Alongside a familiar black Bentley. Walter Cobb's motor car.

I pulled up at the road entrance and switched off the ignition. The two men climbed out of the Transit and went into the warehouse. I sat in the Healey, listening to the ticking of the engine block and settled back in my seat to wait.

I was bored within minutes and invented something to do. I got out of the car and walked back to the map of the estate standing on the corner. The tenant of number 9 First Avenue, was an outfit called *Futures Ltd*. The name didn't give any clue as to what the company did or sold, which was probably the intention. I walked back to the car and decided to try using whatever credit I still had with George Hood.

Hood wasn't at his desk and the call was diverted to Harvey Butler's office.

"Jack," he cried, joviality zooming down the line. "Nice to hear from you. I imagine there is something we can do for you."

I decided not to rise to the bait. "I need you to track a registration number for me," I said.

"Okay," Harvey said. No argument, no attempt at irony. "What is it?"

I recited the details I had read on the back of the Transit. He repeated them back to me and told me to hang on. The line clicked, then clicked again. I waited. Thirty seconds later there was one more click and Harvey came back to me.

"The Transit belongs to a roofer we know as second storey man, Reginald Pearce. Are you by any chance near this Transit as we speak?"

"I'm looking at it," I said.

"In which case, Mr Pearce isn't in it," he said.

"That's right. He and his mate are in a warehouse in Avonmouth."

"No, Jack, I mean Mr Pearce is not there. He's in court today. Right about now, I'm told, pleading guilty to seven counts of earning money under false pretences, and two counts of illegally taking lead from a church roof in Brislington. He will be in Horfield prison by the close of play, beginning an eighteen month stretch at least."

I absorbed the information.

Harvey broke the silence. "Does that help at all?"

"No."

"Can I help you in any other way?"

"No."

"Then have a nice day."

He was about to end the call. But took time to ask how May was. I told him she seemed okay the last time we spoke, and asked him about progress on the Len Coleman murder. Which changed his mood slightly.

"There is none," he said. "How are you progressing with finding Bill?"

"I'm not," I said.

I heard another phone begin to ring.

"Sorry, Jack," Harvey said. "I want to take this. Go gently."

And that was that. Another dead end. Well not entirely, but I couldn't see where two men in a borrowed Transit was going to lead. So I tried road testing an assumption... Men in the employ of Walter Cobb, visit the miserable domain of a group of people with no assets, no self-esteem and nowhere to go. They attempt to persuade one of the group to leave with them. Failing to do so, as the result of the unpleasantness that follows, they drive to their boss, to fess up.

That worked as a scenario, but I had no idea why. And that was the issue. The people who could tell me, were sitting round a table across the road and would certainly not rise to shake my hand if I were to interrupt.

Assuming that Walter Cobb had no plans to flee the country, I could catch up with him later. The time and effort involved in following his employees around until they did something unpleasant once again, didn't bear consideration. I fired up the Healey, U-turned in the road, and drove back into the city.

CHAPTER FOURTEEN

Molly was alone, sitting in one of the battered armchairs when I ventured under the flyover again. She stood up as I walked towards her. She was wearing a bulky cardigan over the boiler suit.

"Are you going to do this regularly?" she asked. "Visit us I mean."

I told her not too often and asked if she would answer some questions. She responded by saying she would, providing I didn't pry too much.

"Is asking for names prying too much?"

"Not necessarily. I gave you mine."

"Yes you did."

"But I didn't get yours."

"Jack Shepherd. I'm a private investigator. Trying to locate a friend."

Molly considered that information. She stared across the concrete and beyond to the gorge and the river.

"His name is Bill Marsh," I went on. "You may know his wife, May. She runs the Drop-In Centre in Bedminster."

Molly turned back to me, nodded, but said nothing. I went on.

"I think a group of people are trying to get the centre closed," I said.

"People are doing that constantly," Molly said.

"Alright… But I'm finding things which appear to be a lot more sinister. Which might be connected to the men who visited earlier. Their boss sent them here to find somebody, and they chose your friend. Can you tell me his name?"

Molly knew there was more by way of explanation. She said nothing and waited. I pressed on.

"All of you here have visited the Centre, right?"

"Yes. Some of us still do so."

"Including the man the Transit drivers wanted to take away?"

"Yes."

"Will you give me his name?"

"Donald. Don, he likes to be called."

"His full name," I said.

Molly shook her head.

"I promise you this isn't about him." I said. "It's about the visitors you had. I'm trying to find out why Don should be a target."

Molly looked steadfastly into my eyes.

A voice called from our left. "Weaver."

Molly and I turned and looked at the man we were talking about. He walked across the concrete towards us.

"Donald Malcolm Weaver," he said.

We stood stock still, three corners of a triangle. Above us, the sound of traffic rumbled on. Weaver stood straight and tall. His thick soled black shoes were scruffy, his grey trousers were dirty at the knees, but the heavy tweed jacket looked clean by comparison. He wore it well. Like a man who, at some time, had been able to afford a bespoke suit or two. Somewhere, he had washed his face and cleaned the wound on his forehead, but the skin was torn and needed stitches. He anticipated what I was about to say.

"I'm not going to a doctor." He spoke with no recognisable accent.

I asked a routine question.

"Do you think the men in the Transit came looking for you, personally? Or were they on a fishing expedition?"

Weaver thought about this for a second or two. The wail of an ambulance siren faded up onto the soundtrack above us, passed over our heads, then diminished as it raced on.

"I don't know," he said. "All of us here, are as anonymous as it's possible to get," He surveyed the cavernous concrete space that passed for home. "At least Martin's okay now. Way beyond all this."

His eyes filled with tears. He sniffed and pressed the fingers of his hands into his eye sockets. Then he dropped his arms and apologised. Molly moved to his side.

"It's alright. You're allowed to cry for Martin. That's the one thing you can do for him now."

He talked to me. "Where will Martin be?"

"I don't know," I said. "He may still be in the morgue."

"Is there a chance that he's already…?"

Don wasn't able to finish the sentence. Molly gathered him into her arms. I tried to help.

"His body will still be in cold storage," I said, attempting to be upbeat, recalling my recent brush with the regulations. "No vagrant is buried or cremated, until the local authority is satisfied that all attempts to trace a relative or the next of kin, have been unsuccessful. I'll find out what I can on your behalf." I paused. Thought about how to how to phrase the next bit. "In Martin's case, there is another consideration. He has only one lung. He probably sold the other."

Molly and Don stared at me; neither of them, it seemed, able to speak. I looked at Don. Asked him how old he was.

"Thirty-six," he said.

"And in spite of living like this, are you well?"

"I think so."

"What do you do if you become ill?"

"We don't," he said. "Become ill I mean. Colds, flu, sprains, aches, pains... We try to ignore them."

"Seriously ill then. Where do you go?"

"To the NHS Walk-In Centre, in Broadmead."

"Is that where your medical records are kept?"

"I guess so. I've never thought about it."

"Okay. And the only other place which has information on you, is the Drop-In Centre in Bedminster?"

"Yes."

"And is this the same with you, Molly?"

"Yes. Now will you tell us what this - "

I held up my right hand. "Just one more thing. And it's very important. Have there been other disappearances or deaths among the homeless groups that you know? Recently, I mean. Say during the last nine to twelve months."

Molly and Don looked at each other. I waited. Don spoke first.

"A man called Ted Morris used to live here with us. He disappeared during the summer last year. Late August."

"How old was he?" I asked.

"Late 20s," Molly said. "He had been living on the streets for seven years he told me. Just a day or two before he disappeared."

"How did he disappear?"

"He left here mid-morning, to see if he could find something to eat. And he didn't come back."

"Could he be living with another group? Or on his own?"

Don answered this question. "That could be so," he said. "But he isn't. We don't have much of a network, but if Ted was around somewhere we would know. The Drop-In Centre would know."

Molly was impatient now. "Jack, please, tell us what this is all about."

I looked at them both. Then told them about following the Transit.

"I think those men were supposed to collect you. Like they did Martin and Ted."

"Why?" Molly asked.

"This isn't much beyond an educated guess," I said. "But it could be that their boss has copies of your personal records, such as they are."

Molly opened her mouth to speak. I held up my hand again and talked to Don.

"You have no kin at all, right?"

Don shook his head. "No."

"How many people know who, and where, you are?"

"I don't know," he said. "A couple of dozen maybe."

Molly interrupted. "Come on, Jack. Explain."

"I believe you are on the list of those two latter day resurrection men. A list of people whose loss to the world will not cause the slightest ripple. Who are being offered money for body parts."

I waited while Molly and Don absorbed that rationalisation. Then I asked him if he would consider selling a kidney for five hundred pounds. He looked at me, dead centre.

"I might," he said.

I turned to my left.

"Molly?"

She responded with another question. "Are you sure about all this?"

"No," I said. "And I don't want to believe any of it."

"Because you're telling us… that someone, somewhere, is running his own private enterprise, from his own operating theatre. In secret."

"Yes."

We stood in as much quiet as a traffic underpass allows. Then I decided on an upbeat line.

"Did you have lunch?" I asked.

"No," Molly said.

"Let's go do that then," I said.

Sid Swift's Meals on Wheels van was a few hundred yards away, along the riverbank, parked at the entrance to a garden centre with no café. Sid conducted his business on the understanding that the garden centre staff could eat and drink at mates' rates, and a percentage of his earnings went into a charity box.

I have known Sid for years. He's 50 something. A stocky character, broad shouldered, bearded and a devoted City fan. He cooks seven days a week, dawn 'til dusk, save for the Saturday afternoons City play at home, half a mile away. No prejudice shown, no judgements ever made. When they had money, Molly and Don were customers.

Sid nodded a greeting at them and turned to me.

"Jack Shepherd, as I live and breathe."

From inside the van, a foot or so above me, he reached across the counter and extended his right arm. I shook his hand.

"How are you, Sid?"

"Never better, Jack."

Burger and chips all round were accompanied by large mugs of steaming thick brown tea. Molly and Don ate without speaking, as if any lack of attention would see the food whisked away. After we had finished eating and Sid had presented us with a second mug of tea, Molly and Don told me their stories.

Molly was forty-two years old; a nurse with two marriages behind her. Her first husband died at the age of 28; trying to save himself and the family dog, one bank holiday when they were trapped by the tide and the mud at Burnham on Sea. She had become addicted to anti-depressants as a result, then prone to serious mood swings. She was prescribed more pills to keep her stable, but had difficulty getting up in the morning and getting on with the day. She began to steal from hospital medication cupboards. She was fired. And lost in a regime of uppers and downers, attempted suicide. In the end she beat the drugs; but not her second husband, who at the slightest upset, beat the shit out of her. She left him. He refused to buy her out of the house, simply banned her from entering it again. Molly rented a flat and took the best job she could find, with an office cleaning company. She lost that job when the company downsized. Then ran out of money trying to keep body and soul together and was thrown out of her flat when she fell three months behind with the rent. She had been on the streets three years.

Don was a long-distance lorry driver. He loved the job. Did it for fifteen years, until he ran down a seven-year-old child on a zebra crossing. It loaded him with guilt, destroyed the joy and the freedom the job gave him, and broke his spirit.

"It still comes back to haunt me," he said. "Through cold, wide-awake nights, and long empty days."

"What about your family? I mean, way back."

Don unveiled a potted history, without any sentimentality.

"No parents anymore. My sister died when she was six. My mother died weeks later, of a broken heart. My father jumped off the roof of the office building he was working in. I spent years in and out of foster homes. I left school as soon as I could, got an apprenticeship in a garage and trained as a mechanic. Then got an HGV licence. I've never really had a long-standing relationship of any sort."

On the surface, there was nothing about Molly and Don which said 'victim'. Nothing about them, apart from the threadbare clothes, which said 'homeless'. Nothing about their conversation which said 'ignorant'. Nothing about them which said 'loser'. Ignored until forgotten maybe, but somehow, managing to stay alive under seriously brutal circumstances. I asked if either of them knew a lady called Lily.

"She had that name on a chain around her neck."

"She was run down by a car," Don said. "I heard about it. I knew her. We shared a squat for a while. She told me she came from somewhere in the home counties. I lost touch with her after we were evicted."

Molly sipped her tea. Don stared into the distance.

"I'll try and find out what's happening with Martin's body," I said.

I got up from the table, waved goodbye to Sid, and walked back to the office.

CHAPTER FIFTEEN

I drove to the Drop-In Centre. Sat down in the office with May. She introduced me to Harry – a young man born and brought up in Bedminster.

Over tea and biscuits I told them the story of the day. Asked how many people were on file.

"Seventy-six," Harry said. "No seventy-five now, without Martin."

"And all the hard copy was originated on this pc?"

"Yes."

"Information which was stolen during the break in," May said.

She looked at Harry. He nodded at me.

It focused our attention. The speculation that the Transit men were picking up to order, now had substance. I asked May and Harry the question about regular visitors disappearing from their radar.

Harry blew out his cheeks. "People do stop coming, of course. Sometimes, thankfully, it's because their situation has improved."

"And you get to hear about those cases?"

"Usually, yes."

"And the others?"

"Sometimes we hear of them living in other communities."

"So who has gone missing recently?"

"Three I can think of," Harry said.

I waited. He looked at May, checking his assessment.

"We last saw Alice Davis three or four months ago," May said.

Harry nodded. "Late January," he said. "I remember that because she told me it was her birthday in a couple of days. I told her we'd have tea and cakes. She smiled. It was a great smile when it arrived. Ear to ear. She left still smiling. But she didn't come back."

He looked at May, who said softly, "Yes I remember."

"Was Alice fit and well?" I asked.

"Yes, she was," May said. She searched the files in her head. "Somewhere in her 40s. She seemed to thrive on misfortune, no matter what she had to face. I don't remember anything getting her down."

"And the other two?"

Harry contributed again. "Ted Harris," he said.

"Yes," I said. "Molly and Don told me about him."

"Did they tell you about Brian Watson?"

"No."

"Brian was a gentle man," May said. "Self-contained. Listening to music the rest of us couldn't hear. The kind of person you have to look out for. He never told us where he lived. We tried to find out, of course, but that's a delicate exercise at best. The risk is the person you're trying to help will discover what you're doing, and then move on."

"Is that what happened with Brian?"

"No," Harry said. "We had given up digging into stuff about Brian. Just welcomed him without questions."

"And when did he disappear?" I asked.

"Between Christmas and New Year. We had a bit of a do here on New Year's Eve. Brian didn't show. And hasn't done so since. Does that help?"

"Yes, unfortunately."

* * *

In the office building lobby, Jason waved to me from the reception desk. I nodded and raised my right thumb. Upstairs, Linda had slipped a note under my office door.

This is so foolish Jack. I'm back late afternoon. Can we sit down and talk?

With a lighter heart I made some coffee, filled a mug, sat in my chair, leaned back and put my feet on the desk. The inside pocket of my jacket began ringing. I found the mobile and answered the call.

Bill Marsh asked, "Where are you, Jack?"

I swung my feet off the desk and sat upright in my chair.

"No no, Bill. The question is, where are you?"

"We'll get to that," Bill said. "You first."

"I'm in my office."

"We need to meet," Bill said.

"Fine. Name a place and I'll be there with bells on."

"It's just after four, yes?"

I looked at the clock on the wall. "Three minutes past."

"I'll meet you at 5.30."

"Where?"

"I'll figure that out and call you back."

"Why? What's to figure out?"

"Just go with this, Jack. Please."

"Do you know that Len Coleman's dead?"

There was a long pause. Difficult to tell whether Bill was absorbing the news, or trying to work out a reply.

In the end he said, "No more questions, Jack. At least not right now."

He ended the call. I switched my mobile off, placed it on the desk and stared at it. It rang again.

"Bill called from an address on Rycroft Road," Harvey Butler said. "George is on the way. Holmes and a couple of uniforms with him."

"Have I your permission to join the posse?"

"Best, I think. You'd probably go anyway."

"Is it a home or a business address?"

"We're checking that."

I called May. She wasn't at the Centre. I called home. Got the answering machine and left a message. "It's Jack. I've just had a call from Bill. He's alive and well. More later." I rang May's mobile. Same result. I left the same message.

Harvey called again, as I crossed the car park and reached the Healey.

"We think Bill was calling from *Faversham Funeral Services*," he said. "Has he gone into the undertaking business?"

"Not that I know."

"Well if you get there swiftly enough, you might get to ask him."

I headed northeast, towards Filton. It took me nineteen minutes to get to Rycroft Road. A patrol car and George Hood's Vauxhall were sitting in the car park to the left of the funeral parlour. PC Deeley, who I'd met on a couple of occasions, was stationed at the door. He bade me a good afternoon and waved me inside.

Funeral parlours are odd places; the atmosphere part church, part morgue and part library. I haven't spent too much time in them, but they are always as I expect them to be – a breathless hush underscored by organ music. Like a reverent department store lift. The lighting in the lobby was low wattage, provided by small, soft glow bulbs. A dado rail stained in dark oak, ran all the way round the lobby at waist height. Below it some sort of textured lining paper was painted a silver grey. Above the rail and across the entire ceiling, the colour was a soft off white.

PC Laker was standing in the hall. She nodded at me.

"Nice to see you again, Mr Shepherd."

I returned the compliment, both of us speaking in hushed tones. PC Laker pointed along the hall.

"The Funeral Director's office is to the right."

It was a big room, with a big window clothed by a long vertical strip blind, and otherwise furnished in the accepted mortician's vernacular - polished light oak panels around all four walls, with discrete lights shining from a suspended ceiling. A dark brown upholstered chesterfield and two matching chairs made up the guest accommodation. The place was uber tidy. Sitting behind a big desk, a tall man with a long face and an expensive haircut was staring, in vehement denial, at Hood and DC Holmes. All three looked at me as I slipped in through the doorway. Holmes nodded a greeting. Hood made the introduction.

"This is Mr Berling, Jack. The Senior Undertaker here. He says he hasn't seen his boss Mr Faversham, since this time last week."

"Has he any idea where Mr Faversham might be?" I asked.

"He says not."

"Does he know if, or when, Mr Faversham is coming back?"

"He can't commit himself."

"So ask him if — "

Berling interrupted, irritated by the third person conversation. "I am in the room," he said.

Hood turned to him. "So make a contribution to the debate."

"Mr Faversham is the Funeral Director," Berling said. "This is his company. He is the man in charge."

"Okay," Hood said. "As we're here, do you mind if we look around?"

"Have you got a warrant?" Berling asked.

Hood stared at him, then transferred his attention to Holmes and me. We both looked suitably disappointed. Hood turned back to Berling.

"We usually find that those who have nothing to hide, agree readily to such a proposition."

"Ah yes… er Detective Sergeant. But this is something of a special place. We have clients lying at rest here. I simply cannot allow you to disturb the peace and tranquillity of any room in this establishment."

"We will do our utmost to respect that," Hood said.

Berling swallowed and breathed in, exhaled and swallowed again. Hood helped him out.

"I can send PC Deeley to find a magistrate and get a warrant issued. And in the meantime we'll just sit here and wait for him to return."

Berling got to his feet. "I must register a serious protest at all this."

"Noted," Hood said.

Berling moved around the desk, ushered us out of the room, and we embarked on a guided tour of the place. Beginning with two more offices. Followed by the embalmer's work place, and the 'Design Room', where the range of coffins and accoutrements were on display. We were then allowed to inspect the 'Dressing Room', the place in which the client was prepared for his last resting place. Berling allowed Hood to take only one step into 'Rest Room One' and 'Rest Room Two', both of which contained occupied coffins. Finally, we all got to see the store room; stacked with a range of wood panels, drapes, gold plated coffin handles, corner plates, screw toggles, shelves of paraphernalia and tools of the trade.

"We design and build everything to order," Berling said, pride in his work getting the better of him. "In our workshop in Horfield. But we assemble the final bespoke product in this space. We have a first-class carpenter and a fabric designer on contract. Now if you don't mind…"

Hood thanked Berling for his co-operation and allowed him to escort us into the street. PCs Laker and Deeley had begun to recce the building's exterior. The exercise didn't reveal much. The curtains were drawn across the windows facing the street. Behind the building there was some architectural confusion. The funeral parlour had once been two semi-detached homes, re-modelled when the use was changed to business. The space which had once been the garden, now housed the rooms we had just visited.

Hood, Holmes and I had a conference by the Vauxhall.

"Okay," he said. "Bill was here, looking for Faversham who wasn't. And that provoked the phone call to you. Which isn't much of a result, given that we are three clever detectives."

No result at all, in essence. And now, Arnold Faversham had joined the platoon of persons missing.

Hood spoke to Holmes. "Another house to house for you to organise, Sherlock. All doors within a fifty-yard radius. Armed with a description of Bill and a picture."

Holmes collected Laker and Deeley and gave them some instructions. Laker got on to her phone and called for reinforcements. I moved to my car, Hood alongside me.

"What the hell is Bill doing?" he asked. "I mean, look who we've dredged up so far. Freddie Settle, whose organisation is known for dealing in dead people, Len Coleman who is dead, and the disappeared Arnold Faversham, who has two dead people in his parlour."

"Presumably for reasons other than criminal," I said.

"Hard to assess, when he's not here to ask. Do you think Berling's in the loop?"

"Probably not," I said. "Seeing that he's still at work, and not in hiding somewhere."

I unlocked the Healey driver's door.

* * *

I was back in my office by half past five, with nothing to do but sit and wait for Bill to call. He didn't. At half past six Adam did, offering to buy me a drink. I told him I didn't want to leave the office. That I was expecting a call, and if lucky, a visit from Linda.

"I'll come to you,"

I did some more waiting. Bill still didn't ring, and Linda didn't appear. Adam was the first to show.

"I've been digging around for the last couple of days," Adam said. "Downloaded everything the Post has on the Settle family, and called an Inspector I know in Serious Crimes." He waved a data stick at me and pointed at the laptop on my desk. "May I?"

He sat down in one of my client chairs, shuffled up to the desk, swung the laptop around and fired it up. Inserted the data stick, tapped a key or two and swung the screen back to me.

"The highlights," he said. "Take a look."

There were a dozen *Post* pieces on the stick. Stories about the Settle empire which cut close to the bone – though not close enough to make Freddy call his expensive lawyers – and a selection of photographs.

One featured a group of people at a charity fund raiser. Daughter Freddie on her father's arm, beaming into the camera lens. Another starred Bill and May, in company with Walter Cobb, the Regional Director of a local children's charity and Freddy Senior. A third displayed the two Freddies in the foyer of the Hippodrome, at a reception for the English National Opera, on tour with *Don Giovanni*. Freddy Senior was smiling that smile he had bequeathed to his daughter. There was a photo taken at a garden party to launch a new environment initiative, with Walter Cobb, the Lord Mayor, the city council Finance Director and Freddy Senior side by side. And the most bizarre picture – celebrating the opening of a new hospital wing – was a line-up of two surgeons in dark blue suits, a nurse, and the Westcountry Hospital Trust Administrator standing in front of an ambulance. All of them smiling at the camera, with the nurse shaking Freddy Senior's hand.

Adam moved around the desk and looked over my right shoulder.

"Freddy paid for the hospital wing" he said. "Got his name on a plaque inside the entrance. Inspired, isn't it? Money laundered courtesy of the NHS."

I looked at the next photograph, taken on Bill Marsh's front lawn. His sixty-fifth birthday bash a year ago. Two lines of local worthies. Bill and May front and centre, next to the two Freddies.

"Look at them all," Adam said. "Is that really the sort of company we would expect Bill and May to keep?"

"Maybe," I said. "Maybe not."

The last photograph was the most interesting. Taken with a long lens across the floating harbour, it showed Freddy Senior sitting at a window table in a waterside bistro, facing a man I didn't recognise. Adam straightened up and moved back to his chair.

"That is James Warburton," he said.

I shook my head. "Doesn't mean a thing."

"He owns eighteen hundred acres on top of the Mendips. *The High Combe Estate.*"

"So Freddy Settle is having lunch with a well-heeled landowner," I said. "What can you make out of that?"

"Not much, if you have a cheerfully unsuspicious mind. However, if you know Freddy and are inclined to believe the worst of him, then all sorts of possibilities occur."

"Is this a *Post* picture?"

"Taken by a stringer."

"But you didn't use it?"

"No. We sent a reporter out to the estate to talk with James Warburton. On the pretence of doing a series on managing the countryside."

"And?"

"Warburton wasn't interested in talking to us. One of the subs put a researcher on the story. She discovered that a couple of the quangos helping to fund the estate had been dissolved. And the remit of two government agencies, also involved, had been reviewed. She believed that Warburton was about to run out of money."

"So, being the suspicious souls we are, we presume that Freddy was prepared to fill the financial holes."

"First response, yes."

"And...?"

"The trail went dead. The researcher couldn't find anything else."

I looked at the photograph again. Adam waited for my response.

"Alright," I said. "What would Freddy Settle want with eighteen hundred acres of woodland?"

"Something to think about," Adam said. He moved to the door. "I'll leave the data stick with you. Love to Linda."

He walked out of the office. I stared at the open doorway. The phone rang. I grabbed the receiver. Jason asked me if I had any letters to post. I told him 'thank you but no'. He said he hoped I would have a good evening and rang off.

The time slid painfully on towards 8 o'clock. Evening was signalled by the sky darkening outside.

Bill still didn't call.

At 8.30, Linda appeared and tapped on the open door. Framed by the architrave she looked terrific. Blue silk blouse, and blue denim skirt, the hem an inch or so above her sensational knees.

"Hi," she said.

I stood up and walked round the desk. Linda stepped into the office, closed the door, locked it, and leaned back against it. I moved into her arms. We kissed. Linda arched her back, lifted her hips and pressed close. I started to shake. She felt it. Swung us both round and reversed our positions. The door took my weight. She leaned the whole length of her body against me and began, very slowly, to rotate her hips. I groaned. For a split second I thought "Christ, Bill, don't ring now." Linda pulled me away from the door, reversing slowly towards the desk, then eased out of the embrace. She dropped to her knees on the carpet. I did the same. She leaned into me again. I rocked back, slid my heels out from under me and lay down. Linda slid into position beside me.

"Now you," she said.

We rolled through one hundred and eighty degrees. I looked down at her. I have a history of buggering up great moments like this. 'Take it easy, Shepherd,' I said to myself. 'Just make it work.'

"Don't think about this, Jack, for fuck's sake," Linda breathed. "Just do it."

CHAPTER SIXTEEN

"Are either of us contemplating work today?" Linda asked.

Saturday morning, five minutes past nine. We were lying with our heads propped up on pillows, looking out of the bedroom window at a vast expanse of the Bristol Channel.

Linda had moved into the best-preserved bit of old Portishead, a year and a half ago. Woodlands Road runs west to east behind an avenue of houses built perilously close to the Severn Estuary cliff tops. Her home is a two-storey art deco house, which feels as if it's hanging over the cliff edge. The windows in the living room and the bedroom above, are big and wide; like the view across the water to Wales. The spring equinox is always a bit of an adventure on this exposed bit of clifftop. When the prevailing wind is blowing with the rain streaming sideways, it hits the windows with some force, beating a tattoo on the double glazing. This morning, the wind was blowing gently and the sky was clear.

"I have tickets to a shindig at the Royal West Academy. Champagne and canapés at noon."

"In aid of what?" I asked.

She looked at me oddly, as if I was a child who had spoken out of turn.

"Art," she said. "The launch of a new gallery space and a celebration of an endowment from somebody. Take your wallet. We may be asked to contribute."

"No such thing then, as free champagne and canapés."

A mobile rang from somewhere. I looked at Linda.

"It's not mine," she said.

I sat up. My phone was ringing on the chest of drawers

facing the bed. I got up to answer it.

Bridget Dean had news.

"I've found my late, greedy bastard employer's old iPad," she said.

"An old one. How many has he got?"

"He thinks he has one only. In all the office upheaval, I found the one he thought he'd lost. I think we should talk."

"Okay," I said. "Now?"

"I think sooner is better than later," she said. "Have you had breakfast?"

"No."

"Come and have it with me."

She gave me her address. I looked at the bedside clock again, told Bridget I'd be with her before ten, and rang off. I turned back to face Linda.

"Where will you be before ten? And with whom?"

"Walter Cobb's secretary and long-established right-hand person," I said.

"That's a pity," Linda said, looking directly at my crotch.

Suddenly I felt vulnerable. No man can make rational explanations trouser-less. Linda eased out from under the duvet and crawled along the bed towards me.

"You not going to breakfast with another woman without something to remember," she said.

I managed to extricate myself from the bed twenty minutes later, struggled into jeans and a shirt, and said I'd be back in an hour or so. The Saturday morning traffic was light, and twenty-five minutes later I was across the Cumberland Basin and into Hotwells. Bridget's house sat on one of the narrow hillside terraces which run down from lower Clifton. I found a parking space about fifty yards from her front door.

Whereupon my mobile rang. Helen was on the other end

of the line, disturbed and frightened.

"May has disappeared," she said.

"You mean she's not at home?"

"I mean she hasn't been home since breakfast yesterday."

I sat in the car, staring through the windscreen. Helen took this hiatus at my end of the line, as less than encouraging. She broke the silence.

"What do I do, Jack?"

"Nothing until I get to you. Within the hour, I promise."

"Okay, thanks," Helen said and ended the call.

Bridget answered the door before the echoes of the doorbell died away.

She ushered me into the living room – knocked through into the kitchen, and occupying the whole of the ground floor of the tiny house. It was simply furnished, but the cushions were big, the fabrics and curtains brightly coloured, which made the room feel more substantial than it was.

"It's a pleasure to see you again, Jack," Bridget said.

I returned the compliment. She was wearing a pale blue tee shirt and dark blue jeans She pointed at the sofa, moved into the kitchen area and called back to me.

"Cereal, eggs, toast…?"

"No breakfast," I said. "Just coffee please."

She poured coffee into a mug from a coffee maker. Launched straight into the story.

"The Receivers are on the way," she said. "They'll be in on Monday. And as I'm the only one who knows how the business works, they've kept me on the payroll temporarily."

"Is there anything you can tell them?"

"I've no idea. I don't know what Walter's actually doing, or how he's managing to do it."

She handed me the mug and sat down at the other end

of the sofa, leaving two feet of space between us. Reached behind her and picked up an iPad sitting on the side table alongside the sofa arm.

"A real house of secrets this."

"How did you get into it?"

She grinned at me. "I know all his passwords."

"Does he know you know?"

"Yes. A breach of security perhaps, but neither of us imagined he'd be in the shit and we'd be in this situation." She paused for effect, then went on. "I think Walter has been doing business in the Channel Islands."

"Since when?"

"Not long I imagine. There is folder in there, created during the summer of 2014. Labelled *Cobb CI*."

"What's in it?"

"Stuff to do with a place called *Channel Skies*."

"And that is…?"

"I don't know."

"No contact addresses or phone numbers?

She shook her head. We both pondered for a second or two.

"If CI does mean Channel Islands," she said, "ten to one it's where Walter's stashed money he doesn't want any of us to know about."

"Can the Receivers get at it?" I asked.

"I doubt it," she I said. "That'll be why it's there."

I sipped at my coffee mug. Bridget put the iPad on the sofa between us.

"And…" she said. "I found a series of emails between Walter and Bill Marsh." She reached behind her and picked up a data stick and some sheets of A4.

"I've printed them out. I didn't get round to other stuff. I thought I could leave that to the super sleuth."

The emails covered a period of five months over the late summer and autumn of 2016. They were about money – basically Cobb spending huge sums of it and asking Bill for more.

"So what do you think? What was going on?"

We sat on the sofa in silence, for some time, shrouded in wondering. I drained the coffee mug. Then I told Bridget that May had disappeared too. She groaned. Leaned back into the sofa cushions and stared up at the ceiling.

"Christ… Can you sort all this out, Jack?" she asked.

"I don't know." I nodded at the iPad. "May I take this?"

"The Receivers will want it on Monday."

"I'll get it back to you by then."

Bridget stood up and moved to her desk. Wrote the iPad password on a piece of paper, then ushered me to the front door. I stepped outside and walked to the Healey. When I turned to look back, Bridget waved, reversed into the house and closed the door.

I drove to Syme Park going through the expanding list of missing persons. First Bill, still alive at the time of yesterday afternoon's phone call. Len Coleman, dead on his living room floor. Arnold Faversham hiding. Walter Cobb, somewhere, counting his money. And now May, just somewhere.

I pulled up in Downs Avenue at 10.45. The press corps had melted into thin air. I told Helen Bill had called me, but it didn't diminish the stress levels much. I asked her if anyone had phoned to speak to May.

"No… Do you think she might have found where Bill is, and gone to see him?"

"Not without telling us. Unless there's another secret being kept."

Helen looked distressed again. I suggested she should go home. She nodded.

"Yes, that's probably best. Yes, I'll do that."

"Do you want me to give you a lift?"

"No no. That's fine."

"You know where I am," I said.

I used the phone in Bill's office to call Chris Gould.

"How are you at getting into hidden files on an iPad?"

"Fairly useful," he said. "Bring it round and I'll take a look."

I drove into Bedminster and handed it over.

"Are you looking for anything in particular?" Chris asked.

"Stuff on the Channel Islands. And anything you can dig out with the names of Bill Marsh, Walter Cobb and Len Coleman attached."

He wrote the names down. I told him about the police phone tap. He took an old 3G mobile from a drawer and handed it to me.

"Keep this for a few days. The number's on the piece of masking tape on the back. I'll call you on that phone until you tell me otherwise."

I got back to Portishead ten minutes before noon. Linda was dressed and ready for the champagne gig. Smart casual was never so sensational. We drove in the Healey to my house. I changed into the closest I ever get to smart casual. We left at 12.30, for the heart of the city's gallery land.

* * *

The Royal West Academy is one half of a small outbreak of Victoriana at the end of Queens Road, in Clifton. The other half is represented by the Victoria Rooms, situated forty yards from the academy on the other side of a roundabout.

The former is an understated, classically restrained, example of the oeuvre. The latter, all swirls and ridiculous detail, is an over-the-top gothic revival meets retro-Corinthian statement, fronted by lions and nymphs, a fountain and a statue on a sculpted plinth. Miraculously, we found a parking space behind the RWA.

Walking to the gallery, Linda fished the invitation cards from her hand bag. She stopped walking and froze on the pavement.

"Bloody Hell…"

I turned to face her. She held one of the cards under my nose.

"Look who the heroine of this little gathering is."

I read the card. Writ large was the name of Freddie Settle, philanthropist and art lover. Linda synchronised her deep breathing with mine.

"Does this revelation change our minds?" Linda asked. "Are we the sort of people to be intimidated by this?"

"Probably not. For we are strong and our cause is just."

Linda smiled at me. "Hell yes."

We walked into the front door of the Academy, past a life size photograph of Freddie dressed to the nines. By the time we reached the first-floor gallery, she was drawing to the end of her welcome meet and greet, standing on a rostrum under a massive splurge of red and brown by an artist I didn't know. Flanked by her accountant Cyril and the Gallery Director. Gareth Thomas, wearing a light grey suit and a charming smile, was standing on the floor in front of the rostrum.

"That's a twelve hundred quid outfit she's wearing," Linda whispered.

"Bringing exhibitions of this quality to the Westcountry takes time and money," Freddie was saying. "And while I can't claim to have done any of the hard work, I'm only too pleased to take all the credit for paying the bills."

There was ripple of polite laughter from the assembled art supporters. Freddie acknowledged this and scanned the room.

"Unfortunately, I have a busy afternoon ahead. So I can't stay long."

She saw us loitering at the rear of the gallery, stopped working the room, and aimed the smile in our direction.

"Please enjoy the reception and these glorious works of art. Thank you all for coming."

The art supporters applauded. Freddie shook hands with the Gallery Director and stepped off the rostrum. Cyril joined Thomas. A raven-haired teenager with a smile to rival Freddie's, thrust a plate of vol au vents at me.

"Can I tempt you, Sir?"

"No thank you," I said. "Perhaps later."

Linda stepped to my shoulder. "What do we do now?"

"Do you want to be introduced?"

"I should say so. A once in a lifetime opportunity to meet the crime boss."

"Let's hope it is only once."

A colleague of the raven-haired teenager swung into position in front of us with a tray of champagne glasses. Linda took one and nodded her thanks. I was still looking at Freddie. Linda picked up a second champagne glass and nudged my elbow.

"Jack…"

I took the glass. Freddie was flowing across the gallery floor. Managing to acknowledge everyone she passed, but clearly heading for us. Thomas and Cyril followed, two strides behind her.

"Jack," she cooed, and directed the nuclear-powered smile straight into my eyes. Before turning to Linda. "Hello, Ms Barnes."

Linda blinked a couple of times, surprised that Freddie knew who she was. She took a deep breath and swallowed.

"Ms Settle," she said.

"Call me Freddie. So pleased to meet you. Unfortunately, I must fly."

"I had no idea you were a patron of the arts, Freddie," I said.

"Something my father did. So we carry on the tradition. So important. Places like this would be forced to close without the support of local businesses."

Hard to disagree with that. Nonetheless, Freddie's expansion, and the malignant growth of Settle influence over long revered city institutions, was no cause for cheer.

A mobile rang. Thomas took a phone from his inside jacket pocket and clamped it to his ear.

"Thank you," he said. He returned the phone to his pocket. "The car is downstairs, Ms Settle."

She looked at us and shrugged politely.

"Sorry. Come and have a drink with me. Soon. We have lots to talk about."

Really? That was the most loaded invitation I'd been offered in a long while. Linda looked alarmed. Freddie flowed past us and out onto the landing. Thomas nodded at me as he followed.

"Mr Shepherd…"

Cyril offered no acknowledgement at all. Simply slid by. Linda grabbed my hand and leaned close.

"She's good. Really good. And she frightens the shit out of me."

"You're not alone in that. However…"

Linda thought that I was about to resolve something. She let go of my hand. When I didn't say anything more she changed tack.

"You've got that determined look in your eye," she said.

I stared at her. "What look?"

"The one you get when you're determined."

"It's only there to fool the public."

"Is there any chance that Freddie wants to discuss something constructive?"

"'We have lots to talk about' loses something in the translation. What she meant was, 'I'm still on your case'."

Linda took that on board, then resolutely moved things along.

"Okay," she said. "In the meantime, let's have some more champagne and give this art the once over."

CHAPTER SEVENTEEN

The art was exciting. Brand new. From painters and sculptors throughout Britain and Europe. The vol au vents were rather good, once we got around to them. We set off for home, mid-afternoon. I turned the Healey into the lane behind my house. And drove towards the silver Audi, parked outside my garage.

"Is that erm…?" Linda asked.

"Gareth and Dylan, yes."

Back to lean on my car and wave guns at me. No doubt a more substantial dose of menace guaranteed this time, with Linda included. I reacted with the first idea that entered my head. Put the Healey into reverse and floored the accelerator pedal. Gareth and Dylan were slow to react. We were well ahead of the Audi as I braked at the lane entrance and swung out into the bus lane. A number 83 bus pulled away from the stop about twenty yards behind us. I found first gear, moved forward and eased right into the designated traffic lane. The bus crossed the lane entrance as the Audi scorched out of it. The engine roar behind us was overwhelmed by a loud tearing noise and the sound of buckling metal.

I swung back into the bus lane and stopped the Healey. Looked across the car at a remarkably cool Linda.

"Go home and wait for me," I pointed through the windscreen. "Left up ahead then twice again. You don't have anything to do with this."

"Neither have you," she said.

"That's something to be discussed."

"No no," she said. "The Audi driver charged out of the lane and into the bus. You didn't cause this. If anyone did, it was those two in the car. Freddie even. If she hadn't sent – "

"There is no need for you to be part of this," I interrupted. "I'm going to find out how badly hurt Freddie's employees are. Sitting in my living room, waiting for her to ring and ask me what I did to her car and her enforcers, isn't an option. She will lay all this at my door whatever. Please, go home."

She stared at me for what seemed ages.

"Okay. I'll sit in your living room and drink your brandy. So don't be long."

I got out of the car and left Linda sliding across the front seats. Took a deep breath and walked back along the bus lane.

The Audi was crushed to about three quarters of its length and was jammed into the bus doorway. Inside, the driver had manged to get out of the driving seat and around the Audi bonnet. He was checking on his passengers. He moved to the rear emergency door and opened it.

Inside the Audi, all four airbags had exploded into action. The interior was a mess of bent plastic, broken glass, torn leather, tangled upholstery and twisted metal. The two front deflated airbags were streaked with blood. Both Thomases were unconscious. Gareth behind the driving wheel, his head way over to the right of his neck, glass and blood in his hair. Dylan, head down on his chest with an ugly wound in the side of his neck, which was bleeding steadily. One of the passengers, moved to my side clutching his mobile.

"I've just called an ambulance. The fire brigade is on the way too."

The bus driver joined us. Stared at the men in the front seats.

"Jesus Christ…" He looked at the two of us. "The car

came out of the lane so fast..."

* * *

The paramedics couldn't get at the two men in the Audi. The Fire and Rescue team set to work. The medics checked all the bus passengers and treated the driver for shock. They wrapped him in a blanket and made him sit in the ambulance. A couple of police patrol cars arrived. Uniformed PCs talked to all of us about we had seen.

It took some time for the rescue team to cut away enough of the tangled remains of the car to allow the medics to get inside and work from the rear seats. They managed to stop the blood flowing out of Dylan's neck. He regained consciousness, at least for a moment, then floated in and out. Gareth was still unconscious when the medics loaded him into the ambulance.

I walked home up the lane. Linda moved into the kitchen as I opened the back door. In the living room, I poured a large brandy and sat down in the nearest armchair. I looked at Linda, perched on the sofa like a maiden aunt waiting for the little boy who has spent the day getting into trouble, to fess up.

Chris Gould's mobile began to ring. I found my jacket and retrieved it.

"*Cobb CI* is in Jersey," Chris said. "I'll email the folders and files to you. Not much I'm afraid. There is no communication with Len Coleman, and no more about Bill Marsh than you know already. But there are one or two emails between Cobb and somebody called Arnold Faversham."

I thanked him, and said I'd pick up the iPad first thing the following morning.

"That's a new, very old phone," Linda said. "What is it, a spare?"

I changed the subject. "How much do you know about banking in Jersey?" .

"A bit. Why?"

"It's where Walter Cobb keeps his money."

"You mean the money he's not telling the receivers about," Linda said.

There was a pause. I waited for her to assemble information.

"We tend to think of offshore, in terms of exotic sounding places like the Cayman Islands, Barbados, the Seychelles, Belize," she said. "But there's a long list of prospects closer to home – Andorra, Luxembourg, The Isle of Man, Jersey…"

"And all these places offer the same kinds of service?"

"Basically, tax avoidance and serious opportunities for money laundering," she said. "Jersey is an odd place. It obviously doesn't have the glamour that exotic places flaunt. It's ruled rather like a medieval bailiwick, according to laws written in Jerriais – a kind of ancient muddle of French and English. The islanders are British but not European citizens. Jersey isn't in the EU."

"Effectively, a foreign country then."

"And these days the island's business isn't about cows and tomatoes. Agriculture makes bugger all contribution to the economy. Finance makes up close to fifty percent. Ninety-something thousand people live on, or to be correct, in the island. Two thousand of them are accountants." She paused, to give that statistic weight. "Compare that to Bristol. A population of four hundred and thirty-eight thousand. With maybe five hundred working as accountants. And if you remember from *Bergerac*, Jersey is famous as the sunny well-to-do haven of retired old money, unscrupulous new money, retired criminals, chancers and law-benders, and rich yacht owning non-doms."

"And you're saying that's not far from the truth?"

"It's close enough. Income tax is low, VAT practically non-existent. So if you can slide all you earn through your Jersey bank account, you're quids in. There's a glut of private banks. Which provide anonymous accounts, low interest rate loans, and investment opportunities you won't find anywhere else."

"So, if you like sun," I said, "quaint place names, a touch of French life without having to learn a foreign language, a place you can circumnavigate in a morning, and all sorts of opportunities for tax avoidance, then Jersey is the place for you."

"In a nutshell," Linda said.

"So how do we find Walter Cobb's company?" I asked.

"You've got a name. Fly out there and mooch around. Shouldn't take you long to find. Even if you have to explore the whole forty-seven square miles."

I found my laptop and read Chris Gould's email. The main business of *Cobb CI* was a surprise.

"Care Homes," Linda said. "I don't believe it."

It did take a substantial leap to lock into the idea of Walter Cobb the carer.

"There's not much in the folder," I said. "The emails passing between Cobb and Arnold Faversham are interesting though. Lots of talk about plans kept close to the chest. Budgets full of massive costs for the tools of the undertaker's trade."

Linda looked at the pages. "Code words," she said. "Meant only for those in the loop. The budget cost for 'flowers' is £25,000. For 'disbursements', £58,000. For 'cleaning and maintenance' £18,000. 'Deliveries' £26,000. For 'materials A' £343,000, for 'materials B' £127,000."

"Arnold must be running a multinational undertaking organisation," I said.

"Whatever," Linda said. "If the ratio of profits to costs is 3 to 1, which is the least you'd expect from a successful business, then he and Walter must be rolling in it."

I looked at her. "Do you fancy a weekend in Jersey?"

"At those prices, absolutely."

* * *

The flight from Bristol to Jersey takes forty odd minutes with the wind in the right direction, and costs twice as much as it does from London City Airport and Gatwick. I gave myself up to the vagaries of domestic flight tickets and shelled out £298 for two returns.

CHAPTER EIGHTEEN

"Have you been up all night?" Auntie Joyce asked. "You look terrible."

"Nobody looks their best on Skype," I said. "How are you and Uncle Sid?"

"We're well," she said. "He's got grand designs for his new piece. He's thumping something right now. The noise is torture. I'm surprised you can't hear it."

"What about the neighbours?"

"They're away for the weekend, so he's getting some extra thumping in this evening."

This was our weekend hook up. It's a regular thing but never a chore. Uncle Sid is a mild-mannered retired engineer, Auntie Joyce is a miracle, and they still love each other to bits. We always find plenty to talk about. I told her about the imminent Jersey trip.

"You could probably do with a break," she said. Then had second thoughts. "It's not a trip is it, it's part of some investigation."

"Linda is going with me," I said.

A bit lame that. Auntie Joyce thought so too. She took a deep breath and kept her own counsel.

"Ah the noise has stopped," she said. "I'll go and fetch Sid."

She moved out of shot and I was left with a view of the bookshelf in the study. Uncle Sid arrived thirty seconds later.

"You look a bit knackered," he said.

I told him we had done that bit and asked him about his new creation. He told me it was an abstract and would be a work in progress until he realised he had finished it. He feared however, that it might prove too big.

"All of them are," I said.

"Yes," he said. "But I fear this one may be a creation too far."

We talked for ten minutes or so. Then Auntie Joyce came back and we resumed our conversation. She asked about Chrissie and Adam and Sam.

"In genuine rude health. And Sam is… well he's just Sam," I said.

Then Auntie Joyce grimaced. "He's started thumping again. Take care in Jersey."

I told her it was no more than a fact-finding mission. She said that was the sort of thing UN envoys said in war zones. She finished by ordering me to find time to visit Suffolk. I promised I would, soonest. We said 'goodbye'.

I rang Helen on the loaner mobile. Asked if May had called. She said no. I told her I'd be away for a couple of days but I'd stay in contact. She mumbled her thanks and we ended the call.

I drove to Chris Gould's shop, picked up the iPad and returned it to Bridget, as promised. She asked me what the next step was. I said two days on Jersey and wished her luck with the Receivers.

Back home, I called George Hood's mobile.

"Hell, Jack, I'm watching *Final Score*."

"May is missing now," I said.

There was a moment's pause, then Hood asked, "Since when?"

"Maybe as much as thirty-six hours. And this is more than run of the mill."

"Yes," he said. "It is. I'll see what I can do. Call me if you find out anything your end. Otherwise, we'll meet on Monday."

"Can't do that I'm afraid. I'm in Jersey."

"So you are taking a spring break while I do your leg work?"

"No. I'm checking on Walter Cobb's business dealings. He has money over there. I'll only be a couple of days."

"Call me as soon as you get back."

"Thanks, George."

"As I said, I like May."

I pulled a brown holdall out from the bottom of my wardrobe and considered what to pack for a trip to Jersey in the last week in April.

* * *

There was no word from Helen or Hood the following morning. Linda and I flew across the Channel mid-afternoon. After spending almost twice the flight time standing in a queue at Bristol Airport, checking in, waiting in the lounge at Gate 16 and taking a bus ride to the plane.

We got out of the Jersey taxi at the eastern end of St Clement Bay.

"I'm not getting any French vibe yet," I said.

The taxi driver pulled away. Linda stared at me.

"The only Jersey soil you've touched, is the thirty yards between the plane and the arrivals lounge, and the square foot you're standing on right now."

She led the way into the hotel lobby.

"I suppose, eventually, I will get round to being pleased you talked me into this."

The Hotel de Bretagne has an unimpeachable French name, some of the building is art deco, and the interior has a resolutely old-fashioned feel. The big bonus is, the front door is not much further than a triple jump from the beach.

I introduced myself to Meg, the lady behind the reception desk with her name pinned on to her jacket collar. She had an expensive, flowing haircut and was extremely beautiful. She asked if I had been to Jersey before. I admitted I hadn't. She smiled at me.

"I'm sure you will fall in love with the place."

Linda and I filled in the registration forms. Meg handed me a room key.

"Room 216," she said. "At the front, facing the sea. Do you want a hand with your luggage?"

"No thanks."

She pointed across the lobby. "The lifts are over there, Mr Shepherd. Enjoy your stay in the island."

Linda and I were the only people to step into the lift. She pressed the second-floor button. The doors closed. There was a slight jerk and the lift began to rise.

"You were ogling her," Linda said.

"What?"

"Meg. You were ogling her."

"I do not ogle," I protested. "I've never ogled in my life. Well, except a time or to at Emily. And now you. I'm allowed to ogle you."

She looked at me dead centre. I wavered a bit.

"Well erm…"

Fortunately, the lift came to a stop and the doors opened. I gave Linda the room key, picked up the bags and stepped into the second-floor corridor.

216 had a no-nonsense sea view. And French windows and a balcony from where we could see the whole of St Clement Bay. I was swiftly warming to the place. Linda tested the bed by lying on it and bouncing up and down. Then she

lay back, raised her arms, put them behind her head and relaxed. Poetry in motion.

"I'm ogling now," I confessed.

"So, show me how ogling transfers into action," she said.

* * *

We were out of bed, showered and changed in time to go to dinner. Linda ate fruits de mer, I had pork and beans. The dessert was no contest. I had éclairs and Linda chose tarte au citron. By the time we were sitting in the lounge drinking coffee, the French vibe had arrived.

And so had the sunset. The tide was out and we walked along the beach. Hand in hand, like teenagers in a stolen moment.

"I hate to break the mood," Linda said. "But what's the MO for tomorrow?"

We stopped walking and turned and stood shoulder to shoulder; looking at the horizon slowly morphing from orange into magenta.

"We'll begin by finding the beating heart of the Walter Cobb empire and then we'll pay a visit."

We lapsed into silence again. Walked a little further. The magenta sky was navy blue now. And the temperature had dropped. We shivered in turn.

"Back to the hotel for Ovaltine," Linda said.

What we actually did was have brandies in the lounge, sitting in two wing backed chairs by a log fire blazing in a big granite fireplace. Close by, on a sofa table, there was the usual clutter of 'things to do' information leaflets and 'lifestyle' magazines. Linda got up to root around in the publications. She came back with one of them.

"Did you notice that the first advertising hoardings we

encountered in the arrivals lounge at the airport concerned finance?" she said, waving the magazine at me. "Well, there's the same mantra in here. Promising 'tax advice', 'wealth management' and 'asset protection'. This is Jersey's headline act. And look at that."

A half page advert from a company called *Westcountry Offshore*. I stared at it. Linda leaned against the chair and looked over my shoulder.

"See what this company does? It buys Jersey and Guernsey businesses and sells them to buyers in the UK, who continue to have them registered here."

I scanned the advertising copy. The company was looking for a property within a price range of three million pounds to five and a half, to convert into a health spa.

"Nothing wrong with that, in essence," Linda said. "But the system is ripe for exploitation. Especially as both buyers and sellers know that Jersey corporations enjoy close to zero percent tax."

Upstairs in 216, I checked my mobile inbox. There were two recorded calls. Hood said he had made no progress. Helen said May hadn't been in contact. I threw the phone onto the bed.

"Is this par for the course?" Linda asked. "This frustration."

"The major part of any investigation is spent in thinking and asking questions. Or the other way round."

"And the rest of it?"

"Leaping into action. Well, sometimes."

In no time at all, the wonderful evening had lost its mojo.

CHAPTER NINETEEN

The following morning, the Ford Fiesta hire car arrived at the hotel as we finished breakfast. We drove into St Helier and found the island Archive. We were in and out in twenty-five minutes. *Cobb CI* was indeed registered in the island, its major business listed as care homes. We looked up *Westcountry Offshore*. Its business was investment. And there was a bonus prize. The CEO was one H.W.Cobb.

We left with two printouts and took a walk around the harbour.

"Walter Cobb and concern for the elderly," Linda said. She considered the proposition for a moment. "No no. Let's face it. No one could accuse him of being concerned about anybody."

"Adam and Bridget cautioned me not to be deceived by his south Bristol wide boy act. Said he was capable of playing several ends against a pile of middles. Not in the same league as Freddie Settle, but still devious and clever."

"Okay," Linda said. "But care homes...?"

"It's the perfect front, for just about anything nefarious," I said. "Totally straight arrow."

"Perhaps, deep down in Walter's black soul, there lurks a caged philanthropist."

"Well, when we get him cornered, we'll put that to him."

"So we have a plan do we?" Linda asked.

"I don't know what I've said to give you that impression."

"I know we just got lucky, but I had assumed that your investigations were driven by theories rather than guided by serendipity."

"All investigations have a story arc," I said. "One discovery leads to another. And if the sleuth is on form, he makes the right connections."

Back at the car, Linda studied the map the hotel had given us. *Channel Skies* had a St Brelades address.

"South west corner of the island," she said. "There's a lighthouse. Can't miss it."

"Okay, got that."

Linda looked at me. "Why are there question marks in your eyes?"

"*Channel Skies* will be exclusive," I suggested. "But it can't be making Walter millions."

"We are in Jersey," she said. "And presumably, multi-millionaires can afford to pay top whack for care. I doubt it's another… what was the Bristol place?"

"Winterbourne View."

"I bet the old folk hereabouts sleep in satin sheets," Linda went on. "And every room has a balcony and satellite TV. Whatever, there's also *Westcountry Offshore*. Based at an address on the north coast."

"Let's go and visit the senior citizens first," I said.

We drove the nine and a half miles to St Brelades in no time at all.

Channel Skies was a hotel conversion. An enormous Victorian place, with a semi-circle of mixed woodland and expensive landscaping bordering the landward side. The big, cast-iron gates were open. I pulled up so that we could read the sign at the edge of the drive. The words of welcome made the place sound only a little short of paradise. Which, on reflection, is no more than any care home resident deserves.

It took us an age to cruise up the drive. I parked the Fiesta in the visitors' car park, bounded by shrubs and small trees.

At that moment, the clouds rolled by and the sun came out. Linda looked up at the sky.

"An omen," she said. "How can we fail on such a bright, bright, sunshiny day?"

I looked at the front of the building, a bit gothic but welcoming enough. The entrance was arched, ten or twelve feet high, with two sculpted oak doors which were open. We stepped inside and onto a flag-stoned floor. Ahead of us was a wide stone stairway, which rose to a landing, then split left and right and continued up to the first floor. The right-hand side had been re-structured to take the weight of a stair lift. There were big rooms on both sides of the hall with big doorways. We stood and marvelled.

"Crikey," Linda said. Her voice hushed and soft.

I looked at her. "Crikey?"

"I didn't want to swear. It feels a bit like being in church."

A lady rose from a chair to our right, circumnavigated an oval mahogany table and stepped towards us. She had short brown hair, sculpted around her face and brown eyes to match. She smiled.

"May I help you?" she asked. "I'm Sophie James, the Deputy Manager."

Her suit was made to fit. She looked smart and stately and welcoming.

"My name is Jack Sanderson and this is my wife Linda," I said.

We shook hands with Sophie, who asked how she could help us.

"We live and work in Bristol. My mother is getting older and a little unsteady. She has few friends now. She talks about Jersey more and more as the weeks go by. Her mother was born in the island." Sophie smiled at my correct use of the participle. "And although she has the best of day care in her house, she doesn't get to see enough of us. To put it simply, she wants to come home. *Channel Skies* was recommended to us by a friend of the man who owns the business, Mr Cobb."

Sophie smiled again. Genuine and unforced.

"Yes," she said. "Mr Cobb is a real ambassador for the work we do here."

Tricky moment over, I tried to keep a straight face. Sophie, now in full public relations mode, asked us what we would like to know.

Linda spoke up. "Jack and I would like a tour of the home if that's possible. It's important that my mother-in-law should like this place one hundred percent. I don't want to go back to Bristol with any reservations."

"Of course not," Sophie said. "So if you would both follow me…"

We toured the ground floor. The living room first, with big windows and big comfortable chairs, a high ceiling and plenty of light. All the residents in the room seemed to be occupied; reading, talking, playing bridge and chess. No one was lolling comatose in a chair, or staring mournfully into the middle distance.

Sophie spoke softly. "We have brilliant staff who keep a close eye on the residents but never get in their way. That's the secret to this work."

The reading room and library had bookshelves around all four walls, sofas to sit on and read, desks to write at. The dining room was neatly furnished and the tables laid with some care. It wouldn't have disgraced the Dorchester. The kitchen, a modern, gleaming stainless-steel workshop, had a chef, a sous chef and two assistants, who were preparing lunch. But the room with the most going for it, at the rear of the house, was a projects room.

"We can organise all sorts of stuff in here," Sophie said. "Visits by guest speakers, drawing and painting, sculpting, aerobics and workouts, music, and even our own little bits of theatre."

She crossed the room and we followed, towards what felt like the rear of the building. She opened the venetian blinds across two windows and revealed an indoor swimming pool, stretching into the garden. A man and a woman were in the water; not floating about relaxing, but swimming lengths with some determination.

"Colin and Esther," Sophie said with some pride. "The over 60s Island Champions. There is a competition every year."

She guided us back into the hall and we began to climb the stairs.

"We have thirty-four residents currently," Sophie explained. "We can take up to thirty-eight." She paused on the first-floor landing. "Six of the care staff are residents too, living in converted apartments in the stable block. We have a doctor on call 24/7." She pointed ahead. "The second suite on the left is not occupied at the moment."

Sophie unlocked the door, made way for us, and we stepped inside.

"Take a look around," she said. "Close the door behind you and come downstairs when you've done."

The suite had a bathroom, a bedroom, and a living room complete with flat screen TV, CD and DVD player. The room was comfortable and spotless. We sat down in two armchairs.

"Nothing wrong with these facilities," Linda suggested.

All that a wealthy senior citizen could wish for. But it was difficult to see what Walter Cobb could possibly squeeze out of this place, other than the average yearly stipend of an up-market business person. *Channel Skies* wasn't going to get him into the super-tax bracket.

Downstairs, Sophie was back where she had been stationed as we came in. She picked up some leaflets from the table and offered them to us.

"Take these away," she said. "Read them. I'm sure they will provoke lots of questions. So please do call me. And thank you for visiting."

She shepherded us to the front door.

I sat in the Fiesta staring through the windscreen, Linda in the passenger seat perusing the literature.

"You have to be King Midas to put your old mum in there," she said.

"The ultimate respectable front. Here's Walter posing as Albert Schweitzer. I tell you he's at it. Getting away with murder."

"Not actually, we hope," Linda said.

"You can tour the shops in St Helier," I said, "while I drive up to St John's and knock on Walter Cobb's door."

I switched on the ignition. Linda looked at me, malice in her eyes.

"Oh right. Women shop while men go hunting."

"What?"

"If Adam was here you would not be – "

"If Adam was here, I'd be telling him the same thing."

"Oh yeah?"

"Yeah. I'm paid to get beaten up and shot at. You aren't. Besides…"

I was about to say something else incendiary, so I stopped. Linda picked up her cue however.

"Besides what?"

"Nothing. It won't come out right and it'll sound condescending."

"Spit it out, Shepherd."

"Alright. I might have enough on my plate without worrying about a sidekick as well. And that's not just because you're a female sidekick."

She paid me the compliment of considering that, but stayed resolute.

"No no," she insisted. "We drive up together. If Walter is at home, we will have achieved our object. You can do the testosterone fuelled macho PI bit, after which we can spend the rest of the day as tourists."

"What I meant in all seriousness was, if Walter is at home, there may be some unpleasantness. In which case I'd rather you weren't there."

"I shop as infrequently as possible. And I can be as unpleasant as the next person."

I gave in.

"Okay swop seats. Drive us there, but please stay in the car. This must be one to one. I want Cobb to deal with me, not both of us."

She relented. "Yes, okay. I get that. Just keep your mobile on. And shout if you get into trouble."

La Greve House sat on the seaward side of the road into St John's Bay. There was a pull-in twenty yards or so beyond the drive gates. They were electronically operated and they were closed. I didn't want to announce myself, so I set off on a recce of the boundary wall. The western side, running inland, was lined with trees and screened the wall from the house. I went over it, dropped into the garden behind a substantial ash tree well into late spring foliage, and looked at the house across God knows how many square yards of lawn. Granite, but in the style of one of the later French Louis. Three floors, with a line of dormer windows along the roof. Six bedrooms at least. Hell of a place for a bloke with no money.

I decided I had a reasonable chance of getting around the side of the house without being seen. I accomplished that bit. At the corner where the western and southern walls met, the trees were barely ten paces from the house. There was an art nouveau style glass covered terrace running the length of the south side. And at this end, a door which looked like it opened into the kitchen.

So what next? Climbing, creeping and running was not the sensible way to do this. Having got beyond the front gate and into the grounds without anyone in the house knowing, the obvious ploy was simply to knock on the front door.

I rang the doorbell. Walter Cobb opened the door and stared at me.

"Well well well…" he said.

"May I come in?"

He thought about that for a moment or two, then beamed at me.

"With great pleasure…"

He moved to his right. I stepped over the threshold.

Even in the hall, I could tell this house was as wonderful as the mock Tudor riot in Bristol was hideous. This was the home of someone with taste and understated style.

"You didn't have to scale the wall," Cobb said. "You only had to buzz at the gate."

"Would you have let me in?" I asked.

"Probably not. How did you find me?"

"Courtesy of your old iPad," I said. "Bridget discovered it."

"Clever girl. Which is why I hired her."

"She sends her regards."

"No, she doesn't." He smiled at me. "So… Would you care for a drink?"

"A bit early for me."

He asked me if I'd had lunch. I said that was the next item on my agenda. He asked me where I was staying. I told him. He said the Hotel de Bretagne was comfortable for a mid-list sort of place, and suggested I should have phoned him for a recommendation. All this without a trace of spite or malice. Walter Cobb, stoked with bonhomie, minus all the bluster and bollocks.

"Coffee then."

"That would be nice."

He led the way into the kitchen, fifteen feet square or thereabouts, fitted with stuff that was custom made. As he made coffee, he told me about the house.

"It's Louis the Sixteenth. Built by a rich French merchant, Henri Carpentier, in 1778. A bit of a pirate by all accounts. He came to live here in 1784 at the height of *The Terror,* intending to go back to Paris after Robespierre's enemies had dealt with him. He did go back for a while, until he discovered he didn't like Napoleon either. So he returned, and lived here until he died in 1826. Another Frenchman, Philippe Giraud, engaged in the slavery business I'm afraid, bought the house, added this space and what is now the laundry and the garden room. He lived to be 85 and died up there above us in what was then the master bedroom, in 1879. His son continued to live here, and he managed to move most of his family into the house during the Great War. They all went back to France in 1919… Black or white?"

I was so engrossed in the tale I didn't know what he

meant. He pointed at the coffee machine.

"Oh, white. No sugar."

He began to pour the coffee.

"The place was empty during the 1920s. Until it was bought by a hard case Yorkshireman called Edward Blagrove. He had a factory making washers, which in turn made him a fortune. I bought the house six years ago from his granddaughter. Thought we might enjoy family holidays here."

"But you didn't?"

Cobb went on without any obvious sentiment. "One of my daughters died of a drugs overdose. The other two left. And shortly afterwards, Claudie moved out."

"Your wife?"

"Yes."

I muttered something about not knowing. He said the cold-hearted bitch could go fuck herself – that was the Walter I expected – then transferred the coffees to the breakfast bar. We sat on stools on opposite sides. I wondered why I was getting all this guff, but I decided that while he wasn't threatening my life and limbs, I'd let him go on. He had finished however. He picked up his coffee mug and drank from it.

"Mmnn, that's good."

I drank in response. And it was good. He looked at me without blinking for several seconds, then asked what I thought was going to happen next.

"I mean, is this a visit to catch up? Do you want to prise something out of me, or have you a firmer purpose?"

"Where's Bill Marsh?" I asked.

He didn't pause. "I don't know."

"Where is May?"

"At home I guess."

"No, she's missing too."

He seemed genuinely disturbed by that news.

"Visiting someone perhaps," he suggested.

"No," I said. "Missing. As in lost, gone, disappeared."

"She can't be. She has nothing to do with this."

"With what?"

Cobb put his mug down on the polished teak, got up from his stool, turned and moved to the window overlooking the terrace. He was not going to tell me, so I changed the subject.

"Did you kill Len Coleman?" I asked.

"I didn't know he was dead."

This conversation was likely to go on as long as we could both draw breath. I drank some more coffee, and when I looked up again, Cobb had turned round, silhouetted against the sunlight bouncing in from the glassed-over terrace, and inviting the next question.

So I asked it. "What pays for all this? It can't be *Channel Skies*."

That surprised him a little. He shifted his weight from one hip to the other.

"Maybe it's *Westcountry Offshore*," I said.

He didn't answer. So I ploughed on.

"And what's all this cloak and dagger stuff with Arnold Faversham. I've seen some of your budgeting. £25,000 for 'flowers', ridiculous amounts for 'materials'. And then 'disbursements', 'cleaning', 'coffin lids' and all the other shite. How long did it take you to come up with all that?"

"It actually works well, as long as you remember what everything means." He decided that was that. "Enough, Jack. Drink your coffee and go."

We had come to the point at last. And having made the journey from England's western shore, it would be a waste to return uninformed. I put the mug down on the teak and slid it away from me. He took that business for the statement it was intended to be and took a couple of steps towards me. Now no longer silhouetted, I could see his face. Cold and expressionless.

"How do you manage this Jekyll and Hyde thing?" I asked. "Switching from charmless buffoon on the mainland, to laid back businessman here?"

"It's never going to come up again. I'm going to stay here. I'm not going back to Bristol. At least not permanently. Just long enough to put the house on the market and pick up anything I need. Like to buy it? I'll knock down the price for a quick cash sale."

I stared at him. He grinned.

"You're way out of your depth, Jack, did you but know it."

He was undoubtedly right, but I wasn't going to give him the satisfaction of agreeing with him.

"Walter, I have spent almost a week on this adventure. Lost contact with everyone except for you, been thumped around by a couple of Freddie Settle's employees, and had a close encounter with the corpse of Len Coleman. I'm now running with a very short fuse. I'm not leaving here without learning something."

"Okay. So what are you going to do? Beat it out of me? Go on." He opened his arms wide. "You don't want to go home wondering what I'm going to do next. Give it your best shot."

Cobb was a truly infuriating bastard. And I suddenly realised what Adam had been talking about. Schtick or no schtick, Cobb was unassailable. He was Mr Punch. Boss of his own crazy world, the hangman his only foe. He wasn't frightened of me at all. It would have been easier if he had been pointing a gun at me, or wielding the living room poker. I was simply never going to get him worked up.

"Look," he said. "I can just stay here. You could spend a fortune on bed and breakfast at the Hotel de Bretagne, and we could sit it out. Eventually one of us would crack but by then we'd both be too old to care. I have nothing to hide here in Jersey."

He made a great show of pondering for a moment. Then he snapped the fingers of his right hand.

"Do you play golf?"

I stared at him. He went on.

"No? Pity. Tomorrow I'm playing eighteen holes with my bank manager. Then I'm hosting lunch in the club house. Had you been a golfer you could have joined us."

This self-congratulatory bollocks was not going to stop until I left the house. I moved to the kitchen door. He escorted me into the hall.

At the end of the drive, I stepped through the gates, which opened as I reached them and looked back at the house. Cobb waved at me from the front doorstep. The gates closed like a fadeout in a movie, with him waving still.

* * *

We had dinner at a fish restaurant at the western end of St Helier promenade. Along with a bottle of Muscadet; Brittany's contribution to the great French wine list, especially good with oysters. The sun went down again. We were a bit gloomier the second time around.

"You're better than this," Linda said over the dessert.

I looked at her, not sure what she meant.

"A better detective you mean? In which case that's a 'must try harder' in the report."

"No, I mean you're tougher and more resolute," she said. "And I'll help you with this. So will Chrissie and Adam. We will find Bill and May."

We finished our meal. I paid the bill and Linda drove us back to the Hotel de Bretagne. We were booked on the 7.45 flight the next morning. I re-filled the Fiesta's petrol tank, called the Hertz hire desk and reminded them to pick up the car from the hotel. We checked out before we went to bed, booked an early alarm call and a taxi for 6.15.

CHAPTER TWENTY

"I apologise for asking this of you," the cab driver said.

He was a little overweight, with a round face and round eyes and a round posture. But for the latter he would have been all of five ten or eleven.

"Do you mind if my brother-in-law rides with us? He's catching the same plane as you. He will pay his share of the fare."

He pointed to a long, thin nosed man with a razor haircut standing a few yards away, holding a small suitcase. It was a twelve-minute drive to the airport. Hardly the journey of a lifetime. I consulted Linda.

She shrugged. "Why not?"

The thin nosed man said 'thank you' and introduced himself as Eddie.

Linda and I introduced ourselves to him. The cab driver loaded Eddie's suitcase into the boot of the Vauxhall, along with ours.

We cleared St Helier a few minutes later. Then the driver turned the car north, pressed a rocker switch to his right and locked all the doors. Eddie reached inside his jacket and produced a revolver. He turned in his seat and raised the gun so Linda and I could see it clearly. A compact, snub nosed .32. The driver called over his shoulder.

"As you see, we're not going to the airport. We are driving north east."

"Courtesy of whom?" I asked. "Walter Cobb?"

Neither of the men in the front seats responded to that.

Linda weighed in with, "We have a flight to catch. When

the check-in desk realises we're not getting on the plane they'll inform the police."

"Have you any idea how long it will take them to consider where you might be?" the driver said. "And then to check all the hotels in the island until they find your registration. Or, alternatively, how soon the real cab driver is discovered."

"He's tied up in a skip," Eddie the gunman said.

The driver summed up. "By the time everybody involved starts chasing around, you two will be dead, the car will be parked in a St Helier back street, and Eddie and I will be on the ferry to St Malo."

That was all clear. I could feel Linda next to me on the seat, shaking.

I began to think. Eddie wasn't going to shoot us sitting here in the back. And out of the car we might have an opportunity to do something about the situation. At which point I noticed both men were wearing gloves. That should have registered with me before we got into the cab.

Linda looked straight into my eyes. She mouthed 'what do we do?' I raised my right hand in what I hoped was a clear 'don't worry' gesture. She sat back in the seat and stared out of the side window. We were now travelling along a lane with grass growing up the middle and pointing straight at the sea. The driver pulled up. I looked around, trying to get the lie of the land. The place was less busy than a hermit's cave at bedtime.

"Nobody lives in this part of the valley," Eddie said. "There's no decent path down to the beach and we've driven the only road to get here."

The driver unlocked the car doors. Eddie was out double quick. He opened the door at Linda's elbow and waved the gun at her. Suddenly he seemed impatient. Or maybe nervous...

"Out this side," he said. "Both of you."

He stepped back a pace or two. Linda got out of the car. I shuffled across the seat and followed her. The driver slid out from behind the wheel, walked around the car, shut all the doors and looked at Eddie, who gestured towards the cliffs dropping down to the sea.

"Now, here's how we do this," he said. "You go first, followed by Nick." He nodded in the direction of the driver. "He knows the way down. You will move as he tells you." He waved the .32 at Linda. "She will follow you, with me behind pointing the gun at her back. Any fucking about and I'll shoot her. Off you go."

Nick stepped up close. "Turn round." I did. "Move to the edge." I did that too. And looked down thirty yards of cliff side to a small beach.

The tide rippled gently below. There was a rib at the water's edge, with an outboard on the back. Out in the bay, a trawler yacht was riding at anchor. The way down to the beach looked like an animal track – made by goats or sheep perhaps – sand studded with small stones.

"That's it." Nick said. "I'm right behind you."

I was wearing a pair of soft soled shoes. Linda was wearing jeans, but her knee length boots with stacked heels were not designed for an exercise like this.

Eddie pointed the .32 towards the cliff edge. "Let's do this then."

The track wasn't impassable. But it was easy to see why, in spite of its location, this little bay was well off the tourist trail. It took us ten minutes to get down to the beach. Linda slipped a couple of times, and was hauled to her feet by Eddie without much ceremony. At the foot of the cliff, Nick walked to the water's edge, pushed the rib clear of the sand, unlocked the outboard and let the propeller drop into the sea. Eddie rotated his wrist and waggled the revolver again. Linda and I walked to the rib.

"Sit side by side at the front," he said.

All of us got our trousers soaked moving between the water's edge and the rib. Eddie sat in the centre of the boat, facing us. Behind him, Nick pulled the starter. The outboard fired up the second time. We skimmed the surface of the water away from the beach. I realised how substantial the trawler yacht was, as Nick cut the outboard and slid alongside the swim platform at the stern. He reached out, grabbed the platform and held the rib steady. Eddie pointed the .32 at Linda.

"First again," he said and jerked the thumb of his free hand. "Up there."

Linda shuffled upright, stepped onto the swim platform and then up onto the stern deck.

Eddie stood up. "I'm next. You follow when I say so."

A couple of minutes later, Linda and I were sitting on the deck. Eddie was looking steadfastly at us from a padded bench seat backed by the stern rail. Nick had disappeared into the lounge behind us. I don't know a great deal about boats. I tried to look around, but the field of view is limited when you can't swivel. Eddie provided the specifications.

"The master bedroom is underneath you," he said. "And two up front. Two bathrooms, a galley, and right behind you the lounge and the bridge. I happen to know it's up for sale. You can buy it for a million and a bit."

"From whom?" I asked.

Eddie grinned at me, and shifted emphasis. "Not that you'll be in any position to do so, because you'll be roped and weighted and a fathom or two down."

He looked beyond me and shouted for his associate. Nick said he needed a minute. So Eddie pressed on.

"Basically, we're just going to drop you into the sea."

He paused for that to sink in. Linda swallowed and looked down at the deck.

"Teak," Eddie informed her. "And we don't want blood stains on that, or the crushed mulberry furnishings."

Nick stepped out of the cabin behind us, hove into view, hands full of a circular steel object about nine inches across, with spokes like an alloy car wheel.

"Christ, this is heavy," he said. He put it down on the deck, managing to avoid crushing his fingers before letting go. "The spare. The other one's at the front."

He walked around me and out of vision again.

"It's a mud weight," Eddie said. "Twenty kilos. You use it for inland waterways, instead of the sea anchor."

"You know about boats then?" I asked. Hoping to keep him talking long enough to consider how to get Linda and me out of this.

"Just what I need to know," he said.

Like stuff about mud weights for instance. Nick came trundling back with the other one. He bent over and put it down. As he straightened up, he yelled out and grabbed at the small of his back.

"Oh fuck!..."

He was directly between Eddie and me. I leaned forward onto my hands, swung my feet out from under me launched myself at him. I hit his rib cage and propelled him sideways into Eddie, who was rising from his seat and attempting to sight the .32. Eddie hit the stern railing behind the seat, joining in the chorus of pain. Nick hit the floor, I stepped over him. Eddie was sprawled against the rail, his arms and feet splayed out like a starfish. I grabbed his right forearm and smashed his wrist down onto the rail. I heard a crunch of bone, he yelled again. The .32 spiralled upwards and overboard into the sea. I hauled him to his feet and jammed my right elbow into his throat. He gurgled, choked, reached for the source of the pain with both hands and sank to his knees. Behind me, Nick yelled again. I turned just in time to see Linda bounce his forehead off the teak. She stood up. I heaved Eddie across the deck and dropped him on top of Nick. Linda offered a high five. We smashed the palms of our hands together.

"Find a knife," I said. "Must be one on the bridge somewhere."

"Aye aye, Skipper."

She went into the lounge and moved towards the bridge. Nick was unconscious. Eddie rolled off him onto the deck. He lay on his back, moaning and trying to take in huge chunks of air. I looked down at the mud weights.

Linda came back holding a chunky steel knife with all the bells and whistles - blades, files, screwdriver, corkscrew, bottle opener, scissors, pliers and the thing for cleaning out horse's hooves.

The rear mooring rope was coiled neatly under the stern rail.

"Cut a couple of three feet lengths off that," I said.

We double wrapped each length of rope around Nick and Eddie's wrists and tied them to the mud weights. Then we moved into the lounge and raided the cocktail cabinet.

After the second brandy, Linda suggested we go back to St Helier in style, and asked if I knew anything about boats.

"Not much. Enough to drive I guess."

We moved onto the bridge. The key was in the ignition.

Twin lever throttles meant twin engines. I switched on the ignition. The heavy marine diesels roared into life and began throbbing away under our feet.

"Er Skipper…" Linda said. I looked at her. "We won't go anywhere unless we weigh anchor."

She left the bridge and moved out on the foredeck. Looked down at the steel casing covering the anchor hawser. She pressed a button on the casing and the anchor rose swiftly and quietly. I felt the boat stir as she became free of the sea bed. Linda returned to the bridge. I pulled back the left engine lever and pushed the right. The boat turned through one hundred and eighty degrees and pointed towards St Helier. I pulled both throttles back to neutral, then gently eased them forwards together. I offered Linda the controls, walked to the stern to check on the contractors, found my mobile, and called 999.

* * *

There was a polite knock on the interrogation room door. The PC stationed at the door, opened it, and another PC ferried a tray of coffee and sandwiches to the table. He put the tray down, nodded at us, and left the way he had come in.

Linda and I had been guests of the Jersey Constabulary for a couple of hours. We had been questioned separately, and now we were in the same room, about to have lunch.

Detective Inspector Ayres came into the room and motioned the PC outside. A smart, dark haired, five feet five or six, she looked as if she worked out. She began by addressing me.

"I have just spent ten minutes talking with Superintendent Harvey Butler. He says that despite being a dipped in bronze pain in the arse, you were once a hell of a Detective

Sergeant. And though you now ply your trade as a private detective, a breed it appears he has no time for on the whole, he does nevertheless vouchsafe that what you are telling us is more likely than not, to be the truth."

I felt I ought to say something. Ayres held up a warning hand. She took in both of us.

"The airline has confirmed your arrival on Sunday afternoon. The taxi company recorded the ride to the Hotel Bretagne, and confirmed this morning's booking. We found the taxi where you said it would be. The hotel agrees that you stayed two nights and checked out earlier. The Deputy Director of *Channel Skies* confirmed your visit to the home, albeit under aliases. And thirty-five minutes ago we located today's bona fide taxi driver, in a skip. Apart from the bump on his head and the pervading smell of wet cardboard and rotten veg, he's not much the worse for his ordeal. You may now leave the building and book yourselves on the next flight out of the island."

The look in her eyes said 'don't hurry back if this is the way you intend to behave'.

Then she remembered something else.

"Oh yes. Superintendent Butler also asked me to convey to you the news that Dylan Thomas is dead. Does that mean something?"

I breathed in and out. "Unfortunately, yes. Did he say anything about Gareth Thomas?"

Ayres thought I was taking the piss. She opened her mouth to say something but I managed to get to the point first, and explained. Ayres decided to believe the tale.

"Finish your lunch and leave," she said.

"I think that Nick is a Jersey resident," I added. "He talked about being 'in' the island and not on it. And he drove us from the hotel to where we got out of the car like he did it every day. No map, and no pausing at any moment to figure out where he was."

"Okay. Thanks."

"Is there any sign of Walter Cobb?"

"No."

"Do you think he's left the island?"

"Looks very much like it. Do you want me to show you out?"

* * *

We managed to book ourselves on to the 5.15 flight to Bristol. The Constabulary gave us back our suitcases, and we lumbered them to the nearest quayside bar.

"I've never seen you in action before," Linda said.

"You seemed at your finest. That head thump was the business."

She grinned. "I enjoyed it."

"Oh dear…"

"This sort of encounter comes up regularly, doesn't it?"

I paused, small glass of beer in hand. "You're beginning to sound like Chrissie."

"Only because we both care about you."

I put the glass down again.

"What I do is…" I began. Then tried to sort out what I really meant to say. "I liked being a cop. It may not seem so now, but I did. You get massive highs, like when a court convicts someone you've put in long days and sleepless nights to arrest. And bloody awful lows, like…"

I paused. Linda looked at me.

"The seventeen-year-old kid in the alleyway."

"Yes, like that. And it's what makes me do what I do now.

On good days I make things right."

"And is that enough?" Linda asked.

"Not yet. But I'm hoping someday it might be."

She reached across the table and laid her right hand over my left.

"You're a good man, Shepherd. But there are times when you sound as if you're on a mission. It's right that you care about what you do, but…"

She didn't finish the sentence. Instead, she sat back and sipped at her Shiraz. I waited.

"Oh shit, I'll just mind my own business," she said. "It's probably old ground anyway."

"Probably," I said. "But go over it if you want."

"No," she said. "It's clear we both know what I mean." She raised her glass of wine again. "It's been an exciting couple of days. So, cheers."

CHAPTER TWENTY-ONE

Chrissie and Sam picked us up from the airport and we drove to Redland making a detour via Linda's house. At 7 o'clock, we were sitting in the living room catching up. Sam was lying across the doorway into the hall, snoring. Adam was working late and due to knock on the door within the next half hour.

"The point is," Chrissie said, "are you any further forward?"

"Not much," I said. "I've no idea which side anybody is on. And I won't improve the shining hour until I find someone who will confess."

The phone rang. I picked it up from the coffee table. George Hood was on the other end of the line.

"The Murder Team duty DC has just received the answer to something I asked him to check over the weekend. Arnold Faversham, is not really Arnold Faversham. He is in fact, Mr Andrew Featherstone. Once a consultant surgeon in the city, and by all accounts, one of the best in the trade. But no longer. Now disgraced and struck off the medical register."

"Because…?"

"Under the influence of drink, he cocked up a bowel operation and his patient died."

I asked the obvious question. "Why didn't someone notice he was drunk?"

"First, he kept his drinking under wraps," Hood said. "Secondly, operating theatre staff question the consulting surgeon at their peril. He is the man in charge and his word is law. And thirdly, the Registrar assisting Featherstone during the operation and the only person who knew about his drinking problem, was a close friend."

"Was?"

"She is now a GP in the Orkneys."

"So Featherstone re-invented himself as an undertaker. That has a certain neatness about it."

"Still not part of my brief," Hood said. "And there may be nothing nefarious going on at all. Faversham may have changed his name simply to put the disgrace behind him. And kept the initials to match his monogrammed shirts and suitcases."

"On the other hand…"

"There is that," Hood said.

He wished me a good night and ended the call. I put the phone receiver back on the coffee table. Chrissie looked at me.

"Well…?"

Impossible to believe, but we had a lead. After eight days of getting nowhere. I must have been grinning from ear to ear. Chrissie looked at me.

"Are you alright, Dad?"

Out of nowhere it seemed, a light had come on. Low wattage maybe. But now I had choices.

Adam arrived twenty minutes later. Sam woke up and went barmy for a minute until the novelty wore off. We went through the obligatory 'what did you do in Jersey?' stuff and then I asked Adam if he knew anything about Andrew Featherstone. He thought about that for a few seconds.

"A bit, yes. Surgeon who lost his job after being drunk in charge of an operation."

"Do you remember any more?"

"No, but the Post archive will. I'll get my pc out of the car."

"Use mine." I pointed to the ceiling. "In my office."

He stepped over Sam who was lying in the doorway

again. The dog got to his feet, excited because Adam seemed to be going to the front door. When it turned out that he was doing no more than going upstairs, Sam's interest waned. He lay down again and sighed.

Two minutes later Adam called from the office.

"Hey guys, come and look at this."

Chrissie and I stepped over Sam. He looked up, realised that something was happening upstairs which might, after all, hold something of interest. And being the optimist he is, he decided to follow. All four of us crowded into what was once the third bedroom. Adam gestured at the screen.

"This was a big story a couple of years ago. Ran for days and days, as stuff came tumbling out of the closet."

Andrew Featherstone's life appeared to be a bed of roses. Just about to turn 50, living in a mansion facing the Downs, with a stunning looking wife who did more good works than Mother Theresa. One daughter reading Classics at Brasenose College, Oxford, the other at Durham University reading Earth Sciences. Featherstone was consultant to a couple of Swiss health trusts, and a European heart charity masterminding research into new lung treatments for cystic fibrosis, with a huge grant from the US drugs company attempting to persuade the NHS to buy in. No one in any position of importance in these organisations, realised he had a drinking problem. His wife wondered if perhaps he had, but couldn't be sure. The person who knew he had, was his long time extra-marital partner, 46 years old hospital registrar Joanna Harper – the aforementioned GP in Kirkwall.

A week before Christmas, a car overturned on the iced up A36, south of Bradford on Avon. The 22-year-old driver died on a trolley on his way into A&E. His donor card authorised doctors to harvest any, or all of his organs, suitable for transplant. Featherstone was consulted. He ordered a test on both lungs for a potential cystic fibrosis recipient, and a kidney test for a patient who was unlikely to see Christmas without two new ones. The bowel transplant didn't work, and throughout it, some members of the theatre staff wondered about Featherstone's concentration. There were several moments when the Registrar was forced to intervene.

There was an internal enquiry two days later. Journalists were barred from that, so they sought out the car driver's parents, looking for an angle. The day after Boxing Day, the back story began to leak out. By New Year's Eve, the surgeon was under siege, his drinking and his relationship with Joanna Harper headline news. There were public cries for justice from the driver's parents. Ultimately Featherstone was deemed culpable, disgraced and dismissed. He was sentenced to eighteen months in a low security establishment in Wiltshire. By which time, Joanna Harper had resigned and was speeding on her way to the far north.

"Featherstone dried out in prison," Adam said. "He was released after sixteen months and no longer news. Mrs Featherstone is now living in the Loire Valley and the mansion has been sold."

We all pondered. Chrissie offered a question to the room. "And so... what now?"

Adam nodded in my direction. "He's the sleuth."

He and Chrissie and Sam stared at me. I picked up the ball.

"I may," I said, "have to do a little bit of breaking and entering."

All three looked alarmed. Sam barked and shook his head. Chrissie asked what I was going to do.

"You don't need to know. So it's best if I don't tell you."

After some objections and dog wrangling, I escorted all three to the front door.

* * *

The accomplice I needed was a retired safe breaker, appropriately named Joe Locke. His mother had named him Joseph after her favourite singer, the great Irish tenor. He of *Galway Bay, Hear My Song*, and *I'll Take You Home Again Kathleen* fame, and Inland Revenue fugitive.

The Joe Locke I know is in his 60s, and overqualified for the work he pursues as a part time locksmith. Among all the con artists, blackmailers, burglars, enforcers, murderers, adulterers and pornographers I have met in the course of twenty-one years as a detective, few have driven me to grudging moments of admiration. Joseph Locke is one who has. A man with a heart bigger than a circus tent. A gentleman, a scholar and a skilled professional.

I considered calling him on the loaner phone, then decided this next conversation should be done face to face.

"Jack Shepherd," he said. "By all that's wonderful."

We swapped catch-up stories for a minute or two, then he asked me why I was visiting. I told him some of the story and gave him time to respond.

"Is the man who runs the place good people or bad people?"

"Bad people."

"Mmm... Which helps us to justify this breaking and entering?"

"Correct."

It was my turn to be silent for a while. This was a huge

favour to ask of a man who had resolved, twenty-five years ago, never to risk going back to prison. So I told him the whole story. He listened without interrupting. And when I had finished, he took a moment to sum up.

"We need to get into his emporium, without being apprehended, and dig around until we find… whatever it is?"

"Yes."

"And the aforementioned premises, is likely to be alarmed."

"Certain to be, but not linked to a police station," I suggested.

Joe picked that up. "Because if this Faversham bloke is bad people, the last thing he will want, in whatever emergency, is to have a bunch of coppers tramping round his property and peering into things. So the proposition is…?"

"You need to visit the place during business hours," I suggested. "Give Mr Berling, the senior undertaker, a false name and address. Tell him a relative of yours is nearing his end and only the best will do. Ask him to show you round, and recce the locks and the alarms."

"Okay," Joe said. "When do you want me to visit?"

"Tomorrow morning," I said. "Then call me afterwards."

CHAPTER TWENTY-TWO

I remember when I was toying with the idea of becoming an English teacher, I wrote an essay on Shakespeare's obsession with the curative powers of sleep. I think I discovered about a dozen references in the plays and sonnets I read. And now, during the course of a long night, I re-acquainted myself with all the similes I could recall – from *nature's soft nurse* to knitting up *the ravelled sleeve of care*.

I set my alarm for 8 o'clock, lay back and waited for the mattress and the lateness of the hour to take over. But thoughts of tomorrow night's barmy scheme crept into my head and stuck there. I drifted in and out of sleep, checking the time with the bedside clock twice an hour it seemed. Nature's Soft Nurse gave me no more than a cursory examination and went off to find a paid-up member of BUPA. I was still punching the pillow at 3 am. Then after what seemed mere seconds, I was rewarded with the ringing in of the new day.

It was some time before I worked out where I was, and that I had stuff to do. I clambered out of bed, crossed to the window, drew back the curtains and squinted into the sunlight. I put on a dressing gown and sat in the kitchen drinking coffee, while outside, the sun tried to warm up the garden. I went back upstairs, showered and shaved and returned to the kitchen. After toast, two eggs and more coffee, I retired to the living room sofa to think. My mobile rang.

"Your friend Molly is here," Jason said from his desk in the lobby. "She wants to speak to you. I'll hand her the phone."

There was a silence, then a rustle, and then Molly's voice. She apologised for interrupting what I was doing.

"Not at all," I said.

"Do you think it would be possible for Don and me to see Martin? Assuming he hasn't been… erm…"

I remembered I had promised to help find where he was.

"I imagine he's still in the city morgue. I'll find him and organise a visit."

"If you could."

"Of course. I'll get back to you later today. Where will you be?"

"There's no place like home," she said.

"Give me back to Jason."

Another rustle, then his voice again. "Mr Shepherd…"

I asked him if he would be in a position to take a message across the road later. He said that would be no problem. I wished him 'good day' and ended the call.

I got on to Irving again. This time, the body in question was in cold storage in front of him.

"Will Molly and Don be able to give us some information about their friend?" he asked.

"Maybe," I said.

"The Coroner's Office and the police are checking databases, records and census info. But nothing has surfaced so far."

"How much more time will they spend on this," I asked.

"Perhaps another ten days," Irving said. "In which case, your friends should visit soonest. I'll find a space in the diary and call you back."

I thanked Irving. He told me it was a pleasure.

So, next?

The weather forecast was good, why not go out for the

day? In fact, why not go and see James Warburton, the man with 1800 acres on the top of Mendip and interest in his welfare from Freddy Settle senior?

The Mendips are not very high. Really not much more than a wide ridge of hills running across north Somerset. *The High Combe Estate* sits between the villages of Priddy and Charterhouse. A piece of land given to a Warburton ancestor, the adjutant to General Lord Thomas Fairfax, after his troops had lifted the siege of Bristol in September 1646.

Old property and old money have always been the backbone of the English aristocracy. Recalling the photograph taken with Freddy and letting supposition run free, it seemed James Warburton might be close to losing both. And his backbone too, come to think of it. He was in hock to the worst person he could have chosen. Perhaps he hadn't yet come to realise what he'd done; or felt the noose of Freddie's real scheme, whatever it was, tightening around his neck.

I googled *The High Combe Estate*. The centrepiece was still the manor house, sitting inside its own twelve hectares of Capability Brown magic. It had been a number of years since those lawns and gardens had played host to an event. Although it was said that James Warburton would be only too happy to run out his collection of sports cars and play host to all who bought a ticket. I spent an hour cleaning and polishing the Healey.

I used the loaner phone to ring the *High Combe Estate*, and got through to the Estate Manager, Arthur Mayfield. I told him the details of the proposition I had rehearsed and he asked me to hold. The line clicked and buzzed and clicked again and rang twice.

"James Warburton…" the man said.

His voice sounded efficient, if a bit weary; but neither overbearing nor pompous. I repeated what I had just said to the Estate Manager. Warburton's voice cheered up. Of course he was interested, he said. I asked him if he had anything special in the diary today. He said absolutely not, we could have the place to ourselves, and yes why didn't I drive up to see him straight away? He would make sure there was someone at the gates to meet me.

I put on the best countryside visiting clothes I could muster and climbed into the beautiful, shiny Healey. I took the old coach road out of the city and drove up the Wellsway onto the top of the Mendip ridge. I parked outside the double wrought iron gates at the main entrance to the estate and buzzed the intercom. Warburton drove his Range Rover down the drive to collect me. He smiled when he saw the Healey.

"1965 is it?" he asked.

"67."

"Well you really have looked after her, Mr Shepherd."

We shook hands. I told him to call me Jack. He suggested in that case I call him James. He looked at the Healey again and asked me to follow him up to the house. The mixed woodland on both sides of the drive was dense. Even in late April, with the deciduous trees between the conifers just greening, the impression was that once you got forty or fifty yards into the wood, closed your eyes and spun round twice, you would have no idea which way was out.

The manor house, shaped like two 'Ls' lying down and meeting at the heads of the letters, sat in a huge bowl in the landscape. The front door, protected by a substantial porch, sat in the middle of the centre section. The house was three storeys high, the two wings had tall leaded windows, and the whole effect oozed solidity and a sense of permanence. It looked stunning, with the morning sunshine warming the Bath stone. I pulled the Healey up behind the Ranger Rover, got out and looked around. The landscaping made the setting work brilliantly.

"Done by Capability Brown, during the 1760s," Warburton said at my shoulder. "Beautiful, don't you think?"

"Absolutely," I said.

"We keep it up as well as we can with two grounds people, the Estate Manager, a Gamekeeper, and an Arborealist. We hire in tree surgeons, planters and labourers on contract when we need to."

Warburton waited while I drank in the view.

"Enjoy that for as long as you wish," he said. "I'll go and put the kettle on. When you come into the great hall, shout and I'll hear you."

He walked to the porch, swung open the ancient wooden front door and disappeared into the house.

Lancelot 'Capability' Brown needs no testimonials from me. He re-designed and re-shaped hectare after hectare of rural England during the mid-eighteenth century. He re-built mansion gardens, dug valleys and moved hills, made lakes and serpentine rivers, and planted hundreds of trees which still flourish in all their massive grandeur today. He had two simple rules for his kind of landscaping. Everything should work seamlessly, nothing should star in the design, and all of the estate should serve the needs of the house.

Oh to be in England, now that April's there...

Browning may have gone to Italy because his wife was consumptive and because that's what romantic poets did, but *Home Thoughts From Abroad* betrays his longing for the English countryside.

The lowest boughs and the brushwood sheaf

*Round the elm tree bole are in tiny leaf,
While the chaffinch sings on the orchard bough
In England – now!*

Those words are simple, the cadence is light but the imagery shimmers. There is a suddenness about the arrival of April, a great surge in nature, and within moments it seems, the countryside begins to turn green. Capability Brown's art was Browning's verse made flesh. Both men get my vote.

The Great Hall had a flagstone floor and massive stone fireplace. And it was cold enough to warrant two vests and a thick jacket. The centrepiece was a long oak refectory table with eight, thick cabriole style, turned legs. I counted fourteen dining chairs, actually arranged around the walls, rather than the table. There was no other furniture in the room; the table and chairs a token of what there once was, or, in the best of all possible worlds, what there could be again.

Warburton re-appeared before I had to shout; carrying a tray with teapot, cups and saucers, milk and sugar. He put the tray down on the table. I asked him how old it was.

"All of thirty-five years," he said.

I stared at him, then back at the table. He explained.

"Made for us by John Makepeace. At a time when the family had money to burn. Now there is enough furniture left to eat in the kitchen, relax in the drawing room, sit down in the library and sleep in three bedrooms." He looked round the hall. "I'm sorry it's cold in here. It costs a fortune to heat the place. I switch off the central heating on the day after Easter Monday, and on again on October 5th."

"That's very precise," I suggested.

"My birthday," he said. "And my present to myself. Warmth."

All of which explained why he was wearing a thick

sweater under his Harris Tweed jacket.

"I'm sorry, I should have warned you to wrap up."

I studied him properly for the first time. Early 40s probably. He looked like I expected a countryman to look. Warm working clothes, albeit properly tailored. Probably expensive when they were bought, just a little shabby now. He was taller than me. Well over six feet, he had a graceful smile and an easy manner. But there were dark bags under the eyes, and the lines across his forehead seemed to suggest he frowned a lot.

He picked up the milk jug and looked at me.

"Yes please," I said. "No sugar."

"It's just plain old Earl Grey I'm afraid." He nodded across the hall. "Pull up a couple of those chairs."

I gathered two chairs and placed them at a table corner. Warburton poured out cups of tea for both of us then pushed a saucer to me across the beaten oak. We sat down. He began the conversation by asking me where I lived and what I worked at. I was honest about the first matter but I lied about the second.

"I live in Bristol, in Redland. I work at a bookshop in Clifton."

I was on relatively safe ground there. A friend of mine is the owner of a small independent bookshop, and if the occasion demands, can act as my answering service and business filter.

"And what is this plan you have for a classic car weekend?"

I lied to him again. "I belong to a car club. And we're looking for somewhere to hold a gathering in mid-September. The landscape outside the front door with the house as a background would be terrific."

Warburton nodded. "Yes, it would. And maybe we can open the old stable block Tea Room again. Like old times."

This was hurting. Firing bullshit at a man I'd only known ten minutes, but who had struck me as genuinely likeable. However, I had started so I had to finish.

"I guess you've done this sort of thing in the past," I said.

"Oh yes," he said. "In the good old days." He looked away from me and smiled as he recollected better times. Then he came back to me, brisk now. "Drink your tea and I'll give you the one guinea tour."

He began by escorting me around the house, which was no National Trust re-furb. The place was old and venerable and looked like it; in some sections more so than others. Warburton had managed to find money over the past few years to restore the drawing room and the library to their former glory. He had patched up the dining room to a degree and the kitchen worked, but the other rooms downstairs were in the grip of rising damp, dry rot and wet rot. The main staircase from the great hall to the first floor, had been re-built by a decent craftsman and the landing floor re-laid. But there, the money and the work had run out. There were six bedrooms on the first floor. Two of them were furnished, the other four looked like their counterparts downstairs – damp wallpaper, peeling plaster, rotten floorboards and leaking windows. We didn't explore any further. Warburton said the rooms above weren't safe.

After which cheery note, he offered me a tour of the estate, and led me into the old stable yard. We climbed into a battered Toyota pickup.

The woodland was fabulous, as thick and flourishing as the house was disintegrating. We travelled a hundred yards down one track, turned left on to another, then two hundred yards later right again. Warburton pulled up and we got out of the Toyota.

It was amazingly quiet. There was some birdsong, and some rustling in the undergrowth to our right. The surrounding woodland looked impenetrable.

"You may think there's nothing going on here," Warburton said. "But I can assure you there is. It takes a lot of work to keep woodland looking like this. Not quite as nature intends perhaps, because we can't allow her to run riot, but we do enough to make sure she stays strong and well."

"Don't you ever get lost among all this?" I asked.

"Sometimes I have to think about where I am," he said. "A little test for you. Can you point in the direction of the house?"

I looked around me. Tried to recall the lefts and rights we had just taken.

"Okay," I said. "That way."

Warburton grinned at me. "You're almost one hundred and eighty degrees out."

I turned round. "You mean it's that way?"

"Or thereabouts."

We climbed back into the Toyota and moved on. We spent the best part of an hour, trundling around the tracks in the woods. Warburton told me how to recognise beech trees and birch and ash and oak and sycamore. And spruce and larch and a host of pine trees. He was clearly passionate about what his father had bequeathed him along with the death duties and the unpaid bills.

"All this must cost a bob or two," I said.

He looked glum. "Indeed. We have grants from central and regional government. This quango and that. But it's a hell of a struggle to make ends meet. All the money goes into the woodland schemes of course. As to the house... well you've seen it."

"What about Westcountry businesses? Have you tried mining that source of supply?"

"We're beginning to, yes. In fact, among them we have hooked quite a substantial donor."

"And who's that?" I asked.

"I can't tell you I'm afraid. The person wishes to remain anonymous."

Assuming that person was Freddy, I wondered why – considering all the posing outside the hospital wing. I asked Warburton what his donors got out of the deal. He happily warmed to the subject.

"Depends how much they offer. The donor we're talking about is given exclusive access to the estate every Sunday."

"To do what?"

"Whatever he likes. As long as he doesn't uproot the trees or shoot the wild life. Orienteering, paint balling, clay shooting... that sort of thing."

"And you just leave this person to it?"

"Yes. I usually take a train to London and visit my daughter."

Suddenly it felt like I was asking too many questions. I apologised.

"Not at all," he said. "Would you like to stay for lunch? I've got some pork pie and a bottle or two of cider. And we can talk about your proposal."

Probably not a good idea. Especially as I was being so disingenuous. I looked at my watch and told him I had taken up too much of his time. I suggested I give him my phone numbers and that we swop email addresses.

"I will relay all we've talked about to the club committee and get back to you soonest."

He said that would be fine. We were about to climb into the Toyota, when my mobile rang. The contract one. I apologised to Warburton, turned away from him and pressed the receive key. Irving at the mortuary offered ten minutes at 8.30 the following morning. I thanked him.

In front of the house once again, Warburton and I shook hands.

"The drive gates open automatically from this side," Warburton said. "I look forward to seeing you again."

I drove away from him and the house, feeling like my head should be cut off and spiked on the gates. I liked James Warburton, and I was concerned that he seemed to know nothing about what Freddie and her mates got up to every Sunday. As the gates closed behind me, I reflected that I didn't either. And I was the detective.

* * *

I drove through Chew Valley and over Dundry Hill into south Bristol. I called at *The Junction Retail Park*, bought a chicken mayonnaise baguette in one of the cafés and sat down to eat. As I looked out of the window across the mega-car park, it began to rain. Stair rods, bouncing off the tarmac. The Healey was all of a hundred yards away and if I left my seat I'd be soaked within feet of the café doorway.

I called Jason. Told him to let Molly and Don know I'd pick them up at 8.15 tomorrow.

The sky darkened like a November dusk and the steady, demoralising downpour went on. I bowed to the inevitable and ran to my car. By which time my jacket was soaked, rain was seeping down my neck behind the collar, my country-casual-look trousers were glued to my thighs and my hair was plastered flat. Inside the Healey, the windows were steamed up. I turned the engine on and switched the blower to full. The windscreen began to clear and I switched on the wipers. The blade directly in front of me, juddered across the screen, swung back in the opposite direction, then began to squeak.

When I pulled into the office car park, I was still cold and the wiper blade squeak had morphed into an insistent scraping noise. Jason respectfully refrained from making any comment on the apparition that dripped its way across the lobby to his desk. He handed over my post and wished me a good afternoon.

There was a spare shirt in the office, on a hanger on the door. I collected it, walked along the corridor to the third-floor shower room, took off the shirt I was wearing and towelled the bits of me still wet. It didn't really improve matters, because I had no trousers to change into. What the hell… I took them off, dried my legs, put on the replacement shirt, stuck my head out of the shower room. Having ascertained the corridor was empty, I strolled back nonchalantly to my office door, as if I swanned around the building without trousers on a regular basis.

Going into the office this time, I saw the note which had been pushed under the door. I picked it up and dropped it on the desk. I turned the thermostat up, draped my trousers over the radiator under the window and sat behind my desk in my underpants. I opened the note.

Linda had written *Knock on my door when you get in*. I had done the trouser-less in the corridor bit. I rang next door. There was no response. So I sat in my chair thinking, hoping for inspiration to strike, waiting for the phone to ring and my trousers to dry. They were still steaming on the radiator when

Linda opened the door and walked in half an hour later. I rose from behind my desk, stepped to my right and posed for effect in my socks.

She didn't blink. Began by staring at my socks, then worked upwards to my shirt.

"It's a new, casual office look I'm trialling," I said.

"I hope so," she said. "Because if it's an attempt at some foreplay statement, it's not working."

I gestured in the direction of the radiator. "I got soaked."

"Sit down again for God's sake," Linda said.

I did. She asked if I'd had lunch. I said, if I hadn't paused to do so, I wouldn't have been soaked. She asked if I wanted something to drink. The clock on the wall said 2.30. It was too early to raid the Laphroaig in the bottom of the filing cabinet.

"Coffee," I said.

"Coming up," Linda said.

She took the cafetière from the top of the filing cabinet and left for the kitchen along the landing.

There is not a lot you can do without your trousers. Well, that's not true; you can do most things you normally do. I'm speaking here of comfort and confidence. Even in quarantine behind my desk, the thought of picking up the phone and talking to a client, whilst trouser-less, was unsettling.

Linda returned with the cafetière, two mugs, and a milk jug on a tray. She looked in the direction of the radiator.

"How long do you estimate this no-trousers interregnum will be?" she asked.

I looked behind me. The trousers were still steaming, though less than earlier. I stood up, moved to the radiator and turned them over. Linda averted her eyes.

"I'm not sure how soon our relationship will recover from

this," she said.

I turned to face her and posed again. She put the tray on the desk.

"It's the socks, Jack. No trousers is a little alarming, but socks on regardless, is no look at all."

We sat down; Linda in one of the client chairs, me behind the desk, visible only from the waist up – if you discounted the view between the desk pedestals. She poured the coffee and sat back in her chair, cradling her coffee mug.

Joe Locke knocked on the office door and walked in. He looked at Linda, switched his gaze to the view between the pedestals, took a beat, then apologised for intruding.

"You're not," Linda said.

She got to her feet, explained that she occupied the office next door, said she had a thing about knees, and that I often helped her indulge in this minor fetish during the course of a wet afternoon. She bade us both 'goodbye' and took her coffee with her.

I pointed to my trousers. "I've been out in the rain."

"I've been to the funeral parlour," Joe said. "Piece of cake."

"Even the alarm system?"

"That's the easiest bit. Do you want to do this tonight?"

"Err…" That needed a simple straightforward 'yes'. But without my trousers on, all confidence in breaking and entering had evaporated.

"There is a way into the place from the back of the car park," Joe went on. "Hidden from Rycroft Road."

He paused, waiting for a response. In my mind I was now putting my trousers on.

"Jack…"

Suddenly my trousers were on again, and I was aglow

with confidence.

"Tonight, yes. What time?"

"I'll pick you up at midnight. We'll go in my car. Wear dark clothes."

"And a black ski mask and brothel creepers?"

Joe laughed. "Brothel creepers. Haven't heard that for decades. Later, Jack." He nodded at the radiator. "But not in those trousers."

He left the office. A couple of minutes later, Linda returned.

"Are you free tonight?" she asked. "With or without trousers. Depends if we're at the pictures or in my house."

I swallowed a mouthful of coffee. "Actually I'm not free."

Not exactly true that. But if we spent the early part of the evening together, I'd have to dodge questions about why I was off to work when sensible people were on their way to bed.

"Why aren't you free? What have you got to do?"

"I can't tell you."

Linda stared at me. Then shrugged. "Okay. Later?"

"Err no… What I'm doing will go on until much later than that."

She thought about that for a moment or two. "This is something I shouldn't be asking you about, isn't it?"

"Afraid so," I said. "I'm sorry. Are you alright with this?"

Linda nodded.

"Are you sure?"

She smiled. "Yes, I'm fine."

"Because this is what I do."

Well not breaking and entering. At least not often.

Linda raised her empty coffee mug. "I'll just take this back to the kitchen."

* * *

I called at the *Cotham Fish Bar* on the way home. Checked there were no messages on the answering machine, left it in answer mode and ate my fish and chips at the kitchen table.

The clock on the wall said 7.30.

I made coffee, took it into the lounge and sat down on the sofa. Did the round of TV channels and decided I didn't fancy anything on offer. I searched the DVD collection and found a copy of the re-mastered version of *Farewell My Lovely*. One time hoofer Dick Powell was Hollywood's first Philip Marlowe. A rendering of the character three years before Bogart's and still a defining piece of work. But even this seminal slice of noir, which usually seems fresh and exciting, couldn't hold my attention. I switched off the DVD player and took myself for a walk.

I began to think about Emily.

I do so at some point most evenings when I'm alone. The human mind has an eject button, of sorts. And if you possess a kind of super resolve, you can use it in moments of regret and pain and anger. Until you discover it's not really what you want after all. Because you still pick up the photograph and choose to remember the moment it was taken, or listen to the song and reap the memories it evokes. That time was over. I could handle all the 'once were' moments now, without too much hurt. Able to go back through the photo albums, share the memories of Emily with others. She would have hated what Joe and I were about to do.

So I switched to thinking about body parts; given up, like Martin in the old privy and perhaps Don's friend Ted, and Alice Davis and Brian Watson and Lily. All this operating would need a top surgeon. So enter, one of the best. Now disgraced, desperate for money and unable to practice the skills he was so proud of. Slightly more plausible than the return of Doctor Frankenstein. And if there was the remotest chance…

I sat on the sofa, to wait out the hour and a half until Joe arrived.

CHAPTER TWENTY-THREE

Joe knocked on the front door at 11.45, in tracksuit and sneakers, looking like he was about to visit the gym. Except everything he wore was black, including a woolly hat covering his bald head. I was in dark blue jeans, a black high necked sweat shirt and black soft soled shoes. Joe looked me up and down.

"You'll do," he said.

I held up my hands. "No gloves."

"We can solve that," he said.

I closed the front door and followed him to a five-year-old dark green Volvo. Inside the car, Joe went through a check list.

"Mobile phone?"

"No."

"Money in your pocket?"

"No."

"Nothing else on your person that jangles?"

"Ah… house keys."

"Put them in the glove compartment." I leaned forward and did as I was told. "No identification of any sort. Wallet, credit cards, driving licence?"

"No."

He handed me two pairs of white surgical gloves. "Put those on when I tell you to."

"Both pairs?"

"Yes. To be sure. You can't do the fiddly stuff with leather gloves. And woolly ones can be too slippery."

He reached out, turned on the car ignition, depressed the

clutch and engaged first gear. He took a deep breath.

"Okay," he said. "Here we go."

Suddenly I broke out into a sweat. And grew more nervous, street by street, as we drove northeast across the city. Joe recognised the symptoms.

"Talking sometimes helps," he said.

I picked up my cue. "What did you say to Mr Berling?"

"I told him all about my Aunt Edna," he said.

"Your Aunt Edna has been dead for over ten years."

Joe glanced across the car at me.

"I told him I wanted the best he could provide. He gave me a brochure. The superior deluxe service offers an exotic hardwood coffin with satin interiors and gold-plated handles, two limousines and four members of staff on the day. There's a long list of other stuff before we get to that. 'Disbursement costs' they're called. Death certificate documents, preparation of the body, announcements and invitations, burial or cremation fees, minister or celebrant fees, flowers… Even an online memorial, costing eleven hundred quid. Everything but a gilded carriage and four black horses with plumes."

"And what does Berling charge for all that?"

"Fourteen thousand pounds."

I stared across the car at Joe.

"Of course you can have it done by the Co-op, with all due care and attention, for around three and a half. I've got that."

I was still staring at him.

"Best to get your affairs in order when you're as stricken in years as me. Have you made a will?"

I was about to tell him I had, when he swung the Volvo into the western end of Rycroft Road. He pulled into the pavement, midway between two street lamps and shadowed by a tall hedge in a front garden. The funeral parlour was fifty or sixty yards ahead of us. Joe switched off the ignition.

"Put your gloves on," he said.

A bit of a palaver at the best of times, surgical gloves. It took me a while. Joe waited patiently. I raised my hands for his inspection.

"Got all the wrinkles out?"

"Yes."

"Okay. This is what we do. There's a small gate at the back of the car park. Padlocked. It should take thirty seconds. Don't get out of the car until that's done."

"How will I know when it's done?"

"Watch me move along the street. As soon as I step into the car park and disappear from view, start counting. Then get out of the Volvo. Lock it with the key, don't alarm it. Then follow me, at a reasonable walking pace. Turn left, go through the gate and close it behind you. By the time you join me, I'll be ready to open the funeral parlour side door. I'll tell you about the next bit then."

"Okay."

He opened the car door.

"Remember, softly softly. Don't rush. If anybody sees us, we're just a couple of blokes a bit late getting home."

He reached into the back seat, picked up a small black shoulder bag. He took the key out of the ignition and handed it to me, eased out of the Volvo, closed the driver's door gently, leaned against it to ensure it was shut tight, then set off along the pavement.

I watched him with my heart thumping. He disappeared. I started counting. I got out of the Volvo, closed the passenger door carefully, walked round the car, locked the driver's door and followed Joe.

The car park gate was slightly ajar. I pushed it open and closed it behind me. The yard was dark. The side wall of the funeral parlour cut out direct light from the street. Two black limousines were parked in the yard; the hearse was obviously quartered elsewhere. Joe and I were standing in the corner of an L created by the main building and an extension I hadn't expected to be there. I tried to recall the geography I had logged on my visit to the place with George Hood. The inside layout didn't match with the view from the yard I was getting now. Joe was at the side door; solid with no windows. I joined him. We talked in stage whispers.

"This door opens to the left," Joe said. "The alarm box is on the wall to the right." He handed me a torch. "When we get in, close the door and point that, at eye level, to the wall on your right. You'll light up the box. It'll be ringing like all buggery but don't let that get to you. I'll have it disabled in less than a minute. Once that's done, we'll take a rest and have a cup of tea."

"Have a what?"

"Never mind. Ready?"

I grunted. My mouth was so dry I couldn't actually speak. Bill's shoulder bag was on the ground at his feet. He took a small pencil torch out of the bag, clamped it between his teeth and started to work on the deadlock. I couldn't see what he was doing. I couldn't hear anything but the sound of distant late-night traffic. And all I could feel was the thumping in my chest. Suddenly the door alarm burst into life. At a thousand decibels it seemed, the noise hurting my ears. Joe opened the door. I followed him into the building, closed the door and lit my torch. Joe took his torch out of his mouth. I counted the seconds, helpless and unable to do anything else. By forty-two, Joe had the alarm casing off and thirteen seconds later had disconnected the battery.

And then there was silence. Deep and dark and the most welcoming I had ever heard. Joe exhaled loudly, turned and slid down the wall, his knees up against his chest. I sat down next to him. He turned his head and grinned at me.

"Tea now," he said. "Point the torch this way."

And, amazingly, tea it was. He took a small vacuum flask out of his bag. Unscrewed the cap, handed it to me, and produced another small plastic beaker.

"I hope you like tea with milk and no sugar," he said. "Not the place for milk jugs and sugar bowls."

I managed to find my voice. "That'll be fine."

I put the torch on the floor in front of us, pointed it at our feet, and we drank our tea. The only sounds were of Joe and me sipping and swallowing. I felt like William Hartnell's character in *The Yangtze Incident*. In peril and under fire, Leading Seaman Frank is handed a cup of tea. He drinks and says *Loverly!!*

"There are no windows in this lobby," Joe said. "The light switch at this end is just above your head. I'll check the other end."

He picked up the torch. Navigated his way along the lobby, checking for places light could leak out. The door at the other end was closed. He leaned to his left and flicked a switch. The sudden shock of light made my eyeballs dance. Spots flickered in front of my eyes like shapes changing in a kaleidoscope. I closed them, re-opened them slowly and got to my feet.

Joe walked back to me. "So far so good," he said. "Finish your tea."

I did. He gathered the flask, the cap and the beaker, put them into his bag and we moved to the door which led into the body of the building. Joe half opened it, told me to stay where I was, and stepped through the gap into the hall where PC Laker had been stationed. I waited.

I heard him say, "Keep the torch beam low, come into the hall and close the lobby door behind you."

We both checked where we were and in which direction we were facing.

"Front door behind us," Joe said, "to our right, the waiting room and secretary's office. In front of us, to the left, is Berling's office. The two doors at the end of the hall lead to the preparation room and the resting room. The first door on our left is er…"

He paused to think.

"The storeroom," I said.

Joe turned to face me. Shone the torch at me, just below my eye line.

"So go back to the 'L' shape," he said. "Question one… If we have the geography right, and that door opens into the storeroom. And if we accept the evidence of our eyes which tell us it's little more than twelve feet square, then what takes up the rest of that bit of the 'L'?"

"And question two," I said. "How does one get into that space, whatever it is?"

Joe added question three. "And finally, why does the alarm system control operate from the yard door and not the front door?"

I began thinking about that. Joe continued, answering his own question.

"Because," he said, "most of the traffic into the building comes that way."

I considered that. "Hardly a surprise though. It's the work access. More discreet than hauling corpses across the front door threshold."

"And also handy for other discreet bits of business," Joe said.

He unlocked the Yale on the storeroom door in moments. We moved into the room, found the light switch and flicked it on. It was mainly as I remembered it. Full of stuff but with an avenue of space running across the room.

Joe pointed along it. "There has to be something behind that back wall."

We inspected the shelving system. I began from the left, Joe from the right and we worked towards each other.

Joe suddenly said, "Bingo. Take a look at this."

I moved to his shoulder. He was standing in front of a shelf section, three feet wide, separated ceiling to floor from the shelves on each side, by a gap he could slide his fingers into.

"I think this is a door," Joe said. "I bet you this section swings open somehow. You take a look at that side."

Joe handed me the big torch, stuck his between his teeth and peered into the gap in front of him. I started from the top on the left and worked down. The torch didn't help much. The beam was too wide and bouncing reflections back at me from the steel-edged frames. I turned off the torch, twisted my wrist, held my left palm and fingers vertical and reached inside the gap until I touched the wall. I drew my hand downwards. Then at eye level, my little finger came up against a horizontal piece of steel.

"I've got something here, Joe. Some kind of catch."

"Press it, or twist, or jiggle it a bit," he said.

I tried all three, but couldn't apply enough force with the ends of my fingers. I took my hand out of the gap.

"We need a tommy bar or a narrow tyre lever."

Joe dug into his bag and produced exactly that. I stared at him.

"Normally the work I do is more subtle than this. But when brute force and ignorance are required…"

I took the lever from him, held on to the curved end and slotted the other into the gap. I slid the lever downwards until I felt it reach the piece of steel. Raised it an inch or two, then struck down onto the steel catch. Nothing happened beyond sending a shock wave through my wrist and along my right arm.

"Shit!"

I hauled the lever out of the gap, dropped it and massaged my elbow. Joe picked up the lever.

"I'll do it." he said.

I stepped back to give him room.

"That was from the top," I said. "Try underneath."

Joe did. Slid the lever under the catch and moved it upwards. There was a double click. The steel catch responded to the pressure. It lifted. Joe took hold of a shelf and pulled. The whole thing swung open from the left to the right. Like Joe had suggested, it was a door. There was another one behind it and another deadlock. This one tougher than the last, and taking a minute of Joe's time to crack open. He looked at me.

"Okay… If this room is blacked out, as it appears to be from the yard, then you can switch the light on. On the other hand, you might do that and light up the yard and the whole side of the building. But what the hell…"

I pushed the door open, reached round the left-hand side of the door frame, located a light switch, and clicked it down. The room lit up like the lobby had done a few minutes earlier.

I moved into the room. Joe followed, stepped to my right shoulder.

There was a long silence, eventually broken by Joe.

"Jesus Christ," he whispered.

We were standing inside an operating theatre.

"Is this...?" He couldn't finish the sentence.

I have never been in an operating theatre. But it looked like all the places I'd seen on TV and at the movies. Even in this state, under what must have been the general-purpose working lights, the cupboards and storage units around the walls gleamed in polished, stainless steel brilliance. And right in the middle sat an operating table, with above it, half a dozen concentrated beam, high-wattage lights.

I began to walk around.

"Don't touch anything," Joe said. "Even with the gloves on."

There were TV monitors, boxes of electronic gizmos, trays of implements straight and curved, bent and shaped, cupboards with words on them I couldn't read and wouldn't be able to remember. At which point, I realised they were written in German.

Joe summed up what we were both thinking.

"Where the hell did he buy this stuff?"

"All these bits and pieces are German," I said. "Or maybe Austrian. Or Swiss. Yes, that's it Swiss." I faced Joe across the operating table. "In the good old, rich old days, Andrew Featherstone was a senior UK consultant to a couple of Swiss health trusts."

"And when he set this place up he pulled some strings?"

"It would appear so," I said.

I looked round one last time. We turned out the lights and left. Joe checked that both doors were locked. In the storeroom, he re-assembled all his gear, made sure he wasn't missing anything. We skirted the stuff in the room, opened the door into the hall, put out the lights and closed the door behind us. Both of us were breathing more easily now. Joe locked the door. Minutes later, we were back in the street and walking towards the Volvo.

CHAPTER TWENTY-FOUR

"Is this your friend?" Irving asked Molly and Don.

Molly nodded. Don said, "Yes, it is."

We were standing in a squeaky clean air-conditioned room with rows of cold stores along the walls. Don put his left arm around Molly's shoulder. He asked when Martin was likely to be buried.

"Cremated actually," Irving said. "We have done all the work we can. We have determined the cause of death and the coroner has agreed with us. We will hand Martin over to the undertaker once the police are satisfied there are no next of kin to find. At which point, under the terms of the 1984 Public Health Act, the city will pay for a pauper's funeral. Not much grandeur in that I'm afraid. A basic coffin, transportation to the South Bristol Crematorium, a short service and committal, then Martin's ashes scattered in the adjacent Memorial Garden."

"And when is that likely to be?" Molly asked.

"Perhaps in a few days. I will make sure Mr Shepherd is told, so that he can pass on the details to you, and anyone else you would like to inform."

Molly looked down at Martin again, letting the tears flow now. Irving tapped my shoulder and pointed towards his office door. I nodded and he moved away from us. Don turned to me.

"Would one of us would be allowed to say something about Martin, on the day?"

"I'm sure," I said. "And I'll drive you to the crematorium."

"Thank you, Jack."

Don pulled Molly closer to him. I took a last look at Martin. Although he looked older, he had made perhaps half of his three score years and ten. Whatever he had been paid for giving up his lung had been spent or lost. A street person, with no connection to anything remotely close to a dignified life, he had died cold and alone, lying on a pile of cardboard boxes in a back street toilet. It was a dismissive 'fuck off' from the world of plenty around him. A brutal and monumental injustice.

I moved around the trolley, covered Martin's face again, pushed the trolley back into the fridge and closed the door.

I took Molly and Don back to what passed for their home. I drove to Redland, working on a solution to the question on my mind. To tell, or not to tell the police about the funeral parlour operating room.

I could imagine Harvey Butler's reaction as I offered him my version of the discovery. Currently, this wasn't of any concern to MIT. On the other hand, George Hood had told me to keep him in the picture. He could be the bloke to call, in order to avoid the inevitable 'go home and stay there' tirade from Harvey.

Only enter the battles you can win. I decided to talk it through with Adam. He was at his office desk.

"I have something I'd like to discuss," I said. "Are you busy? Can we meet?"

"No I'm not and yes I can. At the new café in Clifton. The place in Caledonia Road. Do you know it?"

"Yes."

"Give me an hour to clear my emails and get through the traffic."

I sat in the kitchen. Thinking about May. I needed to know how the Missing Persons investigation was going. I decided to ring George Hood about that. He wasn't at Trinity Road. The obliging DC Holmes put me through to Harvey before I could rehearse what I wanted to say. Harvey came on to the line. I began by asking him about Hood's promotion. He snorted.

"George was offered it. But not within MIT. No money to replace the previous DI here. The powers that be asked him if he would like to go to Vice. They have money left over in the budget from some initiative they canned because it wasn't working. Vice, for fuck's sake... It's a bargain basement job. Crap hours, investigations that take weeks to get anywhere, moody clientele, pimps with short tempers, massive egos and BMWs..."

"So George is staying with MIT?"

"About which I'm immensely pleased. But he could be somewhere else, enjoying a serious pay hike. He won't give the squad any less than his best. Which only makes it worse."

He decided we had done enough by way of intro chat and changed the subject.

"Are you making any progress in your hunt for Bill Marsh?" he asked.

"No. I'm thinking of hiring Bear Grylls to find him."

"And May?"

"Missing Persons is supposed to be on to that."

Harvey mumbled something I didn't hear, then said, "Stay on the line. I'll put this phone on speaker."

There were a series of button tones, then a voice said, "Missing Persons. DC Hitchens. Can I help you?"

Harvey introduced himself and told Hitchens to put the boss, whoever he was, on the line. There was a click, twenty seconds of mild static, then another click.

"DI Waverley," a new voice said. "Can I help, you Super?"

I've heard some utterly useless conversations in my years as a detective, but what followed was an award winner. It took several minutes of rigmarole from DI Waverley to reveal that Missing Persons had no idea where May was. Harvey ended the call, only just in control of his temper.

"Tosser," he said. "Jack, you have carte blanche."

"As in, whatever I need to do to find her I can do?"

"Anything short of violence or murder. Just keep me posted."

* * *

I met Adam fifteen minutes later.

"About that little bit of breaking and entering I mentioned the other day. Actually, there wasn't any breaking involved."

"Only entering then," he said. "No less a charge unfortunately."

I ploughed on. "The disgraced, former consultant surgeon Andrew Featherstone, is now running a state of the art, illegal operating theatre, out of a room at the rear of his premises."

Adam processed that information.

"Jesus Christ. How do you know that?"

"Because I've seen it," I said.

The tone of his voice changed from astonished to wary.

"What the hell are you getting into now?"

I took a piece of paper out of my pocket and passed it to him. "It's a list of names."

He looked at it.

Bill Marsh, May Marsh, Walter Cobb, Brian Watson, Alice Davis, Ted Harris, Arnold Faversham, James Warburton, the Thomas Brothers, Freddie Settle, Len Coleman (deceased).

Adam studied the list. A waitress brought us coffee and croissants. Adam handed the list back to me. He said 'thank you' to the waitress. She gave him a gigawatt smile, said it was her pleasure and moved away.

"The first seven of those people are missing," I said. "Bill, May and Cobb are probably still alive. Faversham has some connection with Bill, and perhaps with May and Cobb also. Brian, Alice and Ted – connected with the Drop-In Centre – are probably dead. Freddie has James Warburton in virtual chains, but I'm sure he doesn't realise that. And as we speak, I have no idea what Freddie is engaged in, and how far up her hit list I am."

"Close to the top would be my assessment," Adam said. "Dylan Thomas died a couple of nights ago. Gareth is out of IC but still pissing blood. Freddie knows what they were supposed to be doing; and, therefore, will be in no doubt as to who was responsible for the Audi hurtling into the road."

"In which case, why hasn't she been in touch?"

I bit into a croissant and took a drink of coffee.

"Have you considered," Adam said, "that the Jersey excitement may have been Freddie's work, not Walter's? She told you she would stay on your case."

I sucked at the residue of croissant stuck behind a molar.

"Have you any notion of Walter's current whereabouts?" he asked.

I freed the piece of croissant. "He did say something about coming back to Bristol to put his house on the market. But…"

"You're not betting on it," Adam said. "And meanwhile, Freddie is keeping her powder dry until she can make you an offer you can't refuse"

He swallowed the last of his coffee and put down his mug. I asked him if he wanted another. He said no, and offered up a completely new idea.

"Alright. What if all the elements in this scenario are orbiting around Walter, and not Freddie? Could it be that everybody concerned with this grim narrative is waiting for Cobb to do whatever he intends to do? Maybe you have to re-arrange the motives and the relationships. Someone has spent hundreds of thousands on Faversham's operating theatre. And Cobb's resurrection men are kidnapping to order. With me so far?"

I nodded. Adam continued.

"So, considering the money invested, there has to be a full schedule of operations. Not just the odd gig. Which, given the evidence, would be in the hands of whom?"

"Bill Marsh or Walter Cobb," I said. "Or maybe the deceased Len Coleman."

"And not Freddie?"

"It's the sort of thing she could mastermind, yes. It's a high-risk activity, with a lot of people on the payroll come operations time. It's extremely lucrative. Big fees paid by the recipients of black-market boy parts. But Freddie talks about her aspirations for the Settle firm like it was some major public company. Somehow, I don't think illegal transplants would fit the portfolio."

"But they would fit Cobb's?"

"He's confident and sneaky. And we do have evidence, of sorts – a Transit van and the results of an illegal visit to a funeral parlour."

"Which you can take to George Hood," Adam said. "He'll get a warrant, on the grounds of something or other, and discover the place for himself. You may get your knuckles wrapped, but you're unlikely to have the book thrown at you."

That sounded dangerously simple. Adam leaned across the table top.

"Jack… The longer you hang on to this, the more the odds shorten on the bad guys finding out what you know. Faversham and his mates have been doing their Sweeney Todd thing under the radar. They could all go to jail for a long time if discovered. So they must have an exit strategy. Which must involve getting rid of the person who discovers what they are up to."

He looked at me, dead centre. I stared at him.

"I haven't a clue where this is going," I said. "I've lost my client, the person my client hired me to find, and the man who owes money to the person I'm trying to find. Who, it turns out, could probably pay the debt several times over."

"Go to George Hood, Jack."

"No. Only as a last resort."

"And you're not there yet?"

"I hope not."

"I think you might be. Sitting on a towel on the beach, waiting for the tide to come in."

He stared at me. I tried to look resolute. He went on.

"Okay… How rich is Bill?"

"I don't know. I don't think May knows either."

"Why did he call you from Faversham's operating theatre? Is he in cahoots with Walter Cobb? Is he helping to bank-roll the business?"

"Why not? Anything's possible in this spellbinding miasma."

"And could Cobb be blackmailing Bill? Or Faversham? Or both of them?"

My mobile rang from my jacket which was clothing the back of the chair. I found it and pressed the answer button.

Freddie Settle picked out the noise in the background. Asked if I was alone. I said I was in a café. She said I should go to my office and ring her from there soonest, and ended the call. I put the mobile down onto the table in front of me.

"Your face has gone grey," Adam said.

Not surprising. I could feel the blood draining from it. I took a huge deep breath.

"Freddie Settle wants me to call."

"In person?"

"No. By phone. From the office. She wants me to be alone."

"Why?"

"I don't know. Maybe it's a flair for the dramatic."

"Get going then. I'll pay the bill."

I stood up and shrugged into my jacket. Adam told me to take care. I promised I would and, in return, he promised not to tell Chrissie what I was doing. I walked out of the café, into the sunshine and towards the Healey.

CHAPTER TWENTY-FIVE

The quickest route from Clifton to my office is to cross the Gorge on the suspension bridge and drop down to the Cumberland Basin. But on this occasion I reckoned without the zeal of a road gang who had closed the slip road to the basin swing bridge. The 'diversion' pointed me in the opposite direction. If I'd spent less time thumping the steering wheel and swearing at the incompetent bastards who had devised this method of jamming up traffic into the city, my senses would have been ordered and in the right place. As it was, Freddie's ploy caught me out.

I sat imprisoned in gridlock for twenty minutes. To my right, less than one hundred yards as the crow files, I could see my office window. Eventually I managed to turn onto the exit road, coast down and around, and into the turning circle in front of the office. I barely noticed the dark blue Mercedes parked with its engine idling. I drove around the building and along the riverside. At which point I realised the Mercedes was behind me, driving in my wheel tracks. I turned into the car park. The Mercedes stopped at the entrance. I was boxed in.

To my left, a man heaved himself out of a silver Audi; a match for the one destroyed in the road accident. He was a giant; as wide as he was tall, with more chins than the Hong Kong telephone directory. He waddled towards me. I sat in the Healey, waiting for whatever this was about to be, to get under way. He came to a standstill six feet in front of the car, reached inside his jacket and produced what appeared to be a .38 magnum semi-automatic.

Another man stepped out from behind the Giant. It looked like a stage reveal. He was slimmer than the Giant and clearly more agile. He moved to the Healey passenger door, opened it, slid into the car, closed the door and nodded at me.

"Mr Shepherd. My name is Robert."

He had the shoulders of a hammer thrower and hands that could pull bolts out of gate posts. Not a man to argue with.

"The Mercedes behind us will now turn around," he said. His voice was soft and his manner impeccable. "When that is done, you will do the same thing and then follow the Mercedes. The Audi will follow us."

The Giant waddled his way back to the Audi. I followed instructions to the letter. All the way to Walter Cobb's warehouse in Avonmouth.

The Mercedes pulled up on the forecourt, facing the warehouse door. I pulled up alongside. The Audi slid into position to my right. I noticed it had tinted side and rear windows. Robert nodded at me again.

"If you please, Mr Shepherd…"

We got out of the Healey. The Audi driver materialised, shorter than the rest of the coterie and wearing a chauffeur's uniform. He moved to the rear door on his side and opened it. Freddie got out, straightened up, looked at me, and delivered her fabulous smile.

"Jack. How are you?"

I managed to tell her I was okay. The Audi Driver circumnavigated all three cars and opened the side door into the warehouse. He stepped back out of the way, and the rest of us crocodiled inside.

It was maybe fifty feet long and thirty-five wide. With what passed for a mezzanine floor at the far end, which looked like it housed a couple of offices, a small kitchen space and a toilet. Running from the mezzanine back to the front door on each side, were landings six feet or so deep. There were two long, oblong skylights set into the opposing slopes of the roof. The place was empty. Except for two stacks of wooden pallets, a pile of large cardboard boxes with something I couldn't read stamped on the sides. And two men sitting in wheelchairs underneath the mezzanine, flanked by two more burly flat-nosed types.

The man in the chair on the left was Gareth Thomas. His right arm was in a sling and he had a bandage around his left wrist. He was wearing a kind of skull cap on his head and a whiplash collar round his neck. He wasn't moving. Just staring straight at me. Walter Cobb sat in the other wheelchair. He wasn't bandaged, but looked like he needed to be. His face was a mess and his torn shirt was streaked with blood. His head lolled back on his neck, as if it had slipped out of place.

The Giant pointed at the lower pallet stack, and asked to me to sit. I did. My toes just managed to reach the floor. This was intended as a serious confrontation and Freddie wasn't smiling any more.

"You're a menace, Jack," she began.

I sat up as straight as I could.

"I'll take that as a compliment, Freddie," I replied.

"I'm sorry about the welcoming committee," she said. "But I knew you wouldn't come without a formal invitation. I gave orders that you weren't to be hurt."

I dipped my head in acknowledgement of her courtesy.

"We have to talk, Jack."

A masterpiece of précis that. A euphemism for 'answer my questions to my complete satisfaction, before I hand you over to my associates for a trip to the grinder'.

"Talk away, Freddie," I said. "I'm listening."

She looked at me with some regret.

"We have a problem, you and I. Basically I believe it's a lack of understanding. We both know I have been providing all the good will. You have responded by refusing to co-operate, by wrecking an expensive piece of machinery, by sending Dylan to the morgue, and Gareth," – she nodded in his direction – "to intensive care. That is poor reward for the interest I have shown in your health and welfare."

It was an irredeemable load of crap, but she was dishing it out with some urbanity. It didn't merit much of a response as yet, so I simply shrugged my shoulders and looked down at the floor. Freddie accepted the gesture as an invitation to carry on.

She stepped close, folded her arms, tapped the floor a couple of times with an expensive Italian shoe and went on.

"I am a business woman, Jack…"

"No Freddie," I said. "You're scum in a fifteen hundred quid suit."

That did it. Freddie's cool evaporated in an instant. She moved her right arm across her chest, adjusted the huge diamond on her third finger, then swung the back of her hand across my face. The ring tore some skin out of my cheek and I yelled in pain. Blood ran into my mouth. I licked at it, then raised my right arm and dabbed at my cheek with the back of my hand. God it hurt.

Then calm once more, Freddie continued.

"I control a large organisation. I employ a considerable number of people. And in normal circumstances, the business runs very smoothly indeed. However, there are some…" she searched for the right word… "interests, which I can't afford to disclose. You are with me, yes?"

I licked my lip again. "So far, Freddie…"

She stepped back a pace. "Where is Bill Marsh?"

"I don't know," I said. "Where is May?"

"That's for later. Do you know who killed Len Coleman?"

"I thought you did." I looked towards Thomas. "Or rather he did, under orders from you."

Freddie nodded at the Giant. He moved to me, hauled me to my feet, executed an effortless full nelson and presented me to my co-driver Robert, who squared up to me.

"A thousand apologies, Mr Shepherd," he said.

He shifted slightly to his right and slammed his right fist into the pit of my stomach. My whole body seemed to go into spasm. The pain spread to my chest. I choked, gasped for breath and immediately wanted to be sick. The Giant released me and I pitched forward onto my knees. It was some time before the nausea subsided. No one in the warehouse moved or spoke. The Giant picked me up and sat me back on the pallets.

Freddie weighed in again, with another morsel of advice.

"This is no way to carry on, Jack. It's not sensible to be so obstructive. You will only get seriously hurt."

I was hurting so much I couldn't frame a reply. Freddie pointed to Cobb.

"He is responsible for all this." She opened her arms wide to include all those present. "We caught up with him on his way to the airport."

"Must have been after the meeting with his estate agent," I offered.

Freddie gave me an old-fashioned look. Which morphed into deeply suspicious. I dredged up something else to say.

"Is he alright?"

"I hope not," she said. "Apparently, he's not broke at all.

He has a lot of money in Jersey. And a fine house, I understand."

"Yes," I said. "I've been there."

Freddie kept her surprise to a minimum. "Oh, I didn't know that."

"Louis the Sixteenth vernacular. Built by some French pirate in 1778."

If this was news to Freddie, it could only mean that our tourist guides in Jersey were a pair of cut-price enforcers hired by Walter. One question answered then.

Freddie turned her face and looked at him again.

"Did he offer you any other kind of hospitality?" she asked.

"We didn't get on." I looked at Walter too. "Did he tell you much?"

Freddie shook her head. "Unfortunately, no. That's why he's in such a state."

"Did you ask him if he killed Len Coleman?"

"Of course."

"And what did he say?"

Freddie shrugged. We were approaching the end of the conversation, so I asked a final question.

"Why are you looking for Bill Marsh?"

"We have important matters to discuss," Freddie said. "We need to set some boundaries, Bill and I. Get a few things straight."

"About what?"

She looked deep into my eyes. Hers were beautiful. But not at all friendly, and contemplating something or other. She called up to the mezzanine.

"Lester. Bring her out."

There was the sound of chairs scraping on wood. One of

the office doors opened. A man in his 30s with a bad haircut and a cheap suit, ushered May out onto the mezzanine. I stared up at her. She tried to smile at me.

I launched myself at Freddie. I was barely upright before arms came from nowhere and encircled me. I jabbed my right elbow backwards and made satisfactory contact with a ribcage. I was rewarded with a vicious punch to the kidneys. My knees buckled and I slid to the floor again. I rolled over onto my back and looked up. Freddie stepped forward, hitched up the knees of her expensive trousers and crouched beside me. She pasted on her megawatt smile.

"Find Bill Marsh for me," she said. "I'll give you forty-eight hours."

She stood up. The Giant hauled me back onto my feet. I shook off his arms and stared at Freddie. The smile stayed fixed.

"Take Mr Shepherd back to his car," she said.

The Giant stepped towards me. I waved him away, took a couple of steps to test my equilibrium, straightened as much as I could, and looked up at May again.

"I'm fine, Jack," she said; her voice strong and her body language resolute.

I turned away and walked slowly towards the side door. Robert and the Giant followed me outside to the Healey. They waited patiently while I eased myself into the driver's seat and fumbled at the keys still in the ignition. When the engine fired, they walked back into the warehouse.

It was a long and extremely painful journey home.

* * *

An hour later, I lay soaking in the bath. Letting the heat work on the bruises, my anger cool and my pulse rate slow down. Encased in the cocoon of water, I did some thinking. May was the only concern, at least for now. But I had learned something earlier in the evening. Heroic though my quest was, I needed help. Not just ordinary help. I needed muscle.

But not tonight. Tonight... phones disconnected, one drink with a light supper and early to bed. I eased under the duvet just after 9 o'clock, took a while to discover the least painful sleeping position, then mercifully, the light went out.

CHAPTER TWENTY-SIX

I woke up at twenty-five minutes past eight, and a split second later discovered I was hurting all over. At least it seemed that way. I moved and the bruises caught me out. I levered myself upright, swung my feet to the carpet and stood up. That wasn't too painful. In the bathroom, I looked at my face in the mirror. The damage Freddie had done to my cheek looked as bad as it felt, but I concluded I could do without stitches.

I called Harvey to ask if he had time to see me. He asked me if it was urgent. I told him it was bloody serious.

The extremely polite PC on the gate refrained from commenting on my face, wished me good morning and said Superintendent Butler was expecting me. I parked the Healey in the same place as last time and walked gingerly across the car park. Harvey was in the lobby, glaring at me and all but stamping his feet.

"Who did that to your face?"

"I had a meeting with Freddie Settle in Avonmouth."

Harvey raised his arms in despair.

"Now don't get cross," I said. "It wasn't my idea. I was press-ganged."

"Do you want us to check the place out?"

"No point. They'll be long gone by now. But for your information, it was the warehouse owned by Walter Cobb."

"Was he there as well?"

"Yes. A bit under the weather though."

Harvey didn't say another word until we got into his office. Then he pointed me to a chair.

"Sit down."

I did. Slowly and carefully, all the while trying to look like a man about to offer up a great idea.

"So now what?" Harvey asked.

I looked across the desk at him. I still hadn't sorted out the best place to begin. Harvey waited.

"I need to give you the whole story, I guess."

"Always best," he said. "Although I'm never convinced that's what I get from you."

"Okay…"

I began with Mr Berling and the funeral parlour. Two sentences in, Harvey held up his right hand.

"Hang on. Let's get George in here. Save a second trip to the well." He picked up his mobile. Pressed two buttons and waited. "George," he said. "Where are you?" He listened for a second or two. "Okay. Within five minutes. Siren and blues and twos." He glared across the desk at me. "Yes, he's here too."

He ended the call, laid his mobile on the desk, re-adjusted his position in his chair and folded his arms.

"You said Walter Cobb was under the weather."

"Just a bit. His face looked like a yard of bad road, and there was blood all over his shirt."

"So he doesn't know where Bill Marsh is either."

"If he does, he's taken a hell of a beating to keep it secret."

We talked about odds and sods until George Hood walked into the office. Harvey looked at his watch.

"That was bloody quick."

"Blues and twos you said. That's carte blanche."

"He gave that to me too," I said.

George sat in the other chair. Reached out and shook my hand. "Okay, Jack?"

Harvey grunted. "When you two have finished…"

He looked at me with barely suppressed ire, in spite of carte blanche.

Hood knew the beginning of the story. He nodded two or three times as I began to tell it. Then I cleared my throat and launched into a slightly edited version of the stuff he and Harvey didn't know; from the funeral parlour recce, through the break in and the search, to the discovery. I avoided mentioning Joe's name, maintaining I had found a way into the place through a rear window that wasn't alarmed. Both detectives knew that bit was a distortion of the truth, but sensibly chose not to pry.

Hood came to the same conclusion as I had done about the interior space.

I wound up. "I looked round the room. I didn't contaminate a potential crime scene. I wore gloves and I didn't touch a thing, except the door handle. I went out the way I got in. You can raid the place acting on information received. Which you can't disclose at this time, as doing so might damage an ongoing investigation."

I gave Harvey my best 'over to you' look.

"Okay," he said. "You want us to bring Mr Berling in here. Then let George and Sherlock play good cop bad cop, until he folds under the strain and tells us all about the illegal operations. Maybe he genuinely doesn't know anything about them." Harvey sat back in his chair, snorted and opened his arms wide. "In any case, it's not MIT business."

"Len Coleman is. And he is… was, part of this."

Hood looked at me and changed the emphasis of the discussion.

"Do you think Bill Marsh is part of Faversham's set up."

I told him I did.

"Which part?" Harvey asked. "He's clearly not qualified for cutting and sewing."

"Bill has money," I said. "And I believe that, for reasons we will not know until we find him and ask him what they are, he helped finance the initiative."

Harvey asked why he would do that.

"I don't know," I said. "That's why we need to find him."

"And you think Berling may be a person who knows where Bill is?"

"He's the only person we can ask," I said.

Hood seemed to agree with that assessment. I pressed on.

"You two have the badges and the warrants and the weight of the law to hand. I would have to beat the information out of him."

"Heaven forbid," Harvey said. He pushed his chair back a bit. "You still haven't heard from May?"

I sat up straighter in my chair. Cleared my throat and explained.

"Freddie Settle has her. She was in Cobb's warehouse too."

Harvey rocked forwards and laid his elbows on his desk.

"Was she hurt?" Hood asked

"Didn't seem to be. She actually said she was fine."

"Freddie hadn't harmed her."

"Not as far as I could tell."

Harvey rubbed his eye sockets. "So, you're about to suggest that we send the ACC's designer commandos to the rescue."

"Hell no. If you do that, May and whatever this is all about, could perish together."

Hood and Harvey exchanged glances.

"May's a prosecution witness," I offered.

"To what?" Harvey grumbled. "A story that Freddie will deny with such outrage, the echoes won't die away for weeks… May isn't hurt, so there's no evidence of intimidation or violence."

"So long as we get her back. Christ, Harvey…"

He glared at me. "Righteous indignation won't work either."

He was close to throwing me out of the building. I had to be very careful.

"Freddie hoped May would lead her to Bill," I said. "I don't think May knows where he is. The task has fallen to me, knowing that I'll move heaven and earth to make sure May isn't harmed. I have been given forty-eight hours."

"So the intention is, to get on with the crime chief's recommendations while ignoring intelligent suggestions from the proper guardians of law and order."

I didn't say anything.

Harvey put his elbows back on the desk. He lifted his right hand to his face and supported his chin. He mumbled into the palm of his hand, looked down at his desk, then up again at his sergeant, decision made.

"Okay, George. Get up to the funeral parlour and scare the living shite of out this Berling bloke."

"I want to go," I said.

Harvey nodded at Hood. "Take Don Quixote too."

CHAPTER TWENTY-SEVEN

The first ten minutes of our journey were made in silence. Hood stared in front of him, concentrating on navigating his way through the late afternoon traffic. As we drove up Stokes Croft, he opened the conversation.

"How the hell has Faversham been getting away with this?"

"It's one hell of a secret business," I said. "I mean you and I paid a visit, got the conducted tour and we didn't notice a thing."

"But you said it's a state-of-the art operating theatre. With big bits of kit, I should imagine. Must have taken some getting in."

"Sure. But with the bits in crates and boxes, who would know? It went in at the side of the building from the back of the car park, not through the front door. If it was delivered in a hearse, who would take a second look? And apparently you don't need a lot of stuff for routine organ surgery. It's a 'carve up, take out and put back' exercise according to a surgeon friend of Adam. As long as the new organ has been properly harvested and stored, and you join up everything with due care and attention, it works. It's all down to the skill of the surgeon. And we know that before his drink problem, Featherstone was considered one of the best."

"Okay. What about the cost?"

"Obviously he was bank-rolled in the beginning. But he is serving an elite client base. You need to be earning close to a six-figure salary to afford a black-market lung, or heart, or bowel. A bit less for a liver or a kidney. So if he's been at this for two or three years…"

"He has probably paid back whoever it was financed the setup," Hood said.

"A friend of Chrissie has a brother with cystic fibrosis," I said. "He's nineteen. He needs two new lungs. He may get them before he dies, but it's a long shot. His mother was recently heard to say she would do absolutely anything for two lungs."

Hood glanced at me. I went on.

"Supposing you had a spare seventy thousand, and the person dearest to you desperately needed it, would you hand it over?"

"Probably."

"And if it was a matter of life and death? An operation or a trip to the morgue? Would that be any different?"

"Probably not."

"And if the only way for this to happen was to pay Featherstone to do it?"

"Well that's the point," Hood said. "Paying Featherstone. He's making a fortune by trading on people's misery. You're not going to tell me that seventy grand is the real cost. I mean what's his mark up?"

"Sixty percent at least, I should think. But if the recipient's family has the money to pay…"

"Okay. But the bottom line is, the organ will have been harvested illegally and such an operation is against the law."

"And that's all that concerns you?"

"There's no moral issue here, Jack. Featherstone is indulging in stuff for which he can, and should, go to prison. And if, as we suspect, Walter Cobb's men with the Transit are on the payroll, there's a shed load of other wrong doing to add to the crime sheet as well." He turned his head and stared at me. "You're not trying to tell me there's a plus in this?"

"Watch the road."

He turned back to look ahead. He hit the horn, pulled across the road to his right and switched lanes. "Answer the question," he muttered.

"Of courses there's a plus," I said. "The family and loved ones of the recipient get exactly what they stump up for, and are rendered deliriously happy."

"After paying through the nose for something one hundred percent illegal," he said. "The law is the law, and if you break it by indulging in criminal activities you have to be stopped. Featherstone or Faversham or whatever the hell he calls himself, is pond scum."

No denying that, but I couldn't leave the conversation unfinished.

"People living on the streets are there for all sorts of reasons," I said. "But the bottom line is, they have nothing to their name. Only the clothes they stand up in. When someone appears and offers them more money than they've seen in years, the choice is a no-brainer. If the harvesting goes wrong, or it turns out the organs aren't any use, what the hell? It's just the end of a long story of pain and misery. And who's going to miss them?"

Hood stayed resolute. "We the police, the people paid to protect and serve, can't do much to reverse these injustices, but we get paid to try."

* * *

At the funeral parlour, Berling began with the knee-jerk response.

"Have you got a warrant for this search?"

Hood responded with, "Would you like to come to Trinity Road and answer my questions there?"

Berling looked alarmed. Hood ploughed on.

"And in the meantime, we'll get our warrant and the four police officers out in the lobby will begin the search. Everyone on the premises will be held here until all questions are answered. At least, everyone who can talk."

Berling was in no state to find that funny. The colour had drained from his face. Hood finished what he had to say.

"Which could take most of the evening. And you could end up in a police cell overnight."

Hood waited for the emphasis he put on the last few words to hit the mark. Berling said nothing.

"So do you want to make a drama out of this," Hood went on. "Or would you rather it was low key?"

Berling shifted his position in his chair. As squirms go it was a small one, but a squirm it was nonetheless. Now he looked glum. Hood moved to the office door and opened it. He called for one of the uniforms, who arrived and took up position in the doorway.

"This is Police Constable Deeley," Hood said. "He and his fellow officers will escort you to the police station." He took a breath. "Mr Berling, I am asking you to come with us, to answer questions concerning the disappearance of Bill and May Marsh, and the murder of Leonard Coleman."

Berling stood up behind his desk.

"I have absolutely no idea what you are referring to… Go on. Search the place."

Hood turned to Deeley.

"Officer… Will you keep this gentleman here please?"

Berling sat down again. Hood and I left the office. Deeley closed the door. In the lobby, Hood pointed to a chair.

"Sit there," he ordered. "The rest of this is by the book." Then he lowered his voice. "I don't want you anywhere near the discovery. Let us find the door to the operating theatre and then pretend to be surprised and excited."

He turned to the other PCs. "Wareham, you come with me. We'll work this side of the lobby. Green and Arnold, you start with the storeroom."

Hood and the PCs set to work. Ten minutes later Hood re-joined me. We waited another four or five minutes. Wareham came back and stood next to us. Then PC Green stepped back into the lobby.

"Sergeant. We've found a door at the back of the storeroom. We got it open, but behind it, there's another door with a deadlock."

"Go and ask Mr Berling for the key," Hood ordered.

Green walked the length of the lobby, opened the office door and stepped inside. I looked at my watch. Monitored the seconds. Just short of a minute later, PC Green stepped back into the lobby.

"Mr Berling insists he doesn't know what I am talking about."

Hood got to his feet muttering. "What a fucking pantomime… Bring him out here."

Mr Berling was retrieved from his office, then escorted into the storeroom followed by Hood. I hovered in the doorway. Berling seemed genuinely disturbed by what he was looking at. He insisted he had no idea what was behind the locked door, and as this was the first time he had seen it, how the hell could he have a key for it? Hood stepped back into the hall, asking PC Wareham to join him.

"Have you got an enforcer ram in the car?"

"Yes."

"Go and get it. Then smash your way into the room and introduce Mr Berling to whatever's hidden in there."

Wareham went out the front door. Hood dug into a trouser pocket, found his car keys, took them out and turned to me.

"Go outside for a walk. Get off the premises until we've done this. Wait in the Vauxhall if you like."

I did as I was ordered. Walked up to the eastern end of Rycroft Road, bought a KitKat from the newsagent on the corner, and walked back to the Vauxhall. I unlocked the car and returned to the passenger seat.

Moments later, PCs Green, Arnold and Wareham emerged with Berling and escorted him to the patrol car. I watched the car drive away. Hood and PC Deeley stepped into the street. There was a brief conversation, then Deeley went back into the building and Hood walked towards the Vauxhall. He got into the driver's seat and I handed him the key. I asked him if Berling had said anything of significance.

"He moaned about the amount of work he was having to get through without Faversham being in the building. Then he said something about a bloke with a name like a venereal disease. Syfy something."

"Sisyphus," I said. "A Greek. He was punished by the gods for his sins, by having to push a huge boulder up a hill forever."

"Ancient Greek you mean?"

"It's a metaphor for any age. Sisyphus was a great ruler, until his businesses began to make a fortune. At which point he couldn't resist creaming off more than his share. He got rid of anybody who suspected what he was up to, and continued to fleece traders who passed through his land."

"Did he get to the top of his hill?"

"As he tired, the boulder got the better of him. Rolled back to the bottom and he had to start again."

"Sisy who?"

"Sisyphus," I said and spelled it out for him.

"I'll try and remember that."

He turned on the ignition.

"Is that all?" I asked

"The gist… I did ask him where the operating staff came from. He continued to insist the business had nothing to do with him. He had no idea it was going on. And you know what? I'm beginning to believe him."

He looked into the rear-view mirror and pulled out into the road.

* * *

I picked up the Healey and drove back to my office. There was another note under my door. *Why don't you keep your mobile switched on? I'm having dinner with someone whose business I'm trying to hook. I can be all yours later. I'll call you.*

I looked at the clock on the wall. Forty-eight hours Freddie had offered. It was now twenty-six, and at breakfast tomorrow, it would be thirty-eight.

Harvey called me. I asked him if Hood was making progress.

"Not much. And Berling's lawyer will have him out of here by supper time."

"Has he coughed up anything about Bill? Anything at all?"

"Sorry, Jack. And now the bottom line is…" He paused to put the right words together. "Arnold Faversham and his business are no longer of interest to MIT. Unless he resurfaces as part of our investigation into the murder of Len Coleman, which seems unlikely. We are no longer tapping your phones."

He apologised again and ended the call.

"Shit, shit shit shit shit."

I threw the phone receiver across the room. Mercifully, the office door was open and it sailed out into the corridor. It was collected by the heavy curtains lining the window opposite and it dropped on to the carpet. I leaned back in my chair and stared up at the point above the door where the office wall met the ceiling. There was a plaster crack I hadn't seen before, running along the join. I got out of my chair and collected the phone. It seemed none the worse for its flight though the air. Then I came up with an idea.

I called Adam with the loaner mobile. He picked up the call at home.

"Is our no-reply email address still in existence?"

"Yes. I told Chris to hang onto it. Thought it might come in handy again."

"Can we send out a blog this evening?"

"I'll ask him."

* * *

We met in Chris Gould's workshop at 9 o'clock. I gave him back the loaner phone and thanked him. He left a key with us and told us to lock up when we had finished. Adam and I drafted a piece of text designed to provoke a response from Bill.

The Bristol private eye who was left staring down at a pool of blood on his client's parquet floor, has compounded his misfortune. There is still no sign of the AB negative's owner and now, to add to his miseries, his client has gone missing too. The victim perhaps, of a kidnapping by seriously dangerous people. This private investigator clearly needs help. Call him. Somebody.

"We've passed the copy deadline for tomorrow morning's Western Daily Press," Adam said. "But I can get a response to the blog into the early edition of the Post. From which I can then quote, questioning the way fools and fetishists misuse the power of the world-wide-web. Which will leave you with twenty-four hours before Freddie makes her next move."

This really was close to conspiracy. Leveson could certainly make something out of a journalist writing a blog and then responding to it in the newspaper he works for. But we had nothing left in our armoury. Somehow, and sometime soon, Bill had to read the blog and the headlines and put two and two together.

CHAPTER TWENTY-EIGHT

I spent the following morning, the second Saturday on the case, finding things to do.

I woke up at half past seven. Checked the landline by picking up the receiver in the hall and listening to the dial tone. Checked that my mobile had enough juice in the battery. Made coffee, and ate two slices of toast.

Upstairs in my study, I googled the local section of the newsdot website. Our email was first up and writ large. Along with a rapidly developing list of senseless comments.

The sun was hard at work outside and tomorrow was May Day. I opened the kitchen door and stepped out to test the temperature. Warm enough for a bit of light exercise. I put on an old pair of jeans, took all the phone receivers into the back garden, and spent an hour tidying up the beds around the lawn. I looked at my watch for the umpteenth time. 8.55.

Back in the kitchen I made and drank another cup of coffee. Checked the wall clock again. 9.03.

I called Linda's home number. No reply - something of a relief. I called her mobile, achieving the same result. I left a message. *I'm really sorry about last night. I'll explain when I can. I'm stuck at home this morning. Expecting a package I have to sign for. Catch up with you later.*

I sat down in the living room. Put my mobile and my landline receiver on the coffee table in front of me. Stared at them with some malice. Switched the television set on. Looked through the electronic guides of as many channels as my patience would allow, then gave it up when I discovered I had seen all the westerns on offer.

I looked at the clock above the fireplace. 9.40.

Adam rang. I asked him where he was. At home he said, and asked me if I had looked at the newsdot bollocks upload. I told him I had. He said he'd be at home all morning if I had anything to impart. I asked about Chrissie and Sam. Adam said the dog was stretched out on the floor by his desk, and Chrissie was working through her tutor's reaction to her latest assignment. At which point we agreed we ought to keep the line clear and ended the call. I put the receiver back on the coffee table and stared at it again.

What would I normally be doing if at home and at leisure? I decided to update my notes on this case and took the phones upstairs. Not that there was much to write, apart from – 'The police have no idea where Faversham-Featherstone could be. I still have no idea where Bill is. Freddie Settle is extraordinarily pissed off and has May as a hostage'

I leaned back in my chair and gazed at the laptop screen. So much for eleven days work. The clock in the bottom right-hand corner of the screen read 10.15.

My mobile rang. I grabbed it and pressed the green button. It was some pillock from my mobile provider asking me how I was today and if I'd like to enhance my total mobile experience. I closed the line.

There was a cupboard on the landing, full of cardboard boxes which had been on my list to sort for months - most of them from eons ago, which I thought might come in useful someday if I decided to move. It's amazing how long you can hang on to this concept once it takes root. There was a monster box in which a huge, fat, analogue TV set had been delivered back in the 90s, full of bits of polystyrene and bubble wrap. I burst a few bubbles but got no thrill out of the exercise and gave it up. There was an equally large box which had arrived with a fitted kitchen oven (more polystyrene), a big old VHS recorder box (empty), two old DVD player boxes (empty), a wide slim-line box in which the current TV set had been delivered (more bubble wrap), a small fat box (polystyrene again) in which the microwave had arrived, and a solid looking box which had delivered something from Amazon.

So now I had a pile of boxes on the landing. I hauled them downstairs and re-piled them in the hall, beside the front door. Working on the assumption that falling over them five or six times would drive the message home, and I would take them to the Recycling Centre.

The living room clock said 10.50.

Then I remembered something that would help. *The Strange World of Gurney Slade*. A TV series from the early 1960s, starring the late, great, Anthony Newley, which I had first discovered in cult re-runs when I was a student. About an actor who walks off the set of a sitcom which is failing to provoke laughs from the studio audience, and into a world entirely of his own devising. At his own pace, he wanders through the countryside. Bringing to life objects and people on advertising hoardings, passing the time of the day with plants and trees, discussing matters of great import with dogs and farmyard animals, and creating a whole new way of taking on the pressures of the world. Only six episodes were made, inventing absurd TV comedy long before the Pythons and Vic Reeves. Like Gurney Slade, I had time on my hands and an overwhelming need to make the world work my way, at least for the next twenty-four hours.

I found the DVD and sat back on the sofa. I was halfway through episode three when my mobile rang. I stared at it buzzing and vibrating on the coffee table. I picked it up and pressed the call receive button.

"I get the message, Jack," Bill said.

I grabbed the TV remote and hit the 'mute' button. Then Bill and I were talking, if not in the same place, at least in the same conversation.

"We need to talk, Bill," I said.

"How is May?"

I ignored the question. "Face to face, Bill, and within the next hour. I'll come to you."

He offered an arrangement he'd obviously rehearsed. "Meet me in the M4 Services café at Aust. You know it?"

"Yes. This side of the old bridge crossing."

I looked at my watch again, this time with some purpose. 12.15. I could be there in less than half an hour. But better to add a few minutes to be sure.

"1 o'clock," I said. "Be there whatever happens, Bill."

"Slit my throat and hope to die, Jack."

The line went dead. I leant back into the sofa cushions and breathed as if the breaths I were taking were my last. A pulse in my left temple was throbbing, my heart was racing.

Something to do. Finally.

* * *

Now cheerfully re-named *Severn View*, the services area at Aust is accessed from the northern side of the east bound carriageway. It's less tatty than it used to be. The old trucker's café has had a makeover and boasts a new entrance beneath the coffee and burger signs.

The car park was sparsely populated. I arrived ahead of time. Sat in the Healey for a long six minutes thinking about stuff, and hoping that Bill had enough guts for what was going to play out.

I found him in the café. In a hell of a state. Hugging himself and visibly shaking. He had chosen a table by the panoramic window with a view of the channel looking north, but he wasn't enjoying it. He was staring down at the table top. As I reached him, he looked up and tried to smile.

"Hello, Jack."

"You haven't got a drink," I said. "Would you like one?"

Bill shook his head.

I re-located to the coffee shop. It took five minutes to get in line, shuffle forwards, order an 'Americano', and take it back to the table. During that time, Bill stared out of the window, only turning to look at me when I sat down. I took a sip of coffee and burned the roof of my mouth. I put the mug to one side, rested my elbows on the table and leaned forwards.

"Where is May?" Bill asked.

"She is currently enjoying the hospitality of Freddie Settle," I said.

There was a beat rest. Bill groaned and thumped the table. I ploughed on.

"Who has given me until 5 o'clock this afternoon. That's four half hours from now, to find you and swap you for your wife. Are you getting all this?"

"Yes. Yes, I am. Oh Jesus…"

"I've got enough adrenalin inside me to bottle and sell to hospitals. So let's make this simple. Where have you been?"

"In a caravan at Severn Beach," he said.

Possibly the best corner of the Westcountry in which to get lost. If there was one place nobody would dream of hiding in, it was there. Which meant that it was exactly the place to do so.

"Do you remember Libby Mason?" Bill asked. "It belongs to her."

I remembered Libby. A veteran sex worker, with pretend red hair, a second-hand tan and a lumpy face. Bill had gone to her rescue a number of times over the years. Now, she was apparently paying her dues.

"The caravan looks out over the mud flats to the channel," Bill said. "It's rusted to buggery, needs a coat of paint, and a new bedroom window. But it's anonymous."

Bill didn't have to paint a picture. One hundred battered brown and white caravans on the banks of the Severn Estuary was a low rent destination.

Bill went back to the beginning of the conversation.

"Is May alright?" he asked.

I gave him a précis of yesterday's trip to Cobb's warehouse. He looked more hollow-eyed, if that was possible, by the time I had finished.

"But May's alright, isn't she?" he asked again.

"She was then."

"You see, Freddie doesn't know."

"Know what?"

"If she did, she wouldn't harm her."

"Know what, Bill?"

He took his time to say the next four words. Like a cheap actor in a bad whodunit, he gave each one equal emphasis.

"Freddie is May's daughter."

I reached for the mug of coffee and swallowed a mouthful that scorched all the way down. I gasped. Bill thought it was because of the information he had just offered. He asked if I was alright. I nodded as the heat began to dissolve in my chest. He went on with the story.

"Freddy and Lisa, and May and I, sort of grew up together. We all lived in Bedminster, went to the same junior school. We lost touch as the years went by. Until May and I met again. I was working for Uncle Jimmy by then."

"Were you married to May when this happened?"

Bill looked at me, the expression on his face half surprise at the suggestion I had just made and half apology for not explaining properly.

"No. We, er... we were engaged."

He took time to sort out the next bit of narrative. I waited.

"Back in the day," Bill went on, "Uncle Jimmy was killed by one of Freddy's employees, working for himself on the boss's time. The situation was dealt with, the bloke disappeared, and Freddy put some money into my new business. He looked after me. I knew everything there was to know about the betting shops, but nothing about the vultures that were circling. Freddy made it clear my business was a no-go area and they stayed away. May came back to Bristol around that time, and all four of us, Freddy and Lisa and May and I, hooked up again. Freddy married Lisa, because he loved her to bits and was desperate for an heir. They discovered Lisa was infertile. IVF was still a bit science fiction in the 1970s. Freddy spent a fortune on experts and treatments. Until Lisa, broken by disappointment, called a halt. So, he and May..." He offered me a 'you know what I'm saying' gesture. "And Freddy got an heiress. Prematurely. Because the pregnancy didn't go well and May — "

I interrupted him. "Hang on. Wait a minute. What was this? Some kind of deal?"

"Yes... No, not really," he said.

"Did Lisa know about it?"

"Yes. We all did. We were all part of it."

It was my turn to stare out of the window. I was the most not-knowing detective in the Westcountry until this moment. And now... Freddie Settle, May's daughter. The Freddie who had threatened my life, who had Walter Cobb beaten to within an inch of his, and who was now menacing the woman who had kept this secret for over thirty years.

"May only just survived the birth," Bill explained. "She convalesced in a very expensive private hospital, and Freddy paid all the bills. She was told she couldn't have any more children. We got married six months later, in November 1987."

"Didn't you want kids?"

"I was in love with May. I never thought about kids."

"And Lisa?"

"She accepted the arrangement from day one. Freddy doted on the baby. And, some years later, when I told him May was opening the shop and the Drop-In Centre, Freddy insisted he help out."

I could imagine that. And the unblinking eyes and infamous fixed smile, which settled every dispute.

"He paid the set-up costs of both places," Bill said. "He still helps to fund the Centre."

Bill fell silent. He looked down at the table again, as if the answers to all questions lay enshrined in the laminate.

"So, when did everything begin falling to bits?" I asked.

"When I helped out Walter Cobb," Bill said. "Four years ago. I paid his debt to Freddy."

"Fifty-six thousand pounds."

"No, he owed Freddie forty-two. The fifty-six was something else."

"What else?"

"I'll get to that," he said.

"Was any of it on the books?"

Bill shook his head. "No."

I picked up the mug, blew on the coffee and drank some more. It gave Bill time to get the next bit of the story in order.

"I've known Walter since we were in the Scouts. I was

patrol leader of the Kestrels when he joined the 10th Bristol Troop. He's four years younger than me."

The Scouts…? It took me a while to get across that idea. My astonishment must have been stencilled on my face, because Bill waved a hand at me.

"Every schoolboy joined the Scouts back in the 60s." He took a deep breath. "Walter was always a chancer. By the time he left the 10th Bristol, he was running all sorts of mini rackets. A score here, a profit there… And he was a hell of a poker player. One Sunday night, in a motel out on the A38, he won a bundle and the scrap business, in a game of Five Card Draw. At a stroke he was rich. He parleyed that into a bigger chunk of money and set about behaving like a winner. Which I guess he was, for a while. He survived all the fiscal nonsense of 2008. Seemed to be immune. Then he started borrowing big sums of money. For another year or two it looked like he was managing to service his debts. Then suddenly, he was on his arse. Broke."

I couldn't let this down and out and bust story go further without adding my quid's worth. I interrupted the flow.

"Sorry to jump in here," I said. "But you do know about *Cobb CI*, and Walter's Jersey endeavours?"

Bill looked genuinely puzzled. "Jersey? No. What do you mean?"

First Freddie, and now Bill. I told him the story of my recent two days in the island. His eyes got wider as we got closer to the reveal.

"So Jersey is where he stashed all his money," Bill said.

"I think he was working up to a carefully planned exit from the UK," I said. "It was his version of the long con. His kipper-tied arsehole thing was brilliant. He'd worked on it for years."

"And he's not broke?"

I flashed back to the warehouse, to his broken looking body.

"Not in financial terms."

"Fucking hell…"

Bill paused for a moment or two. I asked my next question.

"Did Walter organise the Drop-In Centre break in?"

"Yes. He needed to find more potential down and outs."

"Why didn't you stop him?"

"I didn't know he was doing it?"

I sat back in the seat. "Oh, Bill, please…"

"I didn't," he insisted.

I bowled him one on the stumps.

"I need the truth, the whole truth and nothing but the truth. And I need you sound and resolute. Whatever happens. Okay?"

He nodded. I asked him what he was doing in Arnold Faversham's funeral parlour.

"I wanted to find out where he'd gone." He sat up straight. "How did you know I was there?"

"You rang me. The police were tapping my phones at the time."

"Ah…"

"So where is Faversham?"

"I've no idea."

Of course not. He had disappeared, like every other member of the supporting cast. And I was racking up 'I've no ideas' like meat pies on an assembly line.

Bill sat back again and seemed to relax a little. He hadn't shaved for a day or two. That was unlike him, he was always clean shaven. I looked into his eyes. They were blue, but seemed darker under the shadows produced by the café lights above us. Deep purple rings around them. The proverbial piss holes in the snow. He had lost some weight since I last saw him. And the stress of the past ten days had probably peeled off a bit more.

"Okay," I said. "The blood on the parquet floor?"

"It wasn't mine," he said. "The same blood group though. Andrew provided it."

Of course he did. That should have occurred to me. Where else was Bill to get a pint of AB negative?"

"What was this for? To add a bit of drama to the disappearance?"

"I wanted people to think I was dead."

"Including May?"

"Only until I was clear of Freddy."

"Which is why you left your laptop and mobile behind. To help with the idea that something serious and un-planned had happened to you."

Bill nodded. "A bit of a risk I know. I did consider that May might hire you."

I reached for the mug. The coffee was a bit cooler suddenly.

"I need a real drink," Bill said. "Let's go to the pub."

I looked at my watch. 1.25. I drained the coffee mug, stood up and followed Bill out into the car park. He unlocked a battered Renault Megane.

"My loaner," he said. "It's Libby's."

Five minutes later, we were sitting in the lounge of *The Boar's Head* in Aust village, two pints of Butcombe Gold on the table between us.

"Why did you lend Walter Cobb fifty-six thousand pounds?" I asked.

Bill looked uncomfortable again. I kept at him.

"I need to know, Bill."

He swallowed a mouthful of beer, then put his glass down.

"Okay. It wasn't actually a loan. It was a payment."

"What for?"

"You know May has a twin sister?"

I did know that. She lived in Piraeus. Married to some expat Dutchman. And this seemed miles off the point. Bill assured me it wasn't, then did another long think. Finally, he put the words together.

"It's where the whole business began really. With Jenny. She and May are very close, even though Jenny moved to Greece in 1998. Five years ago, she developed the symptoms of chronic kidney disease. Got on to the donor list, and she and Hugo waited. Eighteen months down the line a kidney became available, but something went wrong, and the operation never happened."

"Did Cobb know about this?"

"Yes. I told him one night, in the *Silver Star*. Around the time he and Andrew were in the process of organising their new business. They met on Jersey late spring 2018. Andrew had fallen off the wagon after leaving prison and had been drying out in a clinic. Walter stumbled across him on a beach, recognised him, and they got talking. It was a moment of… synergy… is that the word?"

"Yes."

"Andrew uses it a lot. Well, to cut the story to the bones… Walter made a great show of sympathising with Andrew. They spent three or four days together and at some point, the subject of what Andrew was going to do next came up. Between them, they dreamed up the operating room scheme. I think even then, Walter was imagining their first patient – Jenny. And back in Bristol they set it up. Andrew ordered all the gear through his Swiss health trust connections. Between them they spent just a bit short of quarter of a million."

"And it wasn't quite enough."

"That's what they said."

"So you offered a little top up finance and Jenny got her transplant."

"That's right. Andrew did the harvesting and the operations."

"And where did the kidneys come from. Who was the donor?"

Bill took a drink, put the glass back on the table and wiped the corners of his mouth with his left thumb and forefinger.

"I don't know," he said. "It's like that in the real world too. The only people fully in the know are the administrators who sign the papers. Donors aren't told where the organs are going and the recipients don't get to know where they come from. Sometimes the surgeons who do the harvesting have no idea who the donor is."

I took a drink too. Bill was slouching again. Not the Bill I knew, not even the Bill I thought I knew. This was a sad, frightened, defeated old man.

"Would you have stopped all this, had you known what was to follow?"

"But I didn't."

"Not the answer Bill."

He shook his head again. He looked up at me. We stared at each other as if we had forever. Question answered, so I moved the conversation along.

"Why did you have to disappear?"

Bill sighed, ran his fingers through his hair and sighed

again.

"Do you want another drink?"

I looked at my watch. Three minutes before 2 o'clock. We had time.

Bill got up and moved to the bar. I watched him. He seemed to shuffle, rather than walk. The core of this bloody narrative, in which he was a leading player, was careless, ruthless and shameful. Events rolling on like a soap storyline; as the actors dropped in and out of episodes which spiralled into darker and darker material as the story progressed. Bill came back, put my glass on the table in front of me, and sat down again. Shrouded in gloom, he stared into his glass as if looking at his reflection in the beer.

"So how did we get to the present crisis?" I asked.

He looked up at me. "Old man Freddy was ill. He'd tripped and fallen down the stairs at home. He had compressed two discs in his back and trapped a series of nerves in the wrong place. It hurt like hell just to turn over in bed. He needed an operation."

"But that wasn't a problem was it?"

"Not in terms of cost," Bill said. "Freddy could afford any bed in the poshest of clinics. The problem was, this city has armies of people who'd love to take over his business. And word that he was out of sorts, in any way, would be enough to make them start planning. He knew that checking into a hospital in this neck of the woods, however private, was a huge risk. Someone was bound to find out."

"So why didn't he charter a Lear Jet and fly to some place in California?"

"He doesn't like flying. He doesn't like abroad. He's never left this country at any time in his life. Hell, he hasn't been any farther north than Gloucester. He copes with south

Wales, even though he hates the Welsh. Won't go to London on so much as a day trip. The op had to be done secretly, and swiftly. Even the most discreet of private clinics would have been bound to record what was happening. So Walter offered him a solution."

"Featherstone's operating room," I said.

"Andrew was terrified. He knew that the odds of the op being successful were long, and if it didn't work, Freddy might end up worse off. Getting bed baths, pissing and shitting into bags. Andrew told us spines weren't his speciality. But if pushed, he knew a bloke who was shit hot. Freddy settled for that."

"And the operation went wrong."

"Nobody but the surgical team knows why – whoever and wherever they are. The last time I saw Andrew, must have been just before he disappeared. He was swearing on a stack of bibles he'd never met any of the team, apart from the surgeon. Who has gone on the run, along with everyone else."

"Where did Featherstone get his theatre staff from? Presumably he didn't advertise."

"There's no shortage of depressed and broke nurses and doctors, knackered after years working against the odds in the NHS."

"When was Freddie's op done?"

"Six days before I er… disappeared."

"And now he is totally incapacitated?"

"Yes."

"So, after announcing that her father had retired, daughter Freddie parachuted in to run the outfit. And set about contemplating what to do to you and Walter and all the rest."

Bill looked frightened again. "Yes. Freddie's not new to

the business. She's been her dad's right arm for some time. She just came out, that's all. On a mission."

I stared into my beer glass.

"Alright... Freddie has Walter Cobb locked away somewhere, Len Coleman is dead, and you're here with me."

Bill reached for his beer glass, changed his mind, and rested his right arm across his knees. He was anticipating my next question. So I asked it.

"Do you know who killed Len?"

He looked up and stared straight into my eyes.

"Can this stay just between us?" he asked.

"Maybe."

Bill shook his head. "Not good enough, Jack. I need your word on this."

"Okay, you have it."

Bill swallowed. "It was me. I killed him."

This was a hurricane of a surprise. Bill's eyes were locked onto mine. He looked guilty, miserable and frightened; all at the same time.

"Back in the day, I caught up with Len after his last stretch in Horfield. He had money in the bank but you wouldn't know it to look at him. He lived in a – "

I interrupted him. "Yes I know, I've been there."

"Okay... Len didn't gamble much, mainly because when he did he lost. Though it seemed that Freddy senior liked him. Len was allowed to sit around in The Silver Star with a beer or two of an evening and enjoy the place, and without feeling he had to risk losing his money."

"Why?" I asked.

"I've no idea." He looked at my disbelieving face. "Seriously."

"So, in the end, what went wrong?"

He looked at me. His body language now ferocious, anger in his eyes.

"Walter fucking Cobb. Again. He was a partner in one of the Settle business enterprises. And all was going smoothly. Until he began brown nosing selected Silver Star patrons. Cherry picking from Freddy's membership. Offering cut price deals for... well I don't know. I never knew. Daughter Freddie found out."

"When?"

"As soon as she took the reins. A week before Walter announced he was bankrupt."

"So when he flew to Jersey, he didn't know what Freddie was contemplating?"

"I guess that would be right."

We sipped our beers. Then I asked about the burnt papers in the fire grate.

"Hard copy of all the recent emails and dealings between me and Len and Walter and Andrew. Freddie was closing in, and I had killed Len. I was stuck with a double whammy. I got the blood from Andrew, who handed it over without asking questions. I guess he figured that what he didn't know couldn't backfire on him."

We both drank in silence for a while. Then Bill rounded off the dismal narrative.

"So, I shacked up in the caravan with a pile of books and an old laptop which just about got onto the net, via the site owner's wi-fi. And I stayed there, to sit out the days until I dared to get in touch with May."

I stared at him. He read my mind.

"Yes I know," he said. "Not the most well thought out plan in the world. No sensible er... what do they call it...? Exit strategy."

I turned to the sentence with the big question mark.

"Why did you kill Len?" I asked.

Bill sighed, took a deep breath and answered the question.

"I asked him for help. We had been friends a long time. He knew the Settle clan well. He said I should throw myself on Freddie's tender mercies. That might have worked with her Dad, but there was no chance of a result from the new regime. As the days went by, Len became more and more agitated. He asked me to meet him in his flat. He began begging me to face her. We had a hell of a row, which ended up with him threatening to go directly to Freddie. Spill the whole lot."

"Did you believe him?"

"Yes." He grimaced. "That's why I hit him with the candlestick."

"Two or three times," I suggested.

"I had to make sure," he said, suddenly without a trace of emotion in his voice.

"Where is it now? The candlestick."

"As far into the channel as I could throw it from Severn Beach," he said. "It's buried out in the mud somewhere."

Behind me, our host called 'last orders'.

"Dick doesn't like working afternoons," Bill explained. "So he sticks to old fashioned hours. Everybody out by 2.30 on a weekend."

He picked up his beer glass and drained it.

We had to plan the rescue of May out in the car park. The Renault interior smelled like a refuse skip. We talked in the Healey until we had something half-arsed worked out.

CHAPTER TWENTY-NINE

I called Harvey Butler's mobile. He told me he was in his office; reading the paperwork he hadn't had time to read Monday to Friday. George Hood was there too, attempting to explain what the short-hand references and the typos were meant to convey.

Bill and I stood in front of Harvey's desk, actually and metaphorically on the carpet. Harvey stared at Bill, radiating some degree of impatience and not a little menace. I fed the story to him bit by bit, beginning with the more palatable stuff and working up to the complications of the current situation. Under orders from me, Bill didn't speak until he was spoken to. Eventually Harvey did that.

"This is something of an ice cream sandwich, don't you think?"

George Hood came back into the office. He had been for some coffee. He put a tray of mugs down on Harvey's desk.

"Go and get another chair, George." He addressed Bill and me again. "Still not enough in all this for MIT."

I looked straight into Harvey's eyes, not daring to look at Bill, and hoping he was staring at the carpet.

Then I heard him say, "I killed Len Coleman."

Neither of us blinked. Hood came back into the office with another chair. He sat down next to Bill, the three of us making a small crescent in front of Harvey's desk.

"So…," Harvey said. "Give."

It took five minutes for Bill to explain. Somehow, he kept the story exclusive to his relationship with Coleman. Throughout, Harvey looked as though he was striving to believe it all. In the end, he opened his mouth to begin asking a barrel load of questions. I jumped in.

"We haven't got time for this Harvey," I said. "I need to talk to Freddie within the hour. If that doesn't happen, May will be killed."

At which point, Bill dropped his other bombshell. "The thing is, Freddie is May's daughter. Only she doesn't know it."

Harvey stared at him, a mighty chunk of disbelief on his face.

"The result of er…" Bill faded into silence and looked down at the carpet again.

Harvey chewed over that morsel of information. He looked at his sergeant. Hood shrugged in response. Harvey sat back in his chair.

"May is a prosecution witness," I offered hopefully.

"To what?" Harvey grumbled. "A story that Freddie will deny with such outrage, the echoes will reverberate for weeks. And if whatever we decide to do turns into a dog's breakfast, we could end up with no witnesses at all."

Hood joined the conversation. "Is May hurt?"

"She wasn't when I saw her," I said.

"So no evidence of intimidation or violence," Harvey said.

"As long as we get her back. Christ, Harvey."

He glared at me. "Indignation won't work either."

He was close to throwing me out. I had to be very careful.

"Look, Harvey, I'm not in denial here. I know that my life won't be worth the price of a taxi ride to the coast once I agree to meet Freddie."

"No question. You may get in to wherever you're going to meet, but you won't get out."

I persisted. "Freddie will let May go as soon as she sees

Bill. We can stage manage the handover. And with a little help from you, Bill and I can get out from under as well."

Harvey was listening, but not agreeing yet. I looked at Hood for signs of encouragement. No evidence of any. I turned back to Harvey, who straightened up in his chair, decision made.

"Okay, George. Call in surveillance and get this lunatic wired up.

"Now?" he asked. "Saturday evening? They won't like it."

"We're fucking working." He pushed the phone across his desk to me. "Call Freddie. Get her out from wherever she is to somewhere we can get to you when it all goes tits up."

Hood left the office. I called Freddie at *The Silver Star*. She was on the line within seconds.

"Jack…"

I could picture the smile.

"Freddie. I've got Bill. Let's meet."

"Put him on the line."

I handed the phone receiver to Bill. He put it to his right ear and said 'hello'. He asked to speak to May. There was a pause, then Bill became animated.

"Are you alright?" he asked

He listened for a few seconds, then shouted, "May, May…" There was another pause. Bill nodded into the phone. "Yes, understood, yes."

He handed the receiver back to me.

"Where are you both?" Freddie asked.

"We'll meet somewhere neutral," I said.

The location took time to negotiate. We ended up agreeing to meet at 6.30, in a redundant church hall in Barton Hill. A place Freddie had recently bought, apparently. A fifteen-minute drive away. I put the receiver down. Hood had come back into the office and caught the end of the conversation.

"There's a Surveillance Officer and an Armed Response Team on the way," he said. "DCI MacIntosh asked who was going to pay for it."

Harvey nodded at me. "He is." Then he pointed at Bill. "He stays here. Find him a cell downstairs."

There was no ceremony attached to being wired up. I was followed into the nearest toilet by the Surveillance Officer – a man with a close resemblance to Les Dawson. I took my trousers and pants off. The radio man offered me a razor and shaving soap. He stood out in the corridor while I shaved off a chunk of pubic hair. I called him back. He taped a tiny transmitter onto my skin and a microphone behind my collar. He asked me to put my pants back on and scrutinised the effect. Then he said I could put my trousers on too.

"Comfortable?" he asked.

Surprisingly so, considering.

We assembled in the car park. A posse, consisting of DC Holmes and two other DCs in an un-marked car; PCs Laker and Deeley and two other uniforms in a patrol car; the surveillance man and a radio operator in a Ford Galaxy with tinted windows; Hood, Harvey and me.

"There's a narrow alley behind the church hall. We haven't had time to check if there is an exit into it. If we find one, the uniforms will cover it."

We moved to the Healey. Harvey reeled off the remaining instructions.

"Leave the car parked under a street light round the corner from the hall. As soon as you know May is fine, tell Freddie that Bill is sitting in your car, and hand over the keys. She'll send one of her broken noses to get him. We'll collar him, then we'll come to the party. You'll have a minute or so to improvise something. Just stay close to the door. If there's bother, I want you where those officers…" he pointed to the un-marked car "…can get to you. Is that clear?"

"Crystal," I said.

We left the station yard in convoy. As we drove into Barton Hill, I could see the Galaxy four or five cars behind me. The backup seemed to have disappeared. At 6.30, I drove past the church hall and parked round the corner in York Road. The Galaxy arrived and pulled up twenty yards away, at the head of the T.

"On my way, Harvey," I said.

The Galaxy sidelights flashed in acknowledgement. I slid out of the Healey, walked around the corner and covered the thirty or forty yards to the hall – set five paces back from the edge of the pavement and up half a dozen steps. Robert and the Giant were by the door. Robert smiled with the enveloping politeness he had displayed last time we met.

"Good evening, Mr Shepherd."

He opened the door and waved me inside the hall. The Giant stayed in the street.

Freddie said, "Welcome, Jack."

She was standing in the centre of the hall, dressed in blue jeans, silk shirt and tailored red jacket. Her father sat in a wheelchair next to her, motionless. He was wearing a black suit. Two employees, one bald the other dark-haired, both in bespoke tailoring, stood behind him. Freddie introduced them as Messrs Kane and Black. There was a plastic stacking chair with metal legs, six feet in front of the group.

Robert patted me down and stepped away. Changed his mind and stepped back to me. Reached out again, rummaged between my jacket collar and my neck and found the microphone. He held it up, shook his head, dropped the mic on the floor and stamped on it. Then took up station to my right.

Freddie sighed. "F for effort, Jack."

That bit of the plan wasn't going to work.

The church hall hadn't been used for years. Broken windows had been boarded up from the outside, damp patches discoloured the walls, there were chunks of plaster scattered around the floor. The stage behind my hosts was missing its curtains. Only half of the fluorescent lights in the ceiling were lit.

Freddie told me to sit down. I did so, eyes fixed on Settle père. He didn't look the man who had nodded at me and grinned 'Just you wait' from the dock fifteen years ago; the moment when Judge Alwyn told him he could leave the court, free and clear. Gangster, murderer, thief, extortionist... Now bogeyman turned basket case.

"Why the hell did you buy this place?" I asked.

The only response from him was a twitch of his bottom lip and a blaze of anger in his eyes. Now I could see what the failed op had done to him.

"My father can't speak," Freddie said. "But he can understand what we say. He doesn't go out any more, but he couldn't pass up this opportunity."

Her father's face twitched again. Freddie got down to business.

"Where is Bill Marsh?"

"Where's May?"

Freddie looked beyond me and called out, "Lester…"

I swivelled around in the chair. Lester stepped into the light on the balcony above the door, May at his shoulder. I asked her if she was okay.

"Yes," she said in a hushed voice. The sound carried in the empty hall.

I told Freddie that Bill was sitting in my car. She raised her eyebrows. I told her where it was parked.

She nodded towards Robert. "Give the man the keys."

I stood up, fished them out of my pocket and handed them over. Robert left the hall and closed the door behind him.

Freddie looked up to the balcony again. "Bring the lady down."

May disappeared from view. I heard footsteps cross the balcony and descend the stairs. She was shepherded into view again.

"A few steps forward, May, if you please," Freddie said. "Stop. And now to your left please… Stop. Thank you."

She spoke to Lester again. "Outside please. Lock the door and wait."

Lester did as he was ordered. Freddie switched her attention back to me. I was beginning to sweat. I found myself counting seconds. If the detective squad was on the ball, Robert wouldn't come back. Improvise, Harvey had said.

"So…" Freddie began.

"Why is your father here?" I asked. "If he doesn't get out any more."

This provoked a response from the wheelchair. Slowly Settle began to move his right arm towards his right jacket pocket, grunting with the effort. His daughter answered my question.

"He wanted to see you again."

I watched, fascinated and appalled, as with all the strength he could muster, Settle extracted a lightweight automatic from his pocket. He supported his arm on his right knee.

"Can he fire that?" I asked.

"I don't know. He hasn't tried," Freddie said.

She moved to her father, took the gun from him, released the safety catch and put it back into his hand. Then stepped away from him and looked at me.

"If he doesn't kill you," she said, "I will."

Settle raised the gun in the slowest of slow motions, panting and grimacing. The gun wavered and moved to his right, my left. He grunted and pulled the gun back into position. It dropped onto the chair, between his knees. Freddie picked it up and put it back into his hand. Settle repeated the sequence he had just taken ages to do. This time he fired. And missed. The bullet shot past my right elbow and thudded into the wall somewhere behind me.

Kane and Black looked at Freddie. She looked towards her father. I stood up and lunged at the wheelchair. Grabbed the left footrest and hauled the chair upwards. Settle was launched up over and back; the chair described a half circle and crashed onto its side. The gun slid across the floor. Freddie stuck out an expensive shoe, halted its progress, and picked it up. Kane and Black moved to help Settle. I moved back and to my left, intending to put myself in front of May. Freddie raised the gun and fired at me. The bullet tore the flesh of my left arm just below the shoulder, sped on in a straight line and into May's chest. She yelled out, staggered back under the force of the bullet, then crumpled to the floor. I turned and knelt down beside her. Blood was soaking the front of her blouse. I struggled out of my jacket, unfastened the top two buttons on my shirt with my right hand, and pulled it over my head. I wrapped the shirt into a hand sized bundle and pressed down hard on the wound. May's blood soaked it within seconds.

I sensed Freddie move up behind me. May struggled to

stay awake, tried to focus on Freddie. Her mouth moved but no sound came. She managed to turn her head enough to look up at me.

"Jack," she whispered, and died.

I looked up at Freddie. Her face was a mask.

"Do know what you've done?" I asked.

A shot was fired outside. Followed by a wave of yelling. Across the hall, Kane had picked up Freddy Senior. Black was heading towards a door at the side of the stage. Freddie pointed the automatic at my forehead. She couldn't miss from eight feet. Outside, the yelling subsided. It was followed by a hefty bang on the door.

Then instead of shooting me, Freddie stepped back a pace and gestured over her shoulder.

"Follow them," she said.

There was a second bang on the front door.

Suddenly Freddie wanted me alive. So there seemed no point in getting shot right then. Something she would surely get round to if I delayed her long enough. The part of the plan where I saved May had disintegrated into a million pieces. I stood up and looked down at her, all bled out.

There was a third bang on the door, accompanied this time by the sound of splintering wood.

Freddie tossed me my jacket. "They who turn and run away…" she said.

I set off in the direction of the door. Beyond it, we followed a passage alongside the stage. Moved into the hall kitchen, smelling of damp, rubbish and rot. Crossed the room and left the building by an exit door held open by Black.

A Range Rover was standing in the lane, engine idling. No straight from the showroom model. It had jacked-up and re-built suspension with a kangaroo bar across the front of the radiator grill and wrapped around the lights. Kane was sitting behind the steering wheel. Settle was strapped into the front passenger seat, his chin down on his chest. Black slammed the hall exit door and caught up with Freddie and me. She climbed into the back seat reached over the head rest in front of her to check on her father.

"I think he's okay," Kane said.

Black pushed me into the back next to Freddie and climbed in after me. Kane slid the gear lever into drive and floored the accelerator pedal. We stormed down the lane towards the patrol car parked across the entrance. Slammed into it, driving it out into the cross traffic. I saw the startled face of PC Deeley behind the steering wheel, then the Range Rover swung left and set off in the direction of the south circular ring road.

To my right, Black bent forward, head between his knees. From under the seat, he produced what looked like an old-fashioned police truncheon. He raised it and slammed it down onto the side of my head. The interior of the car spun round before my eyes, my vision blurred, the light around me turned grey and then black.

CHAPTER THIRTY

The world was still dark when I woke up, lying on a mattress on a stone floor; my hands across my stomach tied at the wrists. There was a six peal of bells ringing in my head. I tried to sit up, using my left elbow as a lever. Whereupon another helping of pain seeped from my upper arm into my shoulder. I could feel a bandage wrapped tight. I slumped back to the floor. I rolled to my left, and this time got up into a sitting position. I was wearing my jacket and my vest, but no shirt.

Then I remembered why.

And then I remembered re-gaining consciousness in the Range Rover with a sack over my head, travelling some distance in the dark and being bundled into a house. Somebody relieved me of the radio transmitter. Somebody else looked at my wound and bandaged it. Then I was dragged down steps, along a corridor, into this room, told to sit on the mattress and had the sack taken off my head

It was pitch black in wherever I was. I decided not to blunder around in the dark and lay back on the mattress. After a while, I drifted off to sleep.

When I woke up again the room was brighter. I got to my knees and from there managed to stand up. I did a careful 360 degree turn and didn't trip over anything. There was a dim light source, above head level, on the wall I was facing. Some sort of reinforced glass window. I could now see across the floor. I took four steps towards the light and realised it was a grating, three feet above me at ground level. I could see weeds growing round the edge of it.

I was in a wine cellar; unfortunately without wine. The place was furnished with empty racks. Obviously, once upon a time, someone had a substantial collection of chateau bottled vintages.

The watch Emily bought me three Christmases ago is a retro design timepiece, with hands rather than digits. I couldn't read them in the gloom. I mooched around a bit and found a couple of wine boxes. I sat down on one and began to ponder. After a while, I realised that the light through the grating was brighter. Which gave some clue as to time. May Day. Dawn at what time? Five, five-thirty? I had stiffened up sitting on the box, so I got to my feet and began to walk backwards and forwards across the cellar. I found myself thinking of the great prisoners of literature… Edmond Dantes, the Man in the Iron Mask, the Birdman of Alcatraz. And my namesake, Jack Shepherd, an enterprising thief who had escaped from Newgate and other prisons on a regular basis, and even from the hangman at Tyburn once. That was four hundred years ago however, and the hangman did get him the second time.

The sound of footsteps approaching the door brought me back to reality. It opened. Kane produced a serious piece of hardware from under his left arm. He stood in the doorway, radiating 'Don't mess me with me pal'.

"Good morning," I said.

He waved me past him into a stone flagged corridor. "Don't rush. Turn to your left at the end."

We took another left, climbed a stone staircase, turned right, and emerged into James Warburton's Great Hall. Kane pointed towards the kitchen.

"That way."

I looked at my watch as we crossed the hall. Just after 6 o'clock.

Black and Freddie were sitting at the kitchen table. She asked me if I knew where I was. I told her I had no idea. She chose to believe that, pulled out a chair from under the table and invited me to sit. Asked if I'd like some breakfast. I said eggs Benedict and caviar were a regular thing in my house. Black offered to punch my lights out. Freddie grinned and told me I'd have to work hard to keep my spirits up as the morning went on. I asked why someone had taken the trouble to bandage my arm. She said she had more substantial stuff scheduled for me than bleeding out on a cellar floor. Lodged in the back of my mind, currently unretrievable, was something I'd been meaning to ask her.

* * *

An hour later the Great Hall had filled up. At least that's what it sounded like from my position in the kitchen, roped to a table leg and scowled at by Black. He was clearly miserable by nature and was wearing a deodorant I could smell from ten feet away.

At 7.45, Freddie materialised again, followed by Kane. All business now.

"Free him from the table."

She waited as Black set to work. Then I remembered the question I wanted to ask.

"What was so special about Len Coleman? I heard he was something of an insider. Never had to pay for his drinks."

Freddie thought about the question for a moment and decided to answer.

"Back in the midst of time, Coleman and my Dad had a thing going. Friends from the old hood. A kinship based on decades of deals, and growing up in the back street badlands. All the old tribal shite. Bollocks, all of it, but you know how it worked back then. Coleman traced the employee who ran over Jimmy Marsh. And my father, as lord of the manor, dealt with the matter. Coleman was loaned to Bill Marsh. Basically to keep an eye on him. The hospitality deal followed."

"So why terrorise Bill? He's not got a role in any of this." For a second, she was almost betrayed by the family smile. "Or has he?"

"He inherited the arrangement my father had with Uncle Jimmy. It worked, in the old backyard honour way. And Bill did well out of it. But in some misguided impulse, he paid off Walter Cobb's debt to the company, so that my father could cut him loose. I can't recall how much it was."

"Forty-two thousand pounds," I said.

Freddie took a couple of steps across the kitchen, eyes suddenly blazing in anger.

"You know what, Jack? Bill just got in the fucking way... I'm tired of the old gangster network thing; a favour here, a drink there; you take south of the river, I'll take the north. I'm pissed off with handshakes and deals which are brokered on the basis of secret ambitions; you look after the bloke I'm chasing, I'll nail this miscreant to the warehouse floor. It means fuck all, Jack. It belongs back in the day, with the Krays and the Richardsons, the celebrity, the gang wars and the paranoia. Bill Marsh, Len Coleman, Walter Cobb, and the unwanted attention they bring to organised crime... They are all in the fucking way."

She looked at Black; the anger gone as quickly as it had appeared.

"Tie his wrists again, and bring him outside."

The Range Rover we had left the church hall in was parked alongside a Defender in the stable block yard. Three people I hadn't seen before – two men and one woman wearing moleskin trousers, boots and camouflage jackets – climbed into the Range Rover. Kane put the cloth sack over my head once more. I was shoved onto the rear seat of the Defender and joined by Black and his deodorant. Freddie got into the driver's seat. No Kane. He was obviously driving the other vehicle.

"Alright back there?"

"Fine," Black said.

Freddie turned on the ignition. And we began a trundle deep into eighteen hundred acres of Mendip forest. I tried to count the rights and lefts and estimate the distances between them, but it was an exercise in diminishing returns. The Defender leant over a number of times, dipped and bounced in and out of holes. Then we stopped, and Freddie cut off the engine. Black opened the passenger door on his side and heaved me out of my seat. I was escorted along a pathway, stumbling ankle deep into holes and tripping over tree roots. I began to feel sick, hoping it was only because of my companion's deodorant. He pulled me to a standstill. My wrists were freed and the sack pulled off my head.

The daylight was fierce. I closed my eyes, opened them again, massaged my eye sockets and looked around me.

We were in a kind of glade; a small, moss coated amphitheatre, about twenty yards in diameter, surrounded by trees. I was standing in the centre, facing the camouflage jackets, all three now wearing baseball caps. Freddie was to my right, Kane and Black behind her.

She smiled, all welcoming bonhomie, and began to speak.

"Lady and gentlemen, welcome to our morning of sport. Your prey is a change from the person billed. A more formidable sample than you might have imagined. In a couple of minutes, each of you will be issued with a .357 light weight rifle, pre-loaded with ten rounds. Mr Shepherd here, will be set loose and given a ten-minute start. You will then be free to hunt him down."

Absurdly, my first thought was 'Does James Warburton realise this is going on?' It was followed by a massive jolt of fear and seriously growing nausea. Three hunters, three rifles and thirty rounds of ammunition. Freddie continued, holding up a circular object about the size of ten pence coin.

"Each of you will have one of these pinned on to your jackets. A wire-less transmitter which will enable us to track you, find you if you get lost, and pick you up when the hunt is over. Mr Shepherd will be wearing a monitoring tag, locked onto his right ankle. We will know where he is throughout the excitement. You will not."

It was small comfort that there appeared to be a uniform and rules to this exercise, one sided though it was.

Kane opened the wooden case at his feet. He took out three rifles and passed them to Freddie. She spoke to the man closest to her.

"Mr Lord… you prefer the lever action I understand. It's a Browning."

Lord stepped forward and took the rifle.

"Ms Baron. Lever action for you, too. A Winchester; it's lighter. And Mr Knight, you requested the pump action. A Remington."

Black pinned a transmitter to the jacket lapel of each hunter. Freddie ordered me to sit down, and Kane clipped a tracker onto my right ankle. I watched him closely, in case there was the remotest chance I'd be able to take it off. The strap was leather, and attached to the fabric of the transmitter case with leather rivets. Freddie told me to stand up. Black climbed into the Range Rover. Moments later the tracker and the transmitters were activated.

Freddie stepped back a pace. "Good luck, Jack." For a moment I felt as if she actually meant it. "Make your choice. Any direction you'd like to take."

I looked around. The woodland was dense whichever way I faced. Freddie looked at the slim Rolex on her wrist. My heartbeat had risen into the hundreds. She lifted her head again and looked straight into my eyes.

"Go, Jack."

I looked at my watch and went. In what I hoped was a straight line.

Experts say that such a thing is an impossibility on terrain which doesn't vary and has no landmarks. They point to pictures of footprints in the desert which simply go round in circles. We lose all sense of direction when we have no idea where we are going. I looked at my watch again. Eight minutes to go. That was when I came up with a kind of plan. If I didn't know where I was, then there was no point in going anywhere. I decided I should leave the hunters to find me. What I was going to do at that point I had no idea. But hell, one step at a time.

I walked on for another five minutes, beating the undergrowth around me, crushing ferns and breaking low branches, leaving a trail to follow.

At zero plus seven, I stopped moving and found a shallow moss-covered foxhole. It had a 360 degrees view. I collected clods of earth and ground covering plants, dragged branches to the hiding place, ringing it as best I could. The camouflage wouldn't have fooled Baden Powell, but it was probably enough for present circumstances. Most of the club sized pieces of wood I found were rotten. I found one which seemed solid. I dug a piece of stone out of the moss, small enough to hold in my hand, moved back to the foxhole and dropped down into it.

My shoulder began to hurt. The moss was soft to lie on. But I had to arrange myself into a position which I could hold without moving, and see around me at the same time. After another frantic minute or so, I managed to do that, favouring my shoulder in the process.

I waited. For minutes. In a world of total silence. Apart from the odd rustle to my right and left. Soft and whisper loud. Small animals of some sort.

Then to my right, maybe thirty yards away, I heard the unmistakable noise of someone on two legs moving through undergrowth. He, or she, passed by, and my world fell silent again.

A minute or so later, the same noise seeped onto the soundtrack from somewhere dead ahead. I looked through the foliage around the rim of the foxhole. Mr Knight and his pump action Remington appeared, stopped, and listened. Carefully, I took hold of one of the ground-cover plants and I shook it; producing a sound just loud enough for him to hear. He looked around. I watched and waited. As he turned his head into my line of sight, I moved the plant a couple of inches to my left, wiggled it, then got down as low as I could. He raised his rifle and sighted it on the plant. He fired. I yelled out in response. I heard Knight pump the next bullet into the chamber. I groaned.

Then he was above me, leading with his left leg. I rose and swung the piece of wood in one motion. It slammed into his ankle. He over-balanced, fell sideways, and rolled on to his back still holding on to the Remington. It took him too long to realise what was happening. I was out of the foxhole and standing over him in tenths of a second. I stamped down hard on the wrist holding the rifle, dropped beside him and slammed the stone onto the bridge of his nose. He screamed. Blood poured from the wound. I prised the rifle out of his hand, tore the transmitter from his jacket, and threw it as far as I could into the woods.

When I looked back at Knight, he was choking and crying in pain.

I'd only seen pump action guns in American TV series and Steven Seagal movies. The Remington was smaller than I had expected, with a custom-made stock and a short barrel. I sighted on his right thigh and fired. He yelled once again and passed out. I pumped another bullet into the chamber, bent down, transferred the baseball cap from his head to mine, unbuttoned his jacket, turned him on to his face, pulled his arms back and up and hauled the jacket off him. I put it on, rolled him into the foxhole and dropped my own jacket on top of him.

Now what? I've never been a fan of TV survival shows. I began to wish I had paid more attention.

Someone was approaching from my right. I added Knight's baseball hat to my costume and turned my back. Stared down into the foxhole. Whoever was coming might believe, at least for a moment or two, that I was him. I listened to the footsteps. They stopped.

"Mr Knight…"

I turned round, and pointed the Remington at Ms Baron.

"There's a cartridge in the chamber," I said.

She stood still, the Winchester in her right hand pointing at the ground.

"Throw it over here," I said. The rifle landed at my feet. "Now lie down. On your face."

She did that. The Remington had eight cartridges left.

The lever action Winchester had ten. I now had more fire power than Mr Lord, but no one can fire two rifles at the same time. At least I can't. John Wayne could, but this wasn't *True Grit*. And there was no time to dither.

I moved to Baron. Told her to roll onto her back. She did and looked up at me. She had looked tough when I first saw her in the stable block, but now I could see sweat on her forehead. I fired into the ground to the left of her. She flexed, as though I'd put a charge of electricity though her body. I asked her if she knew Knight and Lord. She shook her head.

"I met them for the first time, this morning."

"Have you got a mobile?" I asked.

She looked down the front of her jacket. "In the right- hand pocket."

"Take it out."

She found it and clutched it tight.

"Unlock it please."

She looked at the phone. Perhaps working out the odds on me actually shooting her. I counted to five and fired again; this time to the right of her head. She dropped the mobile, scrabbled for it, found it and unlocked it. I pumped another cartridge. She stretched out her arm. I took the phone from her.

"Now roll over again. Back on to your face."

I called George Hood's mobile. It went to message.

"George," I said. "This a matter of life and death. I mean it. No exaggeration. Call me as soon as you get this."

I tried Harvey's mobile. That went straight to message also. I repeated what I had said to Hood. I bent down, picked up the Winchester and ordered Baron to get to her feet. Waved her in the direction of the foxhole.

She stood transfixed, looking down at Knight, still

unconscious.

"Next to him," I said. "Face down."

She got into the foxhole. Shuddered as she stretched out.

The mobile rang. I dropped the Winchester and answered the call.

"Where the hell are you?" Harvey asked.

"I'm on top of the Mendips on *The High Combe Estate*. You get to it from the road between Priddy and Charterhouse. I need your help. There is a manhunt going on. Freddie has three people trying to kill me."

"What?"

I thought I was being succinct enough. I began again. He interrupted.

"No Jack, I've got it. I just don't believe it."

"Jesus Christ, do you think I'd make up something like this? People are creeping around here in the woods with .357 rifles." I raised the Remington and fired it. "Hear that?"

"How do we find you?"

"God knows," I said. "Drive on to the estate with as many cars as you can muster, making as much noise as possible. Keep the sirens running. Bring something hefty to open the gates. They're probably locked. Big cast iron things. And get here bloody quickly. I'll keep this phone live."

I ended the call. Looked down into the foxhole again.

"Ms Baron, do you have a knife?"

She said no. I pumped a fifth cartridge into the Remington. Then I heard Lord shout. "Knight... Baron."

I pointed the Remington at Baron. "Don't say a word."

I stepped back a pace. Fired the Remington into the air. Shouted Lord's name. Pumped another cartridge into the chamber and shouted again. He shouted back. I located the direction of the sound. Moved around the foxhole and crouched into cover on the other side. Now I could hear him moving. He called again. I called back. Then I saw him, twenty yards from me, negotiating his way through a cluster of shrubs and young trees. Fifteen yards. Twelve. Ten... He stopped and shouted again. I stood up and pointed the Remington at his chest. He stared at me.

"Drop the Browning," I said.

He thought about it. I shifted the Remington a degree or two and fired. The bullet smacked into a tree trunk inches from his head. Bits of bark sprayed out. A piece went into his left eye. He flinched, yelled, dropped the Browning, and raised both hands to his eye. I re-loaded the Remington. Three shots left.

Lord was grunting and cursing. He stopped and squinted in my direction.

"Over here," I said.

He moved towards me, still fiddling with his eye. He tripped over an ant hill and fell on to his face.

"Stay where you are."

I moved back to the foxhole and ordered Baron to her feet. I pointed in Lord's direction.

"Over there."

She moved towards him. I stopped her a couple of strides short. I told Lord to sit up and unbutton his jacket. I asked if he had a knife. He mumbled. I pointed the Remington at his head. He said 'yes', fished around in his jacket pockets, found it and tossed it to me. It dropped to the ground a yard in front of me – a slim, stainless steel, short blade case knife. I looked back at Lord.

"Take your jacket off, but don't shift your arse." He shrugged out of it. "Give it to Baron." He stretched out his arm. She looked at me. "Take it from him." She collected it by a sleeve. "Now take off your jacket, and tie the sleeve in your hand to one of yours. A reef knot. You know, right over left and under, left over right and under." She did that. "Now pull on both sleeves and check the knot is tight." She did, and it was. "Okay. Sit down, back-to-back with Lord." She sat down. "Keep the knotted sleeves in front of you and pass the two other jacket sleeves to Lord, left side and right." I crabbed sideways into Lord's line of sight. "Help her." Lord reached behind, groped about a bit, found both sleeve ends and pulled them around in front of his chest. I told Baron to slide her arms inside the ring of jackets and sleeves, and Lord to pull tighter. I stepped closer to Lord; still squinting and blinking. I told him to put his hands into his trouser pockets. He hesitated. With the Remington angled down, I fired a shot over Baron's left shoulder. The bullet ploughed into the ground two yards in front of Baron, kicking up grass and dirt. She yelled out. Lord stuffed his hands into his pockets. I knelt in front of him, laid the Remington down out of his reach, picked up the sleeve ends, linked them right over left and pulled tight. Baron yelled again. Lord arched his back as best he could and shouted, "Alright alright."

I completed the knot, picked up the Remington, walked back to the knife lying in the grass and collected it.

The odds against me getting to the end of the day had shortened considerably. Knight's transmitter was now part of the great outdoors. Baron and Lord were still wearing there's. I was still wearing the tag. But we were all in the same place and not moving. So if Freddie, Kane and Black were awake, they'd realise that the wrong person was in charge. Waiting for the opposition to arrive had been successful so far. And when plan A works, don't invent a plan B. If I sat down beyond where Lord broke cover, I'd be facing the way the bad guys would come.

I dropped to my haunches in front of Baron. She stared at me. She had green eyes. I gestured behind me.

"I'm going over there. You two will be in my line of sight. If there is any commotion from you when our hosts arrive, I will shoot you."

It seemed she believed that. Behind her, Lord hadn't moved.

I called to him. "Did you hear that?"

"Yes, yes."

I stepped back and sat down, opened Lord's knife, slid the blade under the leather sleeve of the tag, and began to saw. It took a couple of minutes before the leather rivets popped and the tag fell off my ankle. I picked it up, got to my feet, swung round to face the other way and threw it as far as I could – the theory being, that if I appeared to be some distance beyond Lord and Baron, then our hosts might feel more inclined to break cover and go to the assistance of their clients. I was also working on the assumption that this kind of incident had not happened before. So telling myself I'd set this up as best I could, I moved into the bushes, picking up the Browning and the Winchester on the way.

There were two rounds left in the Remington and ten in the other rifles. I was the prey and I had done all the shooting, and so far, I hadn't killed anybody. I fervently hoped it would stay that way. *I'm A Detective Get Me Out Of Here...*

I looked at my watch again. Ten minutes since I had talked with Harvey. It would take another half hour at least, for a fast patrol car and the best of drivers to get here from Bristol. Perhaps twenty minutes from Wells. But convincing the Somerset Constabulary that this escapade was not someone's 'film of the day' fantasy, would have used up precious time.

The mobile rang again. I grabbed it.

"ETA twenty-five minutes," Harvey said.

I wanted him to say 'listen out for the sirens, we're tear-arsing down the drive'.

"There are three armed officers in this car, and three in the patrol car behind us. Hang on…"

The sound of detectives talking fast, underscored by a speeding car engine, was all I could hear for a few seconds. Then Harvey came back to me.

"And there's a posse on the way from Wells. The man in charge lives up on the Mendips. He knows the estate. ETA twelve minutes."

That sounded better.

Harvey ended the call. I switched the mobile to silent and put it in a trouser pocket where I'd feel it buzz against my skin.

And sat back in the undergrowth to wait.

CHAPTER THIRTY-ONE

My shoulder was hurting again, but mercifully my arm wasn't bleeding. I began to feel hungry; which I guessed was a good sign. But I was turning cold, despite being wrapped in the camouflage jacket. The sweat had dried on me, the overnight dew was soaking my backside. At least it was a bright morning. No cloud cover and no wind. You could hear a sparrow fart at twenty paces.

I couldn't help thinking what Emily would have made of this. I wondered what Chrissie and the household were doing now. I counted back over the hours. I hadn't seen Linda for almost two days.

And then I began wondering how good Kane and Black were at this revved up field craft. The manhunt business was clearly a regular thing. It had a uniform and rules of engagement. So where did the prey come from? I began thinking about Walter Cobb and his resurrection men. Cobb had clearly annoyed Freddie. Why else would he have been sitting on display in the warehouse, propped up like Billy Clanton in the undertaker's window in Tombstone. You could say that Cobb was working in a related field. Maybe he was Freddie's prey supplier. And maybe she had decided that his moonlighting as a supplier of body parts for Faversham was a breach of security.

It wasn't a bad theory. It was just bloody aggravating to come up with it in the current circumstances. Cobb was probably dead by now. Buried in these woods. Somewhere in the eighteen hundred acres along with the previously hunted.

I wondered how much Freddie charged these perverted rich folk with money and time on their hands. Twenty, twenty-five thousand per ticket? She didn't have any R&D to pay for and no overheads. The guns were good, but still not more than five or six hundred quid each. The ammunition was peanuts. The jackets were around what, thirty quid? In my next moment of boredom I could price up this endeavour and work out how much Freddie was making every Sunday.

There was a noise ahead of me, beyond the opposite side of the glade. I tightened my grip on the Remington. The noise died away. I sat still and waited. Looked at my watch. If the Wells team was on time, we should hear the sirens in a bit less than five minutes. The mobile vibrated in my pocket. I struggled to get at it, trying not to move and give away my position.

"Harvey," I hissed into the phone. "There are two men, maybe twenty-five yards away. They haven't seen me yet, but it's a matter of moments."

"You should hear the sirens in three or four minutes," he said, and rang off.

At least I didn't need to conduct the next piece. I was in charge of this situation as thoroughly as I could be. Just had to sit and wait for Kane and Black to break cover.

There was a rustle at eleven o'clock. The sound grew in volume. Kane came into focus. He stopped. Now he had a view across the glade. He could see Baron and Lord, tied back-to-back. Lord was shaking his head furiously bumping up and down on the moss. Tied to him, Baron was getting hurt in the process. Kane looked back over his left shoulder. There was more rustling, which grew in volume. Black appeared at one o'clock. I turned my head slightly and got both men in my eye line. A moment before I got cramp in my right thigh. It hurt like nobody's business. I tried not to move.

A moment later I had to do so anyway. Lord bellowed out that I had gone that way. He must have jerked his head to help indicate the direction, because it bounced off the back of Baron's. She cried out in shock and pain.

Keeping quiet didn't matter now. I moved my leg, bent it at the knee and massaged my thigh. Black looked at Kane for orders. Baron had joined in the yelling. I lifted my head, sighted to the left of Kane and fired the Remington. The bullet skimmed his shoulder and scythed through the bushes behind him. He dropped to the ground and shuffled back into cover again. Black did the same. I fired the last shot in the chamber over his head, threw the gun away and picked up the Winchester. I waited, listening for the slightest movement.

Baron and Lord had stopped yelling. They were grumbling currently. Appeared to have fallen out. They began wriggling about and bouncing up and down. I fired a shot to their right. They stopped immediately.

If Kane and his associate were thinking, they would each make a wide circle to the left and right and get round behind me. From 9 o'clock I heard rustling again. Then somewhere in the way beyond, the sound of police sirens seeped into the silence. And grew louder and louder. The cavalry had arrived, making enough noise to wake the dead and, in the process, drowning out all the sounds around me. Kane and Black could tap dance up to me with a full orchestra playing and I wouldn't hear them.

Now or never Shepherd...

I picked up the Browning, and with a rifle in each hand, ploughed forwards. Nobody shot at me. I sprinted past Lord and Baron who were yelling stuff I couldn't hear. I dived into the foliage ahead and picked up what I assumed was Kane's track towards the glade. I could retrace his steps back to the vehicles. I was moving now, as fast as the woodland would permit. I stumbled several times and tripped up twice. I was breathing heavily, taking in great gulps of air. I decided to risk calling Harvey. I stopped moving, swung round to look behind me, put the Winchester down and thumbed his mobile number. He answered on the second ring. I told him I was okay, but the sirens were now a mixed blessing.

"Do you want me to call them off?"

"Ask them to leave one running. I can use it as a location fix."

"Roger that. Our driver reckons we are six minutes away."

Kane's trail was still clear enough to follow, even moving along at the miles per hour I was managing to generate. I was spending so much time looking down and left and right, I forgot what might be ahead. It came back to me as I stumbled from Kane's track out into the open.

Where Freddie was standing by the Range Rover, pointing an automatic at me for the second time in a little more than twelve hours.

I stood in front of her. My chest heaving, my arms by my sides, a rifle in each hand. She had turned the Range Rover around. It was facing the way we had come. The left side front and rear passenger doors were open.

"Put the rifles on the back seat," she said.

"I don't think so," I said.

"Don't give me the Bruce Willis stuff again. I may need a hostage to get out of here, but I would rather shoot you than waste any more time. Where are my clients?"

"I left Mr Knight with a broken nose and a bullet in his thigh. Ms Baron and Mr Lord were tied up when I last saw them."

"And my associates, where are they?"

"No idea."

"In which case, we'll quit the field." She waved the automatic at the Range Rover. "Do as I say. Rifles onto the back seat, please."

I walked to the car.

"Stop there," she said. "Throw them in, close the door, and step this way."

I did all that.

"You drive," she said. "But get in from this side." She pointed to the front passenger door. I moved towards it. "Slide across."

I climbed in shuffled across the mid-seats console and slid behind the steering wheel. Freddie climbed into the passenger seat. The sirens was still echoing through the woods.

Freddie stayed cool, eyes fixed on me. "Don't dawdle. But be careful."

I switched on the engine, selected drive, pressed the accelerator, and we began to move.

"Turn left up ahead," she ordered. "We're going out the back door."

Another way to get into and out of the estate. I hadn't thought about that.

Fifty yards later, we broke out of the dense woodland onto a dirt track.

"Right," Freddie said. "And speed up a little please."

I swung right. We took another left and another right and then turned onto the best piece of road so far. Dead ahead, a couple of hundred yards or so, was another double gate. Just as substantial as the version at the main entrance. There was a lodge to our right as we approached.

"You'll have to get out to open these gates," Freddie said. "And they open towards us, so leave room."

I pulled up level with the front door of the lodge. Freddie passed me a big key; the sort of engineering they locked Guy Fawkes away with. I got out of the Range Rover. Freddie got out behind me. I left the driver's door open and walked around it. As I did so, George Hood stepped out of the lodge door and pointed a .38 revolver at Freddie's head.

"This is a far as you go. Please drop the gun onto the ground at your feet."

Freddie did as she was told.

Hood called back over his shoulder. "Get out here, Sherlock." Holmes appeared. "Ms Settle has put her gun down. Go and get it."

Moments later, DC Holmes had all the guns, and Freddie was sitting in handcuffs in the back seat of the Range Rover sandwiched between two uniforms. And I was congratulating Hood on his brilliance.

"Almost didn't happen," he said. "We shot past this gate five minutes ago, doing over eighty. The Super yelled at the driver to stop. We hadn't thought about another way in or out. Glad to see you. Sorry we cocked up yesterday evening."

He grinned. I asked him how Bill was.

"In pieces. Finding May dead on the floor, well…"

"Where is he?" I asked.

"Still in the holding cell at Trinity Road," Hood said.

We both took time to breathe.

"Now what?" I asked.

"I call the others and tell them to turn that fucking siren off. And then we all assemble in front of the house."

* * *

Ten minutes later, outside the house, another battalion of coppers arrived. The rest of the Wells swing shift had been called up, complete with loudspeakers and megaphones. The DCI in charge asked me about the fire power in the woods. He was Welsh; a north Somerset version of Windsor Davies.

"One of the hunters is out of action," I said. "The other two are unarmed. Freddie's two associates have a rifle each. They may have hand guns also."

Then I told him about the tracking system they were using.

"Just leave all that to us. We'll get the buggers out of there, don't you worry."

Harvey tapped me on the shoulder.

"Do you want to have any last words with Ms Settle before we take her away?" He nodded to our right. "She's in the patrol car over there."

I walked over to it. The PC standing by the rear door opened it and stepped to one side. I joined Freddie on the seat. She turned her head and looked at me.

"We'll do this again sometime, Jack," she said.

"Probably not," I said. "There's a wide trail back to you and your wrong doing. And it will get wider as your associates begin singing."

"So what do you want to say to me?"

"May Marsh was your mother."

I stared into her eyes. She stared back, without blinking.

"The result of a brief liaison between her and your father. Deals were done. You were handed over. And nobody said anything more about it. Until Bill told me, yesterday."

Her mouth moved and her lips parted, but she had no words to say.

"You took your own mother hostage and you killed her," I said.

I got out of the car, nodded at the PC and he closed the passenger door. I walked towards Harvey without looking back. Behind me, I heard the patrol car fire up and pull away.

Another patrol car gave me a lift back to Barton Hill.

CHAPTER THIRTY-TWO

The two uniforms in the front seats talked sparingly; keeping the volume fader at minimum and making no effort to include me in any snatches of conversation. I was grateful. I sprawled on the back seat and tried to relax. The adrenalin in my system seeped away. By the time we cruised into the suburbs of south Bristol my chest was no longer thumping and my heartbeat felt as it should.

I was allowed to collect the Healey on the strict understanding I then drove straight to Trinity Road. I unlocked the car and fished my mobile out of the driver's door pocket. No juice in the battery, no way to call Chrissie or Linda. Mercifully. I wasn't ready to re-run the story of my weekend.

I reported to Harvey's office. He began proceedings by telling me that Bill had officially confessed to the murder of Len Coleman.

"The thing is, we had no reason to suspect him. We would have accused Freddie of ordering the hit, she would have denied the charge, and we would have gone on dancing and weaving."

"I think Bill would have considered it untidy not to confess," I said. "Deep down in his broken heart, he doesn't care what happens now. Can I see him?"

Harvey shook his head. Sadly, I thought. "Not right now, Jack."

The truth was, a lot of people's lives would be poorer with Bill and May gone.

We talked about Freddie. I asked Harvey if she had revealed what she did with Walter Cobb.

"No," he said. "Not that she's saying much at all at the moment. When asked about him, she said 'Walter who?' She's down in the basement with her brief. And behind George and Sherlock, a long line of detectives from Burglary, Vice and the Special Crimes Unit are queuing up to interrogate her."

I gave Harvey my theory about Cobb's hubris backfiring on him, and Freddie taking umbrage at his body parts freelancing. He seemed to agree with it. I thanked him for rescuing me. He told me to go and find DC Holmes, who would interview me for the record and take my statement. He stood up and stretched his right arm across the desk. I shook his hand; both of us recognising this moment for what it was. A cease fire, in an ongoing bending and stretching of rights and wrongs, albeit with both of us on the same side.

Sort of.

* * *

I drove home, bought an *Observer* on the way, parked the Healey outside my front door, went into the house and poured a small brandy. I sipped it slowly.

Half an hour later, showered and shaved, I examined the shoulder wound. It needed a stitch or two, but it was clean and not bleeding. I managed to dress and bandage it again, keeping it in place by winding a length of Elastoplast tape around my arm. I glided down the stairs. The answer light on the phone base in the hall was blinking. I pressed the message play button There were five calls; three from last night. The first, timed at 7.04, was from Linda. *Where are you, Jack? Call me.* The second message was from Chrissie, at 7.09. *Hi dad. Where are you? Fancy coming over for dinner?* There was another call from Linda, at 8.54. *Jack, are you so busy you can't pick up a phone?* The fourth, was another from Chrissie, who had called again less than an hour ago. *Are you at Linda's? I'll try again later.* And the last call was a message from Linda, left while I was in the shower. *Jack. Where the hell are you?*

The clock on the wall said 10.05.

Feeling better and firm of purpose, I de-constructed the cardboard boxes still piled in the hall, flattened them, stowed them in the boot of the Healey, and took them to the Recycling Centre in Sainsbury's car park on Winterstoke Road. On the way home, I parked in front of the office building. I walked into the cavern under the road. There was no one there. The villagers had gone. All evidence of their occupation had been cleared away. The noise from the road above pounded on.

I called Linda. It took some time to get the story told. I managed to parley it into some degree of sympathy. I offered to buy lunch; then rang Chrissie and invited her and Adam too. We drove up into the Cotswolds in Adam's Espace. The afternoon went well and I spent the night in Portishead.

* * *

On Monday, shortly after midday, I drove up to the High Combe Estate, intending to call on James Warburton; now back at home, amazed and furious in equal measure. I didn't get beyond the lodge gate. I spoke to him by phone from the Estate Manger's Office.

"I am truly sorry I deceived you, James."

He disconnected the call.

The following day, I traced Molly and Don, living in a damp and draughty shed at the back of a car breaker's yard in Hengrove.

Irving from the Public Mortuary called a day later, with news of Martin's funeral. I drove Molly and Don to the crematorium. Along with the priest, we were the only people there. I found the Crematorium Manager and asked about Lily. The manager recalled a visit from her sister.

"Mrs Maxted paid for a brick in the Wall of Remembrance," he explained. "You'll find it at the end of the Memorial Garden."

The words on it read *Lillian Margaret Barrett. 1973-2018. No Longer Lost.*

Later that afternoon, Chrissie and I, Adam, Helen, Monica and Harry from the Drop-In Centre, George Hood, a host of May's neighbours, and Bill escorted by two police officers, attended May's funeral.

* * *

At 7 o'clock the following morning, Bill was found lying on the floor of his remand cell; blood from his wrists – his own AB negative this time – staining the linoleum; a razor blade a couple of feet away from him. He was pronounced dead at the scene.

THE END

COMING SOON...

THE JACK SHEPHERD COLLECTION
THE BRISTOL THRILLERS
Cloning the Hate | Bending the Rules
VOLUME TWO

JEFF DOWSON

diamondbooks.co.uk

DIAMOND CRIME

DIAMOND BOOKS

DIAMOND CRIME

Passionate about the crime/mystery/thriller books it publishes

Follow
Facebook:
@diamondcrimepublishing

Instagram
@diamond_crime_publishing

Web
diamondbooks.co.uk

DIAMOND BOOKS

Printed in Great Britain
by Amazon